Praise for Don Juan in Hankey, PA...

"A fast, fun read with wit, charm, and can-do optimism at its heart. DON JUAN IN HANKEY, PA is a tale of longing, lust, and love in small-town USA, featuring a sympathetic rake, a bipolar ketchup heiress, a desperate divorcée, a spurned society matron, a pimping balloon entrepreneur, and one plucky ghost. Some authors write comedy with aplomb. Others excel at infusing stories with emotional warmth. Martin combines both in a debut novel that will have you doubled over, laughing, that deserves to be welcomed with a hearty brava."

—Kaylie Jones, author of LIES MY MOTHER NEVER TOLD ME and A SOLDIER'S DAUGHTER NEVER CRIES

"Gale Martin has achieved an unlikely feat: an opera buffa in prose. Martin paints her characters in primary colours and whirls them through a series of improbable events and operatic in-jokes, at a pace worthy of the closing stages of a Rossini overture. And to help us along the way, of course, there's a very particular phantom...."

—David Karlin, founder of BACHTRACK

"Gale Martin has written a clever and enchanting story that sings from the first page to its last. Opera buffs and novices will enjoy the juicy drama and intrigue that happens both on and behind the stage. What a treat!"

—Margo Candela, author of GOOD-BYE TO ALL THAT, LIFE OBSERVED, and THE BRENDA DIARIES

"Like a fabulous production, DON JUAN IN HANKEY, PA seethes with wild jealousies, convoluted mysteries, wry comic turns, resident ghosts, mysterious assailants, bold intrigues, longing, love, lust, and – of course – plenty of opera. Gale Martin's novel is 'meraviglioso!'"

—Lenore Hart, author of BECKY and THE RAVEN'S BRIDE

Don Juan in Hankey, PA

a novel

by Gale Martin

Booktrope Editions
Seattle WA, 2011

Edited by Toddie Downs

Cover Design by Greg Simanson

*This is a work of fiction. Names, characters, places, brands,
media, and incidents are either the product of the author's
imagination or are used fictitiously. Any resemblance to
similarly named places or to persons living or deceased is
unintentional.*

ISBN 978-1-935961-40-6

DISCOUNTS OR CUSTOMIZED EDITIONS MAY BE AVAILABLE FOR
EDUCATIONAL AND OTHER GROUPS BASED ON BULK PURCHASE.

For further information please contact info@booktrope.com

Library of Congress Control Number: 2011941461

For Jessica

Acknowledgments

This book would not have been written without the guidance, patience, and encouragement of some very special people.

First, I need to thank the wonderful people at Booktrope Publishing who believed in this book—Ken Shear and Katherine Sears. I am also indebted to my editor Toddie Downs.

I also owe a debt of gratitude to the staff and faculty of the Wilkes University Creative Writing program, whose comments and suggestions allowed me to formulate and improve this book. Most especially to Nina Solomon who not only gave me the *psychic* license to write this book but also traveled the journey with me and my quirky characters. I am also grateful to my fellow writers in the program for their support at crucial times, most notably, Kurt Topfer, Amye Archer, William Prystauk, and Ginger Marcinkowski, my "soul sister," who kept sending me books on opera she found along her travels, which I relied on heavily on background for this book.

I am indebted to Carol Wenger, school librarian *emerita* and opera-going partner, whose enthusiasm for my writing has buoyed me for years. Thanks also to the Pequea Valley Library Book Club for their generous feedback on an early manuscript—and for the opera fudge.

I so appreciate the friendly counsel and encouragement of Mary Beth Matteo, who generously critiqued each incarnation of this book and was an indefatigable resource at every turn.

Thanks also to friends at Bachtrack, Alison and David Karlin, who gave me the chance to see life-changing opera events and meet some extraordinary performers along the way. I must also acknowledge Dr. Joan Zeidman, my on-call medical consultant for this project, and Kevin Heisler and Luis Sanchez, who helped me bring my opera know-how to a worldwide audience.

No one has been more convinced about the publishing potential of this book than my mother, Jessica Ringler, an avid reader, who tore through chapters faster than I could mail them and shared them with many of her friends in her senior citizen high-rise. Her constant support has meant more to me than I can express.

Lastly, I need to thank my husband Bill for being everything to me and for me that matters in this life (and the next).

The Prologue

For me, the defining opera experience begins with goosebumps and ends with a glimpse into the face of God—and I'm an agnostic.

—Deanna Lundquist

A first kiss, a first love. Neither can compete with hearing opera the way the composer intended it to be sung.

—Dr. Richard Rohrer

A true opera lover can pinpoint that single musical moment that makes her want to sing and sing and sing until she develops nodes.

—Oriane Longenecker

My late husband made me sit through **Parsifal** in Bayreuth. Six hours of shrieking and yodeling. Without electric shock therapy, I would've strangled the next fat blonde with braids to cross my path.

—Paylor Frantz

The first time I heard Delibes's "Flower Duet," I knew what it felt like to be among angels singing. Trust me—I wasn't in the midst of an astral projection.

—Vivian Frantz Pirelli

The conflict in **Rigoletto** tore at my heart. All this dramatic upheaval set to Verdi's incomparable music. I couldn't write stories that well, but I could help tell them.

—Carter Knoblauch

I knew there'd be opera in heaven. How could God not have His hand in something so glorious?

—The Late Mary Rohrer

Like beauty pageant contestants, opera characters live passionately and die violently. It makes Arnaud weep like Arnaud has never wept before.

—Arnaud Marceau

Since you're asking everybody, I don't know nothin' about opera. I don't want to either.

—Donald Longo, Hankey EMT

"A well-born Cavalier, such ev'n as I am, tamely can see such sweet and dainty freshness, such delicate perfections."

—*Don Giovanni*

I
The Cavalier

*Mid-March, downtown Hankey, Pennsylvania. The main
thoroughfare, Henry Avenue, is deserted. Its centerpiece
is the Hankey Opera House—the only handsome building
on a blighted street.*

Like untold other mornings in Hankey, the day had broken like
a farm-fresh egg cracked into a rusty skillet. After such a dreary
start, devoid of possibility, Deanna Lundquist never dreamed she'd
encounter someone who'd change the course of her life.

Needing make-ready time for each meeting she chaired, she'd
arrived at the Hankey Opera House at 9:15 a.m., coffee and Danish
in tow. She was forty-five minutes early—plenty of time to organize
things just so. She leaned against the bank of glass doors at the
entrance, expecting them to be locked. When one gave way, she
teetered on patent-leather high heels into the foyer like a circus
clown on stilts.

The coffee tumbled out of her hands and onto the carpet. A dark,
wet ring began spreading at her feet. She needed paper towels—
now.

She hurried around the corner and down the carpeted steps to
the ladies' room. More than anything else about the Hankey Opera
House, it was the winding, downward trek to the restrooms that
reminded her of the Metropolitan Opera House in New York City.
Hankey productions couldn't approach Met quality. But Deanna did
derive satisfaction from knowing their small-town opera house had
more bathroom stalls.

She threw open the door and set her things on the tiled counter,
surveying the sink. No towels anywhere. Just one of those turbo-
powered hand dryers that sucked the flesh off your bones. She hated

that dryer, needing no reminders that by age forty-two, her skin had lost its youthful elasticity.

What idiot had left the front door unlocked in the first place? Or was it the opera house ghost up to its tricks again?

The Hankey Opera House had served as a ghost motel for generations of spectral intruders. It had been built on the foundation of a jail used during the French and Indian War. Since then, operagoers claimed to have heard war whoops of massacred Lenape captives, most notably during Act I of a 1974 revival of *Rose-Marie*—right in the middle of the "Indian Love Call" number. The latest ghost—no war whooper—was more likely to open doors if your arms were loaded down, that is, when it wasn't floating back and forth between the house and the green room.

Deanna knew she should forget about cleaning up that spill herself and just call Kleen Carpets. After all, she was supposed to be upstairs, preparing the room for the guild and those about to be interviewed. As she reached into her bag for her phone, she felt the air rustle around her. The acrid scent of sweat rushed into her nostrils, turning her empty stomach. Someone grabbed her around the waist and clamped a hand over her mouth.

"Don't move, *signora*," a man said in a husky voice, "or I'll snap your head right off."

Stunned, Deanna froze. She'd taken self-defense classes. In the throes of an attack, her mind had gone blank. What had her instructor said? Don't capitulate. Refuse to cooperate.

He took his hand off her mouth and wrapped it around her neck. "I want you to talk *nice* to me, eh?"

"You worthless piece of—"

He secured his hand over her mouth again, more forcefully this time. "I said, talk *nice*," he hissed through clenched teeth, dragging her toward the freight elevator. "You don't look stupid. Don't act stupid. You better be sweet if you want to live to see your thirty-fifth birthday, *bella signora*." He removed his hand from her mouth.

He thought she was thirty-four? She couldn't think about that at the moment. "If you let me go now," she said, "you'll get off with a hand slap."

She heard him push the elevator button. He nuzzled the back of her neck, and she stiffened. "Please," she cried softly. The feel of his hot breath and moist lips sent nausea climbing into her throat.

"That's better," he purred, his voice becoming melodic. He inhaled deeply. "*Bella signora*, you smell so fresh. Your body—an hourglass. *Perfetto.*"

"God in heaven," she managed to say, but he continued grazing her skin with his mouth. She focused on picturing the size and weight of his lips, which felt blubbery and a little scratchy as if he wore a mustache or a mask. His accent was slight, lilting. Since he wasn't revealing his face, she'd need those details to identify him to the authorities, assuming she survived this. She heard the freight elevator doors clunk open.

"Who are you?" she squeaked.

"Hush! Silence." He tightened his grip on her until she could scarcely breathe and pressed his lips against her ear. "*Signora*, you call me—*il cavaliere.*"

Deanna shivered. "What?"

He inched her closer to the elevator, digging his arm into her chest. Was he going to hurl her down the cavernous shaft? Her body recoiled in terror. If he dragged her inside the elevator car, he could do whatever he wanted to her.

He yanked her closer. "*Il cavaliere*," he repeated in a husky voice.

His Italian sounded perfect, as if he'd studied the language. As if he'd been a student of opera. The irony of it. *Il Cavaliere* was no simple Hankey thug.

"*Il cavaliere*," she said, doing her best to mimic him.

"Louder!" he commanded.

Deanna struggled to clear her throat. "*Il cavaliere*," she croaked.

Suddenly her captor arched his back and cried out in anguish as if someone had just walloped him from behind. With a fierce shove, he pushed Deanna away from him. She tried to break the fall with her hands. But he'd acted so savagely, she'd flown across the hall, landing on an elbow. The pain coursing through her arm was paralyzing. Yet, she had to see his face. She twisted around in time to see the elevator doors close on a mustachioed man with an eye mask battling an unknown assailant, his dark cape flying through the air, à la Don Giovanni.

"Help!" she cried. "Oh, heaven help me."

Then everything went black.

2
The Claque

*Deanna regains consciousness with a blistering headache.
During the assault, she snagged her hose and snapped off
one of her heels. She takes the freight elevator to the third
floor and limps to the entrance of the boardroom.*

Hovering outside, Deanna peered through the glass-paned door, wringing her hands. How long had she been unconscious? Her elbow still smarted, so she couldn't have been out long. And who'd fought off *Il Cavaliere* in the freight elevator, sparing Deanna from his clammy lips and hot hands?

It had to be ten o'clock or later since everyone was waiting on her: Richard Rohrer, a dermatologist, now retired from practice, the only doctor on the guild; Oriane Longenecker, Hankey's finest lyric soprano named for a shining ingénue from French opera; and Vivian Pirelli, the newest member of the guild, a ketchup heiress-cum-New-Age-wacko.

Deanna tugged at her hose. *Il Cavaliere* had wrinkled her gabardine suit and ruined her $300 stilettos. But she was alive. Nothing but her pride had been injured. So she took a deep breath, squared her shoulders, and hobbled into the room, hoping the guild wouldn't notice her torn stockings and graceless gimp.

"It's about time, Madam Chairman," Richard said, adjusting the clasp on his bolo tie, which he did habitually. He glanced at her legs then at her feet. "Why are you limping?"

She seated herself at the head of the table, summoning her inner tigress. "Something happened."

"There's a stain on the carpet in the lobby," Oriane said, nose-deep in a fashion magazine. "Thought you'd want to know."

Deanna cleared her throat. "I've been—" She forced her mouth to form the word she needed. "Assaulted."

Oriane dropped her magazine. Vivian, who'd been organizing her breakfast on a tray in front of her—an assortment of rainbow capsules—stopped and gasped.

"What?" Richard said.

"Wh-where?" Vivian stammered.

Deanna swallowed hard. "On the first floor, near the bathrooms."

Richard jumped out of his chair and rushed to her side. "Are you hurt? Did he—?" He reached for her hand and immediately felt her pulse at her wrist.

"Oh, no!" Oriane cried. "What should we do?"

"Nothing," Deanna said, removing Richard's hand to rub her elbow. She was embarrassed by the incident more than anything else. She should've jammed her high heel into his shin and given him a cross-power punch to the head while he was still hopping around on one foot. When she really needed her kickboxing classes to go into hyperdrive, all that expensive training had meant nothing. "My elbow's a little sore. My neck, too, where he grabbed me. I'm shaken up more than anything else."

"We should call a doctor!" Oriane cried.

"I *am* a doctor," Richard snapped.

"You're a dermatologist," Oriane said.

Richard scoffed. "Oh, never mind." He gently placed his hands on Deanna's jaw line. "Can you move your neck?"

Deanna nodded, letting her head loll gently, side to side, forward and back. She removed Richard's hands from her face. "Why didn't I see him coming?"

Vivian finished downing her capsules and replaced the cap on her water bottle. "No woman expects such things will happen to her." She reached for her purse. "I'm calling the police immediately."

"Don't do that." Deanna herself sounded urgent. She needed to take the emotion out of her voice in order for everyone else to remain calm. "Need I remind you what's going to happen if we don't hire someone today? We have to go through with these interviews."

"You're being an idiot," Vivian said, dialing her cell phone. "We'll just *reschedule* them."

Deanna opted to revisit the *idiot* comment another time and stick to the issue at hand even though Vivian was now mumbling something about a police emergency into her phone. "No, we can't reschedule them. The first candidate . . . wait a minute." Deanna reached into her bag, pulled out some papers, and distributed them. Then she put on her reading glasses. "Don Blank was supposed to have driven all the way from Boston last evening," Deanna said. "And the other one's flying in from Fairbanks."

"Fairbanks, Alaska?" Oriane cooed. "That's exotic."

"Fairbanks, New Mexico," Deanna corrected.

Vivian peered over her bifocals at the rest of the guild. "The police are on their way."

"In regards to this Blank fellow, wasn't there someone waiting outside," Richard asked, looking confused, "when you came in?"

Deanna shrugged. "No one hanging around upstairs."

Oriane's head bobbed to attention. "I'll bet Don Blank was your attacker! I guess he won't be showing up for his interview this morning."

"We don't know that." However, Deanna's assailant spoke perfect Italian, was dressed like Don Giovanni, and knew the Italian word for "nobleman," *il cavaliere*, which Giovanni insists on calling himself throughout the opera. Artistic directors of opera companies were often fluent in other languages. They'd also have access to all of a company's resources, including the costume shop. "I suppose I should've called Blank's references."

Richard looked aghast. "You didn't do that?"

"His references were such prominent people in opera, I didn't follow up with them," Deanna admitted. "I'm certain he'll show."

"What did your attacker make you do?" Oriane asked, her eyes wide with interest.

"None of that now," Richard scolded.

Vivian huffed. "I'd like to know. I'll need to protect myself when he comes after me."

"Why don't you all have a tea party and discuss it on your own time?" Richard said hotly. "We need to get down to business."

"Let me stick my head out the door and see if Don Blank's arrived," Deanna said. "Then, we'll get started."

As Deanna rose from her chair, she felt a kink in her neck, reaching down into her shoulder blades. Now that Vivian had made her blessed phone call, Deanna knew the Hankey police would show. She just hoped the inevitable investigation wouldn't interfere with her spa visit later that morning. Missing her regularly scheduled facial and massage would only compound her suffering. She opened the door, glancing up and down the empty hallway. The elevator dinged brightly, signaling its arrival on the third floor. Deanna gripped the doorknob. What if her attacker was behind those elevator doors? She held her breath as the doors eased open. Out stepped two uniformed city police officers—a middle-aged man so slim he couldn't possibly intimidate hardened criminals, and a second one, so overweight he couldn't run down the heftiest of Wagnerian sopranos.

Deanna stepped forward and extended her hand. "I'm Deanna Lundquist."

"So, uh," Slim began, "are you the, uh, afflicted personage?"

Afflicted personage? "Do you mean the victim? That's me," she said, answering herself before Slim could. "It happened this morning. On my way to the bathroom."

"Give us the 4-1-1," Portly said.

When Deanna repeated what her attacker had made her say, *il cavaliere*, Slim and Portly looked at each other and rolled their eyes. She was telling them about the mystery person who nailed *Il Cavaliere* from behind when she heard raised voices inside the board room. "One second," she told the officers.

"I don't like *Don Giovanni*," Vivian was saying as Deanna reentered the room.

"You're not serious?" Richard asked.

"Why don't you like it?" Oriane asked, apparently ready to launch an opera intervention, if needed.

"It makes light of Donna Anna's sexual assault. That taints the whole production for me," Vivian said. "Look at what just happened to Deanna. We don't need to parade a dashing role model who preys on women in front of our male subscribers."

"It's like Deanna is Donna Anna or something!" Oriane blurted out.

Richard threw his hands in the air. "Not all men are predators. Not to mention, our male subscribers probably have erectile dysfunction anyway."

"Ew!" Oriane said. "TMI, Richard."

"And another thing," Vivian continued. "The talking statue in the cemetery and the demons from hell? Gothic dreck. It frightens people without imparting any genuine understanding about the spirit world."

"I'm sorry Mozart didn't ask your *permission*," Richard said, his voice increasing in volume as he rose from his seat, "to write a heap of *gothic dreck* which is only regarded as the most-acclaimed opera of all time."

Deanna grimaced, scooting back out the door for further interrogation, which she much preferred to getting sucked into the boardroom fray.

She glanced at the officers. "Any more questions?"

Slim looked at his notepad. "The identity of the other personage—the one who, uh, 'saved' you? Height? Weight? Eye color?"

"No idea. He came from out of nowhere," Deanna said brusquely, thinking it was their job to do the investigating. "I did get a look at my attacker finally. He had a mustache. And he wore an eye mask and a black cape. Like Don Giovanni."

"Mask, cape," Portly muttered, pinching the end of his nose. "We'll be in touch."

Slim said, "We got your, uh, cell number, right?"

Deanna nodded. If those two represented Hankey's finest, she better start carrying her snub-nosed revolver again.

She followed them to the elevator. As they boarded, a stranger stepped off, dressed for an employment interview. Average height, on the chunky side, with light curly hair, and an easy smile. Well appointed in a linen jacket, linen shirt, and linen pants, all the color of bland twigs. "Don Blank?" she asked.

"Carter Knoblauch," Knoblauch said, nodding. *"Buon giorno, signora."*

Deanna's eyes tore over his mustachioed face, searching for another sign. Was this the cavalier who'd terrorized her earlier that morning? She had a fraction of a second to decide whether to retrieve the officers or give Knoblauch the benefit of the doubt. "You—you speak Italian?"

Knoblauch shrugged. "I prefer German. Since you were producing *Don G.,* I thought I'd let loose with some Italian for a change."

"That might've cut it on any other day," Deanna said, more to herself.

"Pardon me?" Knoblauch asked, but Deanna said nothing. "What were the police doing here?

"Petty theft this morning." She extended her hand. "I'm Deanna Lundquist, guild chair. I'll see you in."

She led Knoblauch to the boardroom, threw open the door, and clapped her hands. "Carter Knoblauch, folks. His qualifications are on the back," she said, indicating the papers in front of them.

"Knoblauch, you say?" Richard pursed his lips to the right side of his mouth, and they made a smacking sound when he released them. *"Knoblauch* means 'one who grows garlic.'"

"Growing garlic is a job?" Oriane asked.

"It's a Germanic name," Richard said. "Though a number of Knoblauchs were living in the United Kingdom by the nineteenth century—"

"We don't care, Richard," Deanna interrupted, pushing her hair off her face. She kept smiling even though she knew presenting a candidate to this crew was akin to throwing raw meat at a pride of starving lions, that Knoblauch's breezy self-confidence would be shredded like a wildebeest's entrails inside ten minutes. "Won't you have a seat, Mr. Knoblauch?"

3
The Impresario

Deanna introduces all the guild members. Carter Knoblauch greets each one vigorously and seats himself. Oriane removes a pen from her purse. Vivian takes out a digital tape recorder.

"Do you mind if I record this?" Vivian asked.

"Not at all, Mrs. Pirelli," Knoblauch said.

"Call me Vivian," she said into the tape recorder as though she had something of inestimable value to impart. "Did you know that honeybees are disappearing in North America?"

Knoblauch fell silent for a moment. "I didn't know that."

"Tragic, isn't it?" She batted at the volume button. "You may begin."

Knoblauch nodded. Everyone else stared at Vivian like she'd just roared in from the Black Lagoon on a motor scooter, sans meds.

"I'd wager you're a Milwaukeean if I were a betting man, Mr. Knoblauch," Richard said. "Milwaukee has a large German population."

Knoblauch shrugged. "From Cincinnati originally."

Deanna listened carefully to every word Knoblauch said, considering whether he could have possibly been her attacker that morning. He didn't sound like the same man—he almost came off as British. Maybe he was putting on a different accent.

"Welcome to Hankey, Pennsylvania, Mr. Knoblauch," Deanna began. "Basically, we need an executive to provide both artistic direction to our productions and front office supervision. You would be the public face of the Hankey Opera Company, along with Maestro Schantzenbach, our resident conductor and music director."

Knoblauch smiled. "As long as the Maestro doesn't mind sharing the spotlight."

"I'm sure he wouldn't mind," Vivian said.

"What makes you so sure?" Deanna asked.

"I know Maestro," Vivian said.

Silently discounting Vivian's hollow claim, Deanna planted a smile on her face. "We have a few warm-up questions. What's your favorite opera?"

"Righto," Knoblauch said, sounding like a British native. "*Rigoletto*—hands down."

Rigoletto, Verdi's operatic hit parade. A head-on collision of beauty and savagery rooted in the masterful storytelling of Victor Hugo, whose heroines suffered no less than Hugo's own daughters: one drowned in a boating accident; the other was committed to an insane asylum.

Deanna could've predicted their reactions to Knoblauch's choice. Richard, who was estranged from his oldest daughter Marlena, would disapprove. Oriane had longed to sing Gilda's showcase aria, "*Caro nome*," and what trained singer wouldn't want a chance to tackle those trills? Vivian, on the other hand, would hate *Rigoletto* because it vilified a handicapped man, while Deanna would endorse his selection because *Rigoletto* was a potboiler—provided Knoblauch didn't do it as a minimalist production. No one in Hankey would pay to see a show produced on the cheap.

"Fine choice," Deanna jumped in. "What about *Don Giovanni*? Would you contemporize it?"

Knoblauch trembled with excitement. "Call me Knobby," he said, his mouth eking into a smile. "My costumes would be seventeenth-century Seville all the way. The lighting would be textured to release the work's primal power. Especially in the final scene when Giovanni descends into hell."

"You favor *Rigoletto* over *Don Giovanni* for primal power?" Richard asked.

"The first time I saw *Rigoletto* I was in high school," Knobby explained. "It was as deep as the Shakespearean tragedies we were studying." Knobby held his breath for a second then patted his chest.

"Excuse me, too much coffee." He smiled thinly as if he'd been stricken with some sort of pain. Heartburn at ten in the morning? What did Ohioans eat for breakfast? Rusty nails?

He continued. "Then I learned that Victor Hugo's story reminded Verdi of Shakespeare."

"That says something about your character," Richard interjected, "preferring a different show to the one we're producing."

"Interesting," Oriane said in a tone indicating she found the whole Verdi-Shakespeare tangent tiresome. "We have an event called Riverboat Days each summer when the Hankey Opera Company sings a special program with the Hankey Symphony. How do you feel about riverboats?"

"I practically lived on the Ohio River as a kid," he said. "We had all these wonderful riverfront events. Splashfest, Wienerfest. Anyway, your riverboat cruise sounds perfect for your off-season programming. If I were appointed to this post, I'd want to make opera more accessible to people in this town."

"Do you mean ADA-approved?" Richard asked. "We took care of that three years ago."

Knobby's face whitened at this question, so Deanna held up her hand. "Let him explain."

As he breathed in, Knobby's shoulders nearly reached his earlobes, like he had difficulty filling his lungs. "Did you know the average age of opera patrons is sixty-years-old? If we—"

"Are you feeling all right, young man?" Richard asked. "You've lost color in your face. You don't look well—and I should know. I'm a physician."

"I'm fine, really. It's—I flew in on a redeye. May I trouble you for a glass of water?"

"No trouble," Vivian said, excusing herself and heading to the adjoining kitchenette for a bottle of Evian.

"As I was saying, if we don't reach out to young people immediately, opera companies will have no audience in twenty years." Knobby searched their faces for moral support. "How about concerts in the schools and free family programs in your city park in summertime?"

"Summer programs in the park?" Oriane squealed with delight.

Knobby continued, though his voice sounded scratchy. "You could Simulcast productions on the side of this opera house like they do at Lincoln Center."

Oriane sighed. "We could be Lincoln Center on the Schuylkill!"

Richard reached for his tie again, sliding the clasp even closer to his neck. "Free concerts. Open-air movies. We can't have you giving our product away. We have the bottom line to think of."

"Underwriting, Richard," Deanna said. "How hard would it be to find a quality-of-life benefactor? That whole livability thing?" Deanna searched the faces of her fellow guild members for consensus. "Hankey's ready for your ideas, Knobby."

Richard turned to Deanna, continuing to fidget with the clasp of his tie. "You think asking for money is easy? I'd rather be 'tased.'"

"No, you wouldn't," Vivian said, returning with the water and handing it to Knobby. "Inhuman devices, tasers. They should be outlawed."

Deanna ignored Richard and Vivian. "Knobby, any questions thus far?"

Knobby downed most of the water, swallowing hard. "What happened to the last director?"

Deanna hesitated. "Terminated in January over a dispute with Maestro Schantzenbach. He called him a '*time-beater* obsessed with his *sausage dog*.'"

"He was," Richard began, "referring to the use of the term *time-beater* during the Baroque period—"

Knobby interrupted, "When the conductor literally pounded the beat with a stick instead of using a baton."

"Obviously, you know your opera, Knobby. In Hankey, all you need to know is this," Deanna said. "No one calls Maestro's beloved dachshund *a sausage dog*. Remember that, and you two will get along fine."

"As long as I don't have to be around him," Knobby said, then cleared his throat. "The dog, I mean. I'm allergic."

Deanna turned her evaluation form over and laid her pen on top of it. She'd been hoping for the ideal candidate to walk through that door, and, lo and behold, he had. If she'd been disappointed that Don Blank was a no-show, she'd put him out of mind. Why, she'd almost forgotten about her assault, except for intermittent pain around her temples, the crick in her neck, and her sore elbow.

Knobby exhaled as though he'd been exerting himself. "Land-o-Lakes, it's hot in here."

It was hot. At one time, the conference room, on the top floor of the opera house, was coated with yellow grime and reeked of stale cigar smoke. Four years ago, following a capital campaign co-chaired by Richard and Deanna, they'd transformed the boardroom into a pleasant meeting space with a new Scandinavian teak wood table, green paisley wallpaper, and frame-and-panel wainscoting in burnished brown. Unfortunately, the funding ran out before the air conditioning system could be upgraded because the carpeting was pricier than they'd expected, the same carpeting she'd just stained with a coffee spill the size of a dinner plate.

Richard got up and tried the window. He examined the frame and wiggled it up and down a few more times. "I wish I could let in some fresh air. You look like you need it."

"I'm—fine. Really," Knobby said, adding, "I oversweat—like the Albert Brooks character in *Broadcast News*. I'll break a sweat before everyone else in the room."

Richard grabbed the sash of the window and gave it a tug. "The maintenance men nailed the windows shut." He turned to Knobby. "You're from Cincinnati. You know all about Rust Belt towns. We're riddled with crime. At one time, steelworkers made thirty, forty bucks an hour. Then the steel mill closed. Then crack cocaine moved in. Now these guys'll do anything for money, including selling drugs. If they're not peddling drugs, they're robbing and burgling for drug money."

Deanna wished Richard would shut up about Hankey's drug problem and resultant crime wave, since they were supposed to be selling the town to Knobby rather than giving him reasons to look for employment elsewhere.

"Yes—well—Knobby, I think your perspective complements ours," Deanna said. "We've begun production on *Don Giovanni*, which opens May 21."

"I saw your write-up on the Internet," Knobby said with a frog in his throat. "Who's playing Giovanni?" he croaked.

Richard said, "We've have Donato Bianco. He's in town right now, working with Maestro."

Knobby tried to make a whistling sound but it came out as mostly air. "Quite a coup."

Deanna cocked her head. "The last time I saw Bianco perform the role, he was sporting a mustache. I hope we put it in his contract to keep it. It's perfect for *Don G.*"

At that point, Richard rose from his chair to tell *his* story: how he'd met Bianco in Philadelphia outside the stage door at the Academy of Music, how Richard had approached him and said Hankey would mount the show just for him if he'd perform here. Deanna had heard the story at least ten times since Christmas. Maybe she'd never stop hearing it.

Time to wrap things up. Knobby had grown wan, but then, group interviews could be stressful.

Salary negotiations were always the stickiest part of any interview. The guild couldn't afford to pay more than it had to. Deanna really liked Knobby, but she had to stick to the agreed-upon figure. "We're prepared to offer $45K—tops."

Richard nodded approvingly.

Rivulets of sweat streamed from Knobby's head. "My range is $50 to $60K."

"Just offer $50K," Vivian said. "This negotiation is making him uncomfortable."

Knobby's face blanched ghostly white.

"All right. How about $50K?" Deanna asked.

"I'm not feeling—" Knobby said.

Vivian said, "Would $55K make you feel better?"

"I can't—" Knobby pressed his hand to his throat, wheezing. "Not enough—"

"Knobby?" Deanna asked, realizing that more than a salary negotiation was in play. Something was gravely wrong with him. "Richard, do something."

But Richard was already out of his chair, hurrying to Knobby's side. "Are you diabetic? Did you forget—"

Knobby slipped off his seat and hit the floor. He was lying on his back, arms and legs sprawled in all directions, starved of breath. Now paler than the ghost of Banquo in Verdi's *Macbeth*, Knobby clutched at his chest.

"Somebody call 9-1-1," Richard ordered.

"Right. All right." Vivian yanked her purse off the floor, dug out her phone, and punched in the numbers.

"Oh, Lordy," Oriane cried, her hands cradling her face. "Is he going to die?"

"Calm yourself, Oriane." Richard knelt beside Knobby and leaned his head close to his nose. He blasted two quick puffs into his mouth, laid his hand on Knobby's chest, and shook his head. "Damn it, man. Breathe," he said, administering chest compressions.

Vivian began chanting her Eastern gobbledygook. "*Om Mani Padme Hum.*"

Oriane sobbed as Deanna put her arm around her shoulders. "Oh, Knobby," Oriane pleaded. "Don't die on us."

4
The Revival

Same day—11:31 a.m. Knobby has been treated in the Emergency Room of Holy Ghost Hospital in Hankey. Richard is pacing in the E.R. lobby, awaiting word of Knobby's condition.

"Knoblauch family?" an E.R. doctor called into the waiting area. "Any family members here for Carter Knoblauch?"

Knoblauch family? That's me, Richard thought. He rose from the hard plastic chair, waving one hand in the air, supporting his aching back with the other. He hadn't gotten down on his hands and knees to give CPR in a long time. "Here!"

The physician approached, not looking grim. But not looking as though he had good news to impart either. "Are you related to Carter Knoblauch?"

"Close friend," Richard said. "I'm a physician myself."

"He had a life-threatening arrhythmia when he came in. The EKG indicated myocardial infarction. We shocked him twice," the doctor began. "Then we did lose his rhythm for a bit."

Richard's mouth went dry. "He flatlined?"

The doctor laid his hand on Richard's forearm. "Not to worry. We got a stable rhythm and moved him to the cath lab. You can see him in CCU after they open up that blocked artery."

Back at the opera house, as the EMS drivers prepared Knobby for departure, Richard had volunteered to follow the ambulance to the hospital, urging Deanna to get herself checked out once she confessed to fainting outside the freight elevator. Oriane had offered to drive her, but Deanna waved her off, promising everyone she'd see her family doctor right away.

So Knobby was undergoing heart catheterization. At his age, he had a good chance of not only survival but returning to a normal life. Richard reminded himself to call Deanna. He wanted to make sure she had followed up on her own care and to let her know that Knobby would pull through.

Back when he presided over the guild, he established a phone tree in the event of an emergency, one they still used today: Richard would call Deanna, who would call Oriane, who would then call lowest limb on the tree, in this case, Vivian—kind of like whisper down the lane via Verizon. He punched in Deanna's number.

"Did you get yourself checked out?"

"I'm fine," she said, sounding fine at that. "What about Knobby?"

"You've seen a doctor?"

"He told me I fainted because I hadn't eaten anything since lunch yesterday."

"I don't know how you're going to chair the guild if you don't take care better of yourself," he chided. "Crash dieting is for the birds. You've gained weight. Not lost it."

"I thought we were discussing Knobby."

"I'm getting there," Richard began. "Knobby's in the cath lab. He'll pull through—I'm certain of it."

"What a relief," Deanna said.

"He'll be in recovery for a while," Richard explained. "Then they'll move him to the CCU. He'll be out for two to three weeks at most."

"A heart incident at forty. That's sobering," Deanna said. "He's young. He's my age."

"You're forty-two," Richard said.

"You should be so young," Deanna said, her voice back to business-as-usual.

"Have you heard from the police?"

"No," Deanna said. "That suits me just fine. I don't have time to go downtown and look at a police line-up anyway. Too many guild things need my attention right now."

"Just as long as one of those things," Richard reminded her, "includes taking care of yourself."

"Right. Now that Knobby's going to make it, offer him sixty thousand."

"Where does our endowment stand these days?" Richard asked.

"Same as the close of business yesterday. A few ticks over $280,000."

"Ouch," Richard said. He and Deanna worked so hard to raise that money. To see stock market losses siphoning it away was killing him. Richard pursed his lips. "I don't have to tell you what will happen to the Hankey Opera Company if *Don Giovanni* doesn't sell out, if we're not in the black by June 30."

"No, you don't."

"I'm offering fifty, Deanna."

"You can't offer a man who just escaped death's clutches fifty thousand a year. Our benefits aren't that great. We want to keep him. Offer sixty and not a penny less. I'll call Oriane and tell her Knobby's going to pull through."

"Tell her he's *likely* to pull through."

"*Likely.* Got it. She can call Vivian."

"Good!" Richard said. "I can't talk to that woman without becoming aggravated."

Richard pocketed his cell phone, trudged up to the CCU, and plopped himself in a waiting room chair. Sheer and total relief barely described the sensation that enveloped him upon learning Knobby would survive. Despite circumstances that prevented everyone from sharing what they'd written on their evaluation forms, Richard was highly intuitive. He knew they'd all connected with Knobby that morning. Most of the time, that crew never agreed on a blinking thing.

At the same time, in allowing Knobby to survive, Richard felt The Man Upstairs had personally affirmed their selection and that the upcoming season would be blessed with great box office revenues and renewed critical acclaim. He salivated a bit, imagining the headlines: MAN SAYS NO TO DEATH, SAYS YES TO HANKEY OPERA; and DEAD MAN WALKING INTO OPERA HOUSE.

Why, this news offered potential for a regional, national, or even syndicated human-interest story! Publications and radio shows that wouldn't have looked twice at Hankey—the *Baltimore Sun, Opera News*, or, heaven forbid, *Weekend Edition with Liane Hansen*—would be calling for interviews within days. Was this the break—*the* big, sought-after break in the cultural and performing arts—that their little band deserved?

The last decade had been a struggle, scrabbling year to year to raise funds for one more season. Three years ago, when Richard and Deanna had thought things couldn't get any worse, Hankey Steel collapsed. The opera company not only lost a generous annual contribution from the town's largest employer, but many of the executives and their spouses moved out, taking their patronage and their matching gifts with them while the high-toned stores and restaurants they frequented went the way of the steel company.

Deanna had spearheaded some new fundraising events allowing the company to hang on: a frolicsome Winter Carnivale and the Annual Martini Masque (an idea purloined from another company), which was coming up in six weeks. Deanna had even donned an Apple-tini costume herself at last year's event, soaking up the limelight. People paid admission to see her legs in apple-green Lycra.

Sneaking glances at Deanna earlier that morning, Richard could tell that she'd gained weight over the winter—too much weight to wear the costume, especially the narrowed part of the martini glass that hugs the hips. Once word got around she'd have to be replaced by Oriane, who had a lovely face (but even a bowlegged ostrich had a nicer pair of gams), attendance would suffer. What he didn't know was the cause of Deanna's weight gain.

Pregnant at forty-two? Not unheard of, but unlikely. Deanna had divorced Stu two years ago. Richard thought her weight gain was probably related to improper metabolism aggravated by crash diets. Her skin, normally smooth and creamy, had recently become dry and inflamed. Like any other major organ of the body, extreme dieting affected the skin, too. He'd ferret out the truth about Deanna's expanding mid-section after Knobby was back on his feet.

Sooner rather than later, he'd also need to address her request for more help, someone with event-planning experience. She could only increase the quantity and quality of fund-raising events with some expert assistance. Richard knew she was right. He just didn't know where to turn. All of his professional colleagues wanted nothing to do with planning special events. It was everything he could do to get them to attend—period.

The sound of a grief-stricken man wailing in Italian—Richard's ringtone—poured into the guest waiting area. A woman nodding off in the lounge with the latest issue of *People* in her lap screamed and knocked a cup of coffee onto the popular weekly, staining Heather Locklear's newest gown and dripping onto Holy Ghost's beige Berber carpet. While he struggled to mute his ringer, the duty nurse sprang up from behind the desk and came tearing down the concourse in Richard's direction,.

Throughout his career, and more recently because of his wife Mary's illness, Richard had worked with dozens of nurses. They fell into two camps: the kindly, unassuming nurses, sweeter than saccharin; and the bullies, who, as luck would have it, were charged with tasks such as administering enemas. Richard deduced the one stalking toward him was a bully of the enema-giving variety. He wondered what had happened to the sweet nurse who readily gave him updates on Knobby's condition before lunch. He checked his watch. By golly, it was ten after three. Nurse Saccharin was finished for the day. He'd picked the wrong nurse to be violating hospital rules on her shift.

"Turn that off," the duty nurse hissed. "No cell phones allowed—*sir*," she said, and as she called him *sir*, it was clear she found him unworthy of the courtesy title, never realizing Richard was a doctor—or at least, that he had been.

Last year, Richard had retired from his practice at age sixty-four. Within months, Mary'd died unexpectedly. Richard had fully expected Mary to follow him in death. Sixty-four is too young to die, especially a seemingly healthy woman. Most lived decades beyond that in the United States. Her death was tragic unless it was Mary's ticket to serenity, death being preferable to having Richard underfoot day and night in a household she'd had to herself most of her adult life.

After Mary's passing, Richard had fallen into a bout of melancholy and changed his ring tone to Pavarotti's *"Vesti la giubba"* from *Pagliacci*. After knocking back one too many Wild Turkeys, Richard would call his own cell phone over and over, just to wallow in the few measures the ringtone captured—the most moving section in opera's most gut-wrenching aria. He was reduced to sobbing after three phone calls—precisely the outcome he sought. Such a ritual proved cleansing. He felt that by releasing his pent-up blubbering in an expedient fashion, his grief would ease sooner, and he could get on with his life. Besides, playing those same four measures on his cell phone was easier than cueing up his stereo over and over.

His uncultured son-in-law would burst into a chorus of, "No more Rice Krispies! We are out of Rice Krispies!" whenever he heard Richard's ringtone. To everyone else, *"Vesti la giubba"* was an arresting piece of music. If Pavarotti's dramatic tenor could—and often did—jolt operagoers out of their plush seats, it terrified everyone in the CCU that afternoon.

Richard considered making the argument with Nurse Enema that if anyone had lost a loved one that day, they'd find no greater expression of sympathy than in Leoncavallo's famous aria. However, he was forced to admit—now that Knobby was going to pull through—*Pagliacci* made for a gloomy ringtone. In honor of Knobby's revival, he'd change it to something snappy like "The Toreador's Song" from *Carmen*.

And by Jove, wasn't Bizet a master with a march! It was springtime, and marches suited perfectly, heralding the burgeoning promise of the season. They got Richard's blood pumping, just like the sight of creamy shoulders revealed by skimpy halter tops and beautiful firm thighs emerging from short shorts with the arrival of warmer weather. Young women had never come to see him unless they had eczema, acne, warts, or impetigo. Springtime constituted his E-Z Pass to all the perfect skin he never observed while practicing. If opera was his passion, seeing beautiful skin on women was his guilty pleasure.

Now that he'd silenced his ringtone, he checked his messages. A text message? From whom? Oriane? She knew all the trendy abbreviations used in texting. "TMI, Richard"—that's what she'd said. Besides guild members and his daughter, not many others had access to his cell number. During his professional life, all of his calls were placed for him by nurses or administrative assistants. He never developed much tolerance for making his own. Come to think of it, he didn't know how to retrieve a text message. He thumbed his way around the message options until he stumbled upon an inbox and clicked it open: *gr8 news be by soon vivian.*

Vivian? Besides being inarticulate, she didn't believe in capital letters or punctuation either. Well, he'd seen enough of her for one day. She should just stay away. If he knew how to text, he'd have told her as much. But he could never figure out how to add spaces between words or include periods. He wasn't about to ask his grandson for help. And he certainly wasn't sending messages without proper spacing and punctuation.

Pocketing his phone, he approached the nurse's station. He cleared his throat until Nurse Enema raised her eyes to meet his over the counter. "Madam," he said, in complete and utter supplication. "May Carter Knoblauch have visitors?" When he was a practicing physician, his white coat had allowed him passage anywhere in the hospital, thereby eliminating the need to kiss up to bullying nurses. At one time, he couldn't wait to hang up that coat. He wished he had it now.

Nurse Enema sighed heavily, which he translated to mean, *You're a pain in the ass.* "Are you his grandfather, Jocko?" she intoned.

His grandfather? Knobby was forty, for chrissakes. Richard would have to be eighty to be Knobby's grandfather. Had Richard really aged that much since retirement, since Mary's death? And *Jocko*? The nurse had insulted him, but he would contain himself.

"I'm his employer," he explained calmly. "This is not a case of my being fit to see him. The question is whether Mr. Knoblauch is fit to be seen." He stuck his index finger straight in the air, as if he'd suddenly thought of the perfect line to cap off the perfect rejoinder. "'Ay, there's the rub.'"

"There's the *what*?" Nurse Enema had a hundred expressions— all of them variations on a scowl. "Family members only."

Richard scowled back. "I'm a doctor. And a good friend of the president of this hospital. And—"

"You're a doctor?" She leaned in, glowering at him. Richard noticed a raised mole around the collar of her uniform that needed removal and decided not to tell her as much—not that she'd give him credence anyway. "Shame on you for using your cell phone in this hospital. You should know better."

Götterdämmerung, he would not be upbraided by this wretched woman, completely graceless in every way, right down to a hairy neck mole. Most likely, a product of that damned community college, a state-subsidized R.N. mill. Richard was approaching his dotage with more momentum than a Mozart overture racing to its conclusion. One might have thought that he would appreciate an institution pouring hundreds more health care workers into local hospitals. At sixty-five, he was now ripe for all manner of chronic ailments—acid reflux, angina, arthritis, irritable bowel, hearing loss, macular degeneration, incontinence.

One would've thought wrong.

"Madam—" he protested.

"Just a cotton-picking minute, Jocko."

If she called him Jocko one more time, he'd coldcock her with her own clipboard and blame it on his son-in-law who'd insisted he watch a Three Stooges marathon last Christmas.

With overtones of disdain, she muttered, "Doctors," under her breath. "I need to check his chart." She made an elaborate ceremony out of inspecting and reinspecting Knobby's information before finally informing Richard that, yes, he could proceed.

As Richard shuffled toward Knobby's room, he decided to make a request of Mary during their nightly talk, which he always did in his pinstriped PJ's. Would she come back and haunt Nurse Enema who worked Saturday afternoons in the CCU? Since Mary had neither the patience nor the stomach for ghost stories when she was alive, he anticipated her needing further illumination on how to haunt someone.

Richard would say, "Bug your eyes out. Wear something flowing and sweep around making noises like a screech owl," fully aware that Mary knew its haunting call. One had nested behind some loose boards in their garden shed a few years ago. "They have flowing get-ups in heaven, don't they?" he'd add, if she balked at his request.

Oh, how he missed her, especially in the smallest things.

He paused at the entrance to the room. If Knobby was resting, he'd leave a note at the desk when you-know-who wasn't looking, and come back tomorrow.

"Hello—Richard," Knobby said, his eyes open a slit. His voice was faint. Even uttering those few words had taxed him.

"Knobby, old sausage," Richard said with quiet enthusiasm. "You pulled through. Good for you, man." For someone who'd flatlined, Knobby looked calm and rested. "You look—fantastic," Richard said, because Knobby was a vision compared to a dead man.

"They told me," Knobby said, "that my heart stopped beating. That I died."

Richard had plenty of faults. He could be intolerant, pompous, condescending, and bossy. But when he was bedside, he never said anything to deprive a patient of hope. Hope had more healing powers that the traditional medical community was willing to admit. "Your heart stopped for a bit. But you were in the best possible place when it happened."

Knobby took a few labored breaths. "About the job. You're here to let me down easy?"

"Nonsense, man. I'm here to make an offer. We'll start you at—" Richard bit his tongue. "At $60K. But don't think about that now. Just think about getting better." Richard pointed to the armchair by the window. "Mind if I sit?"

Knobby attempted to pull himself up on the pillow and then thought better of it. "Sixty thou? I accept. Can I share something personal with you?"

Richard shrugged. Intimate exchanges, *mano a mano*, had never been his strong suit.

Knobby's eyes widened. "You'll never guess who I ran into? My dog. I saw my dog—" he began, too choked up to continue.

Richard tightened his bolo tie. "In the CCU? Well, that's interesting."

Knobby spoke softly but intently. "First, I saw Figaro."

Richard liked some dogs—the ones he wasn't afraid of. He'd been bitten by a German shepherd as a child and never overcame his fear of attack dogs.

"Figaro, my Doberman. A lamb of a dog, I tell you," Knobby explained. "He was ninety-five pounds of gristle and had teeth like a tiger shark. But as sweet as peanut-butter buckeyes."

Richard reached for his tie again to loosen it. "I thought you were allergic to dogs."

"Oh, I only developed allergies as an adult. Then I saw my grandmother. And then my sweet old mother, God bless her soul. Then, Mrs. Muce, my elementary school music teacher." Knobby laid his head against his pillow and closed his eyes momentarily.

Figaro? His mother? His music teacher? Knobby'd just gotten out of the cath lab. How could he have had all those visitors? He must be hallucinating, dreaming, or fresh from a near-death experience. What was it called? Oh, yes. An N-D-E.

Within seconds, Knobby's eyes fluttered open. "Oh, and I greeted a little woman I never met before, who introduced herself as your wife."

"You saw Mary?" Good thing Richard was sitting down. "You're trying to get a rise out of me, aren't you, with this fabrication about visiting the afterlife? Well, you have my rapt attention, young man."

"Actually, she was waiting for me when I stepped off the elevator. Gave me a big hello." Knobby sighed. "Lovely woman."

Richard drew in his breath sharply to stem the hurt welling up in his chest. "Mary was waiting for you—and said hello?"

Knobby nodded. "At the elevator."

Richard was afraid to put any trust in Knobby's story. But he had to continue questioning him—to determine whether Knobby had a cruel streak, was off his nut, or was actually telling him some version of the truth. "Which elevator?"

"The one just off the E.R. I hung around for a little while, watching everything. But that got old quickly. I could tell the doctors were getting frustrated. So, I decided to go to the top floor—so to speak."

"You—watched—the hospital staff working?" Richard asked, overemphasizing each word.

"Yes, when I was dead."

"And you saw Mary?" Richard said, hoping to poke a hole in his story.

"You'll be pleased to know she's up there where it's all bright lights and fluffy cloud pillows and paisley wallpaper. A lot like your boardroom, in fact. I imagine she was exactly as she used to be when she was alive. Charming woman. A bit cheeky. Fantastic lady." Knobby winced and lightly pressed his hand to his sternum. He exhaled softly. "Sorry for your loss."

Knobby had seen Mary in the afterlife, which was like a great boardroom in the sky? Richard knitted his brow. "I'm not enjoying this little *yarn* of yours."

Knobby grew quiet, presumably considering how to answer Richard's question in a way that quelled his anxiety. "I'm sorry to have upset you. I thought you'd want to know she's well. As well as she can be . . . considering."

Memories of Mary bubbled up. How many performers had commented the house was perfection because of Mary's tireless hospitality work? Freshly brewed coffee, juices, homemade quick breads, and bouquets of flowers, almost a dozen, gracing the green room for the singers and musicians, for each dress rehearsal and performance. "She's a saint, I tell you," more than one performer had told Richard. "You know you're loved when you come to sing in Hankey," others reported. What better legacy could Mary have left than to have made Hankey a place where performers felt welcome and appreciated. She'd done peerless work as a guild member—

never seeking the limelight, all because she believed in the work of the guild and the sheer magic, the glory, of classic opera. No one could replace Mary, especially not Vivian—not only in Richard's heart, but as hospitality chair. Mary was selfless—nonpareil—while Vivian was . . . Vivian.

What had Knobby been nattering about? Still going on about his near-death experience? His N-D-E? Well, TMI, Richard thought. As Knobby continued babbling, he oozed the same kind of spiritual energy as someone speaking in tongues. Not that Richard had ever seen people doing this in real life—only on cable television. Like religious fundamentalists and snake handlers, Knobby had been touched by something otherworldly.

"Someone said, 'Knobby, time to go back to the E.R.' I didn't recognize the voice though it was a sweet one. Here, it was your Mary. Just before the elevator arrived, my family and Mary ganged up on me and pushed me down the elevator shaft. I was falling and falling, terrified I'd never reach a final resting place. I wound up back in my body in the E.R., alive and twitching," Knobby said, his voice gaining strength. "I'm a changed man, Richard. I want to— write a poem about it. No. I want to write a song about—not just a song. An opera. I'll write an opera about it."

"An opera about falling down an elevator shaft? You couldn't produce it in this town. Modern doesn't fly in Hankey, Pennsylvania." Could Richard retract a job offer from a man who'd flatlined without being visited by three of Knobby's dead relatives, the ghost of his attack dog, and Mary herself? "Please, no more stories about seeing Mary in heaven. I can't take it."

"Agreed. As for that opera, I'd write it in a classical style. Like a sequel to *Don Giovanni*—what happened to Giovanni after he got sucked into the afterlife. The high concept would be 'Giovanni's near-death experience.'"

"Giovanni's NDE?" a woman's voice said. "How fabulous."

As promised, Vivian had made an appearance at Holy Ghost. Vivian, who ate pills for breakfast. Vivian, who had friends who claimed to be galactic channelers—whatever in God's name that meant. Of all the guild members, Vivian was the one Richard least wanted to see today. *gr8 news be by soon vivian*. Gr8, indeed.

Vivian pulled out a bouquet from behind her back. "For you, Knobby. A tussie-mussie." She beamed. "Lavender, salvia, and rosemary—they all fight disease."

"That's sweet, Vivian." Knobby blushed. "Guess what? I met Richard's late wife."

Why was he telling this news to Vivian, of all people?

"In the afterlife?" she asked. "Very exciting."

"Take that mussie whatever out of this room right now," Richard said, his voice growing threatening, like he was somehow channeling Figaro. He could feel the blood rising into his forehead. "You can't give flowers to someone in a cardiac care unit."

Vivian's nostrils flared. "They're healing flowers."

"I don't care if they have the power to bring Eurydice back from the underworld," he said, struggling to control his temper. "It's irresponsible," he added, conveniently forgetting he'd just used a cell phone in a restricted area. "They have to go."

"For pity's sakes," Vivian said. "I can't believe the medical establishment totally discounts herbal remedies. The healing effects of flowers have been used for centuries. They're cut flowers, Richard. They're not going to take oxygen out of the room."

"But you're going to put them in water, aren't you? Standing water breeds germs. Get rid of them, or step out of this room." Richard had wanted to grind her down until she was a stump of her politically correct, New-Age self. He was still sore at her for criticizing *Don Giovanni*. He was, however, right about cut flowers being germy. He was only thinking about Knobby when he'd put her in her place. At least that's what he told himself.

"Excuse us," said Vivian. She looped her arm through Richard's. "Come along, *sir*," she said with the same inflection as Nurse Enema while dragging him into the hall.

A woman hadn't taken Richard's arm in a year, and he realized he was enjoying the sensation of it too much to refuse her—even Vivian. He challenged her instead. "What do you think you're doing?"

"Not so loud," she shushed him, unlinking her elbow from his. "This is a hospital."

Richard slapped a hand to the side of his face in mock horror. "Really? You've proven yourself to be keenly observant."

"Oh, cork it," she said.

Richard leaned in, speaking with feigned lightness. "Would that be synthetic cork or natural cork? But there's a scarcity of natural cork. Why not break out a *box* of wine? No danger to cork there. Oh, but then we'd be cutting down trees to make the boxes, poor trees."

Vivian sniffled. "You can scold me about flowers and chide me about cork. But all your negative energy isn't going to help Knobby one bit."

If Mary were alive, she'd have been more tolerant of Vivian than Richard. While sitting under the dryer at the Font-o-Beauty, the salon most popular with doctors' wives, Mary heard that Vivian had been kicked off the hospital auxiliary. No one had ever been booted off that auxiliary. It was inconceivable, a needy non-profit casting off Vivian. A Frantz, no less. Supposedly, Vivian dissolved into tears when the president told her the news. Was Vivian going to cry now? Richard couldn't bear to have a woman start crying on him.

"Rail all you want. That's what bitter old coots do. But don't do it in front of Knobby," Vivian scolded as if speaking to a willful child. "Create more stress, and he'll be dead as a doorknob before you know it," she said, also having a tendency for misspeaking and mixing metaphors.

Bitter old coot? Now, wait one—. Richard was formulating a comeback when he was momentarily mesmerized by the pair of eyes locked on his. What color were they exactly? Aquamarine? Turquoise? Were they naturally that color or was she wearing colored lenses? He was so taken with Vivian's eyes he'd forgotten she'd called him a bitter old coot. He'd barely noticed she'd said *dead as a doorknob.* And her skin. Her skin was pearlescent.

"It was wrong of me to come here." Vivian stepped back and held up her hand as if to prevent Richard from running off at the mouth about anything else until she regained her composure. "But the way you're acting, you're no good for Knobby either. Go home, Richard, and—kick the dog."

He stood slack-jawed in the hallway. "B-b-uh, b-b-uh," he muttered, shuffling behind Vivian as she slipped back into Knobby's room. He was no dog kicker. He didn't even have a dog.

"Nice to see you, Knob," she said. "I'll stop back tomorrow and tell you all about the health benefits of garlic. I'd recommend a regimen right away."

Knobby smiled weakly, and Vivian breezed back into the hall past Richard in the direction of the elevator, without saying goodbye. Richard's gaze followed her the entire way.

For a moment, he thought about chasing after her to apologize, about asking her to stay, but his feet felt as though they were made of stone, just like the statue of the town founder Colonel Henry Hankey, who stood sentinel mounted atop the opera house marquee. He lingered there, dumbstruck, considering what had just happened. Was his personality as grating as Vivian had made it out to be? Mary had never minded his ways—she'd never said anything to him, was never cross with him a day in her life.

He missed her profoundly. The last time he was in a hospital was when Mary was stricken—for which he felt utterly responsible. One of his patients had left an issue of *Cosmo* in his office. He'd flipped through it, lingering over an article on multiple orgasms in women, wanting to try out a few techniques when he and Mary next made love, which they did the day before she died. They'd been to a matinee of *Der Rosenkavalier*. During the tender love duet, "Presentation of the Silver Rose," Mary grasped his hand and wouldn't let go. The music, the sheer beauty of the two voices, had filled her with longing for romance. Whenever Mary was so moved, Richard knew he could please her—and please her he did, later that afternoon, several times, using some of the magazine's tips. For a while, he consoled himself that Mary had known glimpses of heaven the day before she passed. Then a sense of guilt engulfed him. If she hadn't become so emotional at the opera and later, aroused in bed, would she be alive today?

The next day, Mary was in the ICU. A blood vessel had burst in her brain. Richard waited and waited for news that she'd regained consciousness. But she never did. She just drifted away—like something precious that gets caught up in a wave and carried out to a vast ocean, not to be seen again. He never had the chance to say goodbye, to tell her how much he loved her, to kiss her cheek while she was still alive—not that she would have heard him or felt his kiss anyway—but it would've given him some closure.

Then, who of all people gets to interact with his late wife but Knobby, someone Mary had never known in life. If the interaction had taken place at all. Vivian believed Knobby's story, yet she barely knew him or Richard.

Previously, he'd regarded Vivian's eyes to be about as welcoming as two interrogation room lamps. Today, when her blue-green eyes fixed their gaze on him, he had to admit that they reminded him of the water in his backyard pool. Surprisingly, he found himself wanting to slip on a pair of trunks and dive in. Why had he never noticed the subtle shades of red in her hair before? Like a glass of Beaujolais nouveau when you gave it a swirl in a stream of sunlight. All those lush and lovely shades of red.

He was being disloyal to Mary, to her memory. It had only been a year that he'd been without her, the longest year of his life.

But he loved redheads. He always had. Typically, redheads had the creamiest complexions. And sweet little freckles. He was also terrified of redheads, which is why he'd married Mary in the first place. Any woman with Mary's hair color, an innocuous shade of brown, would have to work hard to be treacherous, if half his theory proved correct. The other half being that duplicity came naturally to redheads, though where he got that idea, only therapy might reveal. He did remember loathing the "I Love Lucy" show because Lucy was always scheming behind her husband's back, her idiotic husband, so easily duped. Richard always prided himself on being a resourceful, capable husband. What woman wouldn't want a man like Richard?

Had Mary ever wanted him? At first, of course, but as the marriage endured, had she needed him like he'd needed her? If only he'd paid more attention to her.

If only Vivian weren't a redhead with a creamy complexion.

Perhaps he had been hasty in condemning Vivian for her fascination with channeling and mystical phenomena. Maybe Vivian had a friend who could—how does one put such a thing—get him in touch with Mary if she were roaming around heaven like Knobby suggested.

Richard decided he'd behaved cruelly and would apologize; Mary would've made him say he was sorry had she witnessed his actions. He couldn't bring himself to phone Vivian for any reason, let alone utter the words, "I'm sorry." No, he would send her flowers— a mussie. She deserved that much.

Lavender, salvia, roses, and daisies. He couldn't forget nasturtiums—Mary's favorite. How would he sign the card? *Vivian, I was wrong to be cross and crabby. Forgive me. Richard.* No, he couldn't say *Richard*. He'd write *From Dr. Rohrer* instead. *From Dr. Rohrer?* Boy, that sounded drippy, as his daughter Marlena used to say, when they'd been on speaking terms.

He missed Marlena and wanted to patch things up with her, too. After Mary died, he had shot off his mouth one too many times where Marlena and her family were concerned. He complained that she was raising his only grandson to be a dumb jock—no piano or violin lessons and no proper exposure to things of culture—and that Marlena was turning her only son into a clone of her oafish husband. Had Mary been alive to hear that, she would have taken hold of his upper ear and yanked it, which she had done once or twice during their marriage when she became totally frustrated with him. However, instead of Marlena agreeing with her father, she said she wanted nothing more to do with him.

She couldn't have meant that. With Mary gone, he was all the family that Marlena and the grandchild had.

Today was a day for making amends. He would send two bouquets. One to Vivian and one to Marlena. The message to both: *A sweeter woman ne'er drew breath.* You could never go wrong with poetry, Mary always said. But he wouldn't sign his name. The bouquet's purpose was not to draw attention to himself but to make each woman feel joy, if for only a few seconds.

It was settled. He would send the floral arrangements first thing in the morning.

Richard's face twitched like an insect had just alighted upon it. Reflexively, his hand flew to his cheek to wave whatever it was away. No biting insect; it felt more like a butterfly. A butterfly? Get a hold of yourself, Richard. Why would a butterfly be flitting around Holy Ghost Hospital in March? A housefly, maybe. It simply hadn't been warm enough to see butterflies. More likely, he was having a mini-stroke, a TIA. But there was no history of stroke in his family. Historically, Rohrer men lived longer than junkyard dogs. Not to mention that he'd just sailed through a stress test, using *sailed* metaphorically, since it was all done on a treadmill these days. But not an ordinary treadmill. You'd never see a treadmill outfitted like the ones hospitals used in any Hankey health club . . .

5
The Soubrette

The next day Deanna and Oriane have arranged to see Knobby in the CCU. They ride to Holy Ghost Hospital in near silence. Deanna is absorbed in a 2007 recording of Don Giovanni *pouring from her CD player with Johannes Weisser as Giovanni. Oriane tries to lose herself in her own musings.*

Oriane surveyed the interior of Deanna's Lexus, settling into the buttery-soft leather of the bucket seat. "Spiffy car," she said.

"Who says spiffy anymore? You're one of those millennials, aren't you?" Deanna asked, like *millennial* was a dirty word.

"My mother called this morning," Oriane said, ignoring the millennial barb. "There was an article in the police beat about your being assaulted by an Italian Zorro."

"I never used that term—Italian Zorro," Deanna said. "The officers must've come up with that on their own. I said 'Don Giovanni.' Tell me they've never heard of Don Giovanni?"

"How long have you lived in Hankey?"

"Too long—believe me. What else did those dumb officers say?"

"Well, that you were dragged to the elevator by your neck. And you thought he was going to 'have you.' Oh, and that you warned the ladies of Hankey to be on their guard against the Italian Zorro."

"Enough with this Italian Zorro already." Deanna pulled her sunglasses from an overhead compartment and slipped them on. "I'm trying to listen to this CD. I love Weisser's "Champagne Aria" and don't want to miss a note."

At least the policemen had known the legendary Zorro wasn't Italian. That showed some higher-order thinking, didn't it?

Oriane settled back into her seat, leaving Deanna to her "Champagne Aria," thinking of Knobby. She hadn't wanted to see him all by herself—that might have appeared forward. She already cared what Knobby thought of her. Bizarre, since they'd only known each other a few hours. So, she agreed to visit with Deanna, starting to doubt the wisdom of that decision.

But she had to see Knobby and give him the will to live. Sometimes it seemed like opera was a sea of old people—old performers and old patrons who preferred to do things in the same old way, year after year. At forty-years old, Knobby was no millennial, but he had young ideas, just like hers—how to attract younger audiences and younger singers. Knobby was exactly what the Hankey Opera Company needed, what she needed—an ally who cherished classic opera but had a progressive point-of-view about how to make it relevant in the twenty-first century.

All during the interview that morning, Oriane had envisioned herself and Knobby sharing simple pleasures—snuggling on the love seat at the opening night gala for *Don Giovanni*; standing at the railing of the riverboat with their arms wrapped around each other, watching the world go by from the open-air deck; and giving her special consideration for juicy supporting roles because they'd become affianced.

She'd taken a shine to Knobby. So, she couldn't possibly visit him alone. She would be showing her cards too soon and forfeiting her chance to win the big kitty if she did.

Oriane had spent a year as a novice in Hankey's Convent of the Sacred Heart immediately after high school. She'd thought she wanted to pursue sisterhood, but the reality of living without romantic love had driven her away from cloistered life. That and the fact that she'd never had a smoldering love affair before she got the call.

My-oh-my, how she pined for one now.

Love could only smolder when something, anything—human or inanimate—physically separated the would-be lovers. Be it a river, a mountain range, a magma-filled ravine like in the adventure movies, or an over-protective mother (like her own), obstacles erected between lovers fueled desire exponentially. Though no redoubtable obstacle, Deanna's presence would sufficiently impede the path to romance with Knobby that Oriane sought. With any luck, it might make him want her more, too.

Knobby hadn't been wearing a wedding ring, one of the first accessories a twenty-nine-year-old single woman looks for when sizing up a potential mate. There was no wife to contact as next of kin—only an Aunt Laverne on the outskirts of Cincinnati. The second accessory, according to Oriane's mother, being the wristwatch—a handy measure of income. The third? A diamond stud in the left earlobe. "Steer clear of men wearing those— romantically speaking," her mother had warned with such conviction that Oriane believed her mother spoke from a painful personal experience. "It can only bring heartbreak, falling for someone who can't love you in return." Oriane had gay friends whom she loved and who loved her like a sister. Perhaps her mother really meant "make love to."

If chit-chat was all she and Knobby ever shared in bed, that might suit her fine. Despite a return to the secular world ten years ago, she was still a virgin—which she knew the rest of the guild suspected once they learned she'd been a novitiate. Oriane regularly attended live broadcasts from the Met at the local Cineplex all by her lonesome, squealing and swooning whenever a dashing male star filled the screen—Marcelo Álvarez, Nathan Gunn, Juan Diego Flórez—all gifted and gloriously appealing, especially in high definition.

"Underneath all the star quality," Deanna had once told her, "the swagger, the bare chests, well-defined and gleaming with sweat, a man was a man at the *root* of it," winking on the word *root*. Oriane understood her to mean that men were rather undifferentiated from other men, an unshakable reality a virgin such as herself could never appreciate until she learned it the hard way.

Oriane had remained chaste, but not for religious reasons. Rather, she had never gotten past that all-important third date with any man, the threshold date leading to sex. Now the prospect of intercourse terrified her. She especially feared the dark-complected baritones that opera companies attracted in droves.

The great irony of being both a student and a devotee of opera was that most of the men Oriane met were swarthy beasts who behaved like they needed abundant sexual servicing. The egos of male opera singers were rivaled only by the size of their libidos (and concomitant body parts) as far as she knew, and baritones were, per the divas, the worst of the lot.

She felt downright comfy around fair, ordinary-looking men like Knobby. Not that Knobby wasn't attractive. He had the same quality going for him that wheat germ had going for it—plain, but good for you. Thus far, he hadn't given her the slightest impression that a role in *Don Giovanni* might result from a quid pro quo arrangement— they hadn't shared any conversation to speak of. He just didn't appear to be the kind of guy who'd take advantage of any woman. Oriane knew she wasn't leading lady material and would never be— it was in the opera company's best interest to use principals from the international star circuit because stars sold tickets. But if Knobby felt inclined to award her a juicy supporting role because of her devotion to the guild, or based on their budding relationship, she would feel obliged to accept it.

Because she looked years younger than her actual age, she could play a range of roles—a trouser role like Cherubino in *The Marriage of Figaro*, for instance. Since companies like Hankey Opera had to drag teenage boys off the street to audition, pants roles had fallen to her by default but not always by choice. Her voice, with its light, lilting quality and bright timbre was ideally suited to singing the soubrette. Oriane was eternally optimistic and could do beguiling country innocence like Adina in *The Elixir of Love*, a role she performed exceedingly well, if only in workshop. One of her favorite roles thus far was Papagena from Hankey's 2004 production of *The Magic Flute*, which had prepared her for a larger part like Zerlina in *Don Giovanni*.

They would have to cast Zerlina from the community, and who better than Oriane? Her lyric soprano was perfectly suited to the role. Based on past performances with Hankey, she had earned the privilege of serious consideration. Not to mention that parts like Zerlina only came around once every ten years for a singer of Oriane's caliber. By her mid-thirties, her vocal cords would begin to thicken as did many women's, and she was petrified that her voice might lose much of its lightness and brightness, taking with it one of her last opportunities to sing soubrette roles, relegating her to the opera chorus ever after.

She wanted Zerlina badly. For one thing, she would get to wear a wedding dress—everyone in the audience would see her at her loveliest, dressed as a bride. Thousands more than at a real wedding. Secondly, if she wasn't going to be seduced in real life, she wanted to be someone's love object on stage—to play the true soubrette. So much so, she didn't mind their bringing tired old Donato Bianco to play Giovanni though it confounded her that everyone was making such a fuss over him, like he was the best they could hope for. More of that "same old, same old" thinking. She had seen better—far better. Maybe one of the best Giovanni's ever.

Last summer, while on an eleven-day tour of the United Kingdom, her Scottish auntie had treated her to a professional production of *Don G*. Not Covent Garden-quality but very accomplished. The bass-baritone playing the title role, Leandro Vasquez, was impossibly sexy—like a matinee idol. According to the director's notes, Leandro meant "lion man."

Vasquez was an uncaged simba—sleek and powerful, stalking Zerlina around the London stage, purring *"La ci darem la mano,"* the famous duet between Giovanni and Zerlina, teasing her with her own scarf, pulling her closer and closer, ensnaring her. Later in the act, when he appeared naked from the waist up, women gasped from sheer titillation.

"Where did they find this god on earth?" a woman beside Oriane asked her friend.

"Singing to his cattle, apparently," the friend said. "He was a gaucho in the Argentine outback."

"A gaucho?" her friend asked, which was Oriane's question, too.

"You know . . . a Spanish cowboy," the woman replied.

A cowboy? No wonder his physique was as toned and muscular as a male model's—rippling pectorals atop a vee-shaped frame. And bulging biceps, from roping beefy bullocks—the better to embrace you with, *cara mia*. It was the first time in her life Oriane had ever prayed for a man to remove his pants onstage, too. And to think, the whole time she envisioned the Lion Man completely naked, she had no idea what a naked man really looked like.

After the show, Oriane waited at the stage door for a glimpse of the Lion Man. For once, she was glad she'd listened to Aunt Fee, who'd encouraged her to dress up. Oriane's yellow strapless dress had given her confidence in the way only a favorite outfit can. Eventually, Vasquez appeared, looking like a rock star in a burgundy cape and tight silver pants. She thrust her program toward him. Other women crowded in front of her, but she squeezed through until she was standing paw to paw with the Lion Man. "Mr. Vasquez. Can you sign this—please?"

He took the program from her hands. "Leandro. Call a me—Leandro." He smiled easily. "You—little sparrow?"

He looked younger and softer in person than he did on stage. It must have been the make-up giving him a harder edge. The make-up and the faux grime. The make-up, the faux grime, and the five o'clock scruff. "Oriane. Make it out to Oriane."

"Oriane? *Amadis de Gaule?*"

She nodded. For the first time in her life, she felt proud of the name she inherited from the opera world, that she'd despised from little on up. She'd always wanted to be named Paris, like the city, like the Hilton.

"First opera—ever heard. *Encantadora,*" Vasquez said. "Why I sing—today. Oriane is sweet—like a you." As he signed her program in large, swash characters, time stood stock-still, as did Oriane, petrified in the presence of this sensual, swarthy baritone with an exotic accent and deep brown eyes, whose words fell out of his mouth in running triplets. "In my travel—I never meet—Oriane. I'm take tea—you join me?"

This couldn't be happening. Aunt Fee, not wanting to wait around until the cast members emerged, had gone back to the hotel.

Oriane couldn't refuse Leandro Vasquez an invitation to tea. But perhaps she should. He was a baritone. But he seemed uncommonly gentle, maybe because he was so much younger than Bianco. In her dress the color of buttercups, she would never look better than she did at that moment. At twenty-seven, she had hit the zenith of youth and beauty, according to Longenecker family lore.

Off she went, on the arm of Leandro Vasquez.

While they strolled to the tea house together, Vasquez explained that he only drank tea and never alcohol after a show because he needed to keep his vocal cords hydrated. As he shared other details of his routines, lo and behold, the tearoom appeared around the corner from the playhouse. Management had already reserved the best table in the house for Leandro and guest.

All evening their conversation was light. Oriane wanted nothing from him besides the pleasure of his company, and he must have sensed that. He told her about his cattle, that he missed being out on the range with them, singing to them, and that they missed him, too. He laughed about his rapid rise to stardom, and nearly cried when relaying how his patron Señor Luis Garcia, an Argentine gentleman who fiercely believed in him, died only months ago. She told him how she was a volunteer for the opera guild in her town because every year, there were fewer and fewer helpers, and that the opera house was likely to close. Hankey, Pennsylvania, couldn't find enough selfless people to devote time to the arts while expecting nothing in return.

"My fondest wish?" Vasquez had said, "For opera—to wake up—to young people. You—help opera—wake up—in your town?"

She nodded. Why had she ever feared baritones? she asked herself. Vasquez couldn't have been sweeter or more gallant.

As they finished their tea, he yawned and mentioned how a good night's sleep was part of a regimen that helped him care for his instrument. "*Una pregunta.* Opera diva—a dream?" he asked.

Oriane shrugged. "A silly dream. Once. At one time, I wanted to be a nun."

Vasquez cocked his head. "Qué?"

Oriane was sure she didn't know the Spanish word for *nun*. Sometimes Italian and Spanish words were only letters apart. "*Convento?*" she tried, which she knew meant *convent* in Italian. Vasquez's eyes lit up.

"*Suor Angelica?*" she said. In a workshop of Puccini's one-act opera of the same name, she sang the role of Sister Osmina.

"*Convento!*" he said, recognition flickering in his pupils.

Oriane nodded vigorously.

"*Mi gorrión,*" he said, taking her hand in his and stroking it and then kissing it softly. His eyes pleaded with hers, his lips continued to graze the top of her hand. She knew a little Italian, a little German, and even a little Latin from singing *Carmina Burana*, but almost no Spanish. Classic operas like *Don Giovanni* and *Carmen* may have been set in Spain but were never sung in Spanish. He continued nibbling his way up her bare arm. "*Quiero hacer el amor contigo.*"

Now what was he saying? Oriane shook her head as if to say, I can't understand you. She couldn't translate his Spanish, but she certainly understood his body language. What had come over him? What had she said to rouse the Lion Man, to awaken the lusty baritone inside? That she'd been in a convent? It had something to do with *Suor Angelica*, she figured. He was frightening her.

It was time for their cozy tea party to come to an end. Besides, her tour group would depart at six o'clock the next morning. "I've got to go," she said, retracting her arm.

Vasquez sighed. For some reason, he looked crestfallen. "*Mi gorrión,*" he repeated. Then he bowed, turned away from her, and vanished into the night air.

Mi gorrión . . . what did that mean? My turtle dove? My tearoom pal? My nail-salon slave? And what about *quiero something something amor something*? She whipped out her months-old iPhone, pulled up the translation app, and punched in *quiero* and *amor*. "I would love," the app spit back. He would love what? Me?

The next day, Oriane's tour group left for Scotland—though she would've stayed behind had it been possible. She'd have waited for him at the stage door every night and taken tea with him for a hundred nights had they stayed in London that long. Being in an attractive man's presence had reminded her of how single she was, how lonely she was.

For the rest of the tour, though their days were full of activity, her heart ached every night at bedtime, when it was always hardest to be alone. She kept reliving those magical few hours with Vasquez, sipping tea, talking about arias and roles and every topic she could manage to squeeze in between sips, remembering the feel of his lips grazing her skin. Would she never have a man she could call hers to stroll arm and arm with, to have tea with, to wear her dress of buttercups for?

It was only natural that whenever one of the guild members mentioned Donato Bianco, Oriane's thoughts turned to Vasquez. An up-and-comer—no getting around that perceived shortcoming. But Vasquez had played Giovanni with a raw sexual energy she'd never observed from any opera star before or since. Bianco was a has-been, pathetic by comparison. From his publicity stills, he looked like a middle-aged gasbag, a candidate for a heart attack just like— Knobby. Knobby! She'd almost forgotten. They'd come to the hospital to see Knobby.

As Deanna pulled into the visitor lot, her cell phone rang. "Grab that for me, Oriane. The front pocket," she said. "Oriane! Yoo-hoo? Earth to Oriane?"

Was Deanna calling her?

"My phone," Deanna said, pointing to her purse on the floor of the passenger seat.

Oriane dug out the phone, flipped it open, and placed it in Deanna's right hand while Deanna took the parking ticket from the machine with her left.

"This is Deanna."

Deanna's freshly exfoliated visage collapsed in on itself. She hoped Knobby hadn't taken a turn for the worse. Not before they cast Zerlina.

Deanna gasped. "He—? Are you kidding me? Are you—"

It had to be a tragic turn of events concerning Knobby. But Deanna's tone sounded almost angry—like she'd been cheated out of something. Get off the phone, Deanna. Get off this instant, and tell me what's going on! she said to herself, never able to summon the courage to boss Deanna around out loud.

"I don't believe this," Deanna was saying. "This is beyond comprehension. Why? Just tell me why?" After sitting a minute in stunned silence, she flipped her phone closed and stuffed it into the cup holder.

"What happened?" Oriane asked, now certain something terrible must have befallen Knobby, her last best hope not only for Zerlina but also for the once-in-a-lifetime role of Mrs. Carter Knoblauch. Come to think of it, if they ever were to marry, she'd prefer to call him Carter, since Knobby would sound funny in the bedroom, and a little too close to the truth, perhaps.

Deanna sat motionless for a long minute, dazed. "Unbelievable."

"What?" Oriane pleaded.

Deanna put her Lexus in park, flipped down the mirror on the visor, and checked her hair and make-up. "Donato Bianco pulled out of his contract."

"Pulled out?" Oriane said. "Why?"

"I have no idea." Deanna retrieved her purse from the passenger seat and climbed out of the sedan, slamming the car door. She hustled out of the parking lot, toward the main entrance. "The jerk wouldn't give me a reason."

"Who?" Oriane asked.

"His agent, that's who."

Deanna could walk faster in two-inch heels than Oriane could walk in sneakers, and she struggled to keep up despite having longer legs. She couldn't remember Deanna ever being so upset.

"Nodes?" Oriane asked.

Deanna huffed. "I told you, the agent didn't give a reason."

Though Oriane hardly rejoiced in the hardship this created for the opera company, secretly she was relieved Bianco wouldn't be playing the part. He was fat and old and had needed to retire anyway—at least from parts like Don Giovanni. She couldn't even stand the thought of his hands ranging across her body when she played Zerlina. He would've been much better suited for the old

Commendatore, Donna Anna's father, whom Giovanni slays in the first scene.

"There's a parrot who sings arias," Oriane said with more gravitas than she felt.

"I'm ready to book that parrot," Deanna said, barreling through the double doors at the entrance. "God in Heaven, we needed some good luck for a change. How am I supposed to think about the Martini Masque when I don't even have a baritone for *Don G*. Tell me that!"

"What about that balloon creations guy? The little guy whose name rhymes? He'd help you with the Martini Masque."

"Arnaud Marceau?" Deanna asked. "I can't pay him."

"Put him on the guild. He'd get a charge out of that."

"Arnaud Marceau. I don't think he's guild material. I just . . ." Deanna sighed. "Why does everything about small-town opera have to be so damn difficult?"

Oriane shushed her as they click-clacked past the Sister of Mercy at the information desk. Deanna's heels beat a crisp tattoo on the shiny entrance tile. "Watch your cursing. This is a Catholic hospital."

"Oh, zip it, will you?"

"Do you know where you're going?" Oriane asked.

"I think I know where the CCU is," Deanna said.

Oriane was left to surmise that someone in Deanna's immediate family—probably her hard-driving, philandering, Type A big-and-tall husband Stu had a heart episode before dumping her.

"We'll never get this show on the boards. First Knobby. Now Bianco. We're dead as a doorknob, as Vivian likes to say." Outside the elevator, Deanna jabbed at the up-arrow button, several times. "I swear, somebody's put some kind of curse on us for doing this show. I'm starting to give credence to all Vivian's talk about karma whammies. Though I can't imagine what I did. All I've done is to try to help this company survive." She sighed. "What in God's name do we do now?"

"Stop bringing God into this, will you?"

"Enough with the religious mumbo-jumbo. Or I'm going to tell you to get back to a nunnery. And you'll have deserved it."

In the past, Deanna had never gotten so huffy with her. Sarcastic, yes. Huffy, no. In fact, she'd been a picture-perfect chair. Challenges that sprang out of nowhere seldom rattled her. She seemed to thrive on the adrenaline rush created by uncertainty. Amazing, considering all the variables in live opera performance outside of Deanna's control. Would the shows sell and get strong reviews? Would the special events be well attended if it rained—or snowed? Would the economy impact charitable contributions? If Deanna was pessimistic, then maybe losing Bianco was the death knell for the Hankey Opera Company. Oriane began wringing her hands but then she noticed Deanna wringing hers. She didn't want Deanna to think she was mocking her in her distress. She wrapped her arms around herself instead and squeezed until the elevator arrived.

After an elevator ride that seemed to last as long as a Wagnerian act, Deanna and Oriane arrived at the Cardiac Care Unit just in time for the last visitation of the day, passing themselves off as Knobby's sisters, a credit to Deanna's ability to spin credible lies. They hustled off to Knobby's room before the crabby duty nurse could change her mind.

"*Oh, Isadora. Don't spit on the floor,*" Knobby sang to the tune of Bizet's "Toreador Song," while playing time-beater to a chamber orchestra consisting of an IV machine, a heart monitor, and a blank television mounted on the opposite wall from his bed. "*Use a cuspidor. What do you think it's for?*" He giggled musically and began laughing to the beat of the song. "*Ha—ha, ha, ha, ha. Ha, ha, ha*—hello, ladies."

"Knobby," Deanna said. "You look a lot better than the last time I saw you. In good spirits, then?"

Too spirited, Oriane thought.

Knobby gazed back and forth between the two women. "Wait a minute. You're not my sisters."

"Deanna and Oriane—from the guild," Oriane reminded him, devastated that Knobby hadn't remembered her, with her name being so distinctive and all, and in light of recent developments transpiring in her imagination. Oriane had never seen a patient recovering from a heart catheterization. She thought Knobby looked almost robust. Perhaps painkillers were giving him his happy glow.

"I didn't think I had any sisters," he said, his broad smile enveloping his face. "Guess what? I kicked the bucket yesterday. I was singing 'The Toreador Song' just to cheer myself up—since I gave up the ghost." He burst into a gale of laughter. "By George, it worked."

"Great news," Deanna said, shooting Oriane a quizzical look, the kind that telegraphed the word *artistes*, as if that explained everything about a person's eccentricities. She pulled a chair over to the side of the bed and took a seat. "Do you mind if we visit?"

"Not at all." Knobby bobbed his head as if listening to music, like he was going to burst out singing at any moment, but he wore no ear phones. Then he stopped himself, sitting motionless for half a minute. Was he having a relapse? Another heart episode? The women fervently hoped not. Just as suddenly, he teared up and began to sob. "I'm glad you ca-aa-aame."

From ecstatic to despondent in less than a minute? Oriane considered whether they should just go home and leave Knobby to experience his medication privately. "Now, now. Don't make yourself upset," Oriane said. "You're alive. You're on the mend."

"Knobby, did the doctor say—" Deanna began, then hesitated, "when can you return to work?"

"In two weeks if I don't have any setbacks. Did you—know," Knobby said, haltingly, "that Bizet died at age thirty-six—from—a— heart attack?" Tears streamed down his cheeks. "We lost him—at such a young age. He deserved to live longer. He deserved life— more than me."

This was Oriane's big chance to be the compassionate friend, allowing Knobby to see her as the helpmate he'd always wanted in a woman, assuming he liked women. A reasonable assumption since there seemed to be more straight men in the world of opera compared to the world of musical theater, which she'd also dabbled in at Westminster College. "Once you're feeling better, you'll be glad you're not dead," which sounded more eloquent in her head than it did coming out of her mouth. But the sentiment was there, just the same.

"I need a couple weeks to wrap things up in New Mexico," Knobby said, now sounding more lucid.

"I would like to say take whatever time you need," Deanna began, "but we need you at the helm by the first full week of April."

Could she be any more insensitive? Not likely. "You're going to need some help," Oriane said. "I can help you relocate, Knobby. My mom can, I mean. That's what she does."

Knobby smiled. "That would be great, Oriane. Hook me up, babe!"

"Deanna," Oriane whispered. "Now that Knobby's perked up, I think we should tell him about Bianco."

Deanna groaned, answering Oriane in what those in the industry would deem a stage whisper. "I don't think we have to trouble him with that now." She turned to Knobby, her grin forced.

"What's that? You've lost Bianco?" he asked, his eyes widening.

"Now, you've done it," Deanna muttered to Oriane under her breath.

"I've done it? You're the one pestering him to start work so soon after his surgery."

"Sitting around is going to drive me nuts. At least give me the gossip. The chance to troubleshoot and use my brain," Knobby said, pointing to his head. "This part is working as good as ever."

Deanna turned to Knobby and said calmly, "Bianco pulled out of his contract."

"Nodes?" Knobby asked.

"That's what I said," Oriane offered.

Deanna looked bewildered. "His agent didn't give me a reason."

"Okay, Bianco is out. That's a damn shame." He looked as though he were sifting through possible replacements for Bianco in his head. You could see it on his face—his considering ideas and then weighing their viability. His expression changed from worried to hopeful. "But the show must go on. Cheer up, Deanna. We're down, but we're not out. I've heard of a performer who has it all over Bianco. An up-and-comer, one of the most exciting singers in years. The ladies actually swoon over him. Normally, my recall is fantastic, but I . . . Alejandro? No, Leandro."

"*Leandro Vasquez?* I saw him in London—nine months ago," Oriane said, dying to add that she'd shared a pot of tea with him but stifling the instinct to namedrop. "He's electrifying."

"In every conceivable way," Knobby said. "I watched a clip of him on YouTube serenading a herd of hairy cattle. Moo-ve over, Simon Keenlyside."

"Moo-ve over?" Oriane giggled. "I concur. He's a natural." Oriane wondered if Vasquez had meant it when he'd said he'd never forget her. Was he merely being gallant, still caught up in his stage role, which happened more than actors cared to admit? After the curtain came down, sometimes the misers and misogynists they played exited the dressing room wearing the street clothes of the people playing them. Especially in *stagione* productions, where actors did the same characters night after night. "I met him—after the show. He said . . . he would never forget me because of my name."

"Really?" Deanna asked. Oriane could tell from Deanna's expression that she was doubting not only her claim to have met Vasquez, but also that Vasquez was any good. "Why haven't I heard anything about this balladeer of South American cows?"

Deanna was asking herself, as anyone would have had they been there, if this Leandro So-and-So was so utterly captivating, why had he taken tea with meek, little, might-have-been Oriane Longenecker? But in the interest of a bigger payoff, namely, booking Vasquez, Oriane only said, "He was only recently discovered."

"Now, that's impressive!" Deanna said.

"Don't write him off," Knobby explained. "Newcomers may not have a name people recognize, but they are out there, showcasing themselves. They try hard every day. Unlike the superstars, they never phone it in. And one day—instant fame." He was calmer now, more rational. Perhaps the medication was wearing off. "It's going to happen for Leandro Vasquez. I have a gut feeling that Hankey's going to break out opera's newest male sensation. If we can move on this, the payoff's going to be massive." He laid his hand on his chest and moaned softly, like he had indigestion. "This is too exciting."

"Now, you've overextended yourself," Deanna said. "Besides, this is all speculation. We don't even know how to find him."

"Try the Internet. Young stars are wired. Actually, any singer who wants work these days," he said. "If he's from Argentina but performed in London, he has an agent. On the off-chance he's available, book him."

"Why would he come here?" Deanna asked.

"Mention my name," Oriane said, with uncharacteristic aplomb. "He'll come."

"Mention your name, and he'll accept our offer?" Deanna sputtered in disbelief. "That's too much. Why in God's name would he do that?"

There she goes again—bringing God into it. In years past, Oriane had survived the politics in the guild by choosing her battles. She would not let Deanna get the better of her today, not in front of Knobby, not when the guild needed her connection to Vasquez, however tenuous. The stakes were too high. "If you want a shot at Vasquez, tell his agent to mention that Oriane, his little *gorrión* from London—"

"His little what?" Deanna asked.

"Sparrow. His little sparrow wants him to come to Hankey to sing Giovanni. That we have a new director—a champion—who wants to bring opera to young people. Right, Knobby?" He nodded, and then she nodded, thinking that she had said all she needed to say, proud of herself for taking on Deanna, for bossing her around for a change. "But don't mention our champion is laid up in the hospital at the moment."

"As if I would say anything to jeopardize a deal." Deanna shook her head. "I don't know about this Alejandro. I think we'd have better luck with the parrot."

"Leandro," Oriane corrected. She hadn't thought to search for "Leandro Vasquez" on the World Wide Web until Knobby mentioned it. She whipped out her iPhone, entered Vasquez's name in the browser, and clicked on one of the links. Voilà! A picture from the London production of *Don Giovanni*. "Deanna! Take a look."

Deanna sighed as if she rather be stoned by a fusillade of cabbages. She took Oriane's phone and gazed into it. She zoomed in on Vasquez's face, then zoomed out on the body, then zoomed in on his pectorals. "Oh, my, oh—my." She sighed wantonly. "This young cattle crooner is our Gold Coast and our El Dorado in one iron-hard, swarthy package. I'll call tonight."

Oriane threaded and unthreaded her fingers—vigorously— embarrassed that Deanna bared her middle-aged fangs in front of Knobby. Change the subject, she thought. "What about Maestro? He'll want to be in on the negotiation, won't he? I've worked closely with him."

"As have I," Deanna said. "I'll handle Maestro."

"Maestro loves Wagner," Oriane reminded her.

"Well, who doesn't?" Deanna said. "Besides me."

"Mark Twain hated Wagner," Knobby said, readjusting a pillow behind his back. "He called seeing a whole Wagnerian opera 'the next thing to suicide.'"

"Personally, I'd opt for suicide," Deanna said.

6
The Divina

Saturday evening, a little after seven-thirty. Deanna sits at the desk in her home office, nibbling on crackers and hummus. A photograph of Leandro Vasquez fills the computer monitor. He is shirtless, pleading with a buxom maiden dressed in a wedding gown Deanna barely notices. At her elbow is a very dry martini with two olives. She nibbles one as she eyes Vasquez.

Deanna surfed twenty different sites searching for links to Leandro Vasquez. Two years ago he'd won a talent competition in his hometown. Six months later he won Operatoonity—an international singing competition. Out of all the newcomers invited to compete from around the world, a lowly gaucho won both first prize as male singer as well as the audience prize. Well, no wonder, she thought, staring at his picture. Who could take their eyes off a prize like that? He sang his first operatic role in Chile a year ago and his second in London. Since then, he'd sung in music festivals in the Middle East and Puerto Rico, and made his United States debut as Giovanni in Knoxville. Knoxville? Boy, did their general director have a nose for talent—the best beak in the business. Everyone Knoxville contracted broke out into superstardom before long. He was a shooting star, this Leandro Vasquez, and Hankey had to have him.

By drilling down on a few links, she finally located contact information for Vasquez. He was represented by Bronsky and Greenburg—which she might have guessed since he was a hot commodity, growing hotter by the day. Bronsky and Greenburg had a stellar client list—not just any old troubadours hoping to make names for themselves. She punched in the number. The phone rang and rang. She was dialing a business number on a Saturday evening, after all.

"Answering service for Bronsky and Greenboig," an older woman said. "How may I help you?"

"Oh," Deanna said, startled to hear a live human being on the other end of the phone. The woman's heavy Brooklyn accent barely registered. "I need to speak with Mr. Bronsky or Mr. Greenburg immediately."

"This is an emergency?" the woman asked dryly.

"I said 'immediately.'"

"What is thee nature of thee emergency?" the woman said in a monotone.

Deanna glanced at the monitor. She'd been struck with a vision of the opera house teeming with women of all ages—an SRO crowd. They'd have to schedule extra performances just to accommodate the demand to see and hear Leandro Vasquez. "I must have him."

"Whom is the person," the receptionist began, "of which you are speaking?"

Whom is the person? Who did she think she was, this uppity phone-answerer? Deanna muttered to herself. Not to mention, she needed *who*, not *whom*. "Leandro Vasquez."

"Has Mr. Vasquez violated the toims of his contract?"

"He doesn't have a contract with me—us. Not yet," Deanna explained.

"Why are you calling us on a weekend then? Sheesh! They'll both be in Monday mawning. I'll leave them the message—"

"Don't hang up," Deanna interrupted. "You need to call one of them now—either one—I don't care. Tell them it's an emergency and have them call me at one of these numbers." Deanna provided the operator with her home, home office, and cell phone numbers.

"I'll pass along all those numbahs, but I'm not calling them. I don't work fa you," the woman said, with a hard edge to her voice.

"That won't do. What's your name?"

"What's it mattah?" the receptionist said.

"Tell me your name this instant, or I'll demand your resignation."

"It's Donna. Donna Calamari. C-a-l-a-m-a-r-i. I've been here eight years. Don't go thinking you're going to push me around, Miss Whomever."

"Okay, Donna Calamari, here's the deal. *Don Giovanni* opens in eight weeks. Our leading man pulled out of his contract."

"Yeah, so?"

"Tell them we have no baritone for the title role. That's why I need to talk with one of them right away."

"Whoop-dee-doo for you," the woman grumbled, adding, "I'll leave them both the message," and hung up.

Deanna wasn't used to taking no for an answer. Some people in Hankey considered her a fortress of a woman. She used to be. Then, when she'd turned forty, Stu, her husband of fifteen years, had served her with divorce papers at breakfast and moved in with his legal secretary that afternoon. For the first time in her life, she began to doubt herself, to feel unlucky. Quite an uncomfortable place to be for a woman who believed everyone made her own luck and got all the luck she deserved. The truth was, Stu had wanted out of the marriage—badly. He'd signed away too many assets. She was too embarrassed to tell anyone what she got in the settlement because only a man desperate to leave his wife would give up all that he did.

She'd devoted so much time to the opera guild that Stu had felt neglected. But then he'd exploited her busyness by having an affair. If the opera company failed too, she'd have nothing to show for the last ten years of her life.

Being single—manless—took some getting used to. In a knee-jerk reaction to Stu's leaving, she began sleeping with her kickboxing teacher, whose mantra was, "You have to be selfish. You have to think about yourself," which soothed initially. Of course, her teacher's philosophy about kickboxing also guided the way he lived his life. She quickly learned there wasn't a lot of room in one selfish person's life for another somewhat selfish person and broke off the affair.

Three months crawled by, after which she found herself not only lonely but also hard up. So, she called one of those dating services where you meet men over drinks. Sixteen hundred dollars later, she was seated at a bar outside Philly, waiting for her first date—a dentist from Philadelphia's Main Line. He'd been late, but when he finally arrived, he was good-looking and well dressed. Well spoken, too, and she'd forgiven him his tardiness. When he mentioned that he was the social director for a group of men who bonded in the nude each spring, she walked out. On the second date with a different man, a banker, things were going along well, and they moved from drinks to dinner seamlessly. He selected a top-shelf Cabernet for the meal. Between dinner and dessert, he excused himself to use the restroom, snuck out the back, and stuck her with the tab of several hundred dollars. When the next guy on the list said he'd meet her in the dairy department at the Nifty Mart after he finished playing in his tub full of "Mr. Bubble," she withdrew from the dating service completely, filing a complaint with the Better Business Bureau. That eased her regret at throwing away sixteen hundred dollars but hardly quelled her loneliness.

Then she decided she didn't need a man. Men were useless. She didn't need their money; she had plenty of her own. She didn't need their company; she had a reliable vibrator and lots of batteries. Childless, she channeled all of her life energy and passion into the guild, which had worked fine until yesterday, when she saw the photograph of Leandro Vasquez and realized what she was missing. Not Vasquez exactly, but what he represented.

A man in her bed—a young man with muscles and rock-hard abs and hair, lots of hair, since Stu had lost most of his and was self-conscious about it. And she would find such a man despite the fact that she'd put on a few pounds, or she wasn't Deanna Lundquist. Since Stu was the meat eater of the two, she'd begun a strict vegetarian diet after they split. This past winter, she developed an autoimmune thyroid disorder from consuming too many carbohydrates, resulting in a twenty-pound weight gain. The scaly skin, the extra pounds, were all triggered by unremitting vegetarianism.

One problem at a time. First, to reintroduce animal fat in her diet. Then, find a man. Then, a trainer. Unless, of course, she had a steamy affair with the trainer after a steak dinner. She made a note in her e-datebook to look into it. Right now, she had to call Richard about contracting Vasquez. She punched in his number on her cell. Pick up, Richard. Pick up.

"Are you sitting down?" Deanna asked.

"Now what?" Richard scowled.

"Bianco pulled out of his contract today," she said.

"What? Why?"

"I wish I knew. But it doesn't matter. I've found someone to replace him."

"Already?" he asked, his voice sounding tired and flat. "No teasing. I haven't the stomach for it after all the high drama."

"I'm perfectly serious. A young—" Deanna said, not really knowing how old Vasquez was—thirty, thirty-one? Those publicity stills could be misleading. "Youngish Giovanni? A real up-and-comer?"

"Just how are we going to sell a hasn't-made-it-yet to our subscribers, to the press?" Richard asked, ever practical.

"With his picture. With video and audio clips. We'll make them available everywhere. He sells himself, Richard. Once the public hears him and sees him, they'll flock to buy tickets," Deanna explained, "like hungry birds. Very hungry birds who want to be fed. I'm waiting to hear from his agent as we speak."

"Deanna, are you feeling all right? You sound—well—possessed. I know. The whole weekend has tried us all."

Yes, she'd felt tried—to her limit. She felt possessed, too. If she couldn't resolve this casting dilemma, she'd have to haul her ass over to the gym and exorcise herself. "I was feeling stressed, but just knowing we might be able to book another Giovanni has revived me."

"Can we afford this gentleman?"

Richard had to ask this question. Everyone asked about the affordability of everything these days. "I doubt he's as expensive as Bianco. He doesn't have his reputation. But really, Richard, can we afford *not* to have a Giovanni who'll rock that house to the rafters?"

"What if it's thousands more than what we can—"

The prospect of brokering a deal for Vasquez sent the adrenaline coursing through her system, just like when she finagled a rock-bottom price from a really good florist or wrangled a bunch of freebies out of a caterer. "I'll wheel and deal," Deanna interrupted. "If I can't get the price down, I'll pay it. I'll liquidate something. I must have a painting I can sell." Her pulse raced. Her face felt hotter than Dante's inferno. If Richard didn't endorse her plan this instant, she would self-combust, winding up a few floors lower than Knobby in Holy Ghost Hospital—the city morgue. She gulped her martini. "You won't regret it. I'm telling you. Our blue-haired subscribers will be sticking to their seats by the end of the first act and re-upping at intermission."

"Deanna," Richard said, acting mildly offended, but she knew he was entertained whenever she was a tad risqué. "Well, if you must, then—"

"I must. Oh, and Richard," Deanna began, now feeling the heat of the martini. "Don't say anything to Vivian about Vasquez. Not yet. Her family has its own press connections, and I don't want any leaks about any of this. Bianco or Vasquez."

"Why would I say anything to Vivian?" Richard blustered. "We have nothing in common. I don't—I won't talk to her unless you force me to."

"You know her better than I do."

"No, I only know of her. Only what Mary told me—that they kicked her off the hospital auxiliary."

"She must have behaved very badly to get herself the boot."

Richard cleared his throat. "Dare I say?"

"Oh, do share."

"Vivian was in charge of prizes for last year's Easter Egg Roll, which they always ordered from the Oriental Trading Company."

"I see where this is going," Deanna added.

"As you might've predicted, Vivian didn't like the name of the vendor or their alleged sweatshop goods. Instead of buying three gross of bunny rabbits from Oriental, she overspent the prize budget on, get this, hand-knitted fair trade hedgehogs."

"Hedgehogs? For Easter?"

"If that wasn't bad enough, she doubled the auxiliary's bill while leaving them about three-hundred-and-fifty prizes short."

"How did your wife—late wife," Deanna asked, wincing on the other end of the phone, "find this out?"

"Mary and Vivian's mother had a history. They used to serve on the library board together—until Mary asked her to step down."

"What's with the Frantzes being bounced from boards all over town?"

"There's something screwy going on in that family," Richard said. "Can't put my finger on it, but I blame Vivian's mother. She's certifiable."

"This has been rich," Deanna said, hoping she hadn't slurred any words. "I'll give that agency a call, and let you know how I make out."

"Deanna, are you all right? First, the assault. Then the news about Bianco. You must be rattled and understandably so."

"You're kind to ask, but I'm moving on. We have a show to mount. Ciao, darling," she said, before he'd counsel her otherwise.

If she didn't hear from Bronsky or Greenburg within an hour, she'd keep calling every hour, leaving messages. In a week, she would have this gifted and attractive young man under contract. Within two weeks, Knobby would be ready to start working for the guild. And it would mark the beginning of a new era in Hankey Opera, one Deanna had only dreamed of but had worked toward, for the last ten years of her life.

Ladies and gentlemen, cats and kittens, the *divina* was back. Time to mix another martini and muddle through to the next insurmountable challenge—the Maestro.

7
The Time-Beater

Three weeks later, members of the guild along with Maestro Schantzenbach meet to discuss two possible contracts in the sunroom of Deanna's upscale garden home. Knobby has yet to arrive.

A profusion of color and texture, Deanna's sunroom closely resembled the Pierre Bonnard print that hung on one of its walls. The rattan settee featured richly colored cushions upholstered in a "Summer Garden Splendor" pattern. Silk scarves graced the end tables. Light red paneling, like a wave of scarlet, splashed the wall adjoining the house. Purple iris and gerbera daisies in gilded vases accented the décor. It was a scene straight from Provence.

If it had only been the guild to entertain, Deanna wouldn't have gone to much trouble. Though she scrupulously guarded her reputation as one of Hankey's best hostesses, it was Maestro's attendance that had made the difference between her usual preparations and this week's exhaustive preparations. She'd arranged for the windows to be professionally cleaned and the houseplants dusted. She'd sent out the seat cushions for dry cleaning. Ceiling-high fig trees and generous pots of climbing pothos were clustered to allow room for extra chairs.

If any measure of improvement in the sunroom's appearance registered with her guests, no one mentioned a thing. No matter. She felt more comfortable knowing the surroundings were as perfect as they could get. Except for the weather, which was overcast. Mentally prepared, she could now devote her complete attention to the meeting's purpose once the guests arrived.

And arrive they did, bearing hostess gifts, which weren't as impressive as one might think. Vivian brought a sampler of condiments—ketchup, pickle relish, and Worcestershire sauce. Though the sundries would be useful in her larder, had Vivian brought them in the spirit of generosity or merely to remind Deanna that she was a Frantz?

Despite entertaining the Maestro countless times, he never brought her a gift. Apparently, Maestro considered his silk neckerchief-wearing presence to be gift enough. Always sporting that neckerchief. Who did he think he was? Wagner? On top of a decidedly artistic temperament, Maestro—who insisted on being called Maestro—was a little man barely five-and-a-half feet in dress shoes. People called him "The Teeny Tyrant" behind his back, among other nicknames. As she greeted him, Deanna came up with a new moniker herself, noticing each of his eyebrows made a perfect bushy vee. If this were a scene in opera, and a man with eyebrows like Maestro's came on stage, the choristers would cry out, "Il Diavolo! Il Diavolo!" and cross themselves.

Richard brought a handful of perfect tulips wrapped in tissue paper, handed them to Deanna with a perfunctory "Here you go," and hurried into the sunroom, strolling past Vivian and seating himself on the rattan love seat next to Oriane.

Vivian opted for the chaise longue. No one sat beside *Il Diavolo*. Everyone had left that privilege to the hostess.

Deanna served espresso and circulated a tray of cookies—baci, rococo, biscotti, and amaretti—from the finest Italian bakery in Hankey. "Vivian, the crescents are gluten-free, if you care to indulge," she cooed, and took her obligatory seat beside Maestro.

"Very nice of you," Vivian said. "They were physically touching the non-gluten free cookies, so I can't have any."

Deanna had bought the cookies to try to ensure Vivian's compliance should she need reinforcements as the game progressed. Since Vivian would not be swayed by any of the buttery crescents, Deanna decided it would be wise to concentrate her schmoozing on Richard and Oriane instead.

Deanna's mission? To trick the Maestro into agreeing with two business decisions that, unbeknownst to him, were foregone conclusions: contracting Vasquez for Giovanni and hiring Knobby to serve as general director.

To be clear, the guild could hire whomever they deemed fit for Knobby's post. But without Maestro's blessing, Knobby's professional life would be a miserable one. Usually the general director and the conductor, who also served as the music director, cast the shows cooperatively—pooling their ideas, calling in favors owed them—bringing in two or three star performers per show, the rest of the parts being filled with local talent.

Generally, there's a need for a despot to coordinate all the individual elements of an opera for continuity between music and staging. No one defined small-town despotism better than Maestro Schantzenbach. However, since the guild could not afford to have any production reduced to a concert-in-a-costume, Maestro had to work with Knobby, who'd be responsible for coaching the actors, staging, and coordinating all the technical aspects of the show—sound, lights, special effects. And *Don Giovanni* abounded in special effects—a singing statue, a haunted graveyard scene. Lots of *gothic dreck,* as Vivian had called it. And of course, Giovanni's haunted condemnation to hell in a fiery incineration.

Maestro was quite young for professional conductors. In his previous occupation, he'd been a youth symphony conductor, the perfect proving ground for would-be despots. He'd only been conducting opera for eight years—all of them in Hankey. In performance, the total number of pieces he'd conducted was quite small. But in 2003 the Teeny Tyrant placed in the top twenty in the *Dirigentenwettbewerb Eins,* an international conductor's competition, the same year they needed to hire a time-beater, which made his contest ranking look as pretty as Pavarotti's proceeds from "The Three Tenors" tour.

Soon thereafter, they learned that what Maestro lacked in venerability, he made up for in arrogance, shredding performers and musicians who failed to do his bidding. Everyone assumed he'd mellow as he settled into a position of unchallenged authority—anyone who sided against him was routed. However, the only artists he showed deference to were those higher up on the arts-and-entertainment ladder. It would have been a lovely *divertissement* to watch Maestro grapple with Bianco, who had been at least three rungs above him, professionally speaking.

Richard, who'd hired Maestro, regarded him as his golden boy, and to Deanna's surprise, the two got along famously. As far as Deanna was concerned, Maestro wasn't unnerving or intimidating or threatening; he was just another male authority figure who needed handling. But everyone else on the guild trod guardedly around him.

She'd already signed a contract with Vasquez's agents. Bronsky called her Monday morning, very sympathetic to their unprecedented circumstances. "Yes," he'd said. "Tsk, tsk, tsk, my dear," uncommonly interested in Deanna's husky voice, and the deal was inked. All she had to do was bring Maestro into the conversation without his realizing he'd been the last one to join the party line. If the best cookies in the city, nay, all of Eastern Pennsylvania held no sway, she was prepared to whip out a Bourgeron Blanc with chèvre (which sounded much nicer than goat cheese), a chardonnay that she always served with a really fine Gruyère, and authentic Italian pepper biscuits.

Deanna wasn't above play-acting to ensure Maestro's cooperation. She was a Machiavellian in the most endearing sense of the word. She'd steeled herself to deliver a dramatic spectacle as delicious as the refreshments. Throughout her life, from her Daisy Scout days on up, Deanna Lundquist was nothing if not prepared.

She waited until everyone's mouth was full to start the meeting. "I think we should get going. We don't want to waste Maestro's time. Knobby should be along shortly." Actually, she knew Knobby would enthusiastically endorse Vasquez, a position that would make Maestro wary. Since he and Knobby had yet to meet, to control one of the variables in the unfolding drama, she'd told Knobby the meeting started a half hour later than it actually did.

Maestro had been trying to get Bianco to Hankey for years. After Bianco inked the contract, Maestro had wasted no time calling the arts editor, Benny Lebowski, at the *Hankey Herald* to request a feature, bragging about how he'd been responsible for obtaining

Bianco though it had been Richard who approached Bianco last winter. Subscribers were already behaving skittishly about Bianco's departure—that the opera guild somehow should have known he'd renege when they hired Bianco. Now that Maestro had made the Opera Company and himself vulnerable to criticism, he'd adopt any posture to save face.

"To lose our leading man this late in the game," Deanna began, her delivery unruffled—legato even, "well, I'm not sure we can bounce back. The opening is six weeks away. I think we should cancel the show." She cast her eyes directly at Maestro as she said the words *cancel the show* and watched his countenance droop. She had presumed correctly. He was dying to conduct *Don Giovanni.* She had his time-beating ascot right where she wanted it.

"What did you find out about this Vasquez fellow?" Richard interjected like a noisy trombone. "Is he available?"

"He is," Deanna said, throwing away each word, feigning a total lack of enthusiasm, "but I'm not sure he's worth our time and trouble discussing."

"He's a major talent," Oriane said brightly, like a piccolo introducing a lively motif to advance the drama at a faster pace. Deanna was fine with Oriane moving the conversation along. Whether she knew that was her assigned role was another story. "But I thought you were excited—"

"What do I know?" Deanna interrupted, "Let Maestro take a look. He'll tell us what's what."

"Enough," Maestro blasted in a tinny tenor. "I'll take a look and tell you what is what."

Oriane leaned into Richard. "What did he say? I was chewing my cookie."

"He said," Richard began, *sotto voce,* "he'd take a look and tell us what is what."

Deanna stepped back from the conversation a moment, considering what had just occurred. With everyone talking at the same time, saying the same thing, the last exchange sounded like a fugue for five voices. If this was to be the *tenor* of the discussion this afternoon, the best way to reach Maestro would be the divina's well-delivered, well-timed aria. She could pull it off—she carried herself like a divina because she was the quintessential diva, the only difference being, she couldn't carry a tune in a U-Haul.

Fiercely charming is how Stu had once described her. Perhaps if she'd been less fierce and more charming, Stu might not have run off with his legal secretary. Though it could've been as Oriane once told Deanna, that Stu's leaving had more to do with hating his big, fat philandering self than rejecting her.

After her divorce, ferocity took a back seat to charm where men were concerned. Deanna thought she laid it on thicker than schmaltz in a Jewish deli until she learned that men like Maestro found her utterly beguiling and perceptive whenever she behaved in a subservient fashion. The more cloying the better.

Go figure.

She pulled out copies of Vasquez's résumé and some recent publicity stills and circulated them among the guests.

Deanna sighed, her breast heaving. "Apparently, he's from Argentina. He won two prizes at the 2009 Operatoonity competition," she said as though Vasquez had done nothing more than triumph in a neighborhood game of tiddlywinks. "Is that significant, Maestro?"

Maestro's eyes brightened. "Why, yes! Why yes, it is. Have you never heard of Operatoonity?"

"Sorry, no." Deanna shrugged her shoulders. "I'm but a palm greaser." Then in an unvarnished fioritura, she added, "More cookies, Maestro?"

Maestro lifted another baci from the tray. "Delicious, Deanna," he said, humming with contentment. "Operatoonity is an international contest. That's significant, yes. I'm impressed."

"Maestro's impressed," Richard tooted.

"Maestro's impressed," Oriane repeated.

"But not that impressed," Maestro corrected. "In the past, Operatoonity has been a popularity contest more than a showcase for talent."

He wasn't impressed? Hadn't Maestro's sister participated in Operatoonity when she was younger and won? Had she merely placed? That had to be it. How had Deanna missed that small but important detail? Operatoonity was an ace of a card, and she just misplayed it. She bit her lip before diving into a juicy lie. "Yes, I'd read that about Operatoonity," she began. "In *Opera News*, I think. The judges routinely bypass the best and brightest in favor of contestants with strong publicists."

"Exactly," Maestro said, which is what she wanted him to say, but it got her no further along in obtaining his consent.

Vivian clucked her tongue. "What you're saying is that Vasquez is a wolf in cheap clothing?"

Richard glanced over at Vivian and tittered.

At Vivian's remark maligning a popular English euphemism with origins in fairy tale as a literary genre, instead of delivering a harangue about the sovereignty of words, Richard had merely tittered. Why no foaming at the mouth over Vivian's verbal gaffe? Why was he laying off his game? Why had he not reacted the way everyone had expected him to? Deanna had to know. Was his pacemaker slowing him down? Time for a tweak? She'd pegged Richard for an inflexible man, and in all the years she'd known him, he'd never disappointed. Had she, had they, all of them asked too much of him?

First, he'd lost Mary, then nearly Knobby. Then Bianco's mysterious departure from the show. This followed by the real prospect of having to close their doors if they didn't mount a smashing *Don Giovanni*. Under all those stressors—Mary, Knobby, Bianco, the closing—Richard'd finally cracked. Or—as gluten-free Vivian might say—he'd gone ten pounds crazy in a five-card deck.

Though Richard tittered, Maestro scowled. What should Deanna do now? She hated to do this to Vivian, but since Richard wasn't behaving like Richard, she had to be Richard. Otherwise, there'd be no order in the universe that afternoon.

Deanna rolled her eyes. "Seriously, Vivian. Whether this Vasquez was a wolf in *sheep's* clothing—that's the expression you butchered by the way—is hardly the issue," Deanna said in a voice that implied, *You silly cow.*

Vivian shook following her upbraiding. But Maestro now tittered.

Equilibrium restored.

Now to close the ranks. Or was the expression advance the flanks? She'd have to do both, in short order and stop hanging around Vivian—she was a bad influence. Oh, who cared what Deanna called it as long as she did it?

"Besides this Argentine poseur," Maestro asked, "who else have we for Giovanni?"

"At this late date, no one," Deanna said. "I had a hunch this Vasquez was no contender. He's nothing more than a country cowboy discovered crooning to his cattle."

"'Crooning to his cattle'? Deanna, you slay me," Maestro said. "You're certain all he did was sing to his cows?"

"You never know with lonely gauchos," Deanna said, cracking an artificial grin.

Oriane looked at Deanna quizzically. "But you said—"

Deanna's eyes burned daggers at Oriane. Why wasn't she playing along? Deanna paused, considering whether to pursue her next tack. If Maestro recognized the ploy for what it was, she'd never be able to bring in Vasquez. She might even have to step down from the board; her relationship with Maestro would hereafter be strained. It was a genuine damn-the-torpedoing critics moment. She would press on. "I should have known," Deanna interrupted, "that any descendant of the Mapuche tribe couldn't possibly have what it takes to sing internationally. It's all PC bullshit. What do indigent peoples know about opera?"

Vivian's eyes grew wide as fair trade hedgehogs at the mention of "PC bullshit."

"What?" Maestro's head bobbled like he'd just stepped out of a revolving door. "What tribe was that?"

Deanna examined her manicure and repeated the name of the tribe as though it greatly taxed her to do so. "The Mapuche—of Argentina."

"The Mapuche? Did you know my grandfather Arnold Schantzenbach moved to Argentina after World War II and fell in love with a Mapuche girl, married her, and introduced my dear sweet grandmother to opera? And she, a Mapuche Indian," Maestro said, looking down his long, Palatinate nose at Deanna, "became a lifelong devotee of classic opera."

Deanna stifled a smile. "I didn't know that."

"Of course, it's in the Schantzenbach family history in the Hankey Library," Maestro said. "Had anyone bothered to read it, they might have known."

Thank heavens Maestro hadn't bothered to see who'd signed out his family history. From that same slim volume, Deanna also learned that Maestro's Mapuche grandmother called his grandfather Schatzie. Schatzie Schantzenbach. Revealing that little tidbit, as tempting as it was, would compromise the entire campaign. Wisely, she kept that nugget to herself.

"Hire him," Maestro commanded.

Deanna needed to challenge his directive; she was the guild chair—not too much challenge. Just enough. She shook her head. "We need a Giovanni to take the audience's breath away. Someone who opens his mouth and erases all the doubts Bianco drummed up. A grander Giovanni than we would've had before—not some silly junior gaucho."

"As I recall," the piccolo chirruped, "your reaction upon seeing the silly junior gaucho's picture was more lustful than Giovanni eyeing Elvira's servant girl."

If only Deanna had a silencer she could whip out and slap on the happy piccolo. "Well, he's a good-looking young man," Deanna admitted, "but looks are no measure of talent."

"True, true," the Maestro interjected.

"My personal reaction is unimportant. We need someone *the press* will fall in love with," Deanna replied, "faster than you can say 'Good riddance, Bianco.'"

"I've heard enough," Maestro said. He dabbed a napkin at the side of his mouth. "You have such a talent, Deanna."

Her plan was back on track as if she'd prepared for a possible derailment for months. "Perhaps on paper. Nothing more," she said coyly.

Maestro examined the glossy publicity shot. He moved it closer, searching his face, then he pulled it away, examining his pectorals in the same way a trainer would inspect a stallion at auction. "It's decided," he announced. "We'll take Vasquez."

"But—" Deanna began.

"Hire him," he said. "I'll brook no further opposition on this matter."

Brook no further opposition? Only Maestro was pompous enough to whip out nineteenth-century expressions and drop them into present-day arguments. "No need for brooking today, Maestro. I'll contact his agent," she said, "if you insist."

"I insist," Maestro said.

"Fantastic," Oriane piped up. "I like Vasquez. I really like him. I've seen him singing for a major house in London."

"Maestro," Vivian said, having been unusually quiet throughout the whole meeting. "I'm very much in favor of bringing in Vasquez. I think it's exciting, his having indigenous blood. We need to give the Native American community more reasons to pursue the arts."

As if one hire of one performer with indigenous blood could redress hundreds of years of colossal wrongdoing and mistreatment, Deanna thought. Not to mention that she'd made up the Mapuche Indian connection—not a whit of truth to it.

"Why are you addressing me?" Maestro said to Vivian, as if she were the illegitimate spawn of circus fleas. "This matter is concluded."

Vivian uncrossed her legs and leaned forward. She was unaccustomed to people discounting her opinion—she was a ketchup heiress.

Here it comes, Deanna thought. Another harangue, an indelicate remark, an ill-phrased adage—at least one of the many awful things that had made Vivian infamous.

"I don't like *Don Giovanni*," Vivian said. "It would be irresponsible for us to produce it."

What did she say; what had she said; why did she say that? Deanna had the Maestro fressing out her hand. And it was all slipping from her grasp because the poster girl for fair trade hedgehogs had to go flapping her lips on this topic—again.

Maestro raised one thin eyebrow. "The character or the opus?"

"Both," Vivian said. "There's too much sexual violence in the story—all the female characters are marginalized."

Not this spiel again. O Thor! Throw down a bolt of lightning. That would be a more merciful end, even for the undeserving Vivian, than Maestro gouging out her blue-green orbs with his short fat thumbs.

"What an artistically boorish thing to say," Maestro boomed, his eyebrows arching diabolically, his lips reverberating long after the words left his fat mouth.

Vivian wasn't one to back down easily. She was a Frantz. Her family had made their fortune pulverizing things. She'd emerged from a showdown with the hospital auxiliary president with only minor casualties. She was battle-tested.

"Boorish is a matter of opinion," Vivian began. "Some audience members will be offended by the libretto. Giovanni nearly rapes Donna Anna. He assaults Zerlina. She's terrorized by his relentless pursuit of her. Then she begs Masetto to beat her."

Maestro made a noise like a jet engine had just taken off in his mouth. "Stop. You can't take that vapid, politically-correct posture with Mozart. Your insipidity robs him of his genius—and his work of its historic and thematic intelligibility."

Exactly what Deanna was thinking.

But Maestro was just warming up. "Why did you become part of this guild, madam? To bring about our ruin?"

"That's enough, Jan," Richard said to Maestro.

You could have heard one of Vivian's stuffed hedgehogs skittering across the lawn, it had grown that quiet.

"We're all trying to make this work, Jan," Richard said, the frustration in his voice evident.

Again, Richard called him Jan? *Gott in Himmel.* No one, not even his sainted mother Mitzi called Maestro by his first name any longer. But how about that Richard, showing some backbone on Vivian's behalf! Very curious. Halfway to maddening.

"I'll not have you assailing my volunteers," Richard continued. "Get a hold of yourself, man. Nothing can jeopardize this production. If we offend the founders of Women in Crisis, high-powered women who also support the opera company, we risk losing their philanthropy."

"More coffee, anyone?" Deanna squeaked. She glanced at Oriane, whose hands were hugging her face just as they had been when Knobby collapsed in the conference room. A photograph of Vasquez lay near Oriane's chair. Using her head, Deanna motioned to the photo then to Oriane then to Vivian. "Show her," she mouthed.

"Vivian," Oriane said, approaching Vivian like one would a starving lioness with famished cubs. Oriane, opera's doe-eyed daughter, slipped a publicity shot of Vasquez into Vivian's trembling hands. "I don't think you got to see a picture of the Giovanni we want to bring to town."

"No, I didn't, and I don't want to—"

Oriane shoved the photograph under her nose.

Vivian inhaled sharply, nostrils flaring. She blinked. If this had been a scene in *Don Giovanni*, if she had been one of the woman protagonists such as the hyper-sensitive Donna Anna, with sensibilities more delicate than hummingbird wings, Vivian would have gasped. Then she would have swooned—violently. Someone would've had to catch her before she careened to the floor, given her smelling salts, and then sing sycophantic arias to her for the next year of her life.

"It's good to know we may have detractors," Richard said, trying to tamp down the tension billowing like a scrim in a wind machine. "A good offense is the best defense," he added, which may have been the only sports truism he would ever admit to knowing.

"We'll donate one evening's proceeds to the shelter," Deanna said. "Not to be crass about it, but we're not a social service agency—our mission is to present artistic endeavors."

Vivian shrugged. "It's better than nothing—than not admitting the faults of the show."

Enough with the faults of the show, Vivian!

Deanna had one more score to cinch. "About this new general director, I can tell you, that our first candidate Don Blank of Boston, looked stellar on paper," Deanna said. "But he was a no-show."

"A no-show?" Maestro said, "Boston, I'll have you know, is a first-rate opera town. We'd be fortunate to have a Bostonian in that post. You know, Jimmy goes to Boston summers to conduct."

Jimmy? Was he talking about James Levine. As if Maestro knew him well enough to call him Jimmy. Never mind an ass. Maestro's was a pimple on the ass.

"You must have botched the arrangements," Maestro said, arching his diabolical eyebrows. "You need to reschedule the interview."

Deanna didn't enjoy lying, but she wasn't above telling more falsehoods to get what she wanted. "I called him, Maestro, after he failed to appear for his interview. He refused to return to Hankey to talk with us. He doesn't like *Don Giovanni*. How did he put it? 'A stupid tale. Gothic nonsense.'"

Vivian chirped, as if vindicated.

Utterances of disbelief poured from the Maestro's blubbery lips. "Only an idiot could countenance such a viewpoint," he said, glaring at Vivian. "You'd better've sent him packing." Maestro's arms settled on his Wellesian stomach.

Well, it certainly takes one to know one, Deanna thought.

"Anyone else in that lot worth looking at?" Maestro asked, after cramming a cookie in his mouth.

"We liked a young man fresh from a house in New Mexico. They have splendid opera in the Southwest," Richard offered. He looked to Deanna, waiting for her to indicate she was in agreement. "He would be our first pick, I suppose," he continued. "He had a cardiac incident a few weeks ago, but he's back on his feet and ready to resume working."

"A young man?" Maestro said. "With heart problems? What a pity. Who's left?"

Deanna hadn't wanted Richard to introduce the cardiac issue. However, Knobby's health problems could hardly be concealed. Concessions might have to be made for at least the next two weeks— reduced working hours, more freedom to work from home— regardless of the fact that he wanted to dive right into the job.

Knobby would be installed in the post whether they received Maestro's blessing or not.

"This forty-year-old was the final candidate," Deanna said. "Like Richard said, he received an excellent prognosis."

"Opera's not for the faint of heart," Maestro said. "We'll have to launch another search."

No, they would not launch another search. Knobby was perfect for the job. They had to have him. Deanna met everyone's eyes around the room just before casting the foolproof lure, demanding they all play along, before reeling in Maestro. "As usual, you're right, Maestro. I invited Carter Knoblauch here today so that you could meet him, but I'll tell him thanks but no thanks. Though it was fun having him in town. While Mr. Knoblauch was in the hospital, we had to care for his dachshunds."

Would Deanna sink herself following this dachshund thread? Did Maestro care about anyone else's unnaturally short dogs or merely his own?

Maestro's eyes widened. "Dachshunds? How many?"

"Oh—three," Deanna said. "Cutest little things. I was showing them around Hankey, most of the weekend. Adorable, these— little—bowwows."

"*Drei kleine hunde—wie heißen Sie?*" Maestro said.

"Vee high-senn zee?" Deanna repeated what she thought Maestro had just said, stalling for time and a miracle of the gift of tongues with which to comprehend a Teutonic language. "Well, you're not going to high-senn this, zee—"

No one seated in that sunroom wanted Knobby on board more than Oriane. Oriane was the only one who could step in and rescue her. Deanna's eyes pleaded with Oriane. Deanna was a cresting river, and Oriane needed to be the sandbag. Deanna was a clogged sink, Oriane had to be the Drano. Deanna didn't know her characters from Wagnerian operas, and despite the fact that only moments ago, Deanna had wanted to impale her against the red paneling of the sunroom because no one would notice her bleeding out, Oriane had to come to her rescue, to Knobby's rescue, to the guild's rescue.

"Tristan, Isolde, and—Lohengrin," Oriane said.

"*Ja?*" Maestro said.

"Oh, yah, yah," Deanna said. "Very cute. Especially little Lohengrin." And she sighed as if reliving the joy of romping with Tristan, Isolde, and Lohengrin in Hankey Park. "Did I mention that Knobby's fluent in German and adores Wagner?"

"*Ja? Ausgezeichnet!*" Maestro said, his bushy eyebrows flattening into a unibrow.

"What business have we left undone?" Deanna asked the others. "We need to find another general director. No wine and cheese until our labors are finished, folks."

"Labors?" Maestro said. "Everything's decided. We have this Vasquez and Carter Knoblauch. And you've got a nice something-or-other chilling for me?"

Deanne stood and smoothed out the front of her pants—camel-colored cashmere. "A 2002 Bourgeron Blanc. Oriane? Do you mind helping me bring out the wine?"

"No, not at all," Oriane said and trotted after Deanna towards the kitchen.

Deanna eased the door closed behind them, nearly collapsing onto the kitchen counter.

Oriane burst into laughter. "Knobby has three dachshunds?"

Deanna pushed herself up by the elbows. "Sometimes art becomes life. Deal with it. I'm expecting Knobby any minute." Deanna grabbed a tray from the kitchen island. "While I take these things to our guests, you need to watch for him, stop him just inside the door, and tell him he's the proud owner of three dachshunds named—"

"Tristan, Isolde, and Lohengrin," Oriane finished her sentence. "How do you know he doesn't already have three dachshunds?"

"He's allergic to dogs, remember?" Deanna pulled the door open with her foot. "If he has three dachshunds, I'll hand you the keys to my Lexus."

"Wait," Oriane cried. "How's a man recovering from a heart attack going to care for three dachshunds, especially if he has dander allergies?"

Deanna slid her body between the door and frame. "Can you—possibly—get the door?"

Oriane reached around Deanna and held it open.

"Stu had a stiff walking regimen following his heart incident. Knobby will, too. We'll have to help him," Deanna said, very matter-of-factly and headed back into the sunroom.

"Well, I'm allergic to dogs, too," Oriane said, exiting through the front of the kitchen to the foyer, where she parked herself on the staircase.

Deanna uncorked and poured the wine then raised her goblet. "A toast—to Maestro."

"To Maestro," everyone parroted, and they all drank eagerly to Maestro. And because of Maestro. And because it had been one dickens of an afternoon thus far, thanks to Maestro.

As Deanna refilled everyone's glass, Knobby entered the sunroom. "Hello, folks."

A chorus of "Knobby's" ensued. But where was Oriane? Had she met Knobby and filled him in, as instructed?

Maestro rose from his seat. "Knobby? They call you Knobby?"

"I hope you will, too, Maestro." Knobby extended his hand, and they shook.

"Have a seat—Knobby. By me," Maestro said. "I want to hear about these dachshunds."

"Dachshunds?" Knobby said with a quizzical look on his face. "I'd love to tell you about the—um—dachshunds. All of them?"

Deanna raised three fingers, waving them over Maestro's head, mouthing the word *three*.

"Three," Knobby said. Deanna nodded. "My three dachshunds."

"*Auf Deutsch!*" Maestro insisted.

Though Deanna may have overstated his German fluency, Knobby had to know some German from regularly attending Wienerfest in Cincinnati's biggest beer garden. From his résumé, she also knew he'd done the whole Ring Cycle. She certainly hoped he could recall the words he needed now.

"*Eins first hund ist zo cutezee,*" Knobby said. It sounded as though he started off well. "*He ist mit großen eyes—darkenbrownen,*" he added.

Darkenbrownen eyes? Uh, oh.

"*Dunkelbraun, meinst du?*" Maestro asked.

Oriane scuttled into the sunroom, looking frazzled. "Knobby! You made it. I had to…um…use the little girls' room. Sorry!"

"Glad you could join us," Deanna said pointedly. "You didn't miss *anything*."

"Oh, *ja, ja*. Brown like a Schlitz beer bottle," Knobby was saying. "Like *ein* frankfurter. For certainlich. *Ja*." Then Knobby began singing, "*Ja, ja, ja, ja,*" raising and lowering his wine glass. "*Weißt nicht wie gut ich dir bin,*" he continued singing, finishing the stanza with the cry, "Wienerfest!" His voice, a dark baritone—darkenbrownen—sounded surprisingly robust and clear.

Now Maestro joined in singing the second verse, "*Du, du, liegst mir in Herzen. Du, du liegst mir im Sinn.*"

From her elegant Provençal sunroom to a stinking Hofbräuhaus all because of a few stanzas of a German drinking song: "*Doo, doo. Yah, yah. Doo-dah. Doo-dah.*"

If all this *Deutschland-über-alles* crap resulted in the desired outcome, Deanna would wear a horned helmet, don a breastplate, and warble "The Wedding March" herself, the same CD she ground-up in the garbage disposal the morning Stu served her with divorce papers.

8
The Tragic Flaw

The gathering breaks up at Deanna's. Deanna, Richard, and Knobby are meeting in the den to review the terms of his contract and cover other employment-related matters. Vivian and Oriane wait with one another in the sunroom—both hoping to speak with Knobby privately.

Vivian thought she'd better be getting home—threads of tension were collecting around her temples like cotton candy swirling onto a stick. But she hadn't had a chance to thank Knobby for the flowers and didn't want to abandon Oriane either. So, they finished a bottle of wine together, chatting about modern reactions to the story of *Don Giovanni* and a Mozart forum Oriane belonged to. Their conversation was as easy as piano-by-number until Vivian brought up the flowers Knobby'd sent.

Oriane coughed and a slurp of wine dribbled down her chin.

"The same ones I brought him for healing while he was in the hospital." Vivian fanned herself with her hand. Another damn heat flash. She'd already had one that afternoon. "Lavender, salvia, and rosemary."

With her palm, Oriane wiped the wetness from her chin.

"He signed the card, 'A sweeter woman ne'er drew breath.'" Vivian sighed. "That's Shakespeare. Remember, he said he'd read a lot of Shakespeare when he interviewed."

"Way back in high school," Oriane said grudgingly.

"You never forget your Shakespeare—high school, college, whenever."

"Well, you're wrong. It's not Shakespeare," Oriane said, suddenly appearing crestfallen. "Why—why would Knobby send you flowers?"

Vivian hadn't read as much into the gesture as Oriane had, apparently. "It was nothing."

Oriane laced her fingers and tucked them under her chin, rocking back and forth in silence. Her eyes flashed, and it appeared as though she was preparing to say something. Judging from her varied facial expressions, she kept changing her mind about what to say. She exhaled over her clasped hands and rose from the rocking chair. She gathered a few stray wine glasses in her hands. "I'm off to the kitchen. I offered to be Deanna's chief bottle washer."

"Masque planning meeting next week," Vivian said. "You're the Apple-tini."

"Right," Oriane said, looking like the last thing she was in the mood for was parading around as the Apple-tini.

Vivian watched her run off. What had she said to upset Oriane? That she had gotten flowers from Knobby? Was Oriane sweet on him? Vivian appreciated Knobby's gesture—it was the first kindness anyone extended to her since she'd joined the board. She hardly considered the flowers a romantic entr'acte. Merely a kindness returned. She had no romantic interest in Knobby.

She couldn't entertain a lover anyway, what with her mother behaving so badly of late. Unless Vivian placed the medication in her mother's mouth, or stayed with her until it dissolved, her mother would not take her lithium. Vivian found capsules hidden in planters and on the windowsills. Once, she'd discovered a little pile underneath the standing lamp in her mother's bedroom. Her mother was careening toward another hospitalization—maybe a permanent one—and there was nothing Vivian could do about it, except to make sure she stayed on her own medication or she'd lose all coping ability whatsoever.

Had someone told her how miserable her mother would become because of bipolar disorder, she would have turned around the day she was born and crawled right back in the womb. At least there, she wouldn't have to endure her mother's nonsensical rants.

Vivian was in college when she realized she had inherited more than the Frantz Ketchup fortune—the Frantz disposition toward bipolar disease. Following a hypomanic episode at Wellesley, she'd gotten the family doctor—good old Dr. Jasper, who was a hundred-years-old then—to prescribe medication. Though no foolproof drug, it did reduce the mood swings and lessen the frequency. However, she still became perturbed over inconsequential things.

When she was thirty-five, during the summer she lived in Milan, she married Formula 1 racecar driver Guido Pirelli, a perennial winner of the Italian Grand Prix. Despite the fact that they barely saw one another—he constantly traveled the world with his racing—they divorced within five years. He'd gotten fed up with her mood swings which increased with each of his extramarital affairs. Her manic-depressive episodes became more frequent with every year which was more than the nature of the disease than anything else.

For reasons she couldn't begin to explain, things a normal person cared nothing about incensed her. Throughout her life, people mocked her for unleashing a hair-trigger temper. Vivian suffered their derision rather than clue people in as to what was really going on. Manic depression, like other psychological illnesses, is commonly ascribed to a weakness in character, as if Vivian somehow chose to allow her emotional and obsessive impulses to overrun her life.

After the divorce, Vivian retreated even further from society. That was one way people couldn't find out about her flaws. Yet, she was getting bored staying home day and night. Since she wasn't very active in the family business either, she needed another pursuit. She was expected to contribute to the Hankey community as a volunteer.

She tried the hospital auxiliary—but the directors were rigid and humorless. Despite her interest in supporting the Hankey Public Library, she couldn't join the library board since her mother had been asked to leave. Instead, she'd write a fat check every year while continuing her search for a non-profit home, eventually thinking the Hankey Opera Guild might be the best fit. Opera storylines were filled with characters who succumbed to their primal impulses. Operas wouldn't be very exciting if they lost their primalcy, would they? *Primalcy?* Was that a word? she wondered.

Because real-life people weren't supposed to run others through with steak knives or strangle loving wives, operagoers lived vicariously through the dramatic deeds of the most cinematic characters in Western art. Why else would *Tosca* become a household word and *Otello* one of the most performed operas in the world? By serving an organization that showcased unbridled passion, Vivian assumed she'd finally fit in somewhere. To date, the volunteerism thrust hadn't worked as planned. If other guild members hadn't accepted her by September—the start of the 2011–12 season—she'd give up volunteering and resign herself to the life of seclusion her mother led.

Unlike less fortunate individuals stricken with bipolar disease, Vivian Frantz Pirelli had waitstaff and resources at her disposal. She never needed to go to a pharmacy, grocery store, hairdresser, or to a job another day in her life, if she so chose. She could just hole up in Frantzland—her pet name for her family homestead—until manic depression combined with old age combined with loneliness turned her into Miss Haberdash, Hashish, Haverford—whatever the name of that Dickens character was.

"Vivian," a man was calling. "Vivian."

Richard? Why was he still here? He and Deanna were close— that much she knew. How close, she could only guess. If she were Richard's age, single and male to boot, she'd try her luck with Deanna—who was by anyone's standards a fine-looking woman. Smart, too.

Vivian removed her pocketbook from the handle of the chair and slung it over her arm. She was trying to remember whether she'd worn a coat or not but had no recollection of doing so. Her surroundings, her bearings were becoming cloudy—quickly. An episode was coming on. She had to go home and lie down, maybe even take some additional meds, so she had enough wherewithal to deal with her mother this evening.

"I found you," Richard was saying. "I'm glad you didn't leave— I wanted you to know, that I'm proud of you for standing up to the Maestro this afternoon." He patted her on the shoulder in a paternal way. "What you said needed to be said. We have to be prepared for the fact that some people might think Giovanni takes rakish behavior too far. I shudder to say it, but some might see him as a rapist."

"I don't mind telling Maestro my mind. I'm an outsider. I had nothing to lose," Vivian said. "Though I am concerned that you and the others don't trust my motives. I want the show to succeed and the guild to succeed. You don't want to be blindsided by protesters kicking up a media firestorm about the themes in *Don Giovanni*." She picked up a few decorative pillows and arranged them on the settee. "When I was younger," Vivian explained, as she arranged a throw over the armchair, "I would have picketed outside the opera house if you were presenting *Don Giovanni*. You'll want time to mount a defense against people like me." She smiled at Richard out of obligation and excused herself. "I think I left my wrap in the foyer."

"Vivian—wait," Richard called. "I'll walk out with you."

Vivian scoured the entrance. No coat. Perhaps she hadn't worn one. The fact that she couldn't remember whether she had worn a wrap was nothing out of the ordinary. It was warm enough—she didn't need one. If she ended up leaving one there, Deanna would return it. No use signaling to Richard that she was feeling disoriented.

Was it a full moon? It felt like it.

"So, Knobby's under contract? That's what you and Deanna were meeting about?" she asked. "I was hoping to catch him before I left. He sent me flowers, and I wanted to thank him. I'll see him another time."

"*Knobby* sent flowers, eh?" Richard said, holding the front door for her. He joined her on the cobblestone path leading from Deanna's door. "Very thoughtful of him. I'm not much for sending flowers. Only on occasion. Only to special people."

"I've always thought a certain kind of man sends flowers," Vivian said.

"How about that!" Richard said.

He seemed inordinately interested in this thread of conversation for a doctor, for someone who admitted he wasn't much concerned with posies, and for someone who'd shown her nothing but disdain up until now.

"And what kind of man would that be—if there is such a type?" he continued. "Someone sensitive? Thoughtful? Sentimental?"

Vivian turned to Richard. "One vastly different from my father. Most people don't know this, but the nicest thing he could say about women was that their figures reminded him of ketchup bottles." I could write a book, she wanted to say. But why would anyone want to read a book about a *messagist*, no, um, *massageamist*, no. A ketchup magnet who hated women, she said to herself instead. *Magnet?* Was that the right word?

"Women are shaped like ketchup bottles?" Richard chuckled. "Now there's a fresh perspective on the female form—very interesting."

Was everything she said today interesting, or was Richard being overly kind because that's how men apologized? She had never heard the words "I'm sorry" uttered from a man's lips. She was sure she wasn't about to, either.

"Knobby's signed and ready to work," Richard said, "whenever his doctor releases him."

"He's a perfect fit for us. I loved his idea about the opera raps. A fabulous way to bring in professors and local college students, too. He's level-headed, too. With Maestro being the way he is, so despondent, that's important."

"I think you mean *despotic*, Vivian."

"*Despotic*, yes. Isn't that what I said?" she asked.

"Knobby has just the approach we need—forward thinking, full of ideas. Still, we have to mount a fabulous *Don Giovanni*—to give Knobby a chance to show us what he's made of," Richard continued. "Vivian," he began with hesitation in his voice. "I'm sorry if I was cross with you at the hospital. I get in these moods sometimes—ever since Mary passed."

He said *I'm sorry?* Vivian smiled on the inside. Had Richard seen the corners of her mouth turn upward slightly? "Well, I wouldn't know what that's like," she said. "I'm always in control of my emotions—one hundred percent of the time."

"Really?" Richard extended his arm to help her step off the curb. "How do you do it?"

"I was kidding," she said, considering how forthcoming she should be, opting to cloak her mental illness, yet again. Vivian dug her keys out from her handbag. "That's my ride—there," she said, pointing to the silver-blue Jaguar. "I guess we meet next at the planning party for the masque, huh?"

"I was going to make a corny remark like, 'We can *ketchup* then,' but then I figured you probably get a lot of ketchup jokes."

Vivian stopped herself from saying something snide, soft-pedaling her response. "A lot of ketchup jokes. You could say that, yes. See you next week."

She'd fought back the urge to snipe at Richard for making the same play on words hundreds of other people had made at her expense throughout her lifetime. For his part, Richard wasn't a graceful man, as far as communication skills went. Most doctors weren't. Richard never had to develop much diplomacy—not if one believed he was the smartest person in the room. He hadn't tried to annoy her with the ketchup remark; he was just trying to be cordial.

Richard cleared his throat. "Would you like to go for coffee?"

Was he asking her on a little date? She struggled to keep from smiling, no—laughing. If he only knew the real Vivian Pirelli.

She couldn't go for coffee. All afternoon she'd had that sinking feeling she'd be falling off a cliff soon. She had to get out of Richard's sight before her mood plummeted. And she'd had cravings for pretzels and ice cream and potato chip sandwiches, sure signs that a depressive bout loomed as surely as Aida was destined for a tragic love triangle. She wasn't certain what the trigger had been this time—she rarely was—though she never socialized when it was a full moon. It could have been the full moon. She'd been so busy with guild work she'd forgotten to check her calendar. She had some anti-anxiety medication in her glove compartment. She could rein in her mood swings until then.

"Thanks, but I need to tend to my mother," she told Richard, unlocking her car door.

A minute later, with a Xanax dissolving on her tongue, she waved to Richard, who stood beside the curb as she drifted past.

Her cell phone rang through her car radio—a customization she insisted would save her life one day. It would be just like her to crash her car trying to dig a cell phone from her purse. She glanced at the display. Mother. She let it ring.

9
The Aside

As Vivian steps into her car and pulls away, Richard stands transfixed at the foot of the walkway. He is alone in Deanna's development—no irksome children riding by on skateboards or scooters. He begins talking to himself like he used to in his office, a casualty of too much time spent alone with his Dictaphone.

What in the world had come over him? Why had he asked Vivian out for coffee? Vivian of all people. He wasn't behaving sensibly. It had to be her eyes and her skin bewitching him, both looking exceptionally lovely in the natural light of Deanna's sunroom. And something else, too, which he noticed for the first time as she strolled ahead of him toward her sedan. She had a figure on her. Full in the right places, cinched in others. Like the old ketchup bottles but with more on top.

Why in the world was Vivian single? Richard asked everyone and no one, as she drove away. He could guess why—she never let men get close to her after her marriage went south; she was suspicious of all men because her first husband been a world-famous lecher; and she was an heiress. He wished he knew the real story.

He did know that he'd never been attracted to scrawny women. He couldn't help himself—he had a weakness for an hourglass shape. While Vivian was explaining her father's views about women, he was noticing her light blue sweater, unbuttoned to her sternum and, how could he put this delicately, that Miss PC had one fine pair of headlamps. On her way to her car, she swung her hips from side to side. He had always loved backyard swings—from childhood on up.

How old was she? Early fifties? Would she think he was too old for her? He looked down at his three-piece suit and brogues. According to Nurse Enema, he looked eighty-years-old. What if he started dressing younger? Deanna had exquisite fashion sense. She could help him find clothes that would take off ten years. Ten years younger would put him squarely in Vivian's range. But Deanna couldn't be told why he needed her help. Nor could he confess to Vivian that in the course of a few weeks, he'd become sweet on her.

What if all of this happened because he'd been lonely? Had working alongside another woman on the guild made him feel something for Vivian that was nothing more than animal lust? Then again, he'd been partnering with Deanna all these years. He'd even been alone with her several times after fund-raising calls. He never felt aroused by Deanna the way he had by Vivian—not once. He liked Deanna. But he never desired her because she could pluck a chicken down to its last feather follicle using her eyes alone, if she chose to.

He couldn't tell Vivian how he felt—not yet. His affection might dissipate the next time she insulted his command of the English language or demonstrated a complete lack of verbal sophistication. That would be a sure test. If she mixed a metaphor, and he still wanted her, he would have to ask her out for dinner.

His heart raced. His pants stiffened—for the first time in a year. Being around her, rather, being close to her, Richard realized he had no need for Viagra or any other such medication. Everything his urologist previously deemed as "broken" hadn't needed fixing after all. He just hadn't met the right woman.

Richard felt like singing, "Ah, mes, amis" from La Fille du Régiment, but even a bullfrog had more top C's than he did. When he got home, he'd throw Juan Diego Flórez's version in the CD magazine and lip sync, just to keep himself in an amorous mood. What was Vivian's number on the speed dial? Whatever it was, he'd change it to two. Two for two blue-ribbon headlamps.

10

The Gay Divorcée

Deanna is eyeing the furniture in the sunroom, considering the events of the afternoon—that she emerged the victor from the match today. Oriane tags along behind her.

"Should I put these back?" Oriane asked, lifting one of the straight-backed chairs, grunting, "Heavy!"

"Dining room," Deanna said, pointing to her left. "Take them through the living room."

Deanna moved all the plants back to their usual spots and picked up the last of the empty glasses and luncheon plates, stacking them up in her arms, like a waitress. Not because she'd ever been a waitress. She'd had one job after college, in the fund-raising office at her alma mater, Mt. Holyoke College, which is how she met Stu—her roommate's older brother. Stu was an alpha male who chased a woman, plying her with gifts and sailing trips and tickets to the Met, until she said yes. They weren't married a year before Stu had his first affair.

She deposited the dirty plates on the work island in the kitchen and filled the right half of the double sink with warm soapy water, hand washing her crystal stemware—Waterford—a wedding gift. She lifted a wine goblet out of the suds and held it under hot tap water to rinse it in the other sink. She held the goblet there until the second before the water scalded her hand, the best way to get streak-free glasses.

Knobby stuck his head in the kitchen. "I'm going to get going. Thanks again, Deanna."

She turned at the sound of his voice. "Don't thank me. I'm the one who roped you into owning three dachshund puppies."

Oriane entered the kitchen from the other side, carrying a tray of cheese and crackers. "We'll absolutely help you take care of them, Knobby. I love dogs, by the way."

Deanna grabbed the dish towel from the countertop and dried her hands. "Gee, I never knew that about you, Oriane."

Knobby smiled. "I don't have any dogs just yet, do I?"

"You will," Oriane said. "If Deanna promises something, it's as good as done."

"Your mom's been great, Oriane—helping me find that townhome," Knobby said. "I'll have to take you both to dinner as a thank you."

A crooked grin stole across Oriane's face. "I'll bet my *mom* would like that a lot."

Deanna folded her arms and leaned against the sink. "Okay, kids. Time to skedaddle. You've helped me enough. I need to get me some dawgs," she said with an artificial drawl.

An hour later, Deanna had restored the kitchen to its pristine condition. She put a load of linens in the washing machine and sat down at her computer. She didn't know whether she could buy dachshund puppies on line. If she could find a seller and determine how much dachshund puppies cost, that would be a good start. Were dachshunds one of those ultra-expensive breeds, like Bernese Mountain dogs? She didn't want to spend $5,000 on puppies. Even though she'd gotten a lot of assets in the divorce settlement, she was hardly in a position to spend that kind of dough on something non-essential. To make matters worse, Pennsylvania was a no-alimony state. If she put herself in the position of needing regular income, she'd have to think about getting a job. She couldn't run the guild and hold down a full-time job.

She'd better start looking for those dachshund puppies.

She clicked on the link for PuppyHunt.com. Then she typed in dachshund in the "Breed finder" area, and found 1,500 matches. Fifteen hundred dachshund puppies. Each was adorable. She had no idea dachshunds came in so many colors. Little blonde pups. Tiny chocolate brown puppies with big sad eyes. Black-and-tan long coat pups for only $500—shipping included. Pictures of puppy mommas because the pups weren't due to be born for weeks. Fifteen hundred puppies? How would she ever choose three?

What an efficient search engine that PuppyHunt.com boasted! If only she could find a man as easily. Imagine a site where you could type in "dark-haired lawyer" and dozens of hits would come up, each with specific buyer's data: "He's up-to-date on his current vaccinations and comes with a health guarantee. (That would have come in handy for Stu.) Additional information: He will be dewormed (critically important for lawyers) and ready for his new home by May 1."

If only it were that simple.

She was going to need a generous glass of wine before wading through hundreds of entries of puppy data. She hurried to the kitchen and uncapped one of the Bourgeron Blancs, her favorite, filled a glass, and returned to her computer. She clicked on a tan pup, staring into his big, brown eyes, and felt a sudden urge to call Stu. Just to find out how he was doing and to report how well things were going—that they had a new director and were bringing a hot young star to Hankey who'd put them on the map.

Stu hadn't called her for a year—there was no need. No children involved. No pets, even. He'd moved to Florida because that's where his secretary's family was from. He'd gotten her pregnant, and she'd wanted to live closer to her parents, since she'd be giving them their first grandchild. Funny. Deanna couldn't imagine Stu moving anywhere to please her. But the firm agreed to open an office in Ft. Lauderdale, and off Stu went. She had his Florida number on speed dial. All she had to do was punch it in. She picked up the receiver and hesitated. Then she returned it to the cradle. She couldn't call him. Just couldn't do it.

But what about Facebook? Was Stu on Facebook? Oriane had set up a Facebook page for the Hankey Opera Company. She typed in the login information Oriane had given her and searched for Stuart Lundquist. And there he was—or at least a thumbnail picture of him. One Stuart Lundquist on the whole Facebook network? Weren't there more than 500 million people on Facebook? She took another swallow of wine and clicked on his picture. She lingered on his page, an abbreviated one apparently, since he hadn't *friended* her, but long enough to see a picture of Stu and his new wife holding their baby boy. She hadn't needed to see that.

Would Stu know she'd gone to his Facebook page in search of him? She left his page, as quickly as she'd arrived, vowing never to look for him again.

One Stuart Lundquist in the whole universe of Facebook users? Wouldn't that just feed his Stu-sized ego to know that. More than likely, only one Deanna Lundquist on Facebook, too. She typed Deanna Lundquist in the "Search" box. Clicked on the cursor. Three Deanna Lundquists? Three? She'd never even met anyone named Deanna before. No other Oriane Longeneckers besides their Oriane. No Vivian Pirellis either, although Google generated loads of hits for Vivian Pirelli. She clicked on one of the links that looked especially juicy and pulled up an online tabloid, scanning the first few paragraphs.

So, the sole heir to the Frantz Ketchup fortune had yet to come into a nickel of it. And there was a photo of Vivian Pirelli, identified as the ex-wife of Sicilian racecar driver Guido Pirelli, wearing a shower cap, sucking on a Frantz pickle. Someone on the Pirelli side must have slipped the press that photo. There was even a video clip of one of his Italian cousins saying, "Guido married Vivian for money and got tired a waiting for her parents a croak."

Deanna was starting to feel sorry for her.

Time to check out the competition, which she did routinely. She clicked on "Favorites" and trawled the special events calendars of a half-dozen other opera companies in the United States, looking for fresh ideas. What was that? A Chanukah Music Fest fund-raiser? How enterprising! By using the alternate spelling *Hanukkah*, Hankey could borrow the idea guilt free. She'd bring it up at the next guild meeting.

Enough surfing for one day. She closed that window, which left fetching dachshund puppies crawling across the screen. So what if she had to buy three puppies? She'd tricked Maestro into "hiring" Leandro Vasquez and Knobby. How about that! She'd skillfully manipulated *Maestro*, who was always contrary, a man everyone feared and loathed.

No, she wasn't at the apex of happiness in her personal life. She was, however, ensuring the survival of the Hankey Opera Company, staking her reputation on its success. And they would succeed. Okay, they'd gotten off to a rough start. But things would improve— from today onward. She could feel it in her calcium-fortified bones.

Sometimes she became so embroiled in guild work, she forgot the world around her. Though she knew the dates of every show opening and every fund-raiser, she wasn't always certain what day it was. She clicked on the calendar in the lower right hand corner of her computer. Saturday, April 4. The Masque was in about a month. Opening night of *Don Giovanni* was in little more than six weeks.

It was April 4 already? Was it too early to stop by the polo field tomorrow? She couldn't recall when polo season began. Yet, Stu played for years. Had she blocked out that part of her life? Not entirely. She'd remembered he had some handsome teammates. But she was getting ahead of herself. No use making plans to drop by if it wasn't going to be nice out—weather first. She clicked on the homepage of the local station. A banner across the top said, "Another assault by the **Italian Zorro**, this time in a laundromat. Details at eleven." *Italian Zorro?* A brief surge of adrenaline spiked as she recognized the moniker; she'd have to remember to watch the news tonight.

On second thought, she shouldn't try to seek out Stu's old teammates tomorrow. For one thing, polo season always began later in this part of Pennsylvania. For another, although she was feeling lonely, she couldn't begin to think about dating again. She had an opera to launch. And she needed to get back to the business of finding those puppies, who'd have more going for them than most polo players anyway.

Selecting three puppies from among thousands was a massive responsibility—nothing for the non-committal. She needed to get pumped up. She clicked on her music file. Another click and the overture to *Don Giovanni* came pouring through her speakers of her computer. She inhaled deeply, threw herself into a couple kickboxing moves on selected beats, exhaled completely and reseated herself, ready to do battle within the kingdom of cuteness. Deanna clicked on the PuppyHunt.com tab and was met with a forlorn little face with deep brown eyes as big as half dollars. The little longhair female looked just like a dog named Isolde should look, with her reddish coat marked with dark dappling on her head and ears. For Tristan, she chose a coal black long-haired dachshund with a tiny blue-black nose who looked angelic nestled on a baby blue towel. The minute she saw him, she knew the puppy she wanted for Lohengrin: a little chocolate piebald with coloring like a Guernsey cow and a bitty pot belly.

She could only buy three? Of course, she could only buy three. Three for Knobby. She had no time for puppies, no matter how much she wanted one. No time for men either. She had an opera company to save.

II
The 'Elektra' Complex

Vivian drives home, craving sour pickles. She takes a hot bath and crawls into bed, setting a jar of Frantz kosher dills and a glass of water on the nightstand. After some snacking, she takes a pill and nearly drifts off to sleep when she hears her mother calling. A full moon is rising through her bedroom window.

"Vivian!" her mother wailed like a cow whose calf had been ripped from its teat.

Mother didn't take her medication, Vivian said to herself. She lifted an empty glass off the end table and slid her feet into fuzzy purple slippers jutting out from under the foot of the bed. "I'm coming," she called, shuffling out of the darkened room. Damn it. She'd hardly had a chance to close her eyes. Now, she'd never have the patience to tolerate her mother's needling and whining. Well, she'd take her medicine now. Even if Vivian had to cram it down her throat.

She hurried down the length of the hall as fast as she could so the servants wouldn't hear her mother's undignified cries. Before she entered her mother's bedroom, she stopped herself. Had she taken her own medication? She stared at the empty glass in her hand. It had been full of water a half hour ago. Hadn't it?

What if she only thought she'd taken her meds, but hadn't, and suffered a complete breakdown while caring for Mother?

When had Mother gotten so bad? She'd gone crazy lately—Bedlam-grade insane—all because she refused her medication. God knows, Vivian tried to make her take it. She pleaded with her, threatened her, withheld privileges. Still her mother would not down her pills.

Had Vivian taken her own pill?

She slipped inside the room, pretending to be invisible. Her mother sat bolt upright, her frenzy of white hair protruding every which way, looking like Bertha Rochester, or at least, how Vivian imagined her to look.

"Vivian!" her mother yelped. "Took you goddamn long enough."

"I'm here," Vivian whispered. Why was her mother always shooting off her big, fat, vulgar mouth? Why? Why? Why? She went into her mother's bathroom and filled the water glass. "Where's your medicine?" She scanned the cabinet over the sink. No pills. Then she noticed a plastic prescription bottle stuffed down into the wastebasket. She retrieved the bottle, shook out two pills into her hand, and took them and the glass to her mother, setting them on the nightstand.

"Where were you?" Her mother breathed heavily. You could see her chest expanding and contracting, her nylon dressing gown like a flimsy sail in a stiff breeze. "Your father's here."

This ought to be good, really good, oh, so good, Vivian thought. Another post-mortem communication with Daddy Dearest? How had he contacted Mother this time? Through the flickers of a Partylite candle? By rattling on the windows? No, not Dad. Not the Great Karl Frantz—ketchup magnet. *Magnet*? Was *magnet* the right word? Not the Great Karl Frantz, King of Ketchup. Drumming on windows was too conventional—every ghost tapped on windows now and then. Had he written a message in the pool of unused ketchup on her mother's luncheon plate?

"What about him?" Vivian asked in a monotone.

"He's—he's coming for me," her mother said.

Considering Dad had been six years gone, this was highly unlikely. Another manic hallucination, she guessed. "Really?" she said dully. "And how's he doing that?"

"He—he was floating outside there," her mother said, pointing to the double-hung window. "He kept saying my name. 'Paylor! Pa-a-a-y-y-y-l-o-r-r-r. I'm coming for yo-o-o-u-u-u-u.'"

"Mother, it was the paperboy calling, 'P-a-a-p-e-r-r-r-r,' because he needs to be paid on Saturdays. He always comes around after dinner to collect. Did you hear me, Mother? It's *Saturday*," Vivian said. "The day you pay—for the paper," she said, pounding her fingers into her hand for emphasis. "Not to mention Dad couldn't sing. But don't worry. I'll pay the paperboy. I'll take care of everything. Since you can't take care of anything," she said, adding, "because you won't take your medicine."

"Don't mock me, you hussy. After fifty years," her mother raged, pointing a quivering finger in Vivian's face, "don't you think I know your father's voice?"

Vivian gently rubbed the skin at her hairline. Then she winced. Besides a lead-heavy feeling in her gut, her forehead throbbed. She was in the throes of an episode herself. A full-on big, fat bender. Why? Why now? Unlike her mother, she *had* been taking her meds. At least, most of the time, when she hadn't gotten confused. What had triggered her own distress this evening? The wine? The argument with Maestro? Well, you won, Maestro, she wanted to say. I'm suffering now. Are you happy? You're thrilled because you want everyone to be miserable. Because you're miserable. That's your mission in life. I should introduce you to my mother. "Of course, I—"

Her mother cackled. "No wonder your husband left you. You whore!"

"That's enough," Vivian said, shuddering from the pounding in her head. "Stop talking, Mother." Stop thinking, Vivian. Then you'll stop talking, and maybe she'll stop talking. Just stop. Stop it now. Maybe you should pound your own skull in. Then you'll definitely stop thinking. You won't be breathing either. But then breathing's overrated. "The servants will hear you."

Her mother huffed in and out as if blasting her breath into a harmonica. "I don't care. They need to know what you are," Paylor said, her voice growing louder. "You whore. You frigid, thieving whore."

Pain seared Vivian's head, like a kid having a go at a bass drum smack in the middle of her skull. "A frigid, thieving whore? Really, Mother."

"Are you deaf *and* dumb?"

"How can a whore be frigid, *Mother*? Thieving, maybe. But frigid? A frigid whore would be a starving whore," she said. Her mother called her dumb? Her mother was stupid, an imbecile, a mindless parasite. An old, cackling—. Vivian stopped herself. No sense picking on Mother when neither of them was of sane mind at the moment.

A fiendish smile crept across Paylor's face. "You're getting tubby, Vivvy," she said, using her daughter's childhood nickname. "You're eating too much. Vivvy's a fat whore," she sang, the latter insult sounding like a playground ditty. "A fat whore who loves to snore."

"That's it, Mother. That's the limit." Vivian stalked to the telephone. What's the number? The number? What is it? "I'm calling Dr. Jasper. You're going back to Serenity Acres."

"Don't call that quack!" Paylor yelled.

Dr. Jasper, who delivered Vivian, who'd been the family physician for more than fifty years may have been in his eighties, but he was no quack.

Vivian grabbed the phone and punched in the doctor's speed dial number and waited for the service to pick up. One ring. Two rings. Three rings. Four rings. It shouldn't be ringing like that. Did she punch in the wrong number? What was it? Four? Five? Four or five? Six? Just as the answering service came on the line, something smacked Vivian on the side of her head.

"Yeoww!" Vivian grabbed her left ear and wheeled around to face her mother. Her mother had lifted the drinking glass off the nightstand and hurled it at her. It grazed the side of Vivian's head and fell to the bed with a plop. Before her mother could reach it, Vivian grabbed the glass and threw it to the floor where it smashed into jagged pieces. "You're going away this time. And you're never coming out. Ever," Vivian said, lurching for the phone.

"Over my dead body," Paylor cried. Rising from the bed with uncommon strength, she rushed Vivian and knocked her off her feet. As Vivian struggled to her hands and knees, Paylor clambered on top of her, riding her like a pony, laughing a chilling, guttural laugh.

"No, no, no. Nome not. Nome not. No—ho!" she cried, wrapping her left arm around Vivian's neck, pressing it tighter and tighter across Vivian's throat with each utterance.

"Get off me!" Vivian shrieked, struggling to break free. How could a seventy-five-year-old woman be that damn strong? Now her mother was rocking back and forth, grinding the top of Vivian's head into the wall with each forward thrust.

When Paylor dug her right hand into Vivian's ribs, Vivian realized she had a second's purchase to get out from under her mother. She grabbed hold of her mother's arm and twisted it back on itself until Paylor yelped. Then Vivian flipped her, shoving her head to the floor.

"Now you'll keep your damn hands off me, won't you? Won't you, Mother?"

Her mother didn't answer. She lay on her side, her vengeful fury drained from her. Glass fragments lay all around her head. Vivian rolled her mother onto her back. A shard of glass was embedded in her neck, sticking out from her jugular vein. Blood began gushing from the two-inch gash, and she gagged at the sight and smell of it.

"Oh, God!" Vivian cried as her mother's blood soaked her lemon yellow dressing gown.

"Hello? Hello?" someone's voice poured from the receiver of the phone, lying face-up on the bed. "Whoever's there, pick up the phone. Talk to me."

Hands shaking, Vivian collared the phone and eased it to her mouth. "My mother's been h—hurt badly. Send—Dr. Jasper. Frantz residence. It's an emergency. Hurry," and dropped the receiver.

She peeled a pillow case from one of the bed pillows, bundled it into an unkempt ball, and pressed it to her mother's neck, holding it there, to stem the bleeding. "I'm sorry, Mother. I'm sorry," she keened while her mother moaned softly.

* * *

"They'll be here any second," Dr. Jasper was saying. He sat beside the bed, applying pressure to the wound. "Hold on, Paylor. Hold on, old girl."

"I didn't mean—" Vivian muttered, holding her head.

"Sit down, Vivvy," he said, pointing to a chair. "You kept her alive. Dr. Jasper's here now. Sit still and stay quiet. Do your breathing while I help your mother."

A half a minute after Vivian began her rhythmic breathing, an ambulance screamed for two or three seconds and then it was eerily quiet. Emergency lights flashed outside her mother's bedroom window as if announcing the arrival of an impromptu carnival. Vivian was standing by the chair—she couldn't sit—filling her lungs to the count of five.

Dr. Jasper ran from the bedroom to the top of the stairs, leaving the door wide open. "Up here! Second floor!" he yelled.

Before Vivian could push out all the air from her lungs, the EMT's were racing up the stairs and barreling into her mother's bedroom.

"The external jugular's severed," Dr. Jasper said, pointing out the broken glass. "One of the pieces tore a gash two-inches long into the left side of her neck. We've been applying pressure to keep her alive."

The med-techs raced to Mrs. Frantz's side, did a lightning-quick assessment, then slid her onto the gurney.

"We'll follow you to the hospital. Go, go," Dr. Jasper ordered. Once the EMT's had left the bedroom, he retrieved a hankie from his back pocket and wiped his face. He shuddered a sigh that threatened to snap his frail body in two.

Vivian looked down at her blood-drenched garments. The Lucia di Lammermoor of Elysian Hills—twice as old as Donizetti's Lucia, every inch the murderess. "I must get something else on." She went to one of the dresser drawers in her mother's room and pulled out a velour sweatsuit and ran into the adjoining bathroom to change.

"Hurry, Vivian," Dr. Jasper called. "She's lost a lot of blood."

12

The Deus Ex Machina

Vivian emerges from the bathroom wearing the jumpsuit. She races to her mother's closet, grabs a pair of clogs, throws them on, and bolts out of the room and down the winding staircase, toward the door. Dr. Jasper trails behind.

As Vivian opened the front door, a rush of wind and rain smacked her in the face. The ambulance bearing her mother tore off the property, headed toward Holy Ghost Hospital. Lightning crackled overhead, illuminating the deciduous trees lining the drive—big, angry soldiers, their limbs barren but for buds of leaves. She rushed ahead to Dr. Jasper's Buick sedan, covering her head with her elbow, to keep from getting soaked while he tottered out from under the overhang shielding the front landing. She stopped and turned. "Do you need help?"

Dr. Jasper waved her off, removed the car keys from his pocket, and clicked his fob, so Vivian could climb in on the passenger side. While she buckled her seatbelt, Dr. Jasper eased himself into the driver's seat. He started the engine, flipped on the wipers, and rolled ahead a few feet before braking. The car shuddered to a halt. "This storm came up fast. I can barely see out the windshield."

"I'll drive," Vivian said, throwing open her car door, wrapping her arms around her head to stave off the elements. She hurried to the other side of the sedan while Dr. Jasper slid across the bench seat. She threw her seatbelt on and tore down the drive before Dr. Jasper was safely buckled in. The air smelled like burnt rubber, and she wondered how much traction she'd just scorched off his tires. "Which way should I go?"

"Henry Avenue would be the fastest," Dr. Jasper said.

"What about the train?"

"Wouldn't worry about it. Not at this time of night."

When Hankey Steel was operational, Amalgamated Rail Corporation (AMRAIL) freight trains ran through the downtown several times daily, making and picking up deliveries for towns north and south. Since the plant closed, Hankey'd been reduced to a drive-through for other Rust Belt manufacturers in the Northeast.

Vivian checked the speedometer. She needed to go faster than fifty miles an hour to catch that ambulance, which she could easily do. She had a lead foot. Plus, she could see the road better. Rain no longer pinged the windshield like BB gun pellets. If she held her breath, she could hear the ambulance.

Within minutes, they had reached downtown Hankey, where the streetlights and stoplights improved visibility even more. At nighttime, the most prominent feature of the Hankey skyline was Big Red, the Bobbin' Robin fast food chain's signature emblem perched high on a steel pedestal—a neon beacon rising three stories high, as tall as the Hankey Courthouse, towering over most buildings.

The ambulance was roughly three cars ahead of them, judging from the intensity of its flashing lights. Its screaming siren pierced the eerie stillness of a Saturday night downtown. She barreled through a string of green lights, keeping within half a dozen car lengths of the ambulance. Suddenly red lights nearly as big as traffic lights began flashing from the railroad crossing at 10th Street.

"A train?" Vivian asked. "At this time of night?"

"Son of a gun. Those boys better step on it," Dr. Jasper said.

"I thought it was safe to take Henry Avenue."

"Whodda thunk it."

Vivian eased off the gas pedal. She pulled behind the ambulance whose lights throbbed and siren whined with desperation. "They're caught, too, Doctor."

Caught was definitely the right word. Once an AMRAIL train came barreling into Hankey proper, there was nothing anyone could do but pull out a newspaper and read the box scores or whip out a cosmetics pouch and freshen one's makeup. Their freight trains stopped traffic for ten solid minutes, sometimes longer.

Realistically, Vivian knew she needn't fret anymore than she already was. That ambulance had everything it needed to keep her mother alive—equipment, communications, and well-trained medical personnel.

What happened next was not only outside of Vivian's control—anyone's for that matter—it would make national headlines the next day. A gust of wind blasted up the alley, rocking the old Buick from side to side as if it were at sea in a tempest. The zephyr raced past them, swirling leaves and debris marking its path, surging past them and upward toward the Big Red emblem. A gale-force gust slammed into the big steel bird roosting stories above them, causing the glowing mascot to wobble as if hanging from an industrial-grade teeter-totter in a hurricane. A hollow crack rang out, and the steel pedestal supporting Big Red snapped like balsa wood. The bird came hurtling toward the ground—beak first.

"Look out," Vivian yelled, reaching out her hand to brace Dr. Jasper. The steel robin landed on the back of the ambulance in front of them, crushing it on impact. The ferocity of steel crashing into steel caused the Buick to jump a foot into the air.

"Oh, my God!" Vivian wailed. "My mother's in there. Mother!" As the Buick settled to the ground, she and Dr. Jasper were jostled around like raw eggs dislodged from their carton. She tried to steady herself by grabbing onto the steering wheel with one hand and the door handle with another. Then, as suddenly as it had whipped up, the windstorm now petered out, leaving Vivian disoriented—doubting everything she'd just seen. Tears stained her cheeks as a caboose clattered by. The railroad crossing arm lifted, its bells dinging happily.

13
The Supporting Player

The next morning, Richard's picked up the Sunday paper from the front drive and has settled in his easy chair to enjoy his coffee. Before he has a chance to unfold the paper, "The Toreador's Song" blares from the end table— his cell phone. Since he rarely gets calls Sunday morning, he deduces it's Marlena, to acknowledge the flowers he sent.

Richard scooped up his phone. "Hello?" He would wait another half second for someone to answer—lots of wrong numbers on cell phones, what with people dialing in the dark and having phone conversations in traffic. Absolutely maddening, those idiots dialing and texting from behind the wheel of moving vehicles. "Hello?" he asked again. Just before snapping his phone closed, he heard a woman's small voice.

"Hello?" The woman fell silent for a moment.

He hadn't heard his daughter's voice in a while, but it must have been her. Who else would phone him on a Sunday morning? Not to mention Marlena never identified herself whenever she called home. Like she expected him to know her from the sound of her breathing. He was hoping she'd call once she received the flowers. "Marlena, I'm glad you called, dear," Richard said. No answer. His natural speaking voice was pitched so low, he often sounded like he was growling. When Marlena was younger, his angry-bear voice—that's what she called it—used to terrify her. He pitched his voice a little higher, to sound gentler. "You got my flowers, hon?"

The connection on the other end went dead. She hung up already? God, that girl was sensitive. And it was entirely his fault.

He had babied Marlena—treated her like a princess her whole life. Thirty-four years later, she still behaved like royalty. Because he hadn't recognized her instantly from her first utterance over a bad connection, she'd gotten her nose out of joint already. What to do? What to do?

"Mary?" Richard called out toward the tiled ceiling. "Help me, Mary. I can't do this without you."

He'd call Marlena back. He was the adult—he needed to behave like one. He returned to his chair and held the phone under the floor lamp. Then he pushed the little button that redials the number. He glanced in the display area. That couldn't be right.

"Hello?" Vivian said timidly.

"Vivian? It's Richard." He heard nothing for a long moment. "Did you just call me?

"I shouldn't have—"

Her voice sounded weak and hollowed out, and he wasn't sure if it was a poor connection or whether something was very wrong. "No trouble. Not in the least," he lied, adding, "don't hang up."

"Did you see the morning paper? Something terrible's happened."

All he'd been trying to do was sit down and read his precious paper before the phone tag started. He could hear her struggling to control her emotions. Did the opera house burn down? Did Knobby have another heart attack over night?

"It's my mother. She's dead," she said, her voice breaking. "I didn't know who else to call."

Out of all the thousands of possible connections the Frantz family must have, owing to the power and influence accorded the rich, Vivian called him? She could afford to pay someone to give her tea and sympathy, if that's what she called him for. Suspicious by nature, he allowed a much less flattering image of Vivian to flash through his head: Vivian, the giant octopus, ensnaring him in big blubbery tentacles. Earlier, he'd been taken in by Vivian's eyes, hair, and her spectacular figure. Now, his gut was telling him to keep his distance. If he permitted her to attach her sticky suction cups, maybe he would be pulled under and start drowning, too. What could he say now? Sorry, I have to go? He wanted to. Instead, he cleared his throat. "What happened?"

"She died in a traffic accident."

"I'm sorry for your loss, Vivian," he said, trying to sound sympathetic but not overly sensitive. He didn't want her emotional floodgates to break open. Almost out of habit, he added, "Is there anything I can do? I mean, I'm not available at the—oww." His neck suddenly spasmed, and he reached for the tender spot.

"Are you hurt? There's something wrong?" Vivian asked. "I'm sorry. You're busy, and I shouldn't have intruded."

"No, don't apologize. It's fine," he said, switching the phone to his right hand to massage the folds under his left ear. It was like somebody had just taken a clump of his skin between two fingers and twisted—hard. "Anyway, if it would help, I'll gladly call a relative to come sit with you. Right now, I can't leave my—. Yeeow!" Richard clutched at his right shin, which felt like someone had given it a sharp kick.

"Oh, my stars. Someone's attacking you in your home?" Vivian asked, alarm evident in her voice.

She was the aggrieved, offering him comfort? Now, he felt like a heel. Richard shifted the phone back to his left hand, trying to massage the kink in his neck while leaning over to rub his right shin. "No, nothing like that," he said. "My rheumatoid arthritis flared up just ahead of the rainstorm last night. That was some storm, huh?"

"Listen, I shouldn't have c-called," Vivian stuttered. "This is hard for me to—talk about—over the phone. Did you see the Sunday paper?"

"Not yet," he said, thinking I'd surely like to. "Should I call back after I've read it?"

"Th-that would be great. Or you could just read it and . . . stop by," she added hesitantly.

Stopping by her family estate? Wait a minute. That was more than he'd bargained for. "I'll look at the paper but . . . ," he said, his neck muscles still twitching, wondering how badly he slept last evening to be suffering these spasms this morning. He couldn't let on that he had nothing special to do today, being the important man he was. What if she came to expect him to drop by regularly? Would that be so bad?

It certainly would. He couldn't allow it. Or could he? "Well . . . I'll be by before long."

"Thank you. I'm in Elysian Hills, on Harmony Drive."

"I know the area," Richard said, thinking, who wouldn't? All the local news features over the years. He'd even taken a field trip to see the Frantz family farm when he was in grade school. "See you soon."

He let his phone slide onto the end table. What the hell just happened? he asked himself, still smarting from the kick to his shin. Vivian had told him to look at the paper. He slid back into his easy chair, pulled the *Sunday Herald* out of its plastic sleeve, and unfolded it.

FRANTZ MATRIARCH CRUSHED UNDER SIGN, a headline above the fold read. The photograph accompanying the story was a grainy testament to the tragedy—the back of the ambulance looked like it had been fed through a trash compactor.

Richard's pulse raced—he couldn't scan the story fast enough. The steel bird from atop the Bobbin' Robin fast food restaurant sign had snapped off its pole and crushed the back of an ambulance, killing Paylor Frantz. The ambulance crew members remained hospitalized.

The ambulance had been stopped at the railroad crossing at Hankey Avenue, between 10th and 11th Streets, when the accident occurred. Sixty-mile-an-hour wind gusts trailed a fast-moving thunderstorm that rolled into Hankey around 10 p.m. A single gust caused the pedestal to buckle and the sign to come crashing down on the ambulance. Nothing so far about why Paylor Frantz was headed to the hospital in the first place. The rest of the article was inane man-on-the-street comments, a forte of the *Hankey Herald*.

"My five-year-old son saw that one-ton robin come crashing down on the ambulance," one man said. "He'll have nightmares for the rest of his life."

"They brought in the Jaws of Life to pry that robin's beak apart—to get the lady out," another bystander said. "I knew it was too late, though, when they wheeled her away in that big black Ziploc bag like they do on 'Law and Order.'"

The article ended with a statement from the restaurant manager, "The Bobbin' Robin will be closed for repairs until it reopens." Richard had visions of a smart-aleck late-night host sharing the profundity of that statement with the rest of America: "The restaurant will be closed until it opens."

He'd never heard of a fast food pedestal sign collapsing, let alone killing someone. This would make the national news. He didn't want the Hankey Opera Guild to be associated with such a freakish occurrence. Accidents like this were reduced to one-liners in standup routines in a matter of days when they concerned high-profile families like the Frantzes.

So, he'd committed himself to a trip to the Elysian Hills—Harmony Drive—most likely to hold Vivian's hand now that she'd lost her mother in this improbable accident.

Now that he'd agreed to see her, a sense of dread mounted in him. Sure, he could fall for Vivian. Any guy could. He may have already done so. In his gut, he knew he shouldn't get involved with anyone, not now. The timing wasn't right. It was too soon after Mary's death. Yes, he was afraid of falling in love again. But it wasn't just that.

The nature of the Bobbin' Robin tragedy bothered him. He'd had a successful career in medicine because he was analytical and also intuitive. Much to the credit of his practice and reputation, he had combined both for years. This he'd done, not only to aid his patients but also to grow his practice—hiring the right people, making profitable business decisions. Why hadn't Vivian explained what put her mother in the ambulance in the first place?

His intuition was braying that he shouldn't get any more involved in Vivian's affairs than he already was. He offered Vivian a seat on the guild, following up on Mary's desire to patch things up with the Frantz family. Sure, Vivian had rev'd his engines of late, but so did most redheads. Every redhead he'd ever known—hired, fired, met, worked alongside—had only given him trouble over the long term. Part of him did want to see her and was genuinely moved that she thought of phoning him. Now that he mulled it over some, it would be more appropriate to call Deanna or Oriane on her behalf and have them visit Vivian.

"GRR-AUWW!" he yelped, knocking over his coffee mug. His right hand flew to his ear to cast off whatever was yanking on it. "What? Who—?"

For God's sakes. Someone had just grabbed him by the ear and given it a hefty tug, just like Mary (God rest her soul) used to do when he behaved like an ass. It hurt like hell then, too. He didn't know which to rub first—his ear, his shin, his neck.

All these inexplicable discomforts—the pinching, kicking—all of it had begun with Vivian's phone call. Were they signs from Mary? He'd best hightail it over to Vivian's before the goonies attacked him again—after he cleaned up the spilled coffee and put on his best bolo tie and called Marlena.

He punched in her number but got the damn machine. "It's your father. I was just thinking about you and wondered how everyone was doing. Give me a call when you can."

14
The Supernatural Embrace

The essence of Mary Rohrer, Richard's late wife, paces outside the Frantz Estate a few feet off the ground, waiting for Richard to arrive.

While Mary was living, Richard had a head harder than granite. Why had she ever assumed he might be different after she died? It had taken a pinch to the back of his neck, a kick in the ankle, and an ear tweaking to get him off his rear and over to see Vivian.

No matter how much Mary tried to stop worrying about Richard, she couldn't. It was preventing her from crossing over, and no one wanted to cross over more. She'd gotten a glimpse of heaven when she'd first arrived during her pre-reckoning appointment. St. Peter had invited all the new arrivals to his suite—and what a suite it was. First, they were serenaded by a choir of angels. My, oh my! Nothing like the choir at First Presby. No wobbly high notes from eighty-year-old sopranos either. When she was alive, Mary had sung in the choir for fun. She'd always coveted a soprano solo during the annual Easter cantata. Now that she was dead, she was undone by her ability to reach high A's—like she'd been born to sing them. And luncheon was heavenly—literally. The perfect amount of food, a divine presentation, and every morsel satisfied. The best part? No clean-up. She could get used to heaven in a hurry.

Surprisingly, she was sent back to limbo after lunch. "You're not ready, Mary," St. Peter had said. "You have unfinished business. Get some closure."

"I'm dead," Mary said. "How much more closure could I possibly get? I've been permanently removed from earthly life and everyone I love."

"Figure it out, Mary," St. Peter had said, pointing her back to the celestial transporter. "Then you'll be ready."

Figure it out. As best she could figure, this lack of closure had all to do with Richard's being alone. She'd been such a capable wife that she made him too dependent on her while she was living. He hadn't taken any real interest in another woman, prurient or otherwise, in one whole year—until Vivian.

This was just a theory, mind you, but if she could get Vivian to take a corresponding interest in Richard, and they began spending time together as a couple, then Mary could get the closure she needed. No longer would she be a "Bimbo-in-Limbo," as some women who hadn't crossed over called themselves. Up to heaven she'd go, singing and supping with the cherubim and seraphim and the gallery of saints for eternity.

Was Vivian the best woman for Richard? Maybe not. Not to mention that the two of them were off to a terrible start—she'd probably contributed to that animosity by asking Paylor Frantz to step down from the library board when she chaired it. But no one could say Mary had not given Richard and their marriage her complete devotion. Surely, she couldn't be expected to give more of herself now that she was dead. It was her time to kick back and relax. She'd earned a release—and wanted it more than anything she'd ever desired when she was alive. According to St. Peter, her task now was to *figure out* how to get it.

Since Richard was en route to Vivian's, she glided around to the back of the estate and peered inside the kitchen window—she didn't feel right about letting herself into Vivian's house without Richard being there. Vivian waited for Richard in the kitchen, her hands warming around a cup of tea or coffee—Mary couldn't tell which.

The intercom buzzed, startling Mary and Vivian. It was the gate attendant. "Mrs. Pirelli? Dr. Rohrer to see you."

"Let him in," Vivian said.

Since Richard was nearly there, Mary could, in good conscience, allow herself in through the window.

She followed Vivian into the powder room, where she checked her appearance. That was a good sign. Why would a woman care how she looked if she wasn't interested in her visitor? Peering in the mirror alongside her, Mary thought Vivian definitely needed a little primping. "Look at that stray hair sticking out from the side of your head!" she whispered in Vivian's ear. She must've tossed and turned in her sleep or been running her hands through her hair, that is, had she gotten any sleep. The harrowing events of the previous evening had caused her to look disheveled. However, even overtones of dishevelment couldn't disguise classically beautiful features— prominent eyes, creamy skin, full lips, and good teeth. No wonder Richard was attracted to her. If Vivian had met Richard while she and Richard were courting, Mary would've never captured Richard's eye, let alone his heart.

Had Vivian served on the guild while Mary was living, Mary would've felt threatened. Partly because of Mary's own widely publicized feud with Paylor, who'd leaked confidential board dealings to the press. And partly because of Vivian's looks, wealth, and her penchant to surrender to her personality quirks.

Being dead gave Mary a fresh perspective on things. She now understood why Vivian was so quirky, that it was a coping mechanism. Since Vivian joined the guild, Mary popped in once in a while, to check on things. She'd heard them arguing about producing *Don Giovanni* and gossiping about Vivian being run off the hospital auxiliary. Before her death, Mary had little sympathy for Vivian. Now she saw how Paylor had mistreated everyone around her, but most especially Vivian. Paylor, off her meds, would rail about anything, acting up in the middle of the night. After what Paylor put her daughter through in the daytime, Vivian should've been allowed a restful sleep.

Mary hovered in the foyer as Vivian waved Richard into the great room of her family home. Vivian had a hollow, nervous crescent of a grin on her face and gestured to Richard that he seat himself in a stately armchair. "Thank you for coming," she said.

As Richard took in the surroundings—the gilded fixtures, the hardwood floors, the Persian rugs—Mary did as well. On a recent drive-by visit, Mary overheard Vivian prohibiting the wait staff from using the term *Oriental* in reference to rugs or any other housewares, for that matter. (That was Vivian for you!)

From the wrought-iron gate to the grounds to all the furnishings in this formal sitting room, as far as anyone could see—everything now belonged to Vivian. She was the sole proprietress. The weight of her inheritance—the prospect of managing it all—must have felt like a grindstone, wearing her down.

"I read the news story about your mother," Richard said. "I'm very sorry."

Vivian said, "I don't mean to burden you with my problems. It's just that—I'm feeling overwhelmed."

"Isn't there a family member who can bring you comfort in your time of need?" Richard asked with more impatience in his voice than Mary thought was polite. Not to mention, that he sounded like a cheap greeting card. And wasn't that just like him to make Vivian feel self-conscious about asking for assistance.

Richard had always been self-absorbed. Ever since he was in medical school. Mary had found his cockiness appealing then. She assumed it would lessen as his practice became more established and his reputation grew in the Hankey medical community. But he only became more puffed up with himself.

Mary knew she was partly to blame. She'd coddled him, catered to his whims. Wherever he wanted to go on vacation, whenever he wanted to go, that's where and when they went. Truth was, she was tired of Nantucket and wanted to go somewhere warm and tropical for a change. But she'd always put his needs before her own throughout their marriage. And look how he turned out. More wrapped up in himself than ever. She brushed up against him and whispered in his ear. "Ask her what happened. Ask her! Or I'll tweak your ear a good one."

"What happened?" he asked, brushing Mary away from his ear like a pesky fly, looking puzzled about what had been circling the side of his head. "I don't mean the accident with the ambulance. Why were they taking your mother to the hospital?"

He certainly was direct—directness being the province of physicians and others at the top of society's food chain.

Vivian winced as though her back had tightened up on her. She pressed the small of it into the chair. "I'm having tea. Would you like some?"

Richard shook his head. "No, thank you."

Obviously, Vivian didn't know how to begin to tell Richard what really happened last night. She would have Richard's undivided attention—Mary would see to that. If Vivian could just come out with it, then Richard would be drawn into someone else's life and stopped being so absorbed in his own.

"My mother was manic depressive. When I returned home from Deanna's, she was having a bad episode. In a manic fit—" Vivian paused. Could she continue? "She threw a glass at me. We scuffled. She accidently got a piece of glass stuck in her neck."

Richard cocked his head, trying to process what Vivian had just told her. "Who else knows about this?"

Vivian sighed and re-draped her arm over the love seat, pulling up her legs alongside her. "Dr. Jasper, our family physician. And now you."

"Then for pity's sake, Vivian. Don't say another word. With regard to the fight that resulted in your mother being injured, you really should talk to a lawyer. I may know medicine but I'm no legal beagle."

Ain't that the truth, Mary thought.

He recrossed his ankles. "Did you speak with the family attorney?"

Vivian gasped. "I will. I just needed to tell someone what really happened. I didn't have anyone else to talk to."

What would he say now? Mary wondered. Would he stick his size 10EEEE wingtip in his mouth?

"I see," Richard said. "Promise me you'll call an attorney today."

Vivian drew her knees to her chest and wrapped her arms around them, like she was retreating into a cocoon. "I'll take care of it."

"As a doctor, there is one piece of information that interests me. What was her prognosis when they loaded her into the ambulance? Was she going to pull through?"

"Dr. Jasper thought she would."

"So, it was an act of God, legally speaking, that toppled the sign unit onto the ambulance?"

"If that's the correct legal term," she said, sighing. "You know what's odd about this whole thing? Bobbin' Robin is a huge account for Frantz Ketchup. Our best customer, our biggest to date," Vivian said. "How ironic is that? The company whose business created the most wealth for the Frantz family brought about my mother's end?"

"You may have grounds for a lawsuit," Richard said, fiddling with his bolo tie.

When he touched that tie that meant whatever had come out of his mouth was either falsehood or filibuster. Like Richard would know which acts of God were precedents for what lawsuits.

"I'll just talk to the attorney," Vivian said.

The next moment, she heard the buzz of the intercom. Vivian rose from the love seat, smoothing her skirt. "I need to get that."

Richard rose, buttoned his jacket, and tightened his tie. "I'll see myself out."

Vivian hurried through the hallway, past the French doors, back into the kitchen, and reached for the phone on the countertop. "Hello?"

"Mrs. Pirelli?" the gate attendant said. "There's a Detective Donovan from the Hankey Police Department here to see you."

Well, Richard was going to be involved now—whether he liked it or not. The arriving detective would watch him depart. Maybe he'd even interrogate him on the way in and make him feel all kinds of itchy and uncomfortable. If that happened, Richard had deserved it—for checking his heart at the door.

Mary hadn't been very successful today. But she would find a way to draw Richard and Vivian closer. The guild needed her—her influence and her resources. Richard needed her.

Apart from Deanna needing Mary's help with the Italian Zorro—one well-placed jab between the shoulder blades when he least expected it (which could have been construed as an *intervention*, she conceded)—Deanna could take care of herself. Vivian couldn't. She needed a Richard in her life, someone smart and capable, who could be loving when he chose to. And, now that her mother was gone, Vivian would need the guild to fill the huge void left by taking care of Paylor to the extent she had. Mary hadn't done right by the Frantz family when Paylor was alive. But she would make it right in death, with Richard's help.

She was desperate to cross over. She wasn't comfortable prying into people's private lives all the time. It constituted too much interaction with the human world. Most importantly, it was excluding her from taking her rightful place in heaven.

Where was Richard most vulnerable? It used to be his wallet, when Mary was alive. But he wasn't lonely then. He was sitting pretty. Retired, free to follow the pursuits of his heart. She had a feeling that his vulnerability was riding a little lower than the back pocket of his pants and down in front. Vivian and her big blue-green eyes, bountiful breasts, and fat inheritance was a good foil for Richard. How she would get them together, well, that was another problem whose solution was hers to unfold.

15
The Understudy

Two days later, the guild meets in the Opera House to discuss the death of Paylor Frantz and review details for the Annual Martini Masque, their biggest fund-raiser of the year.

"What a bizarre way to go," Oriane said as she and Deanna waited in the opera house boardroom for Richard. "I've never heard of a Bobbin' Robin sign collapsing like that."

"Richard advised us not to give any media interviews," Deanna said, handing Oriane a freshly dry-cleaned Apple-tini costume.

Unceremoniously, it seemed. It was obvious Deanna didn't want to give up being the Apple-tini. She lived off all the compliments she got on her legs for months to follow. What would she do for strokes this year, Oriane asked herself? Deanna was nothing if not resourceful—she'd come up with something to fill her cup.

Oriane laid the costume on the back of an empty chair and seated herself beside Deanna. "People are already making jokes about the whole Bobbin' Robin thing," she said. "I heard them at church saying, well, I'd rather not repeat it. Let's just say it had to do with a pecker. At mass, of all places."

Deanna glanced at her watch, which could only mean that Richard—who believed if you're on time, you're late—was now officially late.

"Richard thinks we might have to replace Vivian—that she won't have time for us now that she has to manage her family's estate." Deanna chuckled. "If I had her money, I'd just pay someone to manage it."

"Why don't you like her?" Oriane had to ask; it had been bothering her. "I know Vivian annoys people. Her ultra-political correctness. Her Buddhist chants. Her malaprops. Beyond those little issues, what's so bothersome about her?"

"I think she's a phony-baloney," Deanna said. "If her heart is with people suffering in third-world countries, why hasn't she followed it? Why is she volunteering with an opera company and not working to help the poor? What's holding her back? Certainly not lack of resources."

Oriane had no idea what living in an atmosphere of wealth and privilege was really like, but that hardly stopped her from offering her own opinion. "I kind of like her."

"There's something not quite right about her," Deanna said. Her back was facing the door and as she spoke, Richard entered the room.

"Right about whom?" Richard asked, removing his overcoat and laying it over an empty chair.

Deanna gave Oriane a not-a-word-from-you look while spinning a little white lie faster than Mimi shacks up with the viscount in *La Bohème*. "Oh, the woman at the answering service—for Vasquez's agent. She's—rude, extremely rude. 'Answering service for Bronsky and Greenboig,'" Deanna parroted in spot-on Brooklynese. But then, she originally hailed from the same island, albeit the other end.

Richard took a seat at the head of the table. He removed a yellow legal pad and a pen from his briefcase and placed it in front of him. "Has our contract with Vasquez been jeopardized?"

"Nothing like *that*," Deanna said in answer to Richard's question while carrying on another conversation with Oriane with her eyes. "Sometimes women don't hit it off. We can be at odds with each other for no apparent reason. Women can be very territorial. You wouldn't understand."

Richard shrugged. "I had a wife. I have a daughter. I understand more things about women than you realize."

Oriane cringed. To keep Richard from realizing they'd been gossiping about Vivian, Deanna slipped her designer-shoe into her pretty painted mouth. Deanna needed an intervention from Queen Frostine. With her white angel hair, blue taffeta gown, and snowflake scepter, Queen Frostine was the most benevolent character from Oriane's favorite childhood game—Candyland. No one could be mean or dishy under the spell of Queen Frostine. Oriane imagined Queen Frostine waving her wand over Deanna's big head.

"You're absolutely right," Deanna said to Richard. "I apologize."

Ha! It worked, Oriane thought.

Richard removed his reading glasses from his jacket pocket, popped the case, and slipped them on until he was looking down his nose at Deanna and Oriane.

Oriane turned to Richard. "So, how is Vivian? Is she in shock? She must be devastated, right?"

Richard ran his hands through his hair, and a few dandruff flakes uncustomarily littered his shoulders. "I stopped by to see her Sunday. I brought her onto the guild—I owed her that. I think she's overwhelmed. I doubt she'll make it tonight."

"You were at her house?" Oriane asked. She thought she knew the answer to her next question but had to ask it anyway. "Is there something going on between you two?"

Wincing, Richard leaned back in his chair. Or was it the look of annoyance? He ignored Oriane's question, staring straight at Deanna. "I don't like all this chit-chat. Don't we have work to do?"

Deanna smiled thinly. "Let's get started, shall we?" She glanced at her notepad. "Old business—the need to add new guild members." Deanna surveyed the room. "Our ranks are thinned and thinning, yet the special events keep coming. The Martini Masque in one month, exactly. I've already obtained catering contracts for the winter fund-raisers."

"I hate discussing winter fund-raisers in April," Oriane said. The flowering trees had just begun to bloom. Spring was her favorite season. Why was Deanna always trying to rush things?

"Someone's got to think ahead," Deanna countered, looking at Oriane overtop of her reading glasses. "Or you and I will be stuffing canapés for Winter Carnivale."

Oriane made a face. She wasn't sure she even knew what a canapé was.

"Not to despair, everyone," Deanna said. "I wanted you to be the first to know—after me, that is—that we have a new guild member."

"Really?" Richard asked. "Who?"

"Boy, do we need another body!" Oriane said.

Deanna added, "If everybody's on board with this person."

"How did he find us?" Richard asked. "Or is it a she?"

"*He'd* like to tell you himself." Deanna pushed out her chair, opened the door, and in walked the balloon creations guy who decorates for the Martini Masque every year. Funny. Oriane and Deanna were just talking about him.

"Say *hello*," the little man said, sweeping into the conference room, "to *Arnaud!*"

He flitted around the table in the conference room, handing out his business card.

Arnaud Marceau, Oriane read. That's how you spell his name, huh? She continued reading his card: Hankey's premier balloon décor—balloon centerpieces, balloon drops, balloon arches, & confetti cannons—makes any event extra looney-tooney.

"What brings you to volunteer for the guild at this time?" Richard asked.

Arnaud threw his head back and cocked a hip. "Deanna is most persuasive. She needs help with events. And Arnaud loves planning and managing special events."

"Won't you have a seat?" Deanna said.

"Want to know more about me? Grill away, peoples," Arnaud said, flopping into one of the armless chairs and resting his chin on a bridge made from his knitted fingers, looking surprisingly like Audrey Hepburn. "Arnaud wants to be interrogated."

"All right. What can you do besides—make things out of balloons?" Richard asked.

"Arnaud can sew. Arnaud can make things grow. Arnaud is a tennis pro. Arnaud makes a mean *anisette de bordeaux*. Secret family recipe," he added in a stage whisper.

Oriane was certainly entertained by him and all his cute little rhymes. He was like a nursery book character come to life—Wee

Willie Winkie morphed with a platinum blonde Orlando Bloom. She looked over at Richard, who looked skeptical that Arnaud had the right stuff for the opera guild. She hoped Richard hadn't already written him off. Arnaud would be fantastic with those awful fund-raisers Oriane hated so much. Deanna always needed helpers with aesthetic flair for parties and galas. "Anything else we should know about you?"

Arnaud shrugged. "Arnaud is type O. And Arnaud talks to dead people."

That was a freaky answer. After sewing and growing and tennis pro-ing, who would've expected him to say that?

Richard sat up straight. "Dead people?"

"Absolutely," Arnaud said. "If they haven't crossed over, they talk to Arnaud."

"Hmm. I'm not sure why, but I like you," Richard said. "Maybe you'll have us communicating with Mozart, eh? Getting the precise tempi for all the numbers in *Don G.*"

"*Don G.* goes up in less than six weeks, lest anyone has forgotten. You have my permission to channel Mozart, Arnaud." Deanna sighed. "Next order of business. I was surfing the Internet—"

Oriane braced herself. This usually meant trouble—another idea Deanna intended to import from some opera company in the South or the Southwest.

"And it gave me an idea for a new fund-raising event—a Hanukkah Music Fest," Deanna explained, "to bring in donations from our small but affluent Jewish community. It worked beautifully for Knoxville."

"Do we have to talk about it now?" Oriane whined.

Deanna locked eyes with Oriane. "Yes, we do. We have to have enough help and enough lead time to pull it off."

"Arnaud would love to help," he said. "I love Hanukkah music."

"Perfect, Arnaud," Deanna said, lauding him with praise because she always did that to people who never challenged her.

"What Hanukkah music do you like?" Oriane asked, to put him on the spot.

"How much did they net?" Richard said, ignoring Oriane's question.

"About $25,000," Deanna said. "Not too shabby. I say we try it, on one condition."

"If we're still in business after June 30," Oriane said. "Is that the condition?"

"You of all people should have some faith, Oriane," Deanna said. "Our luck is changing. We have Leandro Vasquez as Giovanni." Deanna paused, drumming her fingers on her lips. "And we have Arnaud. Only one challenge to doing our own Hanukkah Music Fest, as I see it."

"What's that?" Oriane asked.

"We need someone on the guild who's really visible in Hankey's Jewish community, to help us reach out to Jewish donors. Put your heads together, people. Anybody know anybody?"

"Is there a Jewish community in Hankey?" Richard asked.

"Oh, for heaven's sake, Richard. There's a temple right down the street—Oheb Shalom."

"I guess I never noticed it before," he said.

"What about the law practice three doors down from your old office—Levy, Weisberg, and Katz?"

"It's not ringing a bell," Richard said.

"Did you work in a bubble, Richard?" Deanna said. "Think, people. You must have served on a committee at some time with someone of the Jewish faith. Arnaud?"

"Arnaud mostly talks to dead people. They're not much help on committees. But he will keep trying for you, Deanna. Anything for you," he said, smiling sweetly.

Deanna stared at them. "Nobody here served on Hankey Steel's Celebration of Cultures?"

Oriane raised her hand. "I know someone. My mother had a mah-jongg party yesterday and invited a friend of hers from high school, Jeannie Weisman. It used to be Weisman when they were in school. It's Jacobs now. Anyway, she's a widow. Her husband was Sol Jacobs, president and chief executive officer of Horst Newspapers. She has a house in Hankey she's been subletting to medical students. She has two homes actually. One in Manhattan and one here."

Deanna screwed her eyes together, riveting them on Oriane. "Your mother's friends with Jeannie Jacobs? *The* Jeannie Jacobs?"

"Never heard of her," Arnaud said. "She must not be dead."

Oriane giggled. Arnaud was going to be fun to work with. Even Richard cracked a smile.

"And you never mentioned it before?" Deanna asked because once she got on a tirade it was hard to get her off it.

Oriane shrugged. "Oh, well. I wouldn't know it now if my mother hadn't gotten onto this midlife mah-jongg kick."

"Why would anyone come back to Hankey if they lived in a New York penthouse?" Richard asked.

"That's a terrible thing to say, Richard," Deanna said. "Hankey definitely has its charms."

"Used to have its charms," he countered.

"My mother thinks that New York reminds Jeannie of her late husband," Oriane interjected, trying to change the subject. Everyone knew Richard found Hankey loads more livable when Mary was alive. He should be able to relate to Jeannie.

Deanna leaned forward, resting her elbows on the table. When Deanna abandoned decorum, it was the equivalent of her being on a mission. "I don't care what it takes, Oriane," Deanna said. "Convince Mrs. Jacobs that the guild needs her, that Hankey's first Hanukkah Music Fest can't happen without her."

Oriane was fishing for something to say, that was uncharacteristically assertive for her.

"She means business, Oriane," Arnaud said. "Better get on it."

Was Arnaud going to be Deanna's little enforcer? Maybe he wasn't going to be that much fun after all. Oriane threw up her hands. "What can I say? I'll try like heck to make sure she joins us."

"Invite her to the masque," Deanna said, waving a hand in the air, dramatically, as if to say, *Duh*. "Now, I have another bit of news about someone special who'll be crashing the Martini Masque."

Deanna's was probably overstating the significance of the mystery guest's appearance. "The mayor?" Oriane said.

"He'd better come," Deanna said. The mayor was counting on a big Lundquist contribution towards his reelection campaign—everyone in Hankey knew that.

"Gene London?" Richard said.

"Gene London?" Arnaud and Oriane repeated at the same time.

"Gene London was a big star in the children's television market. Huge. Lots of kids in the Philly area grew up on Gene London," Richard said. "He's back in town, you know."

"As exciting as that sounds, it's not Gene London." Deanna swallowed hard and threw her shoulders back. Oriane needed to remember that—swallow hard, straighten up—when she was in a similar situation. "Try . . . Leandro Vasquez."

Oriane shrieked. "Tell me you're kidding. You're kidding, right?"

Deanna beamed. "He's singing *Don Giovanni* in Maryland in a co-production with Gotham City Opera. He agreed to drop by our little party en route to his New York performances."

Oriane's face felt flushed. Her body was heating up faster than the fluorescent fixtures in the overhead lights. "You better *not* be joking or, so help me, Deanna—"

"I swear on a stack of bibles, he's coming."

"Who is this Leandro Vasquez?" Arnaud asked.

Deanna turned to Vasquez and lowered her voice. "An Argentinian baritone."

"I'll show you," Oriane said, pushing a couple of buttons and handing Arnaud her iPhone. "Take a gander at this guy."

Arnaud sighed. "Ooohhhh."

"Ooohhhh is right," Oriane agreed.

Deanna rolled her eyes. "You two sound like twin loons on Lake Pocono."

Richard smacked his hands on the table. "Terrific, Deanna. You have the gift of persuasion. Way to go, woman."

"Woman? You're going to have to pay me not to tell Vivian you called me *woman*," Deanna said.

"I'll pay you anything," Richard said, nodding approvingly. "You're worth your weight in gold."

Deanna shot him a look that Oriane interpreted as, *Don't say another word about my weight.*

"Excuse me," Oriane said. "Let's not forget who met Vasquez in London." She searched for something clever to say. Something droll and entertaining, like Deanna would say. "And charmed the pants off him."

"I'll bet you did," Deanna said, totally discounting Oriane's significant connection to Vasquez.

Oriane'd have to remember that trick someday, when she was in power—taking the credit for others' accomplishments.

"Now, let's think about how to make major hay out of Leandro's appearance," Deanna continued, still refusing to acknowledge the role Oriane had played. "What can we do with Vasquez? Any ideas?"

"Ho, ho, ho. Arnaud can think of some," Arnaud said, pouring on the French accent.

"Not those kinds of ideas," Deanna said. "I asked Knobby to stop by to lead us in some brainstorming. I expect him any minute."

"Should he be coming into work, Deanna?" Oriane asked. "His surgery wasn't that long ago."

"Yes, he should. He's ready," Deanna said, tapping her pencil eraser on the table for emphasis. Someone rapped lightly on the board room door. "That's Knobby now." Deanna rose to her feet and ushered him in.

"Knobby! You're looking well," Richard said.

Oriane thought Knobby looked better than well. He looked handsome—ready to be ensnared by the guild's indispensible soprano with connections to Hankey's small but influential Jewish community. "Nice you could join us," Oriane said, smiling demurely. "We won't work you too hard."

"Knobby," Deanna said. "This is Arnaud Marceau. He's a new guild member."

"So nice to meet you. And thank you, Mr. Marceau, for serving in such a vital capacity," Knobby said in an uncommonly charming fashion. He was an accomplished administrator, Oriane thought. The more she saw him in action, the more his skills became apparent.

"As you Americans say, 'back at you,' Know-bee," Arnaud said, pronouncing his nickname as if it rhymed with *Moby*. Arnaud beamed from ear to ear while taking in Knobby's Brooks Brothers apparel.

Knobby seated himself in the empty chair beside Oriane.

Why had he chosen that chair? Did Knobby feel the same fondness for her that she felt for him? "How are you feeling these days—Carter?" Oriane asked because she just couldn't see herself calling him Knobby once they were married.

"Actually, I'm anxious to get to work. First things first. Thanks for the sausage dogs, Deanna. They have me hopping and itching—already."

"I'm coming to visit. Forewarned is forearmed," Deanna smiled warmly, which Oriane hoped was directed to the dogs and not to Knobby.

Knobby laughed. "Anytime you want to drop in, feel free. I could use some help with those three." Deanna was closer to his age than Oriane was. But Deanna carried herself like a much older woman sometimes—like when she chaired their meetings. He couldn't possibly be attracted to Deanna, could he?

At this point Oriane fervently wished she didn't hate dogs so much. First, Knobby sent Vivian flowers. Now he was flirting with Deanna. Why hadn't she realized this before? On his résumé, he called himself an *impresario*. Oh, he was something ending in –o all right. A *gigolo!*

"I have an idea about how to use Vasquez at the masque," Knobby added, "unless you've already thought of something."

Richard pointed his index finger at Knobby as if to say, You're up. "What's your recommendation?"

"I don't know what the program is customarily," Knobby said, "but it would be *fantastic* if he could sing a number. 'La ci darem la mano' would be perfect."

"Fabulous idea," Deanna said.

"Now why didn't we think of that?" Richard added.

"Beats a kissing booth," Oriane said. "That's all I could think of."

"One number—to whet their appetites," Knobby explained.

"*La ci darem la mano*"? This was Oriane's big chance to make her wishes known regarding the role—one of the greatest if not the greatest soubrette roles written by Mozart. "You'll need a Zerlina to do that number."

Knobby smiled. "Exactly. Can anyone locally sing that role? There's no way that Catherine Carnahan's performance schedule would allow her to do the masque."

Oriane drew in her breath sharply. "You're bringing in someone—from New York—to sing Zerlina?" Her chest heaved up and down.

"What's the matter, Oriane?" Deanna asked. "Why are you acting like a startled chickadee?"

Oriane sat there stunned, immobile. "Wh-what about Elvira and Donna Anna?"

"Maestro and I agreed we should contract those two—that was a given," Knobby explained, moving his hands up his forearms to scratch his elbows. "Amazingly, we both were of the same mind with Zerlina—that she's not a throwaway character. She needs to be sung by a professional, too."

"What about Don Ottavio and Masetto?" Oriane asked. "You'll have to hire one of those two parts. The local pool of men is tiny." Oriane clasped her hands together fiercely, which must have looked like little steamed lobsters at the end of her arms. She had to get a hold of herself. A display of temper wasn't going to get her what she wanted. She inhaled deeply and exhaled cooing, "Knobby, you have more talent here in Hankey than you realize. You need a Zerlina who projects the raw sex appeal of a country wench," Oriane said, leaning into Knobby, making her voice husky, like Deanna's. "She's right here, *Signore* Knoblauch. Right at your elbow."

Deanna stifled a snigger. Richard smiled broadly. Arnaud resumed ho-hoing. It always sounded lascivious whenever Frenchmen ho-ho'd. Then all three of them burst out laughing. What was so hilarious? Oriane wanted to know.

Knobby turned his head, slowly, deliberately, without moving his body, just like Chuckie from the horror movies—all *Child's Play*, no hint of Candyland anymore. "You can sing a proper Zerlina?"

Did he just ask if she could sing a proper Zerlina? Her frustration was reaching a fever pitch and must have been evident on her face. "I have sung Papagena and Adina under a music director who's now at Julliard," she said with confidence that this new information decided everything.

"Oriane's very talented," Deanna added, in a motherly tone, though Oriane hadn't asked for her help and certainly didn't want it. She had hoped to win the role based on her ability first and out of gratitude for her work with the guild second. More importantly, she at least deserved a chance to try out for the role.

"It's settled then." Knobby's face brightened. "Our little Zerlina problem is solved. Oriane can sing the duet with Vasquez," he said to the others as if Oriane wasn't even in the room.

"Our little Zerlina problem?" Oriane cleared her throat. "You want me to sing Zerlina for the masque but not the show?"

Knobby stroked his chin. "You can understudy the part for the performance. We'll need a stand-in until the week of dress rehearsals anyway."

Oriane had just devoted the last five years of her life to the guild, weathering Deanna's slights, Richard's patronizing, and Maestro's temper tantrums, asking precious little in return. And all the opera company could offer was a role as an understudy in the greatest opera ever written by the world's greatest composer? She wanted to vomit. "A stand in?" Oriane shook her head back and forth, squirming in her seat. "I'm not a stand in. I can sing that role. Let me audition."

Knobby shrugged. "Maestro has already spoken to Carnahan's agent. A contract is in the works."

Oriane got the picture, all right. They wanted her to bring Jeannie Jacobs? Well, they'd better ante up. "I want that role."

"Oriane," Richard scolded. "Knobby just said it's out of his hands."

"If you don't give me that role, I won't bring in Jeannie Jacobs. If you don't give me that role, I'll—resign from the guild." Oriane wasn't absolutely certain if she'd just said that latter part aloud or merely thought it.

Deanna swung around to face Oriane. "You're the Apple-tini this year."

"I'm the Apple-tini because you're too fat for the costume."

Deanna's chin dropped into her neck like a turtle's. "That was nasty, Oriane."

Richard leaned over and whispered something in Deanna's ear, which returned her chin to its proper physiological position. He folded his hands in front of him and cocked his head, in a fatherly way. "Knobby, I know you're new here. But Oriane is quite a talent who—merits—*special* consideration for roles."

Knobby recoiled. "You're asking me to nullify a contract, one that Maestro and I already authorized, just to keep one of your volunteers happy?" He turned to Deanna. "Did you not give me steep revenue goals? Did you hire a general director or a yes-man?"

"Well—I—guess—I," Deanna stammered. She must not have expected such a reaction from Knobby. Frankly, Oriane hadn't either.

Richard puffed himself up, taken aback. "Watch your step with our guild chair."

Deanna turned on Richard. "You don't need to play Prince Valiant on my account. It's not the Middle Ages, in case you haven't noticed."

"I wanted Knobby to realize that we, you and I primarily, gave him this job," Richard said. "He who giveth can also taketh away."

Knobby started to say something, but then stopped himself. "You're a good man. I'll pretend I didn't hear that."

"You and Deanna 'gave' this job to Knobby?" Oriane blurted out. "I'm a guild officer. I had a say in the decision. Vivian was part of the decision, too. Does anyone else on the guild matter, besides you two?" She stopped, suddenly realizing that her job on the guild was to serve as a warm body—someone to don an Apple-tini costume, someone to fill a guild roster.

What was left to do? Oriane was their sole connection to Jeannie Jacobs. Storm and storm some more. "Good luck finding someone to sing with Vasquez, because it's not going to be me." Oriane left the costume hanging on the back of the chair. "Your little Hanukkah

Music moneymaker? Without my connections, it will be a big, fat flop!"

And with that, Oriane stalked out of the meeting.

16
The 'Gothic Dreck'

Mary Rohrer hears an unprecedented amount of yelling and hollering coming from the opera house board room and decides to pop in, to see what gives.

Richard sat in stunned amazement at Oriane's display of pique. "What just happened to Oriane, of all people? Our little soprano that could."

What had Richard done to upset that girl? Mary never heard a cross word out of her before. Lately, he'd been on a tear. He must have stirred up more trouble, this time hurting Oriane.

Knobby scratched at his chin. "Did I just screw things up royally for you folks?"

Deanna shook her head. "Oriane's sensitive. Talented and giving of her time to the guild. Sometimes she gets stars in her eyes. Yet, we need a smashing *Don G.* And a successful masque that generates buzz like no other masque before it—which will happen if Vasquez makes an appearance."

Richard lowered his voice. "It's Knobby's decision. I apologize for losing my head."

"Quite all right," Knobby said, the resignation in his voice apparent. "Comes with the territory."

Was nobody going to go after Oriane? Mary wondered.

Deanna drummed her nails on the blonde wood of the table. Mary leaned in close and whispered, "Bring her back."

Arnaud stiffened. "Uh, oh, peoples. Someone's here."

Richard scoffed. "Yes, yes. You're here. I'm here. Knobby's here."

Arnaud shook his head vigorously. "No, no. A presence. Arnaud hears a presence from someone who recently departed from this

world. Someone who has not crossed over, who is close to—to—"
He turned to Richard, throwing his hands in the air as if to say, *But of
course!*

Mary clapped her hands and said, "You tell 'em, Arnaud."

"Mary's here?" Richard asked.

"What in heck is going on here?" Knobby asked.

"Arnaud talks to dead people," Deanna explained, sounding
skeptical because she needed convincing, too. "Now isn't the time,"
she said to Arnaud and turned her attention to Richard and Knobby.
"We can't lose Oriane. Or a potential member, like Jeannie Jacobs. I'll
go talk her down."

"Not so fast. I want to hear what Mary, I mean, Arnaud has to
say," Richard said.

"You talk to Mary. I'm going after Oriane," Deanna said,
gathering her things and leaving the room.

Mary hadn't wanted to draw this much attention to herself.
Things would have been better had this new Arnaud fellow not been
present. He was a bit of a fly in the ointment with all his gifts for
hearing dead people talking. Deanna was headed in the right
direction though—off to find Oriane, to use her influence and
powers of persuasion to ease the little sparrow's ruffled feathers and
bring her back into the nest. In view of that, Mary supposed she
needed to say a little something to Richard.

Richard sat back, lengthening his spine, folding his hands in his
lap. "Is Mary trying to reach *me*, Arnaud?"

Arnaud pressed his fingers to his temples and fell silent for a
long moment before nodding. "Mary is standing right beside you,
Richard. For some reason, Arnaud is having a hard time
understanding her clearly."

"It's time to let go," Mary whispered in Richard's ear.

Richard reached toward his ear, trying to grasp the energy force
swirling around him, with the hope of holding some piece of Mary
in his hand.

Arnaud's head snapped forward like a dog reacting to a sound
no human could possibly hear. "Did you hear that?"

"No! Talking to dead people," Richard snarled. "I knew I shouldn't have trusted you."

"The connection just isn't strong enough," Arnaud said. "Not enough bars."

"Not enough bars?" Richard asked with a healthy dose of skepticism. "There's a taproom on every corner in this town."

"Not those kinds of bars. Too many distractions," Arnaud said, shaking his head. "Arnaud is usually better than this. It could be the tacky paneling."

"Tacky paneling? Nonsense." Richard rose, stuffed his keys in his pocket, and glared at Arnaud. "When you get enough bars, let me know." Then he said his farewells and left Knobby and Arnaud staring at each other across the conference room table.

"Was it something Arnaud said?"

Knobby shrugged. "Richard gets testy sometimes."

"Just you and me, kiddo," Arnaud said, with an expression on his face that looked like he was eyeing an ice cream sundae.

"Right," Knobby said.

"I must say Know-bee, I like the cut of your coat. Brooks Brothers?"

Knobby ruffled his hands through his sandy-colored hair. "My Aunt Laverne always said it's better to invest in a few good wardrobe items than a closet full of crap."

"Want to grab a Coke?" Arnaud asked.

Knobby shrugged.

"Then I'd like to show you what I have in mind for stage décor for the masque," Arnaud added, as Mary watched them leave the room.

Though Knobby had no notion of it, Mary'd been observing him ever since his near-death experience, greeting him in the afterlife when he stepped off the E.R. elevator. When Knobby returned to his mortal coil, Mary realized this was her chance to do more than roam the opera house. She reinvigorated her spiritual connection with those she cared most about on earth because St. Peter told her to get some closure, to "figure it out." So Mary decided to embrace the only course she could conceive of, taking her own destiny under wing and freeing herself from Richard, once and for all.

Lately, he'd been making significant strides with their daughter Marlena, sending her flowers as a peace offering. His heart seemed lighter as a result, and the gesture had weakened Marlena's resolve against reconciling their differences.

Now that Mary had a chance to sit in on some interaction between Richard and Vivian, she was convinced Richard could do better by her. Vivian had issues—there was no denying that her personal and family challenges required patience and longsuffering in a partner. But these same issues would be like flint to Richard's stony heart, sparking him to grow into a better, more compassionate person. Who knew what kind of mean-spirited, self-centered creature Richard would become before growing old and dying?

During the last year in limbo, Mary had not established herself as an influential or potent ghost. She wasn't goofing off. Instead, she'd spent most of that time observing others, watching how and when they tapped into their supernatural gifts. Only fools rush in, after all. Then, when Paylor Frantz sliced her jugular and came precipitously close to dying, Mary quickly gathered up some ghostly friends to discuss a daring action with dramatic consequences— whether to "intervene" on Vivian's behalf.

An intervention was nothing like Mary had ever done before. It was one thing to revisit the people and places you loved during your earthly life. It was another thing altogether to use your supernatural abilities to help or inhibit them.

Mary and her friends were arguing over whether to "collect" Paylor before she could finger Vivian for slamming her head into the pile of glass. Mary pooh-poohed the idea. "Collecting people" was poltergeist territory. Mary and her friends were all endeavoring to be heaven-bound good ghosts. They were still discussing the matter when that AMRAIL freight train came rattling along, stopping traffic in downtown Hankey. They never had a chance to launch their own intervention. Some other supernatural force had already whipped up a massive gust of wind that slammed into the pedestal stand and drove the hulking Bobbin' Robin right into the back of the ambulance, killing Paylor.

Later, Mary learned it was Karl Frantz, Paylor's late husband, who'd grown tired of his wife's treatment of Vivian. He'd whipped up that zephyr and, content that he'd done all he could do, he finally crossed over, though not to the place where Mary hoped to spend eternity. Ketchup was a cutthroat industry, she'd heard. Not even saving his daughter from his wife's cruelty could spare Karl Frantz from the fires of hell.

* * *

Deanna stood in the exit lane of the parking garage, her legs positioned like a law enforcement officer while holding her arms out in front of her to prevent Oriane from leaving the lot. She let one or two other cars exit before it became Oriane's turn.

Oriane rolled down her window. "Move, Deanna. I'll run you over if I have to." Oriane had been crying—around her eyes, her skin was yellow and bloated; her eyes were ringed with red.

"I'm not moving," Deanna said coolly. "If you're not willing to park your car and rejoin us upstairs, I guess you'll have to run me over."

In the meantime, a man in a Ford Bronco pulled up behind Oriane. He shook his head and threw up his arms in frustration, but Oriane wouldn't budge.

"I didn't even get a chance to audition," Oriane cried. "You and Knobby just wrote me off like I was a nobody. Like I never played a part before."

Deanna needed to soften her approach to reach Oriane. Oriane's defenses were as high as they could go, and for a lyric soprano, that's stratospheric.

"I didn't have anything to do with the casting," Deanna said. "I didn't know we were at the hiring stage, believe me. That was Knobby and Maestro. That's what they're supposed to be doing— what we are paying them to do. If I come over to talk to you," Deanna said, her voice softening, "I don't want to make our business that of the whole garage—will you promise not to drive away?"

"Drive away already. Fly away. I don't care. Just get out of *my* way," the guy from the Bronco shouted.

"You stay out of this, buster. It's none of your damn business," Deanna snapped.

"You're making it my damn business with all this yelling back and forth," he hollered back. "I got a right to leave a public garage."

Oriane leaned out the window and called to the Bronco driver behind her. "Back up, buddy."

By this time, two other cars had queued up behind the Bronco. Deanna simply marched over to the line of cars and directed traffic. "You go here," she told one. And he did. "And you go there." And she did. "And you, yelling-boy," she said to the Bronco driver. "Go straight back into that parking space behind you, and let this girl turn around." He was about to make a face when Deanna stamped her foot and pointed a long painted finger at him.

Oriane maneuvered out of the exit lane and into a nearby parking space, while Deanna continued orchestrating the queue of cars until everyone had safely exited. Deanna walked over to Oriane's car and motioned to her to roll down the window. She leaned inside. "I know your feelings are hurt. I know you're sweet on Knobby, too."

Oriane breathed in sharply. "How did you know that?"

"You can see it all over your face whenever you're around him," Deanna said. "Can I sit on the passenger side a minute? My dogs are barking."

Oriane blushed. "I don't like him anymore. He's extremely limited in his ability to discern talent."

Deanna sighed. "You can't mean that." She opened the door and the moment after she slid into the seat, she slipped off her high heels. "Here's the thing." She began massaging her manicured toes. "A chance to sing with Vasquez, even for one night, is a big deal. If you continue acting like a prima donna, Knobby's going to write you off. He's probably thinking exactly that as we speak. You'll jeopardize your chance to earn future parts."

"What future parts? The opera house will be forced to close down by July."

Deanna shook her head. "I'd lay down and die. I'd take a second mortgage out on my house. I'd open up a brothel and service every coal cracker in Hankey before I let that happen."

With white-knuckled hands, Oriane clutched the steering wheel. "They didn't even give me a chance."

"You know Knobby and Maestro—well, everyone—is under a lot of pressure to ensure this show is successful—financially. If you really care about the opera company, you'll suck it up this time."

Oriane burst into a fresh round of sobs. "This is my last chance for a good part."

Deanna scowled. "Baloney. You're not even thirty. Keep yourself in good voice. You'll get good parts for another fifteen years. Plácido Domingo said most singers crest at forty-five."

"I don't give a crap about Plácido Domingo right now," Oriane sniffled. "He's a tenor, for pity's sake. Name a soprano who's had a career in her forties."

Renée Fleming was having a successful career longer than the running time of *Parsifal*. "Well, what about—Renée Fleming?" Deanna said.

Oriane's face twisted with disbelief. "You can't compare me to *Renée Fleming!*"

Deanna collected her thoughts. She was preparing exactly what she was going to say and how to say it. "I'm giving you sound advice at the moment. It's in your best interest to take it."

"Why do you care about the guild so much?" Oriane asked.

"Somebody has to care. Somebody has to put the guild first for opera to survive in this dying town," Deanna said. "I'm the chair. That somebody has to be me."

Oriane released her hands from the steering wheel. She removed the keys from the ignition and tucked them into the front her purse. "I'll do it. I sing Zerlina for the masque."

Deanna needed to let Richard know that Oriane was calmed down. She dug in her purse for her cell phone—no phone. She must have left it in the board room. She'd better hightail it back to the opera house. Maybe Richard was still there, talking to his late wife through Arnaud.

Within minutes, she reached the opera house and was about to lean against the bank of glass doors at the entrance. Then she stopped herself, thinking she'd been in this exact position only weeks ago. She pulled out her can of mace before entering the opera house after hours, her right index finger poised on the nozzle. If the air so much as wafted around her, someone was getting sprayed.

"Miss Lundquist?" a man's voice called.

At the sound of her voice, Deanna whipped around, spraying, then dropped the can immediately. It was Slim and Portly, the Hankey Police officers who initially investigated the assault, waving mace out of their faces, weapons drawn.

"Don't shoot," Deanna cried. "I thought you were—"

Slim coughed violently while trying to reholster his weapon. She hoped he didn't shoot his foot off in the process. "That's what we, uh, came to tell you," Slim said. "We, uh, got your man."

"My man? You mean my assailant?" Deanna asked. "The Italian Zorro?"

Portly nodded, coughing one or two times. "Apparently he tried to assault a woman who lived off Coal Street in Wilkes-Barre."

"Uh, she fought him off and called the police," Slim added, rubbing his eyes. "A foot chase ensued. The officer chased him down Coal Street." He resumed coughing, too heavily to continue.

"The Italian Zorro stepped into oncoming traffic," Portly said, pronouncing it 'Eye-talian,' "right in front of the path of a Softy Don's ice cream truck. Splat! Got mowed down on Coal Street."

"He's dead?" Deanna asked.

Slim nodded, his hand stifling another cough.

"As a doorknob," Portly said. "His name was Donato Bianco. We think you knew the guy."

"Donato Bianco? The opera singer?" Deanna felt faint. Bianco, a once-glittering baritone, world-renowned for his portrayal of Don Giovanni, was dead. Bianco had been her opera house assailant—the 'Eye-talian Zorro.' That was the bigger shock to absorb. "I'm speechless." She bent down and scooped up the mace can and tossed it in her purse. "I'm just putting it away now. Sorry about that."

"We don't blame you for, uh, wanting to protect yourself," Slim managed to say through persistent coughing.

"Is there anything else you need from me right now?"

"One more thing," Slim said. "They found, uh, fake I.D. on this guy. He was also passing himself off to unsuspecting personages as, uh, Don Blank."

Donato Bianco was *Don Blank*? God in Heaven. No wonder the guy was a no-show. Oriane had been right the whole time. She said Don Blank had been her assailant—right before Knobby came in for his interview. Wait until the guild heard this news. More importantly, what kind of damage control would she need to do to keep this news from tainting their current production?

"Did you have any dealings with Don Blank?" Portly asked.

"Yes. I mean no," Deanna said. "He never showed for his interview the morning of my attack."

Slim shook his head. "All righty then. That'll, uh, do it."

Portly tipped his hat, adding, "Just glad we could sew this one up for you."

Right. If it weren't for that ice cream truck, Bianco would still be running around Eastern Pennsylvania terrorizing innocent women, his cape flapping behind him.

She clutched her bag to her chest. "I need to get something I left behind upstairs, okay?" she said, backing into the opera house, then waving them off once safely inside. As soon as she got that phone in her hands, she'd call Richard. Donato Bianco. She prayed since he died in Wilkes-Barre, the media wouldn't come sniffing around the Hankey Opera House for dirt. The guild couldn't afford anymore scandal of any kind.

17
The Lion Man

It is the afternoon of the Martini Masque. Since her mother's death two weeks ago, Vivian has resumed most of her regular activities including hospitality for the guild, which has helped to keep her sane. She's waiting at the Hankey Regional Airport for the commuter flight from Baltimore in the Frantz family chauffeured car, parked just outside the Frantz Family Hangar.

Vivian glanced at her watch, and tapped at it, to make sure it was still running. "What time do you have, Walt?" she asked the driver.

"Uh—two-thirty, ma'am," Walt said.

Vivian rubbed the glass covering the face of her watch. "Okay, okay. My watch is working." The masque began in less than three hours. If she didn't return with Vasquez shortly, panic would overtake the guild. Her phone would be ringing, ringing, ringing. Wait—was that her phone ringing? Where had she put—? There. On the floor. She reached into the side of her handbag and pulled out her phone. She flipped it open. "Hello, Richard."

"No, it's Deanna. My phone died. I'm using Richard's. How's that for crummy luck?" she asked. "Has Vasquez arrived yet?" Deanna talked so quickly, Vivian barely understood her. Deanna talked faster, walked faster, and worked faster than most people Vivian had ever met. But she must have had some freaky thing going on with her metabolism, since she'd gained weight over the winter. If it was hormone driven, Vivian could sympathize.

Vivian didn't know how to respond. Was Deanna asking about luck metaphorically or pointing out that if anyone knew about crummy luck, it was Vivian? Or did she just care about whether Vasquez's plane had come in?

"How's the set up going?" Vivian asked with genuine enthusiasm. It felt good to be doing things again, to be needed. "You sound a little harried."

"Besides my phone dying? Things look good. Hopefully, that's the only bad break we'll have today," Deanna said, her voice sounding freakishly nervous, especially for someone who liked heading up special events. "What's going on with Vasquez?"

"His plane's been delayed," she said. "We're practically parked on the runway, aren't we, Walt?" Walt nodded his head once. "We can't miss him."

"The caterer just walked through the door," Deanna said. "Here—talk to Richard."

Vivian heard a thump, as if Deanna had let Richard's phone hit the floor or something. "Richard?" Vivian called into her cell phone.

"'Tis I," Richard confirmed. "How are you doing, all things considered?"

"Did you tell Deanna about the—fight preceding my mother's death?"

"Your secret's safe with me."

That was kind of Richard, not to go running to Deanna with that information. She knew Deanna already thought she was certifiable. If he had passed that nugget of news along, Deanna would probably have removed her as hospitality chair. How could any person of sound mind trust someone who ostensibly killed her mother with the care of world-class performers, with any task really, even a mundane one like picking up a singer at the airport.

"Why does she sound so out of sorts?"

"Oh, she's still processing the Donato Bianco news," Richard said. "She's waiting for the other shoe to drop."

"She's not hobbling around on one good shoe again, is she?"

"It's an expression—never mind. Has Vasquez arrived yet?"

"I expect him anytime now."

"Instinct tells me he'll arrive shortly," Richard said. "And my instincts haven't let me down yet. Vivian, I'd be remiss if I didn't mention that we're all grateful you decided to stay on the guild. Hospitality is important. Mary would be thrilled to see how you've taken it on."

Vivian debated whether to tell him that she had a feeling Mary was watching everything she had taken on—all the time—every move. Clearly, she hadn't crossed over. But why not? What task had she left unfinished? "It gives me something to do. It takes my mind off—" Something outside the car window caught her attention. A Northeast Air commuter jet was landing. "That's his plane. I'm sure of it. Got to go."

She ended the call and threw her phone back inside her purse. Picking up the soloists and stars and chauffeuring them to their hotels—though no one prior to Vivian had provided a *bona fide* chauffeur for the task—were all part of her hospitality responsibilities. Still, it was thrilling to meet the singers, some of whom would be world famous in a matter of years. Some might consider Vivian world-famous—but she hadn't done anything to earn her notoriety other than being born into the Frantz family. Since she hadn't gone into politics and only married a racecar driver, her fame didn't equate to the celebrity of someone like Leandro Vasquez.

Within minutes, the passengers disembarked. It appeared to be a fifteen-passenger plane. Vivian thought her family business had bigger planes than that at their disposal. Passenger after passenger stepped out of the plane. No Vasquez? Oh, God. What if he wasn't on this plane? Deanna would flip. And Vivian would have failed at one of the most elementary of responsibilities as hospitality hostess.

Finally, a young dark-haired man in a brown tweed coat, a red Ripple wine t-shirt and blue jeans stumbled out of the plane, looking bleary-eyed. Oh, God. Was that him? Oriane described him as wearing puffy shirts and frock coats. Dark hair, brooding eyes, essential good looks, unable to be masked by a scruffy appearance? It had to be him. Who else could it be? Oh, God. He looked totally potted.

Vivian stepped out of the car and headed toward the dazed man. He had thick eyebrows nearly knitted together across his forehead. A clump of his hair carelessly obscured his face. He had a day-old beard, which Vivian always found fetching on a young man, though Deanna wouldn't like it one bit. His beard, his slovenly appearance, his lack of sobriety. Oh. My. God.

"Mr. Vasquez?' Vivian called. "Leandro?"

Vasquez whipped his head around at the sound of his name, then lifted it. Apparently, *Leandro* was a word he liked hearing. With a scant smile on his face, he staggered toward Vivian, toward the sound of her voice. Then he stopped suddenly, whipping his head around to the right, and began drifting in the direction of another car and driver.

Vivian had to wave him in like an air traffic controller. "Leandro? This way," she called. "There you go. Keep coming. You're getting warmer. Warmer. That's it. This way. Just a few more steps." She hurried forward to intercept him before he made himself someone else's fare. Finally, she met his gaze. Stoned as a Deadhead. She reached out her hand. "Vivian Pirelli."

He grasped her hand, first to steady himself, and then raised it to his lips. As he grazed it, she felt the stubble lining his lips. "Ahh. Señora Pirelli." Though his words were charming, his voice had a croaking quality to it. "I delight—meet a you," he rasped.

It took longer than it should have to notice. But even Vivian recognized an operatic bass contracted to sing *Don Giovanni* shouldn't sound like Don Corleone. "Wha—what happened to your voice?"

Vasquez waved his hand in the air, as if his brain was churning through all the English words he knew in search of the right one. "I have—what you call—strip trout."

Strip trout? What was strip trout? Wait a minute. Strep throat? Oh, God. Vivian gasped. "Can you—sing?"

Vasquez shook his head. "I have—how you say—drink a—medicine. No help." He stroked his throat lightly. Then his head wobbled backwards as if it were resting on a toothpick. "Whoa," he said. "It make a me—*muy loco*."

Now what? She had to call Deanna—no Richard. He'd be easier to talk to. The good news was that he wasn't drunk—he was only sick. Maybe it would be better if he were drunk. They could sober him up but were at the mercy of his—what you call—strip trout. Did he always speak like that—in running triplets? Oh, my stars.

She took his arm and wrapped hers around it. "I have a car. I'll take you to the carriage house on my farm—that's where you'll be staying," she explained. "You can rest on the way."

Vasquez held on as if she were a lifeline. "You sweet—dulce—Dulcinea. Your eyes—deep blue—like Hermoso—big lake. I swim—with a cows—*mis niñas*," he said, his voice dissolving into giggles.

Just what did he and those cows do in Lake Hermoso? She shuddered, thinking about the methane gas cows generated. "Shhhh. Save your voice, Leandro."

Walt opened the back door. He helped Vivian in first, and then Vasquez, who fell into Vivian's lap.

"I sleep here," Vasquez said. He yawned until Vivian could eye his tonsils, smiled contentedly, and promptly passed out.

"Oh, no! No, you—" She tried to hoist his head out of her lap. But his medication had made him a hundred and eighty pounds of dead weight. At the moment, his head was creasing her dress purchased for the occasion. Not to mention that his stubble pulled at the rayon fabric in the skirt. Damn. She'd wanted to look as fashionable as Deanna this evening. She thought about having Walt pull over and help her reposition him. They could lean him against the car door. But they were already running late. Since she had to take him to the carriage house, she could change her clothes while Walt cleaned him up.

Having to find another outfit for the masque was the least of her worries. She had to let the rest of the guild know that, at present, their celebrated Giovanni could sing no better than the late great Italian Zorro, Donato Bianco. Who could have anticipated such a young singer would fall ill? Vivian didn't believe it herself. Cancelling due to illness was more the province of big stars whose schedules and bodies were heavily taxed—they often gave recitals and solo performances in ball parks and stadiums in addition to traditional runs in opera houses. Vivian had heard rumors that the stars everyone knows on a first-nam basis feigned illness to get better accommodations, more money, more perks. She had heard all about the tricks the biggest singers used to squeeze something extra out of their contracts—to give penny-pinching employers the shaft. Vivian hadn't realized that sort of thing actually happened until she read an unauthorized biography of a world renowned tenor, that recounted any number of his shenanigans increasing in number and frequency the more famous he became. The younger singers, up-and-comers like Vasquez, couldn't afford to tarnish their reputations thusly.

As they traveled to the carriage house, the more she wondered why no one from the opera house in Maryland had called and given them a heads up that Vasquez was ailing? Maybe he was newly stricken. She'd heard of such a thing happening before. Tales of great performers whose bodies held on, staving off illness until the end of a run, until they somehow knew they could shut down, if only for a day.

Did Deanna have a backup plan? Vivian would soon find out. Oh, God.

18
The Pasticcio

Deanna is on stage with Arnaud, inspecting his work—balloon arches over step units leading to the stage, a balloon mural of the Hankey Opera Company logo on the stage left back wall, a pair of drama masks stage right, and a giant balloon martini glass—center stage. Out of the corner of her eye, she spies Richard hurrying down the aisle.

Deanna leaned into Arnaud and gave him the kind of hug that wouldn't smear her make-up or rumple her dress. "You've outdone yourself."

"Always a pleasure," Arnaud said, looking satisfied. "No one on the East Coast does better work than Arnaud. You find someone better than Arnaud?" He tucked his shoulder-length, bleached-blonde hair behind his ear. "Arnaud will do your next job for free."

Since they'd invited him to serve on the board, Arnaud had done the year's masque for nothing. Just tickets to the opening night of *Don Giovanni*, orchestra section, front row. The guild knew they'd gotten the better end of the deal. Guests loved Arnaud's balloon creations. Year in and year out, part of the masque's attraction was seeing how he would top the previous year's décor.

"Arnaud," Deanna said. "Is Richard's late wife really trying to *reach* him?"

"She is desperate to reach him," Arnaud said. "She wants him to let go."

"Let go of what?" Deanna asked, hoping he didn't mean his guild responsibilities.

"Arnaud will need more time with her to figure that one out."

"Don't go inviting any ghosts to my masque!"

"She's already here." Arnaud beamed. "Wouldn't miss it."

"Oh, pshaw!" Deanna said.

"Sometimes," Arnaud said, "if your beliefs won't allow you to imagine ghosts doing the things they do, it's just better to keep quiet rather than insult them."

Opera was a magnet for wackos. Maestro. Vivian. Arnaud. All of them off-kilter. Of course, Deanna could be crazy, too. She had to be partially insane to take up the cause of classic opera in Hankey, Pennsylvania.

"Deanna!" Richard called, hurrying up the steps.

To make amends, she took Arnaud's hand in hers and squeezed it. "Just exquisite work. Give me a moment, darling," she said and headed toward the proscenium.

It had to be urgent. Once they opened the bar, Richard rarely ventured ten feet from it. "What's the matter?"

"I don't know how to tell you this. It's Vasquez."

What trick had Vivian pulled now? She should've never trusted her with Vasquez. Did another Bobbin' Robin sign fall from the sky and crush the Frantz limousine this time? "I thought you said his plane arrived safely. Or can't Vivian distinguish Northeast from Southwest Airlines?"

"Yes—yes. Listen a moment," Richard said, looking distressed. "Vasquez is sick. He has strep throat."

Deanna felt her heart plunge into the toes of her camel-colored Manolo Blahniks. "He what?"

Richard took her by the arm. "He can't sing."

"I have to sit down," Deanna said. "I need a minute to think."

Arnaud raced to the wings and hauled out a folding chair, opening it for Deanna. "Arnaud has brought you a chair. Here, my pet." He indicated with several hand flourishes that she should sit.

Deanna eased herself into it, and sat silently, slowing her breathing, trying to wrap her head around Richard's news. "Let me get this straight. Vasquez has strep throat. We have no one to sing with Zerlina—no one the audience will get excited about. No one to boost ticket sales. If we don't sell out, we die, as surely as Hankey Steel went kaput."

Sensing trouble, Arnaud bent down on one knee, took Deanna's hand in his and patted it. "Darling, darling. Arnaud will get us Apple-tinis—straight up." He leapt off his knee and sashayed toward the stairs, swiveling around on his heel, striking one finger in the air as if he'd been assailed with an idea. "Arnaud can sing the role for you. Did you know Arnaud can sing? You didn't know, eh?" Arnaud began swaying left and right. "I've got you—under my skin," he sang, stippling the ends of his notes like Sinatra. But that was the only thing that came out of his mouth sounding remotely like Sinatra. "I've got you—"

Richard waved his hand. "Enough singing, Arnaud. We'll take those drinks."

"What are we going to do?" Deanna intoned lifelessly. "Now that I'm sitting down, I don't want to get back up. I'd like to fall off an upstage platform and descend to the underworld along with Giovanni." She threw her head back and groaned. "Does it have to be this hard, Richard? Can't we have one moment of glory before we go down in flames?" She reached around with her left hand and massaged her right shoulder. "We've been doing this for ten years now. I swear it's never been this hard. What nasty karma are we being assailed with? Maybe Vivian can tell us. She's the karma-chameleon."

"Relax, Deanna," Richard moved around to the back of the folding chair and placed his hands on Deanna's back. She sighed as his hands gripped her back, moaning as he rubbed. "Let's talk this out. Vasquez can't sing. But the number is a duet."

"My m.o. is to rush in and fix things. We've hired someone to do that for us," Deanna said, wincing and sighing, alternately. "Ooh. That's—fabulous—Richard. We need Knobby."

"I'll page him. Give me one second." Richard dug into his pocket, punched in a few numbers and pushed send. "That ought to—"

"Vasquez is sick, huh?" Knobby said, lumbering onto the stage in their direction.

"That was quick. So, how can we make a soufflé from a dozen broken eggs?" Deanna said to herself as much as to Richard. She relaxed her head, and it hung to her chest while Richard rubbed the base of her neck. She heard the thud of footsteps up the staircase and raised her head.

"Arnaud is back," Arnaud said, with more musicality in his speaking voice than in his singing voice. "With 'tinis." He handed Deanna a glass of something the color of lime gelatin. "An Apple-tini—for the apple-queenie." He placed one hand on his hip and sipped his drink, surveying the stage. "A masterpiece. Sometimes I amaze myself." He turned to Knobby. "No drink for you, Know-bee."

"None needed. I'm working," Knobby said. "Everything's spectacular, Arnaud."

"You outdid yourself—if that's possible," Deanna said, feeling guilty about snapping at him earlier. She took the chartreuse drink from him. It looked like something flushed from the front end of her Lexus. She considered for a moment that if it was antifreeze, these next few moments would be her last. If she expired in the throes of saving the opera company from eventual ruin, it would be the noblest thing she had ever done. She downed a third of it in one swallow. She didn't necessarily care for the sloppy buzz that followed once the vodka hit her bloodstream, but she loved the heat that rose in her chest immediately after ingesting it. "Exactly what I needed. Thank you."

Richard waved Knobby closer. "Maybe we should move this little skull session to the green room? We're running out of time."

"Let's go," Knobby said.

"I'm timing us," Deanna said. "After fifteen minutes—the best idea is the one we're using."

* * *

Deanna had gathered them in the green room, minus Arnaud, whom she sent to the front of the theater to flag down Vivian's limo and redirect it to the stage door entrance. As they schemed, it was clear; there would be no grand entrance for Vasquez this afternoon. This mission would require stealth, secrecy, and lots of martinis—all around.

"That's our best option," Knobby said, having provided the only suggestion that sounded remotely possible. "What does everyone think?"

"Well, fuck a duck!" Richard pursed his lips to one side. "It might work after all. Yeoww!" Richard's hand flew to his ear, and he grimaced in pain. "I swear to God, someone yanked my ear like—" Richard stopped himself.

"You should have that looked at, Richard," Deanna said. "You've got more than tinnitus going on there."

"Lately, I've been trying out the f-bomb, thinking it makes me sound somehow—younger," Richard said.

How could she put this delicately? "Don't say *fuck-a-duck*. That's something an old fogey would say."

"Oh, blast," Richard said. "I don't get this casual cursing. I suppose I need to be provoked to do it well."

"Just think about Vasquez and his strep throat," Deanna said. "That should provoke you."

"Really, Deanna," Richard said. "It's hardly his fault that he's fallen ill."

"It may not be his fault, but it sure as hell provokes me." Deanna realized while she and Richard were doing all the talking, Knobby looked engrossed in thought. If Knobby felt pressured to come up with a solution, he certainly didn't look pressured. His complexion was fair enough to flush varying shades of red quickly. But his flesh tone was as even as the old Crayola crayon of the same name.

"What I can't figure out is why Vasquez came at all," Deanna said. "No one's going to want to hear a voiceless opera singer—Lion Man-looks or no Lion Man-looks. The bad word of mouth alone will kill advance ticket sales."

"So, Knobby, that's the best you got? That you two are costumed identically, and you step in for Vasquez when it's time to sing?" Richard asked.

"I think it'll work," Knobby said.

"Vasquez won Operatoonity. He's one hell of a singer, Knobby," Richard said.

Knobby shrugged. "Not tonight he's not. Hey, at least he's not singing the 'Champagne Aria.'"

Deanna clucked her tongue. "We're out of time. We don't have a plan other than what you've come up with."

Knobby looked calm and confident. "Remember, perception is reality. We could actually end up building more intrigue into the event than we originally thought."

"Or it could completely blow up in our faces," Deanna said.

"We can't risk that. That means," Knobby reminded everyone, "nobody breathes a word about Leandro having no voice—to anybody."

"What if somebody figures it out—that we swapped Knobby for Vasquez? And Hankey's rich and famous in attendance tell all their friends at the country club that our Giovanni's 'got nothin'?' That he can't sing?" Deanna said. "We've already got this Donato Bianco thing hanging over our heads."

Richard tutted. "That would finish us."

Deanna finished her drink and held up her glass, looking around for Arnaud to refill it. "If this audience catches on that Vasquez isn't singing the role, no one will believe we have the ability to pull off this show."

"I wouldn't normally advise we try this," Knobby said, "but what other choice do we have? We can't risk the audience losing confidence in us. Most of them were expecting a Bianco-caliber singer tonight. We have one shot here to restore their faith in our ability to deliver a quality production."

"He's right, Deanna," Richard agreed. "We have to give it a try."

"Not to mention, Vasquez will have had a little rest. Rest does amazing things for performers." Knobby folded his hands together in front of him and clasped them to his chest.

Richard placed his palm face down in the middle of them. "All for one?" Richard then lifted up his hand, as if to say, more unfinished business. "Where's D'Artagnan?"

"Who?" Deanna asked.

"Our little Apple-tini. She should be swearing with us. Solidarity and all that."

"She's probably changing." Deanna placed Richard's hand in the space between them, palm down. She put her own hand overtop Richard's. Then Knobby reached in, covering Deanna's hand.

"And one for all," they chanted clumsily.

"The three—make that four—Musketeers will prevail," Richard said, throwing his shoulders back, nodding his head.

"More like the three muskrats," Deanna said under her breath, thinking that was something Vivian might say unintentionally.

Just then the green room door flew open. Arnaud paraded inside, his right arm sweeping through the air like Vanna White uncovering a puzzle. "Guess who's here?"

In walked Vivian. Clinging to her arm was Leandro Vasquez— clean-shaven, hair exquisitely gelled, but completely washed out. Even a prisoner emerging from a fortnight in solitary had more color in his face and energy in his gait.

"It's about time," Deanna said, glaring at Vivian, who looked like she'd just picked her outfit up off the floor and stepped into it. All that family money, and she couldn't even pull together a decent outfit for a formal affair. Unconscionable. "The cocktail party is about to start. Vasquez needs to go on in an hour."

"We got here as soon as we could," Vivian said through clenched teeth.

"Welcome, Mr. Vasquez," Deanna said, hoisting her glass in his direction. "I think I need another drink, Arnaud. Can anyone scare up Oriane?"

Vivian shrugged. "I'll see what's keeping her."

"I'll show Vasquez to the dressing room," Knobby said, taking Vasquez's arm. "Come with me, señor."

Vasquez burped. "*Perdóname.*"

19
The Burletta

While Deanna and the rest of the guild mingle with subscribers and guests, encouraging the crowd to drink more than usual, Knobby checks up on Vasquez, who has fallen asleep in the men's dressing room.

"Vasquez! Wake up," Knobby said. Vasquez remained curled up on the chaise longue, snoring lightly. Knobby shook him lightly. "Time to make your debut, young fella."

"Qué? Qué?" Vasquez's eyes fluttered open. "Madre? Padre?"

"Just me, Mr. Vasquez," Knobby said.

"Ahh, Know-bee," Vasquez said, pronouncing his name exactly like Arnaud. "Time to meet—the fans, eh?"

"No, Mr. Vasquez. No meet and greet this evening. You do the performance, and you're done!"

Vasquez waggled a finger at him. "You call me—Leandro."

Knobby held up a pair of long black gloves with cuffs like those used in fencing. "Slip these on, Mr. Vasquez."

"But I—love a meet—my pubic," Vasquez said quietly, yanking the gloves on.

"Not pubic. *Public*," Knobby said, thinking I'll bet some patrons would be happy to meet his pubic. "That's a big mistake in this country."

The edges of his mouth turned upward. "Maybe I—no make a—mistake." Vasquez held his big, fat gloves out in front of him as if he were a zombie. "Big, eh?"

"Tough germs require tough gloves, Mr. Vasquez." Though the extra rest had apparently done him some good, Vasquez could easily overdo it, trying to win over the audience. Knobby couldn't allow Vasquez to succumb to cresting adrenaline—not if he was opening in New York over the weekend. Unlike some managers, Knobby never cultivated a reputation for sending damaged goods onto the next company, and he didn't intend to start now. "The sooner your portion of the event is over, the better for you. In fact, Vivian will be waiting in the wings. After you come off stage, she's whisking you out of here, and back to the carriage house."

* * *

"Well, look who it is!" A stunning older woman in a black off-the-shoulder gown stood in front of Oriane, holding her black demi-mask partly on, partly off her face. Judging from the skin tone around the neck and shoulders, Oriane figured she was close to her mother's age, but she couldn't place the woman.

"Do you remember me?" the woman said, pulling the black mask away from her face to eye Oriane's costume. "You haven't changed a bit, Oriane—other than the fact you've turned into a mixed drink." The woman laughed brightly, and it sounded pitch perfect.

Oriane inhaled sharply. It was Jeannie Jacobs. She gave her a once-over. Designer gown, bejeweled belt, rocks on every finger. Older women sure knew how to dress for the opera. "Mrs. Jacobs?"

"Oh, call me Jeannie, darling," Mrs. Jacobs purred. "You look adorable—right down to the swizzle stick."

"You look wonderful—" Oriane stopped mid-sentence, thinking that her own mother should only look that good. Her mother was supposed to be there. Maybe she wasn't hanging around Jeannie because she'd look like a dull penny beside her. Mrs. Jacobs—Jeannie—looked younger and lovelier than Oriane remembered. What was it Oriane had read somewhere? Single women live longer than married women? Any single woman with Jeannie Jacobs' means certainly lived better than most single women. A lot better than she herself did, eating tuna right from the can some evenings. "I'm sorry about Mr. Jacobs," she thought to say.

"Thank you." Jeannie sighed. "Towards the end, it was very hard on him. He's in a better place." Her smile looked a little strained.

"You're spending more time in Hankey, Mother tells me," Oriane said.

"Yes—I'll be around town more. I love Manhattan, but I like getting away, too."

Oriane sipped her own Apple-tini. "You like opera?"

"I'm a season ticket holder at Gotham City Opera where Leandro Vasquez is opening this weekend," Jeannie gushed. "Where are you hiding him? Why isn't he out here mingling with his admirers?"

"Oriane?" a voice called brightly. Her mother. She wedged herself between Oriane and Jeannie and looked dressed for Sunday school in her beige-flowered dress with lace collar and low heels. "My daughter gets to be the Apple-tini this year. Doesn't she look cute, Jeannie? Lorna? Minnie!" Mrs. Longenecker called into the crowd. "Come look at our Oriane!"

* * *

Back in the dressing room, Vasquez pouted. "But my fans—be a sad."

"If this goes the way it's supposed to," Knobby explained, "your fans won't even know it's *not* you, which means, they'll be dying to see more of you."

Vasquez lifted his ruffled white shirt to his chin, exposed his bare chest, tugged the shirt over his head, and let it fall to the floor. He tucked his thumbs into the waistband of his black skin-tight breeches. "Now there is—more of me."

"Too much of you. Put it back on," Knobby said, scooping the shirt off the floor and thrusting it back at Vasquez. "You're already sick. You can't run around without a shirt. I won't allow it." Of course, the real reason Vasquez needed to wear a shirt was that Knobby couldn't be traipsing around the stage with no shirt. His love handles would hardly serve as any kind of inducement for advanced ticket sales.

"¡Discúlpeme!" Vasquez threaded a glob of gel through his dark locks. "You won't allow?"

Knobby looked over Vasquez's shoulder, barreling in on his heavy lidded eyes, the ones women went wild for, staring back at him through the mirror. "This is my opera house, Mr. Vasquez. If you're planning to work here, you'll have to listen to me."

Vasquez yawned. "*El vaquero*, eh? You shoot me—if I no—listen a you?"

Knobby handed him a black velvet cape. He glanced over Vasquez's head to the green room clock. "Five minutes to show time. Come with me."

Vasquez reached for the black eye mask on the dressing stand.

"I'll take that," Knobby said. "And remember, don't take off your mask. Under any circumstances."

"Where—Zerlina?" Vasquez asked.

"Good question," Knobby said, presuming Oriane had changed out of the costume already and waited for them in the wings.

* * *

Oriane wasn't certain what to tell Jeannie about Vasquez's whereabouts, but she knew she couldn't say anything about his strep throat. "His plane arrived late. He just stepped off the tarmac." She saw Deanna and waved her over. "Jeannie, I want you to meet our guild chair, Deanna Lundquist. And you know my mother Iris, don't you?"

"Very nice to meet you, Jeannie," Deanna said. "Nice seeing you, Mrs. Longenecker."

"Call me Iris," she said.

"Well," Oriane said, wringing her hands, "I have to get ready to sing."

"Oh, you're singing?" Jeannie said.

"I mentioned that at mah-jongg," Iris said, "Remember? Just tonight. Not in the show."

Oriane rolled her eyes. "I'm in the show, Mother. I don't have a role."

"I'm thrilled," Jeannie said. "I haven't heard you sing in ages."

"You'll certainly enjoy her this evening!" Deanna said. "Have you seen *Don Giovanni*?"

"Yes, I saw it with Donato Bianco five years ago," Jeannie said.

Wrong question to ask, Oriane thought. What was that look stealing across Deanna's lightly powdered face? Panic? Or was she jealous of how cute Oriane looked in her old costume?

Jeannie shook her head. "What a shame he came unraveled like that," she continued. "He's created some real exposure issues for you, I'm afraid."

"I knew he was Deanna's attacker—before anyone else on the guild," Oriane said proudly. "He even had Deanna thinking he was coming in for a job interview as *Don Blank*. Here, she never called his references."

"Oriane, don't you have to run off and change—*right now*?" Deanna said through a strained smile.

Since Deanna was giving her the stink-eye for sharing state secrets, Oriane excused herself and tore through the crowd. She had to get backstage to change into her Zerlina garb. Exiting the masque, she grabbed Vivian's hand. "I need help," she whispered. Together, they raced ahead to the dressing room.

Oriane barreled through the dressing room door, followed by Vivian. "Unzip me. Hurry."

Vivian's hands shook as she reached around to the back of the costume, picked up the zipper and pulled. Just before the mid-point of Oriane's back, the zipper refused to budge any further. "Oh, God. It's—it's stuck."

"Places," Knobby called through the intercom.

Vivian tugged and pulled the zipper tag. "It won't move."

"Cut it open," Oriane said. She ran by all the dressing room tables, throwing open the drawers. No scissors. "Rip it off."

"Rip it off?"

"If the masque flops because of me, Deanna will tar and feather me. She's already pissed at me." Oriane breathed heavily, almost hyperventilating. "Tear it. Start from the top."

She placed her hands on the costume, flanking the back seam and pulled hard, wearing down the seam. "It's coming," she said, pulling the first threads open. She gave it short quick tugs until the seam was completely compromised. She even ripped the fabric from around the zipper. "Go!"

Oriane tore away from the costume and ran to the clothes rack. "Tell Knobby I'm coming. Tell him to stall. I need five minutes."

* * *

Out in the house, the rest of the guild was ushering the crowd into their seats. They had all agreed to make sure only women were seated on the aisle. "I'll get Vasquez," Richard offered.

"Richard," Deanna called, pointing to a basket at the end of the aisle. "The flowers for Vasquez."

Richard nodded and headed for the side of the stage. He peered around the heavy drape masking the passageway.

In the next instant, the houselights dimmed, and Richard led Vasquez to the center aisle at the back of the house. As the lights came up, Maestro cued the musicians in the pit. As they vamped the introduction, Vasquez strutted down the center aisle like the Don Juan he was hard-wired to be since his gaucho days, handing out loose roses to women seated on the aisle. He stopped to chuck Jeannie Jacobs under the chin, and she melted at his touch. Those seated around her cooed with envy. No denying it—Vasquez was an Adonis, a Latin Fabio, a Calvin Klein supermodel with pipes—just no pipes this evening. The audience's adoration fueled him—he whirled around and bowed low, sweeping his cape like a toreador. The women swooned audibly. The ones in the back of the house had slipped off their demi-masks and whipped out their opera glasses already. Good thing the lights would be lowered when Vasquez took the stage—all to create the perfect mood for a romantic interlude and for a little subterfuge.

Backstage, Knobby searched for Oriane. She should've been easy to spot in a wedding dress. No Oriane. In fifteen seconds, he had to motion Vasquez onstage to chase Oriane offstage, yet she was nowhere to be seen. He couldn't summon her through the sound system in the event his microphone had been turned on—it shouldn't be on until he appeared on stage, but he never worked with Hankey techs before, and didn't know whether they jumped their sound cues or timed them with Swiss precision. He took two steps toward the offstage headset, ready to call for Oriane into the dressing area himself, like the voice of God, when from the corner of his eye, he spotted ruffles and a flowered headdress sprinting toward him.

"You're late," Knobby mouthed, none too happy with her tardiness.

"I got stuck in the Apple-tini costume," she said, seething.

Vivian appeared behind her. "We had to rip it off."

Knobby shook his head as if to say, I don't want to hear excuses. He turned to Oriane, putting his hand in the small of her back. "Get onstage. Down right. Go," he said, pushing her out of the wings.

Oriane took one last glance downward. She wasn't used to wearing such a low-cut blouse and wanted to make sure she was tucked in before she trotted out there on stage. Close enough.

"Masetto?" she called in character. "Masetto," she cried a second time, petulantly. The audience applauded at her entrance. While singing a bit of Zerlina's recitative, she drifted to center stage just as Vasquez climbed the staircase located in front of the proscenium at center stage. "Oohhh," she cried in alarm, at seeing Vasquez.

Why wasn't she running offstage right? Knobby raised his own half mask over his head to get a better look. Oriane was frozen, as if time had suddenly stopped, gawking at Vasquez, an even more spectacular specimen of a man onstage. She appeared to be melting—and not from the stage lights. Oriane was supposed to throw her hands up in a panic and run away. Vasquez was supposed to follow her offstage. Yet, she allowed Vasquez to skulk toward her, inching closer and closer, Oriane's body undulating with his every step.

"What's she doing?" Vivian said, close to Knobby's ear.

"She's gob-smacked," Knobby whispered back, thinking how am I going to follow that?

At that instant, Oriane remembered her blocking, turned away from Vasquez, and raced offstage. Vasquez followed her, falling into Vivian's outstretched arms when he could no longer hold himself up. He purred, "I'm a have—too much fun—to a stop."

Knobby untied the cape from Vasquez's neck and tied it around himself. "Back onstage, Oriane. I'll be out in one minute."

Vivian tried to lead Vasquez away.

"No—no," Vasquez pulled away from her. "I take—curtain call."

Knobby glared at him and shook his head.

"Sì, vaquero. I sit—a there," Vasquez pointed to a folding chair near the edge of the curtain."I—take a bows—no you," he said, pointing to the middle of his chest.

Oriane trotted onstage like a frisky filly. Knobby's cue. It had been at least a month since Knobby had sung anything—even happy birthday. Though he'd sounded fairly good in the shower that morning, singing to seasoned operagoers was another matter entirely. He crossed himself, pulled the mask over his face, raked his plumed black hat and strutted onstage.

"Là ci darem la mano," Knobby sang in a worthy baritone, lights dimming as he strode onstage. The audience, moved by his singing, broke into spontaneous applause. They liked him. Interesting. Deanna had told him that the mood of the masque makes the audience looser, more spontaneous than on regular opera nights. And she'd been correct. He doubted they would ever be this impressionable during a scheduled performance. Though his voice sounded strong to his own ear, he knew he had about two minutes of singing in him before the voice began fading. Then he would be hoarse for days.

Oriane was milling around the martini glass center stage, waving a handkerchief. Knobby, dressed exactly like Vasquez, came up behind her, wrapped his arms around her waist and clasped her hands in his. He leaned his body into hers, and laid his face on her cheek as he sang, "Là mi dirai di sì." As he sang the next line, he gently, playfully placed his hand over her eyes, and then looked right and left in character, for Zerlina's fiancé. The audience tittered—they knew the story—they knew Giovanni was always looking over his shoulder for the suitors of the women he seduced. The audience was well-schooled.

But how shrewd were they? How long would it take for the audience to realize the opera company had pulled the old switcharoo on them, swapping out the dashing Vasquez for a not-so-sensational Knobby in a mask and a musketeer hat—especially guests with expensive opera glasses. Or would they, these season ticket holders, readily embrace this theatrical convention, willingly suspending their natural tendency to disbelieve, choosing to believe only what they saw—a Giovanni seducing a Zerlina?

"Partiam, ben mio, da qui," he sang, striving through every inch of his body to impart the meaning of the line, "let's run away together—you and me," hoping the audience would accord him a swagger he couldn't attribute to himself. No valiant gaucho, he. Just a wholesome Cincinnati boy. But the women in the audience reacted to his last line. He could feel their affection for him floating onto the stage, enveloping him like a soft breeze off the Ohio on a sweltering summer day. All except for one woman.

* * *

Jeannie Jacobs rose from her seat and strode toward Richard, who stood behind the last orchestra row. She came upon him so swiftly that Richard didn't realize she was headed his way until she was upon him. She tapped him on the shoulder. "What's the big idea?"

"And you are?" Richard asked, with annoyance.

"Does it matter who I am?" she said, in a pronounced whisper. "That's *not* Vasquez onstage."

"What do you mean?" Richard said, with strained incredulity.

"Don't toy with me," Jeannie said, raising her voice. "I'm not one of your blue-haired subscribers with macular degeneration. Why isn't Vasquez singing this number as billed?"

Deanna, who'd seen Jeannie stalk out, breathlessly reached Jeannie and Richard and pulled them out into the foyer, out of earshot of the audience. "Jeannie, please understand. Vasquez has strep throat and can't sing."

"Why are you deceiving your subscribers?" Jeannie asked with a raised eyebrow.

Deanna shook her head. "I don't know why, other than, if this show isn't a blockbuster, there won't be any more subscribers to worry about deceiving. After losing Bianco, the way we lost him, we couldn't disappoint them again. So, we took a risk."

Jeannie was silent for a long minute. "You play to win, don't you?"

"Always have," Deanna said.

"I admire that kind of courage. As long as you don't pull any more tricks on me, I'm interested in joining the guild," Jeannie said. "I like your style, Deanna Lundquist."

Deanna's shoulders fell. She let out a deep sigh that seemed to come from her kneecaps.

"Who's the man behind the mask?"

"He's our new general director," Deanna said, gesturing Jeannie back to her seat.

"He's no Vasquez. But he's not bad."

"You won't—"

Jeannie patted Deanna's hand. "I won't. But *no more* tricks."

* * *

Back on stage as Zerlina sang her first line, Knobby was supposed to let go of Oriane since her reaction to Giovanni was essentially an aside—Zerlina, sharing her doubts with the audience that Giovanni was sincere in his profession of love. Thus far, the audience loved him and believed he was Giovanni. He held onto her—tightly. Her hair smelled like gardenias, and his arms fit comfortably around her waist. He drew her tighter against his body. As she sang her stanza, tugging to break free of him to carry out the blocking they'd discussed, her voice was surprisingly light and melodious.

He removed the gold band he'd planted on his pinky finger and slipped it onto Oriane's ring finger. He then held up her hand for the audience to admire.

"*Felice, è ver, sarei. Ma può burlarmi ancor,*" she sang. At these words, which were all about her heart being ill-at-ease—she hadn't dressed in her wedding garb to marry Giovanni, after all—he began kissing her lightly on the wrist, working his way up her arm. Oriane bristled, he hoped with pleasure. He thought he heard members of the audience gasp, pleasantly surprised.

"*Vieni, mio bel diletto*" he sang, the approval of the audience emboldening him. He should be bolder. More brazen. He tucked his arms just under her breast, pressing her to him, feeling the swell caused by the demi-corset sinking into his forearms. As Oriane sang Zerlina's protestations in response, he would not relent. He caressed her arms—just as he imagined a rake like Giovanni would. He was gazing down over her shoulder, his eyes settling on her plumped breasts. He turned his lips to her creamy shoulders and kissed them—his lips to her soft skin—and kept brushing his lips against her silky neck. At the conclusion of his next line, "*Io cangierò tua sorte*," about changing her life forever, his lips reached for hers and he kissed her on the mouth. This time she allowed his lips to linger on hers, forcing her to gasp for air and rush her next singing line. A woman in the audience sighed quaveringly.

Instead of his dancing around the stage in pursuit of her, which is what he informed her he would be doing—that Vasquez would chase her around the stage—Knobby's portrayal compelled him to continue hugging and caressing her until the end of the song, when he bent her head back, covered her mouth with his, and kissed her full on, slipping his tongue between her teeth. He kept kissing her as the lights faded, the audience clapping wildly.

Oriane elbowed him, to jar him out of her mouth. She slipped one hand between her mouth and his and pulled him offstage with the other. "What do you think you're—"

Once hidden in the wings, he drew her to him again, and covered her mouth with a lingering kiss. Then, with more Zorro than Zorro himself, he ripped off his hat and his mask and threw them at Vasquez. "Put these on," he barked. "Take each one off—slowly, carefully—during the curtain call."

Oriane ran onstage first and courtesied. The applause was generous—deservedly. She sang the role as if it had been written for her. She had acted it masterfully, too, appearing worried, almost to the point of acting preyed upon before giving into the Don's advances in the end.

Vivian helped Vasquez tilt his hat at just the angle Knobby had worn it, and ushered him onstage. The audience stood as he bowed, cheering when he removed his hat and mask.

Vivian leaned into Knobby, while keeping her eyes on Vasquez. "My God, Knobby. I didn't know you could sing."

"I pulled it off," he said, laughing now since it appeared that their scheme had worked, at least judging from the expressed appreciation of the audience.

"I didn't know you could act either," Vivian added.

As he watched Vasquez take Oriane's hand and defer the next bow to her, he thought to himself that he never was much of an actor. That he hadn't been acting just then.

Why had it taken him this long to notice a girl like Oriane? How could he ever turn her attention away from Vasquez?

20
The Dramma Giocoso

Oriane leads Vasquez offstage and hands him over to Vivian, who squires him away from the opera house in her limo before the audience rushes backstage. Knobby has secreted himself in the men's dressing room, hurriedly changing out of the Giovanni costume.

"Oriane," Deanna called through the dressing room door, knocking loudly. "Oriane? I'm coming in."

Oriane was unpinning her headpiece and called back through a mouthful of bobby pins, She pulled out the final pin and placed the flowered arch on the vanity, smoothing its ribboned streamers.

Deanna peeked around the dressing room door and let herself in. "You were wonderful, dear. Some of our subscribers want to greet Zerlina. Jeannie Jacobs is waiting for you. Oh, and your mother, too."

"I'm not Zerlina," she said. It had sounded petulant; she hadn't said it to be petulant.

Deanna stared at her incredulously. "Our guests can't meet Vasquez. At the very least, they should have the opportunity to greet you. Put your headpiece on."

Oriane began unlacing the black bodice that had given her such a fetching bustline. "Don't want to," she said dreamily. Too bad corsets and waist cinchers had gone out of fashion. They sure plumped up and thinned out areas where nature had left women wanting, so to speak. "I'm not up to talking to all those people."

"Don't be childish." Deanna lifted the headpiece and a few pins off the table and placed the wreath back on Oriane's head, securing it. "This is a fund-raiser. You're a board member—first—with fund-raising duties. Get yourself together and get out there."

Oriane shoved Deanna's hands away. "Whatever." She checked her appearance in the mirror, pushed past Deanna and entered the hallway where Jeannie, her mother, and another woman were waiting. "Hello, ladies," Oriane greeted them coolly. "Did you like the number?"

The woman she didn't know wore a fox choker. A night at the opera, and that included any classy fundraising event at the Hankey Opera House, was still one venue for which people were expected to dress—where backless gowns, cutaway tails, and furs were welcome. Her mother had told her that Hankey's most affluent citizens became season subscribers to see and be seen. As long as they bought subscriptions, she'd told her mother, she didn't really care why they came—just that they came.

"You sang beautifully, dear. Tell me," the woman in the stole began. Since Oriane couldn't break away from the beady black eyes staring back at her, she was certain it was no faux fox. "Where's darling Donny?"

"Oriane? You remember Lorna from bridge club?" her mother said.

"Lorna! Of course," Oriane said. "So glad you come could come."

"Yes, what's happened to Donny Giovanni?" Jeannie asked, adding, "He couldn't keep his hands off you." Jeannie examined Oriane with one raised eyebrow, as if to say, I know all about the little stunt you pulled, while her mother and Lorna dissolved into giggles.

Highbrow entertainment laced with sex. That's how Oriane's mother had once described opera. These days when people would leave the theatre after seeing The Marriage of Figaro or Turandot, they might be chatting about how Mozart's such a musical genius or discussing some dramatic theme. They would want their friends to think while leaving a production of Werther, that foremost, this is a cautionary tale about what happens to reckless lovers. But make no mistake, most operagoers would be thinking only about sex, every kind imaginable.

Oriane had to concede that many, if not most, operas are lusty—
the Count who constantly gropes for Figaro's lovely fiancé, Suzanna,
because he wants a quickie every time his wife's head is turned; the
courtesan scene in *Tales of Hoffman* set in a brothel; the breathtaking
Manon Lescaut emerging from her stagecoach, at once entrancing the
chevalier. Sexual themes abound in opera story lines—extramarital
sex, stolen sex, forced sex, sex longing, sex envy. Once she'd heard
someone refer to opera itself as a form of sex—between the music
and the lyrics, between the orchestration and the melody. Opera
without sex is, well, *The Pirates of Penzance*.

"Oriane," Jeannie was saying. "Are you hiding him back there?
Keeping him all to yourself?"

"He had to rush off to New York," Knobby interrupted. He had
slipped into the hallway, having changed out of his swashbuckling
garb back into his street clothes. He stood behind Oriane. "He's
opening in New York City within days. But he'll be back, ladies. May
21—*Don Giovanni*. Opening night."

"Knobby," Oriane said without enthusiasm, "these are my
mother's friends, Lorna and Jeannie."

"Pleased to meet you," Knobby said.

"Well, Knobby. With any luck, your Giovanni will be in better
voice when he returns," Jeannie said. "He sounded cloudy and a
little stuffed-up tonight."

"Really?" Iris said. "I thought he was quite good."

Knobby harrumphed. "My apologies, ladies. Mr. Vasquez had a
slight cold."

"So I *heard*," Jeannie said. Oriane looked back and forth between
Knobby and Jeannie.

"Perhaps," Iris said, cupping Oriane's chin in her hand. "But he
was so passionate. I'd have turned to gelatin and slithered right out
of my corset if he'd kissed me the way he kissed you."

"He's not a very good kisser. Very sloppy. All tongue!" Oriane
said, which made all the ladies laugh.

Now, more than ever she regretted not being cast as Zerlina. She
wanted Knobby to feel some of the humiliation she felt. But he
continued to stand there, meeting her gaze. She might have been

attracted to him once, but that attraction had ceased once she saw Vasquez—in the flesh. Even though he'd been ill, and a shadow of the personality she'd met in London, once again, his magnetism had completely undone her. She'd never wanted anyone more than she desired him.

"We'll be back to see him—and you," Lorna said as the women departed, leaving Knobby and Oriane alone together in the hallway for a moment.

"I'm not playing Zerlina," she called after them.

Knobby slipped his hand over her mouth. "Shhh."

"Don't shush me," she said, wrenching his hand from her mouth. "What was with the tongue-action, Knobby?"

"I was getting into the part, Oriane," Knobby said. "You were very appealing as Zerlina. I got totally lost in the character. You should be flattered."

"Guess again," Oriane said, making her annoyance apparent. "What happened to all the wonderful blocking you came up with, that you insisted I do? You stood behind me the whole time. I was supposed to cross down left and then flit around the martini glass. You wouldn't let go. We just stood there—in one spot."

"I deviated from the script—I apologize." Knobby's voice was gentler than it had been all evening. Perhaps because the number had concluded, the evening was coming to a close, and nothing had gone seriously wrong, he felt more relaxed. "I'm not performing much these days. At first I was mortified. But mostly, I realized if I just stood behind you, they'd be less likely to notice I have about twenty pounds on Vasquez."

More like thirty, Oriane thought.

"There were lots of women in the audience," he said, crossing his arms and leaning into the wall. "I also wanted to ramp up their expectations. They'd see lots of romance and sensuality in our Giovanni."

"If Maestro wants to interpret it that way," Oriane interjected.

"What other way can it be interpreted, Oriane?" Knobby said, though it was clearly a challenge, more like a peer-to-peer response than artistic director to mere chorister. "Giovanni's licentious—

there's no other way to play that. I'm insisting on it. I'm the general director, in case you've forgotten. It's my show."

"A director in London made his Giovanni very sensational—shocking even. He intimated that Giovanni used cocaine. Besides the drugs, he dramatized performing—" Should she mention what other liberties this Spanish director added to Mozart's classic romp to give it an ultra-modern edge? Could she say it? Of course, she could. She didn't want Knobby and Maestro to think her provincial any longer. She was going to start dressing differently. Start acting more cosmopolitan—in ways that would make her more attractive to Leandro—beginning with the casual mention of subjects such as—. Oh, boy. She might as well just blurt it out. "Oral sex."

"Right," Knobby said casually, rubbing his chin. "Bieito's *Don Giovanni* for the English National Opera. I read all about that. All I could think of was *Amadeus* meets *American Gigolo* when I read the write-ups. Not very well received, I'm afraid."

She had come right out and said "oral sex," and Knobby hadn't flinched. Did he think she talked like that all the time?

"Maybe not," she said, "but completely plausible. Since, well, forever, women have been drawn to Giovannis or have been burned by Giovannis or have wanted to murder Giovannis," Oriane said, thinking that the last remark made her sound quite sophisticated, except for the *well* that snuck in there. She looked down past her nose at her bodice. From that angle the laces appeared crooked. She shifted her breasts first with her arms, then using her hands to straighten them, gave him a wry smile, her most sardonic, and began walking toward the house.

Knobby grabbed her arm as she passed him and slid his hand into hers. "You sang very well—this evening. Better than that. You were *fantastic*," he said, squeezing her hand. "Maestro and I should have given you a chance to sing for Zerlina. You deserved it. I'm—sorry."

At one point, Oriane thought she would have never wanted to hear anything more fervently during her earthly stay than the apology Knobby had just uttered. Or to have Knobby take her hand in a gesture of fondness. But her head swam with thoughts and images of Leandro. Only Leandro. The Lion Man. The brooding, handsome, king-of-the-jungle, ruler of her heart, Leandro Vasquez. He was all she could think about. Why had she ever fantasized about making a happy home with Knobby? If she "tuned her piano" correctly, she could be touring the globe with Leandro Vasquez, not merely settling for an impresario who's never lived abroad.

Oriane shrugged. "I've got to meet my entourage," she began, with as droll a delivery as she could muster, and continued down the hall to meet the rest of Hankey Society, "all my *mesdames et m'sieurs*, Knobby."

And didn't that sound chic, using *m'sieur*? Like she used the word frequently, and saying the entire word had become too arduous.

As she rounded the corner, she bumped into Richard. "Oops. Sorry," she chirped.

"There you are. I was looking for you and Knobby," Richard said. "Have you seen him?"

Oriane crossed her arms and indicated with a twist of her head that Knobby was behind her.

Richard, unnaturally effusive, took Oriane's hands in his. "I've seen productions of Giovanni before." He was trying not to gush, but there was the tiniest catch in his voice. "Knobby," he called. "I want you to hear this."

Knobby came forward, but stood on the other side of Richard.

"I have never seen that seduction scene done with more passion, more authenticity than you two performed it tonight," Richard gushed.

Oriane tried to protest, but Richard kept talking. "Most times you see Giovanni chasing Zerlina all over the stage, his cat to her mouse. But the intensity of your blocking, Knobby. Holy Mozart. Everyone was electrified—including me. Well done, man."

"Surely someone realized that we had switched Leandro with Knobby," Oriane said.

"Only one person," Richard said, pursing his lips.

"Jeannie Jacobs! She gave me a massive hairy eyeball moments ago," Knobby said.

"Most everyone in the audience saw what they wanted to see. Anyway, there are still people in the house who want to greet you," he said giving Oriane a gentle push down the hall, towards the first floor box seats.

Oriane wondered whether Leandro had seen her perform? He had to have, she thought, approaching a gaggle of guests. Though he could have been resting, eyes closed, seated off stage. He'd have to have heard her anyway. If she was as good as Richard suggested, maybe even the Lion Man was impressed with her. Did he like talented women? Some men had a weakness for singers. Maybe Leandro was one of them. Leandro. She loved saying his name. This is my husband, Leandro, she said to herself, and it tasted delicious rolling off her tongue. She looked up and saw the patrons in boxes waving at her. She did a deep, theatrical curtsy. "Hello," Oriane said to the group. "Glad you could come."

While their praise washed over her, she was thinking how best to capitalize on her success this evening when the Lion Man returned in a few weeks for rehearsals. Could she achieve a full-scale transformation in three short weeks? All her life, she could do anything she'd set her mind to. She'd shop at King of Prussia just like Deanna. Visit the town's swanky salon—the Font-o-Beauty. It was time for the gorrión to go the way of the gooney bird. Why, Leandro wouldn't even recognize his little sparrow when he returned to Hankey.

21

The Divo

Four days later, the New York cast of Don Giovanni *and one hundred patrons who paid five hundred dollars a plate gather in a bistro about four blocks from City Center for a champagne gala. Sometime after one in the morning, the assistant to the general director gets an early edition of one of the dailies with a review of opening night—Vasquez's New York premiere.*

'LION MAN' PRIDE OF CITY OPERA

by Bitsy Marks, Staff Writer

(New York City – May 8, 2011) No one's better at discovering new talent than Maestro Carerra. His newest protégé is a baritone with an international reputation, the Argentinian Leandro Vasquez, who will ever hereafter be remembered for the first night he played in New York City. If for no other reason than to see Leandro Vasquez, or "The Lion Man" as he is nicknamed, go see Gotham City Opera's *Don Giovanni*. Vasquez is ideally cast as Mozart's most famous anti-hero and plays the insatiable libertine to the hilt with his dark brooding looks and oh-so-muscular physique. His voice has a dark timbre ideally suited to the role. After The Lion Man's stunning performance no

one in the opening audience wanted
Don Giovanni to meet his fiery end . . .

Harvey Harrison, general director of Gotham City Opera, stopped reading the review from the first edition of *The New York Minute.* "I've read enough." He raised his glass. "Bravo, Leandro."

A chorus of bravos and clinking glasses followed. Vasquez removed his arm from the platinum blonde draped on it. He pushed back a gleaming silver chair until it smacked the black leather banquette behind him. He then stood to address the gala crowd, presently monopolizing the downstairs dining area of the 9th Avenue bistro.

"Long live Giovanni," another guest cried as Vasquez was about to open his mouth. Vasquez smiled at the jest, then broke into easy laughter. Once he showed the crowd he understood the irony of the man's remark, the rest of the crowd laughed with him, the males among them anyway, while the women in the room swooned. Someone tapped a utensil against a glass to quiet the room. A hush fell over the bistro. Vasquez had sung for three and a half hours. He thought that should have been enough. Apparently, they merely wanted to hear that soft, mellifluous voice—his off-stage voice.

"Gracias." Vasquez shrugged his broad shoulders deprecatingly. "Can I say—I love you—your city—audience," he said, the first syllable in *audience* pronounced *ow.* "I—love New York. To New York." He held up his champagne glass, nodding to the crowd, adding, "To Maestro—sheer genius."

The bistro erupted in more toasts and robust applause. Vasquez gestured to Maestro to stand and take a bow, the proper thing to do. In truth, Vasquez had objected to the reporter's contention that the Maestro had "discovered" him. That honor belonged to his faithful friend and patron from Argentina, Luis Garcia, who'd provided him with clothing, voice lessons, coaching, accompanists, and plane fare to auditions and performances. Señor Garcia had never stopped believing in him. His death a year ago had hit Vasquez hard. He'd almost abandoned his professional opera career, vowing never to return. Miraculously, as if Garcia was still working on his behalf from the grave and beyond, Vasquez's career took off. The companies hiring him offered to pay for his training and all his travel expenses, among other perks. Vasquez was happy to oblige them.

No sooner had Vasquez sat back down than the blonde slipped her arm through his and eased her thigh onto his under the table. He ran his hand up her leg, pushing the panel of her dress out of the way until his hand reached her hips, where it nestled momentarily.

He, Leandro Vasquez, was the toast of the Big Apple.

Strange how New Yorkers reacted to him like he'd come out of nowhere. They would say things like, "Where were you hiding?" and "Who kept a delectable thing like you under wraps?" And not just female New Yorkers either.

Well, he wasn't hiding now. Leandro Vasquez, who'd been a lowly gaucho in Argentina, was performing in New York City of all places. Now that he'd been seen by New York critics, producers, and agents, finally he was somebody in a way he'd never been before. And he had wanted all that. But tonight, more than anything else, now that he'd earned the applause and the reviews and the critical acclaim he sought, he needed release. He was bursting with sexual energy. He wanted to *get the head*. He needed it. Or he'd self-combust.

He leaned in close to the tall, cool blonde who'd attached herself to him since his first rehearsal at Gotham City Opera. "I want to—get the head," he whispered.

"I want to get ahead, too," she said, "but first I have to use the little girl's room," and slipped out of her chair with a rubbery ease suggesting she was more than tipsy.

"Get the *head*?" That was the expression; he was certain of it. So, why had she run away?

While he considered why his come-on had gone wrong, a matronly woman took the empty seat beside Vasquez. As he turned to face her, she held out a hand with gems the size of coffee beans on more than one finger, but he noted she wore no wedding band. He took her hand, kissing her wrinkled flesh which felt thinner than parchment to his full lips. Though initially the feel of her skin had put him off, her overall appearance was very pleasing. She looked trim in a beaded gown the color of casaba, falling off her shoulders. Her eyes were aquamarine and reminded him of Vivian Pirelli's. Soft, full, dewy.

"I'm Jeannie Jacobs," she said with the confidence of a woman who lacked for nothing. "And you are an incredible talent." Then she shuddered, and the beads lining her décolletage rattled softly against themselves, creating flashes of light tinkling against heaving, freckled breasts.

Vasquez marveled at the reactions of American women. In Baltimore, they were wild for his Giovanni. What was it about American ladies, that they couldn't tear themselves away from bad boys? Unfathomable—this weakness for men who used them and then discarded them. He intended to take full advantage of this baffling inclination.

He wondered if this older lady gave the head. Could he ask her that? Could he pull her aside and say, "Madam, you intrigue me. Would you give me the head?"

"Now that you've conquered New York, Mr. Vasquez," Jeannie said, "What's next?"

"Leandro. Call a me—Leandro," he said, and she gave another little shudder. He couldn't possibly tell her he was supposed to be singing in tiny little backwards Hankey, Pennsylvania, in little more than a fortnight. But he had to tell her something. "I don't know—I am—committed. But ask—agent." Vasquez nodded to his right, where Irv Bronsky sat on the banquette nibbling on the arm of a plump redhead who looked nothing like Mrs. Bronsky. "He'll know." He scanned the room, looking for the blonde that he came in with. Nowhere to be found. Maybe she had passed out in the little girl's room.

Jeannie laughed musically, though he wasn't sure he had said anything funny. In the basement of that trendy Manhattan eatery, he was king of the world.

Leandro took Jeannie's hand and helped her out of her chair. He draped his arm around her shoulder.

"Don't you want to finish your chocolate soufflé?" Jeannie asked.

He shook his head, leaned in close, tasting her flowery scent, and said in a husky voice, "*Haceme un pete.*"

* * *

He slipped the key card into his hotel room door and let her in first. Wordlessly, he removed his jacket from around her shoulders and tossed it on the floor. Jeannie unraveled his bow tie and began loosening the studs on his tuxedo shirt. She slipped her hands inside, first stroking then kneading his bare chest, moaning softly. Leandro slipped the strap off her shoulder and eased her gown down to her waist. He expected to see bare breasts but was surprised by a little strapless bra barely covering her nipples. He unfastened it with one hand and massaged her generous breasts with the other. He bent over and said in a low voice, "*Haceme un pete.*"

If he said that to a girl back in Argentina, she would crack him across the mouth. Then she would go tell her father. Then her father would shoot a hole in his heart.

"What is this '*Haceme something,*' Leandro?" she said breathlessly.

She didn't know Argentine Spanish? How to explain this. You'd think a woman who'd been around the square as many times as she has surely would know what he wanted. What he needed. He took her hand, placed it on his crotch and moved it up and down. She rubbed him a few times before reaching up, unfastening his pants, and undoing the zipper. Little Leandro sprang out from confinement.

"*Un pete. Mi pija. Mi pija,*" he murmured, grazing her lips with his, placing her hands on his penis, trying to impart understanding to her bejeweled hand just like Annie Sullivan spelling "wawa" into Helen Keller's dainty palm.

Jeannie rubbed and rubbed his *pija.* Enough with the rubbing, he thought.

"I could buy and sell you many times over," she said, covering his face with kisses. "But I didn't have to—did I?"

Leandro heard her say, "Buy and sell." She was a prostitute? A little old for a whore, he thought. But if that's what she needed to give him *un pete*, he was in no position to argue at the moment. With his left hand, he fished in his pants pocket and pulled out a few crumpled bills. He wasn't even sure how much he had in his fist, but he knew it was enough to buy a couple rounds of drinks. Probably enough for *un pete* from a woman her age. He slipped the bills into her hand, closing it around them.

Jeannie tightened her hand around the money and stopped rubbing. She pulled her body away from his, yanking up her dress, gasping. "You think I'm a hooker? A filthy hooker?" She raised her right hand, turned her palm towards his cheek and slapped it. She clenched the money balled up in her left hand and threw it at him.

"Wait a—no," he wailed. Where was she going? Why was she doing this? "No hooker. No hooker."

Jeannie grabbed her beaded bag off the stand in the hall. "Here I thought you were a clever boy," she said, turning back to him. Then she stalked out of his hotel room.

* * *

He was sprawled on his back when his cell phone rang the next morning. One ring. Two rings. Three rings. He had wanted to sleep in this morning. He had the worse case of *frustración sexual* last night and couldn't drift off to sleep though his body was plainly exhausted.

He glanced over at the clock, but it took him seconds to focus. Eight-thirty. What *coño'e madre* would be calling this God-awful early in the morning? He clambered over the bed and scooped his phone off the end table.

"Vasquez," he said, realizing his voice sounded very scratchy. Too much rich food and drink last evening. He'd better try to cleanse himself today. Hot lemon water—not even coffee. Though bottles of champagne lined the hotel dresser, he wouldn't be consuming them today.

"Mr. Vasquez? It's Knobby. Carter Knoblauch from Hankey."

What was that idiot Know-bee calling him for? He would already be taking his pound of flesh, for a lot less than Gotham City

Opera was paying him, in about two weeks. Vasquez reached for the end table lamp and switched on some light. "You want?"

"I wanted to congratulate you. I saw the reviews," Knobby said. "I wish I could've seen you. Apparently, you were sensational."

"Yes—a great—night, yes."

"Great? More than great. You're all over the *New York Post* this morning," Knobby said. "You made the infamous 'Page Six'—the gossip column. Leaving the party with your arm around Jeannie Jacobs, one of the richest women in New York. Our Don's a devil."

"The richest—in New York?" Vasquez groaned. "*¡Discúlpeme!*" He'd really blown it, thinking one of the wealthiest women in a world-class city was a prostitute.

"She's going to serve on the opera guild here in Hankey, too," Knobby continued. "As we say here in the States, you did us a solid, Vasquez."

If you only knew, my flabby friend, Vasquez thought.

"Anyway," Knobby said. "Can we bring you in a day earlier than your contract calls for?"

"Talk to Bronsky—" Vasquez said, ready to hang up. Isn't that what Bronsky was garnishing his payments for—to set up things like this?

"I already talked to Bronsky. He said I needed to clear it with you. That you really liked New York. That you might want to hang around a few more days."

He had no reason to stay here after the New York run closed. He had completely ruined his chance to be doted on, favored by, kept by one of the richest women in New York.

Yesterday, May 8, he was "The Lion Man, Pride of New York City." Today, he was the thorn in the lion's paw. Never mind the thorn. He was the green pus infecting the thorn.

"You know the part," Knobby said. "But since you have acting gifts I want to give you some stage directions, some coaching, that may be quite different from what Gotham City's having you do. Can you come in on the morning of the 14th, a day early? That'll give us eight more hours of rehearsal time."

Now that Knobby mentioned Hankey, he remembered the women were very friendly there, too. There was Vivian, who was older, but probably a generous lover. Plus, she had *las tetas grande*—world class. He could see them, almost fondle them if he closed his eyes. Then there was Deanna. He'd lay money on long-shot odds that she was a tigress in bed. Spunky, sassy, maybe even a little bit of a dominatrix. And Oriane, who looked luscious, plumped up in her little corset. Such sweet and dainty freshness. He had his suspicions she might be a virgin, and it had been such a long time—years—since he'd had one of those. He'd love to take from her that special something she could give to no other man. It wasn't that he was becoming a cad—not exactly like the part he was playing. Not at all. Giovanni had many women because he needed them more than the food he ate or the air he breathed.

Of course, he had to avoid seeing this Jeannie Jacobs, which he could do by staying busy. He could think of three things to keep him busy—Vivian, Deanna, and Oriane.

"I'll come," Vasquez said. "Be by—" At first, he thought he should say noon, but two o'clock was more reasonable. He always had trouble getting to sleep after an evening performance. He'd relive certain scenes in his head—selected ovations, too. "Two."

"Two o'clock? Works for me," Knobby said. "Rehearsal begins at two. At the opera house. Don't be late," Knobby said sounding like *el vaquero*, barking out orders. Then he hung up.

Yes, he would return to Hankey a day early. There was something about it. Whenever he stepped into the Hankey Opera House, he seemed to smell femininity.

22
The Séance

While the company rehearses, Richard, Vivian, Deanna, and Arnaud meet in the conference room to plan the opening night gala. Deanna is dog-sitting for Knobby and has brought the three dachshunds to the meeting.

Richard looked at the report Knobby had provided him: one hundred and fifty gala tickets sold. The production opened in three weeks. He pursed his lips to the side and began to click his pen. "That number should be twice as high," he said. "Have we used Vasquez's New York reviews?"

Deanna picked up Lohengrin, the funniest looking of all the pups with his spotty Guernsey-calf coloring, and set him in her lap. "We could spring for some direct mail—a postcard with Vasquez's picture on it and the line from the *New York Minute,* 'Vasquez plays the insatiable libertine to the hilt with his dark brooding looks and oh-so-muscular physique.' Four-color to all the Hankey zip codes."

Immediately, Tristan and Isolde nuzzled the ankles of other guild members, begging for attention.

"I don't—don't know. Would that make us sound desperate?" Vivian said, scooping up Isolde. "This one's eyes are windows to her soul. Such a darling! Who knew dachshunds were so cute."

Arnaud picked up Tristan. "We *are* desperate, darling."

"A full-color postcard to three zip codes. How are we going to pay for 40,000 cards?" Richard said.

"If we get a five percent return, it'll pay for itself." Lohengrin licked Deanna on the face. "You're such a little cutie-wootie pie."

"That's a big if in this economy," Richard said, clicking his pen erratically. "Really, Deanna. Must we have dogs in here? They're distracting us from our work."

"Yes, we must," Deanna said. "You can stop clicking your pen any time now, Richard."

Richard harrumphed. "Damn sausage dogs," he said, under his breath. Immediately afterward, he got a swift kick in the shins. "Yeoww! It's happening again," he said, rubbing his leg.

"Ohhh. Ohhhh," Arnaud said, hugging little Tristan to his chest. "We have a visitor."

Lohengrin howled mournfully, even sounding like a little cow. The other dogs joined, each howling on a different pitch—a sausage dog symphony.

Richard threw his pen down. "I refuse to believe Mary's in this room—she never even liked dogs."

"Why do you think the dogs are howling, eh?" Arnaud asked.

"Don't know. But I wish they'd shut up," Richard said.

Arnaud shuddered like he was having a small seizure. "Mary is here."

"Seriously?" Richard said.

"Of course, seriously," Arnaud said. "Who do you think kicked you in the shins?"

Richard rolled his pen between his fingers. "Why did she do that? What am I doing to upset her?"

"She needs to tell you something—something important. It's about more than these dogs." Arnaud squinted and put his fingers to his temples. "But I can't make it out. What she wants to say to you is all coming out like a big brass band farting in Arnaud's egg-shaped head. This room is not a good place for hearing the dead."

"I know," Richard said. "It's the cheap paneling. Well, it wasn't all that cheap."

Richard could only guess what Mary wanted to tell him. She must be hanging around because she knew he'd been thinking about Vivian—lustful, lascivious thoughts. She'd read his mind or listened in on his mumblings and learned that he found Vivian attractive. Vivian—not her money. Quite frankly, he didn't need any more money or real estate holdings or stocks in his portfolio than he already had. It was cliché but true: money didn't buy happiness. He had accumulated more wealth in the form of happiness than he ever

thought possible back when he was a medical student, when he and
Mary were newly married.

To help pay their living expenses, Mary, with her degree in
home economics, taught middle school students how to broil
grapefruit and stitch between the wales of corduroy jumpers while
Richard studied full-time. He often asked himself if he had been
born twenty years later and had come of age during the "me"
generation, if he ever could have found a woman as selfless as Mary.

"Arnaud," Richard began. "I want to know what Mary's doing
here, what she wants."

Arnaud wagged a manicured index finger at him. "'You can't
handle the truth,'" he said, in a fey imitation of Jack Nicholson,
cracking himself up. "Isn't Arnaud clever?"

"Be serious a minute," Vivian said, her eyes widening. "Why
couldn't we make an appointment to talk to Mary? Summon her in a
séance."

"We could do that," Arnaud said, his eyes growing as large and
round as Tristan's.

"Let's not get carried away here," Deanna said, scratching
Lohengrin behind the ears. "I'm with Richard. I don't believe in
ghosts. When we die—we die. That's it."

Arnaud sucked in air reactively. "You, you don't believe in
ghosts?"

Deanna shook her head.

"What's not to believe? Mary has some unfinished business with
Richard. Perhaps with the guild," Arnaud explained. "She died
suddenly and didn't have a chance to prepare. Arnaud is guessing
she never had the chance to say goodbye. Eh, Richard?"

Richard lowered his head and rubbed his eyes.

"Are we finished talking about gala ticket sales?" Deanna asked.
"I think these little ones need to be watered."

"Do you want company?" Vivian asked.

"Thanks, but no," Deanna said quickly.

"Where are you taking them?" Richard asked.

"The cemetery down the street," Deanna said.

Richard gulped. Not Henry's Grove? Since Mary died, he'd not heard anyone mention Henry's Grove in such a casual context.

"The dogs love it there," she continued. "Henry's Grove always keeps them busy. They are good and tuckered out after a walk around there. They sniff around all the headstones. Sometimes they even take a—"

"Richard," Vivian said, "I'm not trying to be insensitive, but if you don't mind my asking, why did you bury Mary in Henry's Grove?"

Richard bristled at the question. The room grew quiet, waiting for him to blast Vivian, he supposed. But it was a legitimate question and one, he realized, that people seldom asked. Since Mary died, hardly anyone asked him anything about her. In fact, people went out of their way not to talk about her. He didn't think people were trying to be rude. He guessed that they were trying to be sensitive. But suddenly, he wanted to answer Vivian's question. He wanted to talk and talk and talk about Mary. He wanted to—talk *to* Mary. "She loved the oak trees. Those massive—ha!—stately trees that turned all those rich colors in fall. She wanted to be there. I just don't think she was planning on being there so soon."

"Arnaud has an idea, Richard," Arnaud said, putting the emphasis on the second syllable of Richard's name and softening the "ch" to an "sh." He clapped his hands together, overcome with excitement. "If Mary loved that cemetery as much as you say, we will summon her in the cemetery . . . tonight. After Deanna is done walking the sausage dogs."

"Don't get in the habit of calling them—" Deanna started to say.

"That's the answer—" Vivian started to say.

"Are you serious—" Richard started to say.

"Arnaud requires little for a séance. All Arnaud needs," he said, tilting his head back, as if he were already summoning Mary, "are candles."

Deanna hugged Lohengrin to her chest. "I know we have hurricane candles with the banquet supplies."

"A food offering," Arnaud continued.

Richard reached into the canvas duffle he always carried with him. "I have a double cheeseburger from Bobbin' Robin that I let get cold," he said, before he realized what he was saying. "I'm sorry, Vivian. They do make a juicy burger."

Vivian shook her head. "I understand."

"With extra Frantz ketchup," Richard added, trying to make amends.

"Now, we need a group of participants divisible by three," Arnaud said.

Vivian looked around the room. "We certainly do. There are only four of us."

"Let's grab Oriane and Knobby after rehearsal," Deanna added. "They should be done in ten minutes," she looked at her watch, "give or take a minute."

"You have to have groups of three?" Richard asked, the disbelief apparent in his voice. This adherence to ritual seemed ridiculous.

"That's what the spirits want. If you want them to come through, you give them what they want," Arnaud said with the conviction of Scarlett O'Hara when she yanked the rutabaga out the scorched earth of Tara.

"What else?" Vivian asked. "It seems like we're missing something important."

"Arnaud knows everything you need to make every ghost a happy ghost."

"Happy ghosts?" Richard said because he just couldn't help himself when people said illogical things. "Isn't a ghost by definition unhappy? If it were happy, it wouldn't be a ghost, would it?"

"What are we missing, Arnaud?" Vivian said again.

"Nothing much," Arnaud said. "Only a round table."

Richard shook his head. "Of course. How can you summon spirits from a square table? Oval tables are the real deal breakers, I've heard."

"Don't be cynical," Arnaud warned.

Now that the prospect of contacting Mary seemed within reach, Richard was actually frightened. She might tell him something he couldn't bear to hear, something he'd have to live with the rest of his life. "Forget the whole crazy idea," he blurted out. "It's stupid!"

The dogs whimpered as Richard raised his voice.

"You scared them, you bad boy," Deanna said, trying to calm little Lohengrin.

"Richard," Arnaud said, with his signature pronunciation of his name. "Do you want to talk to Mary or not? She has something to say to you."

"Well—I," Richard began.

"Then shush up!" Arnaud said. "A round table is critical to making the symbolic circle. Now, where can we find a round table?"

"Oh, for God's sake—" Richard said.

"*Ferme ta gueule!*" Arnaud commanded Richard and turned to the rest of the group. "A round table! Who has one?"

"There's a couple in the closet downstairs. Big old wooden ones that we used for the Winter Carnivale," Deanna offered. "We could borrow one of those."

Richard threw his hands up. "What are we going to do? Roll a table out the back door of the opera house—all the way to the cemetery? We'll look ridiculous."

"Everyone in town already thinks you're all cuckoo," Arnaud said, the twinkle returning to his eye.

Deanna lowered Lohengrin to the floor and snapped on his leash. "Vivian, why don't you bring Knobby and Oriane over, and we'll get things set up in a while."

* * *

Her pocketbook stuffed with candles, Deanna led the dogs toward the cemetery, allowing them to stop at every tree and fire hydrant. Behind her, Richard and Arnaud were rolling the table out of the opera house, across Henry Avenue, down the sidewalk, past Hankey Park, headed toward Henry's Grove.

"This looks very suspicious," Richard said, lowering his head behind the table, as the two men plodded along. "Can't you go any faster than that?"

"I can't afford to break a nail," Arnaud said.

Richard exhaled heavily. "Here I thought you had a weak back or something."

"That reminds Arnaud of a joke," he said, stopping to rest. "Arnaud has a weak back."

Richard grabbed Arnaud's arm. "Well, you shouldn't be lifting then."

"It's part of the joke," Arnaud corrected. "Arnaud has a weak back."

Richard did say anything. Arnaud prompted him. "Now you say, 'For how long?'"

"For how long?" Richard asked.

"About a week back." Arnaud burst out laughing. Actually, it was more of a snort. Richard realized he'd never heard Arnaud laugh at himself before. He hoped he'd never hear it again.

Richard glanced up and over his shoulder around to see if anyone was staring at them. He saw Deanna up ahead, squatting down, rubbing the heads of all the dachshunds alternately. She'd sure taken to those dogs quickly, Richard thought. "Arnaud, if you don't want to ruin your *nails*, we can have the séance right here," he said, pointing to a little grove of trees in the park not far from the streetlight.

"It would be much better in the cemetery," Arnaud said. "Especially if Mary liked to walk there."

"She liked the park, too," Richard said. A starless evening in the cemetery, growing darker by the minute. Where drug deals reputedly went down with increasing regularity. "She's probably not as fond of the cemetery now as she used to be."

Arnaud shot Richard an annoyed look. "Do you want this to work or not? "

Richard nodded.

"Just a little further, muscles." Arnaud grabbed hold of his end of the table. "Let's roll," he said followed by a snort. "'Let's roll.' Arnaud is too much."

* * *

Vivian and Oriane waited at the entrance to Knobby's office, their ears pressed up against the door.

"What are they saying?" Oriane whispered.

"I can't quite make it out," Vivian said. "But it's not a pleasant conversation."

"Maestro's been a bear all week," Oriane said. "He and Knobby each have a different vision for the show. Maestro doesn't like any blocking that impedes the singer. I like Knobby's staging better. It's more dramatic. More realistic. Maestro needs to back down. It's Knobby's call. But if you tell either one I said that, I'll deny it."

"Don't worry. All the production details don't interest me. I don't want to be involved in any of that," Vivian said. "But we need Knobby to make the numbers work for the séance. I'll have to interrupt."

Oriane backed away from the door. "Go ahead. Interrupt them then. Maestro hates you anyway." She slid into a shadow down the hall, hiding herself.

"I don't care what Maestro thinks of me. He's a bush-league conductor. Hankey could do much better," Vivian said. "And if you tell him I said that, I'll deny it." She knocked on the door a few times.

Seconds later, Knobby stuck his head out the door. "Maestro and I are in the middle of something. Can it wait?"

Vivian lowered her voice. "Wouldn't you like a break—from whatever's going on with the Teeny Tyrant?"

Knobby fell silent for a moment. "Are you kidding me?" he said with great animation. "Why didn't someone tell me this sooner? Maestro, something's up. Gotta go. We'll finish this discussion tomorrow."

"I prefer to finish it now," Maestro said.

"It'll have to be tomorrow," Knobby said and slipped out into the hall, closing the door behind him.

Vivian took him by the hand and dragged him toward the elevator. Oriane emerged from the shadows just in time to climb on the elevator with them.

"What's up, you two?" Knobby said, rubbing his hands through his hair. "I have a lot to do."

"The spirit world," Vivian explained, "responds to numbers divisible by three."

"The spirit world? What are we—" Knobby began.

"How about a thank you?" Oriane said to Knobby. "For giving you a break from Maestro?"

Knobby leaned back against the side of the elevator car and crossed his arms. "Why do I get the impression you two are up to no good?"

Oriane moved to the other side of the car, as far away from Knobby as she could get. "Because you're making another assumption without asking people what's going on first."

* * *

"Are we allowed to do this? Have a séance in a graveyard?" Richard asked.

They stood under an oak tree, a few feet from Mary's headstone. Suddenly, he felt very uncomfortable. Couldn't they just as easily do this around his dining room table? "Now what?"

"Let's put the table on that tree stump there," Arnaud said. "Just set it on top. No need to open the legs."

He and Richard rolled the table over to the stump and laid it on top. Arnaud repositioned the table, lining up its center until it was directly over the stump.

"How long does the whole thing take?" Deanna asked Arnaud.

"Not long. Mary is dying to come out," he said, wincing at his poor choice of words.

Richard glared at Arnaud over the top of his bifocals.

"While we're waiting for the others, everyone have a seat," Arnaud said.

Richard and Deanna looked quizzically at Arnaud.

"Sit cross legged or on your knees—whatever," Arnaud said. He tapped the center of the table. "Put your food there. Deanna, set out all the candles you have. The spirits love candles."

"I also have a few sticks of Dentyne," Deanna said. "Should I dig those out?"

"Absolutely," Arnaud said. "Who's not up for a nice stick of gum? Especially if you've been dead for a while. Talk about morning breath."

Deanna tied the dogs to the tree, giving each a rub on the head or under the chin. "Be brave, my little babies." She stiffened. "There's someone coming," she said, pointing toward the sound of rustling leaves, her hand shaking. "Is it the spirits—already?"

"It's Vivian, Oriane, and Knobby." Richard cupped his hands over his mouth. "Over here!" he called.

Knobby stopped in front of the table, surveying it. "This is interesting."

"It will be soon," Arnaud said, clapping his hands. "Everyone take a seat."

Knobby took a quick intake of air. "Should we be doing this, folks?"

"That's what I want to know," Richard added.

"Too late," Vivian said, sitting cross-legged by Richard. "We're doing it."

"Do you really need me?" Knobby asked. "If it's as Vivian explained, that Mary's anxious to talk to Richard, couldn't she just as easily talk to five people? Isn't five a supernatural number? What about the pentagram? That's a Wiccan symbol. I have designs to finish. I have to locate some vendors."

"What about *The Five Little Peppers and How They Grew*," Oriane added. "Nothing occult in that story." She turned to Deanna. "Have you read it? It's the cutest book about the Pepper family. They live in a little brown house, and they call their mother 'Mamsie'—"

Arnaud clapped his hands together again—briskly, forcefully. "Know-bee, Oriane. Sit! Shut-up. We must have six people, Know-bee. And for the last time, Arnaud is not communicating with Wiccans! Arnaud is a spiritualist."

"What's going to happen when Mary comes?" Oriane asked. "Should we look down? Look up? Is Mary going to fly by like a character in *The Wizard of Oz*?"

Arnaud huffed. "No, darling. Arnaud is clairaudient. Mary will speak to Arnaud who will relay her thoughts to you. Everyone ready?"

"I watched *The Devil's Daughter* once. Don't we have to sacrifice something?" Oriane asked.

"How about one of the dogs?" Knobby said. "Three is about two dogs too many."

Deanna raised a well-shaped eyebrow. "Over my dead body."

Don't tempt me, Richard thought. Dead bodies. Living sacrifices. Headstones hulking in the distance. A lead-in to an evening news story ran through his head: *Has Rover disappeared recently? Maybe it's because of the Hankey Opera Guild, a secret coven sacrificing your house pets in occult ceremonies in the city cemetery. That scary story, coming up, after this commercial break.*

Arnaud held out his hands on both sides of him. "Join hands. Now, say with Arnaud. Wait! One more thing. Keep the candles burning. You extinguish the light, you drive away the spirits. Okey-dokey? 'Our beloved Mary.'" He noticed he was the only one speaking. "Okay, first time through, just say after Arnaud. Our beloved Mary."

"Our beloved Mary," the rest of the guild said.

Arnaud continued, "We bring you gifts from life into death..."

Richard scratched the scruff on his face, realizing he'd forgotten to shave. Nerves probably. "A bacon cheeseburger's not a proper gift."

"Shush!" Arnaud scolded. "It's the sentiment that matters, not the gift."

Arnaud resumed the chant, talking over everyone. "We bring you gifts from life into death..."

"We bring you gifts from life into death," the others said.

"Commune with us, Mary," Arnaud said, adding, "and move among us."

They repeated the entire chant three times total, in unison.

One of the dachshunds howled. Arnaud shuddered. "She's here. She's saying a lot of things in a rush."

Richard felt an unusually cool blast of air rush across his back. "Mary?' he asked. "Mary, is that you?"

"Richard," Arnaud said but it didn't sound like Arnaud. His back was ramrod straight, as if in a trance. "You monkey face," he said in a cheesy falsetto. "What are you doing here?"

Vivian leaned into Richard. "She's talking through Arnaud. Answer her."

"She never once called me a monkey face," Richard whispered back to Vivian. "It must be someone other than Mary coming through. Someone I don't know. This whole thing is bogus."

Vivian made a face that said, *You're blowing it, buster.*

Richard cleared his throat. "We—we came to see you. To tell you we . . . miss you. I miss you." He stopped and whispered in Vivian's ear. "I can't do this."

Vivian squeezed his hand. "Yes, you can."

"The hospital," Arnaud said. "In the hospital, I never got to say goodbye, honey."

"Arnaud just called me *honey*," he whispered to Vivian.

"Not Arnaud. *Mary.* Answer her."

Is that why she was hanging around? Richard wanted to ask her that. Could he ask it? Richard began, "It's okay, schnookums. I sensed that. That you missed saying goodbye."

"Oh, Don Juan. Beware Don Juan," Arnaud said.

"She means, 'Don Giovanni,'" Deanna said.

"Shhh," Vivian said, scolding Deanna with her finger.

"Don Juan. Don Juan is standing at the top of the mountain," Mary said through Arnaud. "On one side of the mountain is a . . . a big pile of dollar bills. On the other . . . a chicken? I mean a turkey. A big, fat turkey. Keep Don Juan away from the turkey."

"Well, we already knew that," Knobby said.

"Why is Mary talking like she's the Oracle at Delphi or something? Is that sort of thing normal, Vivian?"

"Shhh!" Vivian scolded.

"No chance of a turkey," Knobby said. "Not with me at the helm. Never mounted a turkey yet."

Oriane elbowed him. "Vivian said, 'Shhh!'"

Richard sighed. "It may not be as simple as that."

Arnaud spread his arms out in front of them to silence the group. "You have to teach Don Juan. Teach him . . . teach him. Now, Richard, about the beautiful big blue-green pool. Put on your swimming trunks, and dive headfirst into the pool, the blue-green pool. Dive, man, dive," Arnaud said, sounding like a trailer from *Run Silent, Run Deep* instead of a channeled spirit.

Richard turned to Vivian. "Can you tell her I love her? That I miss her?"

"Tell her. Say it to her," Vivian urged.

"I love you, honey-bunny. I miss you," Richard said to Arnaud.

"It's time to let go," Arnaud said. "Take that big dive in the beautiful blue pool. Oh, and one more thing. Stop with all your cursing. You don't sound hip. You sound like an old fogey."

"That's what I told him," Deanna said.

"Good girl," Arnaud said. He shuddered and began blinking violently. "She is fading, fading . . ." Arnaud stiffened again, his voice returning to his normal register. His hair stood straight up. "Someone . . . someone is pushing, pushing Mary away. Someone is here for Vivian."

"Well, push back, dammit," Richard said. "Don't let her go."

Arnaud's head rocked back and forth, as if someone was shaking him by the shoulders. "She's a nasty one, let me tell you. No, I won't say that," Arnaud said, talking to the new spirit. "You tell her yourself." Arnaud quaked like he'd been stuffed into a Christmas tree shaker. As if possessed, Arnaud said in a woman's register, his voice quavering, "Vivian, you're a greedy, mur-der-ing whore."

"Oh, God!" Vivian cried.

"You killed me . . . you killed your own mother!" Arnaud shrieked. "You fat whore! Vivvy's a fat whore, a fat whore who loves to snore," Paylor sang through Arnaud.

"Stop this, Arnaud!" Richard said. "This is out of hand. Stop this now."

Arnaud's eyes rolled up into his head. His face contorted, like he was taking on yet another personality. *"Fin ch'han dal vino. Calda la testa,"* Arnaud sang menacingly.

"How does Arnaud know 'Fin ch'han dal vino'?" Knobby asked.

"He doesn't," Deanna said. "He doesn't speak Italian."

"Does your mother know 'Fin ch'han dal vino'?" Richard asked Vivian.

Vivian shook her head.

"'Una gran festa. Fa preparar,'" Arnaud continued, now levitating above the table.

"Arnaud can sing Giovanni's 'Champagne Aria?'" Richard asked, taking Vivian's hand, clutching it in his, rising from his feet.

"No. He doesn't know it," Deanna said.

"Who does?" Richard said.

Oriane gasped. "Oh, no! Donato Bianco knows it."

"Oh, God!" Vivian cried.

"Ha, ha, ha, ha!" Arnaud guffawed—a deep gutteral laugh. He hovered four feet in the air. His eyes turned to black holes, as dark as the starless night. "'Teco ancor quella. Cerca menar,'" he roared.

"Help him," Deanna cried. "Vivian, help! Bianco is going to kill him."

"I'm going to kill—all of you!" Arnaud bellowed.

"Arnaud just used the pronoun I," Richard whispered to Vivian. "It can't be him."

"Drop hands—everyone!" Vivian yelled. She scrambled to her feet and blew out all the candles. "This séance is over!"

Arnaud's eyes rolled into his head. His body hung in mid-air momentarily, then came crashing down toward the table. Richard lunged to catch him but only managed to cradle his head. The rest of him landed with a thud.

"Arnaud! Arnaud? Are you okay? Arnaud, come back," Deanna was saying, patting Arnaud's face lightly. "I hope he's not hurt."

Arnaud moaned. His eyelids fluttered. Everyone was focused on Arnaud's regaining consciousness. They hadn't noticed something was different in the middle of the table. The double cheeseburger was gone. All that was left was the wrapper.

23
The Fugue

Guild members sit around the séance table, dazed, waiting expectantly for Arnaud to come around.

"Who d'ya think ate the cheeseburger?" Knobby asked.

"Oh, who cares?" Oriane said, shivering. "All I know is I've never been so scared in my life."

The cemetery was deathly quiet, except for the sound of Deanna patting Arnaud's face. The momentary serenity was broken by a deafening crack.

"Behind you—" Vivian cried. The biggest branch of the oak tree had split off from the trunk and was falling in their direction. "Run!" She shoved Deanna away from the table. Then she grabbed Richard, pulling him and Arnaud away from the path of the tree. A limb at least a foot in diameter slammed into the wooden table, smashing it in two.

Terror-stricken, the dachshund pups yanked free of the tree and tore off through the cemetery grounds, howling, trailing their leashes behind them.

"Is everyone okay?" Knobby called. "Arnaud?"

"Still among the living—barely," Arnaud said weakly.

Deanna wailed, "My babies! Help! Babies, come back."

"Your babies? I thought they were *my* babies," Knobby said.

"I'll help you, Deanna," Oriane said.

"You stay with Arnaud, Oriane," Vivian said.

"Make Knobby stay!" Oriane said. "He can't go sprinting around the cemetery. I can."

Knobby decided to ignore that remark. He knew Oriane was still peeved at him for not getting the role. She'd get over it, in time. Once Giovanni was a hit—and with Vasquez in the title role, it would bring in the box office proceeds they needed—there'd be more productions, more roles in Oriane's future. He'd make sure of that.

"Deanna, are you all right?" Vivian asked.

She was sprawled on the ground, near Mary's headstone, looking dazed. "I'm okay," she said, getting back on her feet. "But Richard might need help getting up."

"Here. Upsie, daisy." Vivian extended her hand to help Richard to his feet. "We have to help Deanna find her dogs."

"We better hurry," Deanna said. "What if they fell into an empty grave and broke their itty-bitty legs?"

"Then we'll hear their itty-bitty yelps," Knobby said. "It'd be best to split up. Deanna and I will go north and east further into the cemetery. Vivian, you and Richard go due east. We may be able to cut them off."

"Oriane, hand me that lamp," Knobby said, pointing to the one lying at her side.

"We're not on stage now, *Herr Direktor*," Oriane said, scooping up the lamp, holding it up toward Knobby, as if it were coated with germs. "You can stop barking out orders any time."

Arnaud hauled his body up off the ground, holding his head. "Wait for Arnaud. We can help, too."

"Are you sure you're up for it, Arnaud?" Deanna asked.

"No sweat," Arnaud said, wincing on the word *sweat*.

"Tristan? Isolde?" Deanna called. She swung her candle left and right. "Lohengrin?"

* * *

"Vivian, wait," Richard called. "I can't see a thing, and you've got the only lamp." He jogged until he caught up with her. Breathing heavily, he slowed his pace to a brisk walk.

"I'm afraid for those dogs," Vivian said.

"That nasty ghost?" Richard asked. "Was that your mother?"

"The correct term is *poltergeist*," Vivian said, holding the light in her left hand.

"Can you shine that over here?" Richard said. "The ground is uneven."

Vivian switched the lamp to her right hand. "Give me your hand, Richard."

Richard slipped Vivian's free hand into his. "You're into all this stuff? But you don't know whether that was your own mother or not?"

He was trying to goad her into a response, but Vivian refused to answer. Her hand trembled. "She didn't send you a secret message that only someone with your special sensitivities could hear?"

The moon was veiled by passing clouds. Another tree limb creaked, and Vivian jumped. "Ahh!" she cried. "I think someone's still trying to do us in."

"You mean, your dead friends didn't tell you they were going to shake that tree limb?"

She yanked her hand free from his. "Oh, for God's sake, Richard. I don't know what goes on in the afterlife. I've never been dead, have you?"

"But you do astral projection."

"I guess that makes me a garden-variety whack job. Maybe I'm more in touch with the universe than you."

"Look, Vivian, I—" He didn't want to alienate her. He needed information from her. He wanted to know if Arnaud was a fraud or a real medium. "Who took that cheeseburger? Did Mary take it?"

"You know, you can be a real ass sometimes," Vivian said.

"Is that the way your mother talked to you?" Richard asked.

"If you must know, yes. My mother was a bitch. A crazy, Class-A bitch," she explained, and as she did, the flame in the lamp wavered.

If Paylor called her daughter names and abused her in life, why would she be any different in death? "Was Arnaud putting us on?"

Vivian groaned. "Does Arnaud seem like the kind of person who'd put you through all of this just to be the center of attention?"

They walked on in silence, the light in the lamp nearly extinguished.

"We'd better leave the park," Vivian said. "We're not going to have light shortly. The moon is determined to hide behind the clouds tonight."

Richard glanced up to the heavens. Even the clouds looked as though they'd been menaced, torn into shreds. Was Mary behind one of them? It occurred to him, that when he was a kid, he used to think dead relatives sat among the clouds.

Vivian trod silently toward the sidewalk flanking the park and into the light of the streetlamp.

"So you think Arnaud is authentic?" Richard asked.

"And you don't?" Vivian said. "He could have been badly hurt tonight. Does he have to die before you'll believe he put you in contact with Mary?"

"He's theatrical. It comes with the territory."

"He was singing in Italian, for heaven's sake," Vivian said. "He's as French as they come."

"You look worried," Richard said, though now that they'd left the cemetery, he himself felt calmer, even relieved. Now he could put that silly séance behind him.

"I am worried. Donato Bianco almost killed us!"

Richard had been consumed thinking about whether he'd heard from Mary. He'd not said a word to Vivian about saving his life. Every time he was around Vivian, his manners seemed to go right in the dumper. "Thank you," he said, taking her hand again.

Vivian scoffed. "For pushing you onto your ass? I wish all of life's problems were solved as quickly and easily."

Dive, man, dive, Arnaud had said. Dive into the beautiful blue-green pool. Now that Richard had taken a few moments to collect himself, he knew what pool Arnaud, make that *Mary*, was talking about. Yet, whenever he got close to Vivian, she'd pushed him away. Should he try—one more time? Lower his guard and tell her what he thought? "Did I ever tell you, you have lovely eyes, Vivian?"

Vivian harrumphed. "Like limpid pools, I suppose."

"You're a lovely woman," he said.

"Richard, stop with all this nonsense," Vivian said. "We definitely have a poltergeist problem. What's to stop my mother or Bianco from sabotaging the show?"

"Why, you are, of course! You'll kick their posteriors during your nightly romp in the spirit world."

"You're funny," Vivian said in a tone of voice indicating he was being tiresome.

Richard released her hand and let his arms fall by his sides. "Are you scared to be involved with someone? Afraid they'll find out your nasty little secret and have you thrown in the slammer? Guess what, Vivian. I already know your nasty little secret."

"We'd better find those little dogs," Vivian said. "Or I won't be able to live with myself."

* * *

"Tristan! Isolde! Lohengrin!" Deanna called. "Oh, heavens. I can't hear them barking. Maybe they're lying dead somewhere," she said, her voice breaking.

"Or maybe they're just not barking," Knobby said.

"But dachshunds bark a lot—whenever they are somewhere unfamiliar. Haven't you noticed? They should be barking."

When Knobby first met Deanna, he thought she might have been one of the hardest-driving women he'd ever encountered. And he'd met a number of Type A females at opera houses around the country. But these dachshunds were turning her into someone he barely recognized. In Deanna, they'd brought out a maternal instinct he'd previously thought to be nonexistent. "You're attached to those dogs."

"I love the fact that they totally depend on me for everything. I just wish they would bark. I want to hear one little yip," Deanna said. "How about you go that way, and I'll go this way?"

"It's pitch black just a few feet away. We can't split up," Knobby said. "We'll find them. Don't worry." He hoped the dogs would soon pop up. Though he needed a break, he still had two hours of work at the opera house before he turned in. Should he bring it up? Funny, the first few weeks they'd worked together, Knobby had avoided talking with her. She seemed softer and more approachable tonight. It was now or never. "Deanna, I'm having a problem...with Maestro."

"What's going on?"

"He has antiquated—stilted ideas about staging opera," Knobby began, his nose wrinkling. Wherever they were in the cemetery, it smelled like mold. No, not mold. Fresh earth. There must be newly dug graves nearby. A few short weeks ago, one of those graves could have been his. He shook, but wasn't cold. "No one can afford to have stars to stand like statues and sing anymore. They'll be laughed off the stage. Skewered by the critics."

"You're the general director," she said. "It's your show."

"Earlier tonight, Maestro said I was ruining his show," he said. "I'm not backing down this time. I just wanted to prepare you because this is devolving into a showdown."

A crack of lightning tore the sky. A thunderous boom followed, and they both jumped.

"That was close," Knobby said. It came out of nowhere, too, he thought, wondering whether dead opera singers could whip up little thunderclaps if it suited them.

"Knobby, you once reminded Richard and me that we didn't hire you to be a yes-man. You were right. Stand your ground with Maestro. We'll support you."

Was this the same woman he'd met six weeks ago? Were three little sausage dogs the catalyst for this reformation? "One more favor to ask. You're adopting the dogs, right?"

"If they're still alive when we find them, you bet your Midwestern ass I am."

* * *

Oriane and Arnaud lagged well behind Deanna and Knobby. Oriane didn't want to be left on her own to navigate a cemetery on a starless night. Besides, she wanted to hang back a little to get to know Arnaud better, to find out more about his gifts. She'd heard of people like Arnaud, who could not only talk with the dead but could put spells on living people. Maybe he could cast a spell on Leandro Vasquez to make him fall in love with her.

"Are you sure you're okay?" she asked.

"Do you mind if Arnaud takes your arm? Séances are draining. Arnaud may fall over."

"You'll crack your head on a grave marker if you do that in this place." She looped his arm through hers. "Hold on. And tell me. When did you realize you had a gift?" They strolled through a section of the cemetery Oriane had never seen before. Or maybe it only looked foreign and menacing to her because of the streaky clouds and the random flashes of heat lightning.

Arnaud pointed ahead to a pinpoint of light barely delineating Knobby and Deanna. "Let's head off in a different direction," he suggested. "No need to retrace their footsteps."

"When did you first realize you were a medium?" Oriane asked.

"Arnaud's grand-mère Mimi contacted him after she passed."

"Mimi as in La Bohème?" Oriane asked brightly.

"Mimi, short for Maria, who was a famous paratrooper in Limoges in World War II."

"Your grandmother was a paratrooper?"

"No, she was a chocolatier. Maria was the name of the paratrooper so admired. Back to Grand-mère. She loved little Arnaud. And after she died, she used to come talk to Arnaud when he was taking his bath."

That was weird, Oriane thought. But maybe they did things differently in France. "Your grandmother spoke with you after she died."

"*Passed on* is the better term," Arnaud corrected. "We call it death, but it's really a passing from this life to another kind of life."

"Did you tell anyone about your gift?" Oriane asked.

"Arnaud told his mère about the visit. But she discounted Arnaud's gift to childish whimsy. Imagine. Arnaud whimsical."

"Can you see into the future, too?" Oriane asked.

"No, darling. That's telepathy. Maybe clairvoyance with some mediums."

"You mean the gift varies?"

"Absolutely. Sometimes Arnaud has the A-game—A for Arnaud. Sometimes the ghosts talk to Arnaud. Sometimes through Arnaud. It depends on whether Arnaud has had escargot or no."

"Snails, huh? Interesting," Oriane said, wondering whether she could develop telepathic gifts if she ate snails. First, she'd have to get past the notion of them slithering down her throat.

"Arnaud is not a psychic. But Arnaud knows a good one if you want to see her. Why are you so interested in your future, if you don't mind Arnaud asking?"

"I guess I wanted to find out what's in the cards for me, romantically." Oriane lowered her voice. "I can't stop thinking about Leandro Vasquez. I want to know if there's going to be anything between us."

"You can't stop thinking about Leandro Vasquez? Arnaud cannot stop thinking about Leandro Vasquez. He is completely smitten with the boy."

"I think I'm going to die if I can't have him," Oriane said.

Arnaud blubbered. "Arnaud will have a heartbreak like the Eiffel Tower crashing to the ground if he can't have him."

Oriane rested her hand on his shoulder then patted it. "I'm not sure if he goes for men, Arnaud."

"Arnaud doesn't care if he goes for hyenas. He makes his heart go thumpity, thump, thump."

"I was going to be a nun. There has to be a good reason I didn't become one—because God has the perfect man lined up for me, the one I'm to love into eternity . . . Leandro Vasquez."

Arnaud whimpered like a heartsick teenager. "But he is Arnaud's for all eternity."

Oriane sighed. "You won't help me then? Some mediums can do spells. Do you do spells?"

"Not officially. But I think I have a spell that may work for you," Arnaud said.

"Let's hear it."

* * *

A crack of lightning lit up the canopy of trees. Thunder rumbled around Deanna and Knobby.

"Do you hear that?" Deanna asked. "It sounded like a whimper. They must be frightened to death, poor little things."

"Follow that whimper," Knobby said.

"Tristan? Isolde? Lohengrin?" Deanna called. "If they don't make it, I'll be heartsick."

"Chin up, Deanna," Knobby said. "We'll find them. Besides if they don't make it, I can tell you on good authority—my own—that dogs do go to heaven."

"Don't say that!" Deanna cried, resuming her litany with more urgency. "Tristan? Isolde? Lohengrin?"

* * *

Oriane was so needy. Conning her was going to be easier than any con Arnaud had ever pulled. "First," Arnaud said. "Take your voodoo doll."

"I'm a good Catholic. I don't have any voodoo dolls," Oriane said.

"Then make one out of old pantyhose and socks. Do you need hose?"

Oriane shrugged. "I think I can scrounge up a pair."

"Just checking," he said. "Draw eyes on it. Maybe a little mouth. Wait." He stopped suddenly. "This spell will only be potent for virgins seeking true love."

"Then I guess it'll work for me," Oriane said.

Fabulous, Arnaud thought. She's eating out of Arnaud's hand. She'll do anything Arnaud tells her to do. "Ah, my virginal friend. You have your little Leandro doll, no?"

"Should I put pants on it?"

"What would the virgin like? Leandro, with or without pants?"

"No pants. Now what?"

If she did what he told her to do, the spell would be twice as potent if the doll had no pants. "First, boil some water and pour it over little Leandro's feet."

Oriane shook her head. "How's that going to make him love me?"

"It will keep him from getting cold feet at the altar!" Ha! Arnaud thought. What a clever little lie. Arnaud was outdoing himself. "Then place Leandro on top of an ice cube tray."

"What does that do?"

"That freezes his sex drive--he loses his interest in all women."

"All women besides me," she added.

"Besides you. *Of course,* my love." Arnaud could barely keep from sniggering. "Then stuff Leandro into a cup of plain yogurt and place him outside on your front stoop for a week."

An odor crossed Oriane's nose—a rotten, sulfurous smell. She wasn't certain whether it was coming from the cemetery or if she imagined it. "Yechh! Why would I want to do that?"

"You want to share a life full of culture with Leandro when you two marry, no?"

She nodded.

She was making this all too easy for Arnaud. Surely, this next step would tip her off, that he was toying with her. If it didn't, then she was absolutely, irrationally in love with him. "The last thing is to rub a can of cat food all over him."

"You're not serious?" she said.

"Would Arnaud kid about love? Arnaud is a Frenchman, *ma cherie.*" And a nasty little devil sometimes. "You rub him with cat food because you want him to crave your musk."

"Women smell like cat food?" Oriane asked.

"Arnaud wouldn't know this personally. It's what he's been told." He shrugged. "You do all those things to your little Leandro doll, and the big, strapping Leandro will react to you in ways you never imagined."

Oriane wrapped her arm around his shoulder and gave him a squeeze. "You'd share that spell with me, even though you're crazy for him, too? You're a true friend."

In the next instant, a candle shone in their faces. "You!" Deanna cried, looking startled.

Oriane shrieked in terror. Arnaud jumped and pulled Oriane to himself in a protective clutch.

"But where are the dogs?" Deanna said. "I heard whimpering."

"Sorry, no dogs," Oriane said. "That was Arnaud."

* * *

As Vivian and Richard reached the crosswalk, the first rain droplets fell. The parking garage sat on the other side of Henry Boulevard.

"Still no dogs," Vivian said. "No sign of anyone else either."

"I'm about ready to give up," Richard said. "The heavens are going to open up any moment."

"You can't, Richard. I won't let you give up."

"I've had it. All that *seancing* . . . is that a word?" Richard asked.

"Sounds good to me," Vivian said.

Richard shook his head. "If it sounds good to you, then it must not be a word. I'm heading back to the garage. Are you coming?"

Wind whipped stray leaves around them, blowing rain showers into their faces. From atop the traffic light on the corner, a neon man flashed white for *walk, walk, walk*. Not much traffic in downtown Hankey. Cruising had been prohibited, but tractor-trailers were a frequent sight after eight o'clock.

Vivian put her arm out in front of Richard to keep him from crossing. "Wait. Do you hear—"

Suddenly, three dachshund puppies dashed by them straight into the avenue, their leashes dragging behind them. Less than a block away, a semi with a dirty white cab was barreling down Henry, which they often did to make up time lost in daytime traffic.

"Get those dogs!" Vivian cried.

Shards of lightning carved up the sky, unleashing a sheet of rain.

"Tristan! Lohengrin!" Richard called through the downpour.

Vivian hurled herself off the curb and stepped on Isolde's wet leash. "Got one!"

Tristan, who was the fastest of the three, already crossed the boulevard and skidded onto the sidewalk, exhausted from his travels.

"Lohengrin!" Richard called. "Lohengrin, come!"

Lohengrin, with his little pot belly, who was the most obedient and the slowest of the three, halted in the middle of the street when Richard called his name. The truck was fast approaching. The driver could barely see past the windshield wipers slapping back and forth through the torrent, let alone spy a little brown dog plopped in the center of the avenue. The truck wasn't stopping for anything or anybody. Richard had a split second to decide what to do. He darted into the street just as the big rig reached the intersection. The driver must have spotted Richard because he braked hard—one of those noisy compression brakes truck drivers weren't supposed to use in Hankey after a noise ordinance went into effect two years ago. Undaunted, Richard scooped up Lohengrin and rolled out of the center of the street as the truck went rumbling by. Before scrambling to his feet, he reached out and grabbed Tristan's leash, which dangled from the curb.

The driver rolled down his window, but Richard waved him on and he glanced across the street. He waved to Vivian, who stood frozen on the sidewalk, clutching Isolde. He checked the dogs, who appeared to be soaked but unharmed, and then at his clothes, which hadn't fared nearly as well. He'd torn his pants at the knee. He must've gotten brush burns on his elbows, too, because they began to sting. But he was okay, the dogs were saved, and Vivian was only drenched. He felt a surge of pride for what he had accomplished at his age, for what he might have sacrificed for those dogs. Richard Rohrer, dermatologist and special ops—canine unit. He'd been a Boy Scout's Boy Scout. Mary would never have cause to kick him in the shins again.

Deanna came running from the park onto the sidewalk with Knobby trailing behind. They'd heard the ripping of the Jake brakes through the night air. Deanna was sopping wet but was uncharacteristically unconcerned for her appearance. Her only worry had been the puppies. She rushed forward to Vivian, who was snuggling Isolde to her chest to comfort her.

"Oh, my heavens, you found her," Deanna cried, taking the dog from Vivian's arms. "Thank you. Thank you."

Knobby gulped. "What happened to the others?" He searched Vivian's face, but Vivian said nothing. Instead, she pointed across the street. Richard was standing in the downpour, waiting for the light to change. Holding both dogs by their leashes in his right hand, he reached up and waved to the guild with his left. It must have been Knobby's imagination or a strange instance of skewed perspective because Richard looked about eight feet tall from where he was standing.

Oriane and Arnaud emerged from the park just as Richard, both dogs trotting beside him, reached Vivian.

"You found them!" Oriane cried, dashing ahead of Arnaud to pet the dogs.

"Thanks to Richard," Deanna said. "They're all okay."

Richard arrived just in time to greet his admiring throng. "They really smell like dogs now—dripping wet." He handed the dogs over to Deanna. "You need to thank Vivian, too, Deanna. Without her encouragement, I would've thrown in the towel. She kept me—us going. Give credit where credit is due."

Vivian shrugged. "I was only thinking of the dogs."

"Speaking of the dogs. I can't manage them for the long haul. Their dander's killing me. But do you mind if I take them with me tonight, Deanna?" Knobby asked. "I have to head back to the opera house. In the event Maestro wants to resume our—conversation, it would be great to have a few short canine buffers."

* * *

Knobby unlocked the front office, flicked on the switch, and let the dogs off their leashes.

"Go play with your toys," he said, pointing to some chew bones in the corner. While the dogs sniffed their rawhide yummies, he uncovered some papers from a stack on the side of his desk. He needed to review the technical director's purchase order based on his approved design. He felt tired out from all the goings-on in the cemetery and decided to work for only one hour—his doctor couldn't argue with that. He'd just settled back in his chair, pen in hand, when Maestro appeared in the doorway. Knobby wasn't surprised he was still around. He hadn't looked like he wanted to finish the discussion at a later time.

"I was waiting for you, Carter," Maestro said.

"Have a seat," Knobby said. Maestro looked angry. It would be best to have him park it for a while. "What did you decide?"

Maestro plopped his plump frame in the chair facing the desk and inhaled sharply. "I decided I wasn't going to let you wreck my *Giovanni*."

Lohengrin began howling. "Come here, little buddy," Knobby said to the dog, scooping him into his lap. "Your *Giovanni*?" Knobby stopped himself from a knee-jerk reaction to the criticism, settling for a response he hoped would facilitate some adult conversation. "What's the stone in your shoe, Maestro?"

"Don't tell me you don't know," Maestro said, the spittle forming on his lips.

Since Knobby didn't have Arnaud's special gifts, he couldn't be sure of what Maestro alluded to. "I don't know what you mean," he said calmly.

Maestro fumed and his mustache twitched atop his upper lip. "You can't have the actors crawling across the stage when they are singing. Or turning their backs, looking away from the conductor. This is my show. You're ruining it."

"You think they can't get their cues unless they sing facing forward?"

"Of course, they can't get their cues. What are you, an imbecile?"

Isolde growled and ran up to the Maestro, grabbed his pant leg in her teeth, and pulled.

"Isolde! Let go." Knobby got up from behind the desk, picked up Isolde and carried her in his other arm. If Tristan began acting out, he'd have a problem. With a dog under each arm, he confronted Maestro's criticism head on. "Giovanni works when the staging—the acting—complements   and   doesn't   detract   from   Mozart's incomparable score. Modern audiences expect more than a concert-in-a-costume."

"You think all that I, Maestro Jan Schantzenbach, can offer the good people of Hankey is a concert-in-a-costume?"

"I didn't say that."

"You did, too, you prig."

Knobby set the dogs down, sneezed, and patted them on their rumps. "I'll have an adult conversation with you. But I won't allow this name-calling. You need to calm down. I've already made some accommodations to address your concerns."

"Won't permit? Who are you to disallow me anything?"

"Okay, Maestro, you want to pull rank? Chew on this," Knobby said, walking straight toward Maestro, speaking directly into his face. "I'm the general director. I have the power to hire and fire around here. I can even fire *you*. And I might, if you don't shut up and listen to me for a minute."

"You don't have to fire me," Maestro said. "I quit."

"Fine." Knobby walked back to his desk and picked up his Rolodex. "I know at least ten other conductors with better reputations than you who could do this show. Who would do it—on a moment's notice. I have their contact information right here. Don't let the door hit you on the way out."

Maestro's eyebrows arched into their trademark diabolical vees. "You wouldn't dare."

Knobby picked up the phone and dialed one of the numbers on the card. "Sylvia? Carter Knoblauch here. Sorry to be calling so late. I may have a—"

"Put down the phone," Maestro interrupted. "Put it down."

"I have a conducting gig," Knobby continued, "opening up here in Pennsylvania shortly."

Maestro reached in and yanked the phone from Knobby. "No, he doesn't," he said into the phone and returned the receiver to the cradle.

"Don't ever interrupt one of my phone calls again, Maestro," Knobby said, his face assuming the closest thing to a snarl that he could muster. "Or I promise you, I'll fire you."

Maestro cleared his throat. "I'm listening," he said, which Knobby knew was as close to Maestro's carrying his tail between his legs as he could hope for.

Knobby, realizing he'd won, looked up, and collected his thoughts. "I'm having monitors placed around the stage in locations unseen by the audience—offstage right, offstage left, to the right and left above the apron. I'm even having one placed in the Commendatore's headstone in the graveyard scene and in the floor.

In the height of a dramatic moment, the singer doesn't have to break the tension and turn to the conductor for his or her cue. They'll see you cueing up the number in the monitor. They have to be able to get their music cues or the show falls apart."

"Well—I—certainly—I, " Maestro stammered.

"I don't know who you've worked with in the past, but they haven't done right by your orchestra," Knobby said. Tristan came over and whimpered until Knobby picked him up and set him in his lap. "They're a gifted bunch. All the elements of this show have to work together. Nothing, and I mean nothing, can get in the way of Mozart's music."

Maestro exhaled slowly and rose to his feet. "I'm glad you see it my way, Carter."

"Righto," Knobby said, adding, "Have a fantastic evening," closing his lips around a no-tooth smile, which was the best he could muster under the circumstances. Knobby watched him parade back out the door. What a horse's rear end, he thought, setting Tristan down, urging him to go play with the other pups, then picking up his papers and diving back into his work.

24
The Comprimario

The first rehearsal period for all principals has arrived. All the singers—Leporello, Elvira, Donna Anna, Don Ottavio, and Zerlina, have been logged in by the stage manager—everyone except Leandro Vasquez.

Vasquez had better arrive at the opera house any minute, or he was in violation of his contract—Know-bee had told him as much. Regardless, Arnaud could barely contain himself—and even he had to admit there wasn't much to contain. He was five and a half feet tall and one hundred forty-five pounds soaked to the skin. The evening before, he'd barely slept, trying to come up with a plan to win over Vasquez. Ultimately, he decided to ingratiate himself—to earn his confidence—and maybe, he'd be rewarded with something more, if the young and virile Vasquez had had enough of the temperamental iron maidens of the opera world. Arnaud had tempted more than a few men to the other side with his charm and pluck. Plus, Arnaud was neat, caring, and resourceful, with the ability to set a beautiful table on a shoestring budget. How many men could do that?

"He's coming," Oriane yelled from the street where'd she'd been waiting. She, too, could barely rein in her fervor about Leandro's returning to Hankey. Oriane was a vision today. She'd put one of those "bump-its" in her hair and her new layered cut cascaded around her shoulders. She had French manicured fingers and toenails, no small expense. She had the cutest big belt cinching her shirt dress, which emphasized her boobs and her hips. So, where'd she get the fashion sense in a hurry?

"I see Vivian's limousine now," she cried.

Arnaud smiled. Despite Oriane's fetching appearance, he wasn't at all worried. If Oriane had tortured her voodoo doll in the way he suggested in the cemetery, he wouldn't have to worry about any competition from her for Leandro's affection. He felt the heat of unchecked lust rising into his face. Fantasies about seducing Leandro filled his musings by day and his dreams at night. When Arnaud made up his mind about something, there was no dissuading him from it. Now, to determine what other things Arnaud had access to that Vasquez wanted or needed, then he'd have the Lion Man nibbling out of the palm of his manicured hand.

The heavy backstage door flew open and in strode Vasquez—a commanding specimen of manhood compared to the germ-laden creature appearing at the Martini Masque. A raw sexual intensity, fueled by his critical and artistic success in New York, filled his aura, which glowed as red as the neon sign above the Steel City Diner. He took Oriane's hand and kissed it. "You—are a dream. My dream," he said, his eyes undressing her.

Oriane looked ready to faint.

Overcome by Leandro's animal attraction, Arnaud felt his knees buckle. He steadied himself against the wall. Then he approached Oriane and pushed her aside so he stood right in front of Leandro. "Señor Vasquez!" Arnaud called out, extending his hand. "Welcome to Hankey."

Vasquez wrapped his strong hands around Arnaud's. "Eh," he said, smiling warmly "Leandro—you call me."

"Leandro," Arnaud said, the word tumbling from his lips like rose petals falling onto a gently rushing creek—sweet and soft, scented for love. "You've had a long trip. Arnaud can get you an Evian, some chocolates, a glass of peach tea?"

"Who is Arnaud? You—get a me," Vasquez said. He let go of Arnaud's hands and reached up to remove his Oakley sunglasses.

"But—" Arnaud cleared his throat. He wasn't sure he could do it. He hadn't used first-person pronoun in a very long time, it seemed like a something in a foreign language. "But. I. Am. Arnaud."

"A why you—no say so?" Vasquez chuckled. "Water for—
Leandro."

When Arnaud returned with a bottle of Evian, Oriane was
already introducing him to the cast, who had encircled him on stage
like groupies. That bitch! But Vasquez was a star—a big star in an
ever-widening firmament—of which Hankey was merely a speck,
barely a dot. Vasquez had hit a home run in the beautiful Big Apple.
No longer an up-and-comer, Leandro Vasquez now traveled in a
hansom—make that a *handsome* cab.

Arnaud squeezed past Oriane and stood between the two divas
hired to sing Zerlina and Elvira, Porky and Twiggy, respectively,
now peppering Vasquez with questions from either side. Arnaud
reached out and placed the bottle of water in his hands. "Here—
Leandro," he said, smiling sweetly, making as big a deal as possible
over the fact that he and Vasquez were on a first-name basis.

"Arnaud—too kind," Vasquez said, ignoring Arnaud and
returning his attention to Miss Fat and Mademoiselle Slim. He took
each of them by the hand, one at a time, and bowed gallantly, kissing
their hands when he reached the lowest point in the bow. Disgusting.
If Leandro and Porky were in bed together and she rolled over, she'd
crush him until he was flat as a crepe. Arnaud watched Leandro
making goo-goo eyes at both of these Grade B vixens. What could he
possibly see in such a big bruiser of a woman or a little toothpick-girl
so brittle even Arnaud could snap her like a twig.

Arnaud's heart plummeted into his toes. While scratching his
egg-shaped head, he glanced over at Oriane, who now languished
among the rest of the women in the chorus, a half step behind the
principals. She wriggled her index finger at him to wave him over.

"Thanks for pushing me out of the way," Oriane said. "If I didn't
know better, I'd think you didn't want Leandro and me to be an
item."

Arnaud shrugged. "Arnaud meant nothing by it. He simply
wanted to give Leandro his water."

Oriane rolled her eyes. "Look at that *thing* they hired to sing
Zerlina," she whispered. "She's a house. A house with big, sagging
udders."

Arnaud sighed. "He called Arnaud—Arnaud."

"Did you *hear* me?" she snapped. "How can they sick that house on Leandro? My Leandro."

Arnaud clasped her hand in his and squeezed. "Not to worry. Arnaud has a plan to oust the house cow. Did you make your voodoo doll?"

Oriane nodded, and Arnaud squeezed her hand. "But I haven't had time to do the spell yet."

"You better get cracking, you!" Arnaud said. "This is the greatest chance of your life."

"Okay, folks," Knobby was saying. "Let's start blocking the crowd scene in Act I. Giovanni's 'Champagne Aria.'"

Arnaud waved goodbye to Oriane. While trotting his well-creased and tight-fitting chinos past the orchestra pit, just for fun, he winked at Maestro. Maestro winked back. Now, there was a surprise. Suddenly, Arnaud's world brimmed with romantic possibilities. He slid into the third row. Vivian slipped into the seat to his right. A few seconds later, Deanna joined them.

"I thought I'd hang around a bit, to see how good Vasquez really is when he's healthy," Vivian said.

Maestro cued up the orchestra. Notes as rounded and robust as French red wine poured from the prized baritone. "*Fin ch'han dal vino. . .*"

"That's the same aria the ghost sang," Vivian said.

"Yes, it is," Deanna said. "You sang that, Arnaud, when you were channeling Bianco."

"Impossible," he said. "Arnaud is tone deaf."

"You sang that well, and you can't sing? Incredible," Vivian said. "Speaking of incredible, listen to Vasquez!"

"Considering he's only marking the songs, yes." Deanna laid her arm on the upholstered rest. "I can't wait to hear him in full voice."

"I'm going to close my eyes and listen to the voice of the gods," Vivian said.

"Close your eyes? And miss the best part?" Arnaud said, which made the other two women laugh.

"Stop, people!" Knobby said, taking Vasquez aside. "As each woman in the scene comes near you, Vasquez, make sure you reach out and touch her. Her hands, her hair. You could pat one or two on the rump. Okay?"

"Is natural—for me," Vasquez said, grinning.

The number resumed with Giovanni's second stanza. Chorus members as country folk filed past the proper gentleman of Seville. Anyone could see that Leandro's attention lingered on Oriane. Lucky little girl. She needn't have been jealous of Porky or Twiggy. Even to Arnaud, it was obvious that Leandro had nothing more than an iota of sexual interest in either. His greatest competition for Leandro's affection might come from Oriane. How in the world would he handle that little challenge if Oriane didn't follow through on the spell to make Leandro despise her?

* * *

After rehearsal, Vivian stopped by all the star dressing rooms, to make sure Vasquez and the other principals had everything they needed. She knocked on Leandro's door. "Mr. Vasquez?"

He opened the door, wearing a towel around his mid-section and nothing else. Vivian gulped. "You're not dressed? I'll come—"

"Bibian! Come in," he said, pulling her into the middle of the room. He closed and locked the door behind him. Then he dropped his towel.

Holy ghost, he was hung like a *caballo*, she thought. And I'm trapped. Trapped like a lost calf facing a starved mountain lion in the Argentine outback. "Mr. Vasquez, you have the wrong idea about me—" she began to say but before she could finish, he swept her into a passionate embrace. His mouth covered hers.

"I dream—about you. No one—but a you—Bibian," he whispered in her ear, dipping her backwards until her back touched the carpet.

She reached around until she found the bath towel he'd let fall earlier, grabbed hold of it good, and shoved it in his face. "You lost your towel," she said, using the few seconds' purchase she'd given herself to hurry out the door. She was halfway down the hall before Vasquez's door flew open.

"Bibian," he cried with his head sticking outside the door, sounding more needy than Marlon Brando playing Stanley Kowalski. "Come a back!"

She kept barreling down the hall and straight into Arnaud.

"Hey, watch where you're going," he said.

"Arnaud? Look," Vivian said breathlessly. "I'm going to tell my driver you'll be accompanying Vasquez back to the carriage house." Vivian clutched her hand to her chest. "I'll ask Richard to drive me home. Our Lion Man is an untamed beast."

Arnaud rubbed his hands together. "Grr-oww-wlll!" As he was profusely thanking Vivian for the chance to help out, he saw Deanna entering Leandro's dressing room.

* * *

"Knobby said you wanted to see me—" Less than two feet into Vasquez's dressing room, Deanna came to a complete stop. She gasped. "You're naked!"

"No naked. Ready—*dulce*," he said moving toward her.

It had been a long time since she'd been around a naked man who was completely comfortable wearing nothing but his own skin. Either that, or it had been a long time since she'd been around a naked man. She found herself breathless. "Stop!" she commanded. "Don't come any further."

"You come a—see me—a no?"

"A—yes. But not like this," she said, covering her eyes. "Knobby said you needed something."

"You—I need. Sexy—a beautiful—woman," he said.

Interesting. He'd learned the word *sexy* since the last time he was in Hankey. It wasn't as though she hadn't fantasized about making love to this man. But now that she was in his dressing room, something didn't feel right about him standing there, his naked manhood waiting to take her. She wanted to feel desirable in his presence. But mostly, she felt like a piece of meat. On a hook. Hanging in a stinking refrigerator. At a Hankey meat-packing plant.

"If there's nothing else you want, we're finished here," she said, backing up to leave.

He threw his hands in the air—in desperation—and cried, "*La razón por la que.*"

"*No hablas Españolay,*" she said, and slipped out the door, banging Arnaud in the head with it as she exited.

"Ouch!" Arnaud cried, reaching for his nose.

"Sorry! He's all yours, honey," Deanna said, with a wave of her hand towards the big yellow star painted in the middle of Leandro Vasquez's dressing room door.

Deanna took out her cell phone and punched in Richard's number. Not available. She'd have to leave a message. "Richard, we have some damage control issues with the Lion Man that we should address sooner rather than later. Can everyone meet tomorrow at the Steel City Diner? You tell Vivian. I'll phone the others."

* * *

After rehearsal, Arnaud and Leandro rode to the carriage house in Vivian's limousine. During the ride, he offered his services as a personal valet for the duration of his stay at Frantzland since Vivian had informed Arnaud she had neither the will nor the temperament to "wait on Vasquez."

With the help of the driver, Arnaud unloaded Leandro's luggage. He dug down, mustered up some butch, and followed him inside, dragging an overstuffed rolling tote behind him. He set it by the door and was returning to the driveway for another piece when Leandro called him in.

"Come here," Leandro waved him into the living area and motioned for him to sit down. "You play Leporello, eh?"

Arnaud recognized the name as a character from *Don Giovanni*. "Oh, no indeedy. Arnaud can't sing a note, sweetie."

Leandro shook his head. "You *my* Leporello," he said, patting his chest. "Help Leandro—with women—this a week. Oriane, Bibian, Deanna. I love—all a them."

Arnaud didn't know what Leandro wanted him to do. Play pimp for him? Of course, Arnaud had no objections to the assignment, nor to the fashion statement such a role would entail. Arnaud knew he'd look delectable in leopard skin and a fuzzy feathered fedora. But what about his own quest for romance? He had to do Leandro's bidding. He had to do that much to earn his trust and ultimately, his affection.

Leandro rose from the love seat and wandered into the kitchen. "I want a—write letter—to each. Love letter. You write!" he instructed Arnaud.

"Arnaud is not the greatest speller. He always got C's in penmanship."

"You write—tonight. Give a them." Leandro opened the refrigerator and surveyed the shelves. Fully stocked—Arnaud had seen to that. Leandro grabbed a beer and cracked it open. "Beer?" he called to Arnaud.

As good as beer looked tumbling into a glass, Arnaud couldn't stand the taste of it. "Thank you, no. But Arnaud could go for one of those nifty little wine coolers."

Leandro shrugged, apparently not understanding what Arnaud meant by *wine cooler*.

"Arnaud will get for himself. Have a seat. Relax, sweetie," he said, pointing to the love seat. "Look," he said, demonstrating the recliner feature on an upholstered chair.

Leandro chuckled and seated himself, raising his feet with the handle, beaming. "Bibian—a goddess." He groaned. "So hungry."

"Oh, goody!" Arnaud said, setting his wine cooler on the counter. He reached down and lifted up a large wicker basket filled with delicacies he'd gone to a lot of trouble to assemble. "Here's dinner. Baked chicken, salad, homemade rolls, a lovely berry trifle for dessert."

"Ah—hungry—for love," Leandro said. "No *ensalada*."

"If you don't put any gas in your tank, Lion Man," Arnaud said, "your engine won't purr."

It was dark outside the carriage house by the time they finished dinner. Leandro had knocked back three beers. Even though his face was too rosy, almost bloated looking, Arnaud thought he was the most handsome man he'd ever been with—hoped to be with.

"I learn—from opera," Leandro said, popping the top on another beer. "I visit—women—in the night."

Well, you should try men sometime, Arnaud thought. We're lots of fun and loads more simpatico.

"Bibian—I want," Leandro continued. Though he was deadly serious, Arnaud had to stifle a laugh. Arnaud had to get a hold of himself, or he'd forfeit all the trust he'd earned as Leandro's valet and dinner companion. Just as he suspected, Leandro wanted to visit Vivian. Nothing mysterious there. It was her big, fat hooters.

"Vivian hides a key under the back doormat," Arnaud said.

Leandro shook his head. "No key. Climb," he said, making the motions of someone ascending a ladder. "*Romántica*, eh?"

"*Romántica*," Arnaud parroted. Wasn't there a trellis beneath one of the bedroom windows? Holy ghost of Saint Joan. He'd struck upon the perfect plan for the luscious Lion Man. "Leandro, come with me." He extended his hand, but Leandro pushed it aside and followed him to the front door of the carriage house. They stepped outside. Excitedly, Arnaud pointed to the south side of the house, which had a sturdy trellis leaning against it, leading up to a balcony. He pointed to the second floor. "Your Vivian awaits."

"Ahh," Leandro said. "*Perfecto*. I climb tonight."

Arnaud yawned. "Almost time for Arnaud to go nighty-night. Arnaud could stay, Leandro, to make sure you have everything you need, and Arnaud does mean *everything*," he said.

Leandro waved him away.

No time for Arnaud, huh? "Don't forget!" he said, pointing to the bedroom on the south wall though Vivian told him that one was strictly for guests. "That's Vivian's room—right there. She told me she'd be waiting for you—tonight." He lied. He didn't know who'd be sleeping there tonight. But it wouldn't be Vivian.

* * *

In the Frantz mansion, in the study, Vivian and Richard shared a split of port.

"I appreciate your bringing me home," she said, thinking to herself how calm and peaceful Frantzland was in the evenings, now that her mother was gone.

"If you weren't comfortable riding home with Vasquez," Richard said, "I'm happy to help."

But she couldn't bring herself to tell him the reason she'd wanted to ride home with Richard. And why not? Would Richard have been so obliging had she told him Vasquez dispensed with his bath towel when she dropped by to inspect his dressing room? Did Mary have to put up with these kinds of shenanigans when she did hospitality? Vivian had earned the license to discuss it as a business matter by virtue of her volunteer position—and not just because it was a personal concern.

"What do you think of our Lion Man?" Richard asked.

Vivian swallowed a sip of port. "Wh—what do I think?"

"Weren't you sitting in on rehearsal today?" he asked gruffly. "Is he going to blow people's minds in this town?"

Oh, he'll have something blown if he keeps dropping his towel. "Of course, Vasquez is captivating," Vivian said. "He'll sell tickets once people hear him. Never mind hear. Once they see him. Do you think we've done everything possible to ensure opening night is a packed house?"

"I'll have Knobby send out his picture to all the online subscribers. You know, one of those fancy emails with the fonts and the colors—that's at least thirty or forty more touches. We'll keep reservations for the gala open until Wednesday morning. That will help, too," Richard said.

"All women have to do is see him, and they're in love with him," she said.

"And how about you? Are you being won over by the dashing and handsome Vasquez?"

"Hardly," she said, tipping her glass to ninety degrees to finish the port. "It takes more than a beautiful face to turn my head," she said, thinking, or a big phallus, especially if the man was acting like a big phallus.

Richard set his drink on the sideboard. "Vivian," he began. "I know I haven't always treated you as well as I should have. You deserved much more than what I dished out when you first joined the guild."

"You mean, like a month and a half ago, when we visited Knobby in the hospital?" Vivian said. "And you behaved like a brute?"

"Let's forget that for the moment. Can we?"

Vivian bit her lip, not ready to let go that he had humiliated her several times.

"I sent those flowers," Richard said.

"What flowers?"

"The bouquet of lavender and nasturtiums. I sent them. Not Knobby."

Vivian huffed. "Why did you let me go on thinking they were from Knobby?"

"Because the flowers weren't about me. They were about you—and for you."

"It would have been nice to know you were making a gesture of conciliation."

"It wasn't a gesture of conciliation," he said, then pursing his lips and falling silent. "I had nothing to make amends for."

"Okay, fine then," she said.

God, he was infuriating. She noticed Richard reaching for his neck. One of his phantom irritations. Or was it Mary prodding him? His decidedly orange aura had taken on a yellowish cast. He was trying to open up about something. Should she mention it? No, she'd merely distract him, and he'd go off on some New-Age-beliefs-are-bunk tangent.

"I was—I *am* apologizing for behaving badly," he said.

"Apology accepted," she said, adding, "I'm not a grudge holder," though as she said it, she wasn't convinced of the claim herself. No, she wasn't a grudge holder. She was scared to become close to someone—emotionally. Nothing good had ever come of any of her romantic entanglements. "Can we move on?"

"In a minute. I have something else I want to say. I know this might seem out of the blue," Richard said. He fell silent a moment. "I think about you—all the time. You're bright, energetic, passionate, funny—"

Vivian bristled. "I'm funny? No one's ever said that before."

"No, I didn't mean funny. That was the port talking. I meant to say laughable. No, I mean, lovable."

"I think laughable is more like it," Vivian said, laughing herself. "Certainly not lovable. Most people find me insufferable."

"You can be insufferable, God knows. But let me—finish," he said gently. "For many reasons that I'm bad at articulating, including the fact that it takes more than a handsome face to turn your head, I've taken a shine to you, Vivian Pirelli. I'd just love to walk into a crowded room with you by my side." He turned to face her. "Would you be my date on opening night—to the show and to the gala?"

Voice shaking, she said, "That's kind of you to ask. I'll have to—" She stopped. It was time to lower the shield and lose the breastplate. "I'll definitely be your date."

A smile swept across his face. "This calls for another drink." He scooped up her snifter and his, walked over to the desk and poured them more port. He handed Vivian her glass and raised his. "To opening night," he said, then he tossed back the wine in his glass in two swallows. "And if it's not a whopping success, at least I'll turn heads at the gala with you on my arm." As he headed to the desk for a refill, he staggered a bit.

"Are you sober?" Vivian asked.

"Whoa!" he said, adding, "I've. Had. Enough," trying hard not to slur his words.

"I'm ready to retire," Vivian said, setting her glass aside. "Maybe you shouldn't drive home. I can have my driver take you."

"No, no. He's probably retired for the evening."

"Maybe you should spend the night," she said.

Richard wobbled as he made a sorry plea for his sobriety, then acquiesced. "Perhaps I could—that is—if I wouldn't be imposing."

"You can stay in the guest room. Top of the stairs, the first door on the right." She crossed to him, kissing him on the cheek. "Thank you, Richard, for asking me to the show."

"And the gala," he said.

"And the gala. You really can be sweet, you know. See you in the morning."

* * *

Richard had a date for the gala. Well, golly be. He'd wanted to skip up the stairs but because his current state approached inebriation, his light-footedness could only be realized as a stumble up the stairs. When he reached the guest room, he felt his way into the bathroom since he hadn't been able to find the light switch on any wall. His arm raked the wall of the bathroom until he found the light and flipped it on. He closed the door—he had to take a leak. After he finished, he shook himself off and stared at his reflection in the bathroom mirror. He looked bleary-eyed. In the future, he'd try not to drink too much around Vivian. He didn't want to turn her off just as she was getting interested in him. Why, he hadn't gotten lucky yet. Maybe on opening night. If the show and the gala were wildly successful, Vivian might be willing to engage in a little hanky-panky—Hankey style. He could feel himself hardening at the mere thought of spending the night with Vivian. She was a beautiful woman with big beautiful eyes, creamy skin, and full breasts. No pajamas tonight. He'd sleep in the buff, something he'd always wanted to do, but that Mary never allowed. She'd always said she hadn't wanted to wake up to his waggler. Ha! His waggler.

So, he'd enjoy the freedom of sleeping nude. Everything was easier that way. That is, if Vivian realized she wasn't as tired as she thought and stole into his bed. He could only hope.

* * *

Vasquez threw open the window to the bedroom, surprised that it had been left unlocked and that he hadn't triggered the security system. Perhaps it was only in New York where people were obsessed with locks and guns and law and order. He saw light streaming from underneath the bathroom door. He stripped down to his birthday suit, his manhood already rock hard at the prospect of fondling Vivian's generous breasts. He crawled under the covers, raising them over his head, waiting to surprise her. He had come to Hankey to bring back the panky. Which is just what he intended to do—one beautiful guild member at a time—starting tonight.

* * *

Richard pushed the door to the bathroom open a crack. He'd leave the light on since he couldn't find the switch in the bedroom and would need to get up to go to the bathroom at some time during the night. Well, at least he wouldn't be wrestling with pajamas in the dark.

* * *

Vasquez heard someone heading toward the bed. Wouldn't Vivian be pleasantly surprised to find him, the Lion Man, waiting for her, waiting to take those pendulous breasts and suckle them like a calf to its loving mother?

* * *

Richard thought he saw the outline of someone already in the bed. Vivian had directed him to the guest room—knowing she'd be the evening's special guest. What a woman! How about that Vivian, showing her lusty side. She had the right color hair after all. He might be a little intoxicated, but by God, he could still get it up if he had to. Even at eleven o'clock at night. He lifted the covers and climbed in, hoping to cop a feel.

* * *

Vasquez felt a pair of hands reach out and grab hold of one his nipples.

"¡Ay de mí!" he cried, leaping out of the bed.

Richard threw the covers back. In the moonlight, he could just make out a man's shape. A man who was muscular and well-proportioned and spoke Spanish. Vasquez? What the hell was—"For chrissakes, Vasquez!" Richard hollered. He stared him up and down. "What the hell are you doing here, dressed like—not dressed. Explain yourself."

Vasquez grabbed the blanket off the bed and covered himself. "What you do—a here?"

"What I do—a here?" Richard mocked. "What you do—a here."

Just then, Vivian entered the guest bedroom. "What's going on in here?" she cried.

Vasquez dropped the blanket and sprinted for the window, throwing it open and hauling his bare ass back down the trellis until he was safely back in the carriage house. From the front window, he saw two shapes illuminated by the moonlight—Richard, and Vivian—hands flying left and right, like they were arguing.

He went barreling into the kitchen, throwing open the refrigerator and every last cupboard, desperately searching for something stronger than beer to swill. Not seeing anything, he uncapped a cold one and downed it in two gulps. Then he headed for the shower, locked the bathroom turned on the water, and letting the water's warmth trickle across his skin, allowing the steam soothe him into oblivion, until he no longer heard the persistent pounding on the front door of the carriage house. Arnaud! He'd set him up for that shameful episode. Tomorrow, once he found Arnaud, he would grab him by the nuts and twist hard, until each one fell off. Kerplunk. Kerplunk. Just like he used to do with his cattle.

* * *

Richard grabbed a bed linen and wrapped it around his waist like a sarong. "So, that's why Vasquez is staying in the carriage house. Looking for some *night moves*, huh?"

Vivian huffed. "I offered because I was trying to save the guild the expense of a hotel room."

"'It takes more than a beautiful face to turn my head,'" Richard said in a falsetto voice, mocking her earlier declaration. "And to think I believed you."

"Don't believe me then. Believe what you want," Vivian said. "You will anyway. Goodnight, Richard. You're not fit to drive, so I don't care if you stay here for the night. But it will be the last time you stay under this roof." Vivian turned on her heel and left, without waiting for a response, slamming his door behind her.

"'Believe what you want,'" Richard whined in imitation of Vivian, crawling back into bed. "'You will anyway.'" Now that he'd seen another man's goods, this was the first time he'd ever found himself lacking by comparison in more years than he could remember. It wasn't a feeling he wanted to have again anytime soon.

25
The Pedal Point

The next day, Richard heads to the Steel City Diner for the breakfast meeting of the guild. Since he's the first to arrive, he obtains a big table, since Deanna is expecting everyone to show.

Richard looked at his watch. Quarter to nine, and Vivian still hadn't arrived. He'd snuck out of her house before she arose, returning home to shower and shave. He'd left a note on the kitchen table, saying where and when they'd be meeting for breakfast. Would she bring Leandro? He hoped not. Then they couldn't talk about him.

There was no other reason Leandro would have climbed that trellis but to slip into bed with Vivian. Maybe she was telling the truth, that she hadn't invited him into her home. But it was obvious, he wanted her. In which case, she was as good as lost to Richard. While he was quietly inviting her on dates, Vasquez would make irresistible declarations of undying love. And how could a Pennsylvania Dutchman like Richard possibly compete with a Latin lover like Vasquez?

Leandro had been in town less than a day and was already turning things and people inside out. Women swooned at rehearsal. Patrons waited at the stage door just to watch him leave the opera house. Richard had no overall objection to the extraordinary buzz Vasquez created as long as ticket sales remained brisk. No, it was only the specific concern of his making a play for Vivian on his mind. Obviously, Deanna had gotten herself into a lather for other reasons.

The waitress returned with the coffee pot. "Still waiting?"

"Give me a warm up, Arlene," Richard said, thinking that Arlene had worked at that diner as long as he and Mary had been married. In all the years he and Mary volunteered for the guild, Arlene had never seen an opera. A man like Vasquez could change that. His movie star looks and animal magnetism had the potential to attract a new breed of operagoer—women who watch soap operas. "They'll be along soon. Go ahead and put in an order for a Belgian waffle—with whipped cream. Tell me," he said, pulling a poster with Vasquez's picture on it from his briefcase, and shoving it at Arlene. "Would you come to the opera house to see this man on stage?"

"He's a hottie," Arlene said. "He's in one of your shows?"

"He's starring in our newest production, *Don Giovanni*. Opening Thursday."

She tucked the picture in her apron. "I need to show this to the other girls. He's better looking than the guys in our story."

"Your story?" Richard asked.

"You know, 'One Life to Live,'" she said, and hurried toward the counter. "I'm sure that was Mary's favorite story, too."

Not possible, Richard thought. Mary never went for pap like that. She rarely watched TV, and only PBS when she did.

As Richard brought the cup to his lips, he looked up over the rim and saw Oriane strolling past the counter. He raised his free hand and waved. Deanna and Arnaud were right behind her. Still no Vivian. Surely she'd gotten his note by now. Maybe she'd gotten mugged or carjacked. Even though it was daytime, the Steel City neighborhood was a heaving carcass of abandoned buildings now being used as crack houses and by homeless squatters. Couldn't be too careful in "Rust City" these days.

"Here we are!" Oriane said, looking ravishing in a buttercup yellow dress Richard had never seen before. "Tee minus five days until opening." She slid into the seat opposite Richard and flashed him a generous smile.

Richard was pleased with Oriane's appearance. Especially glad that she wasn't moping around about not singing Zerlina anymore. Had she had her teeth whitened? Had she'd finally gotten laid by none other than the oversexed Argentine? Just when Vasquez had fitted Oriane into last evening's schedule, he didn't want to know.

"Good morning, Dr. Rohrer," Deanna said, taking the seat beside him. Deanna only called him Dr. Rohrer when she was in an extremely good mood or was being sarcastic. He heard no sarcasm in the delivery. She, too, looked lovely this morning. Her complexion was less splotchy, her skin tone brighter. She even seemed about five pounds thinner—perhaps from all the walking she'd been doing, watering and exercising Knobby's pups. He heard of therapy dogs but never thought dachshunds were one of the breeds used for this purpose. No, it had to be something else giving her that spring in her instep.

Could Deanna be in love? In lust? He would know if she'd been seeing someone. Was she seeing Vasquez on the sly? Was Oriane? Were all these women being serviced by the Lion Man?

Vasquez had only been in Hankey nineteen hours. Then again, Richard once heard Pavarotti say that sex, like vocal exercises, was good for the voice, and that's why he "exercised" every day. Was Vasquez going to exercise all the ladies of the guild? Or maybe he'd already begun—with Vivian? Richard hated feeling consumed with doubt and envy. He decided, right then and there, that he hated single life, and that things would change. Or he wasn't Richard Rohrer, dermatologist, champion of failing opera companies, and savior of sausage dogs.

Deanna leaned in and kissed him on the cheek. Her perfume smelled spicy—expensive.

"Ladies, you all look fetching," Richard said.

Arnaud swept into the room, removing a beret from his head. "Is Arnaud not a vision?"

"More like a hallucination," Richard said. "Deanna, you smell like Salome."

"With or without the head, Richard?" Deanna asked.

Richard laughed. He couldn't remember seeing Deanna this relaxed—at least not five days before a show's opening.

Arnaud looked lost, so Deanna gestured to Oriane that she should fill him in.

"*Salome* is a one-act opera by Strauss," Oriane said, fingering the edges of her French-tipped nails, "now best remembered for the scene where she sings to the head of John the Baptist."

"A one-act opera?" Arnaud said. "Who wants to see a one-act opera?"

The waitress handed everyone a menu.

"I already ordered. A Belgian waffle," Richard said.

"That's so decadent." Deanna glanced at the menu then set it aside. "I'll have one, too—minus the whipped cream."

"Make that three," Oriane said to the server. "But I'll take all the whipped cream. Hers, too." She giggled and pointed to Deanna.

"Can you have milk when you're singing?" Deanna asked.

Oriane shrugged. "I'm not singing a solo."

Deanna said nothing, presumably not wanting to encourage her, but merely rolled her eyes, à la Oriane.

"Arnaud will have the waffle, madam—solidarity's important," Arnaud said.

The waitress took juice orders while filling everyone's coffee cup.

"Arlene?" Richard asked, as she topped off his cup. "How about coming to see that hottie I showed you this Thursday night. We still have a few seats available?"

Arlene cocked her head to one side. "I used to think opera was too long hair for me, Dr. Rohrer. But I'm tempted to see Mr. Hottie in person."

The guild would be on the brink of a revolution in local opera if someone like Arlene showed up to see *Don Giovanni*. The irony was that Vasquez had the same kind of power over women as Elvis, Tom Jones, and that young Depp fellow Mary used to crow about who wore more paint on his face than a bloody whore. Vasquez had the power to attract women from all walks of life.

Richard winked. "As good as done. I'll leave some tickets for you—with the tip, Arlene."

"Thank you, Dr. Rohrer! Now, I have to find something to wear, don't I?" Another table caught her attention. "I'm off to table ten. But I'll be back."

"Arnaud, aren't you a little curious about a character singing to a severed head?" Oriane asked Arnaud after Arlene left. "Actually, she kisses the head."

"Just the head?" Arnaud shrugged. "I guess there are worse places to kiss a corpse, eh?"

Richard leaned into Deanna's personal space and took a deep breath. "What is that captivating scent? I have to know."

Arnaud turned to Deanna. "Never divulge your cologne. Next thing you know, all the women around you will be wearing your special scent. And it won't be special anymore."

"Speaking of severed heads, I'd like to chop off someone's head right about now," Richard said, now convinced that Vivian hadn't arrived because she was engaging in hanky-panky with Leandro. If there was going to be panky in Hankey where Vivian was concerned, Richard wanted to be the universal donor and the universal recipient. "And put it on a silver platter."

"Richard!" Arnaud gasped. "You terrify Arnaud with your violent talk."

Richard reached into his briefcase. "I had more flyers printed yesterday. Deanna, Oriane? While I'm thinking of it, why don't you two hand these out? Maybe the manager would let you hang a few copies in the window."

"Sure," Deanna said, taking the flyers from Richard. She turned to Oriane. "You take the right side. I'll take the left."

"Arnaud will help, too."

"Oh, no. You're going to stay right here—with me," Richard said, taking Arnaud's arm and pulling him back to the table. "What was the meaning of that little prank last evening? I know you were in on it."

"Arnaud has no idea what you're talking about."

"Listen carefully, my friend. You may be in for it. And not just from me. You put Vasquez in a bad position, too. Don't tell me he thought to climb that trellis all by himself."

"Arnaud swears to God, he had nothing—"

"You're a lying little son-of-a-gun, full of more hot air than those balloons you peddle."

Arnaud swallowed. "Arnaud has to use the little boys' room."

* * *

On the way back from the men's room, Arnaud saw Deanna standing at the cash register, jawing with the manager.

"Thanks, Dave. We appreciate the plug," Deanna said.

Arnaud approached her and looped his hand around her arm, and stuffed a note into her hand.

"What's this, Arnaud?"

"A sweet little nothing from someone who adores you," he said, kissing her on the cheek and dashing ahead.

"Aren't you something?" She shook her head and tucked the note into her pants pocket, patting it down, so as not to destroy their tailored line.

Next, he found Oriane leaning over the counter, talking to a waitress her age. Someone she went to high school with? "Here you go," she said, handing her a flyer. "Maybe we'll see you Thursday then?"

"Oriane. Psstt!" Arnaud tilted his head toward an alcove right around the counter.

She left her friend at the counter to join him. "What do you want?"

"Arnaud has something for you from someone who thinks you're very special." He reached into his pants pocket.

"Reaching into your pocket for something special? Isn't that, like, what a pervert does before he whips you-know-what out?"

He frowned, pulling out the note. "Now, it's out of Arnaud's pocket. And in your hands. Promise Arnaud, you'll read it today?"

"Is it from Leandro?" Oriane cried.

Arnaud nodded.

"I'll read it. I promise."

My work is nearly done, Arnaud thought, returning to the breakfast table. He'd left Vivian's note in a fruit basket on the kitchen table. The rest was up to the Lion Man. And when he got what he wanted, he'll be overjoyed. He won't know how to thank his good friend, Arnaud. That's when Arnaud will give him a suggestion or two.

* * *

Deanna and Oriane returned to the table, empty-handed. "We couldn't give them away fast enough," she said, sliding back into her seat.

"You must have had fun doing it," Richard said. "You're beaming. Both of you."

"I forgot to mention. I invited Jeannie Jacobs to join us this morning," Oriane said. "She's back in town and definitely wants to join the guild."

"Fantastic news," Richard said. "Oriane, you never cease to amaze me."

"She had a wonderful time at the Martini Masque, and well," Oriane said, "was very taken with Vasquez. Whatever works, right?"

"Absolutely," Deanna said. "In fact, if I'm not mistaken, that's Jeannie." She pointed toward the entrance. "Who else in Hankey wears a purple cloche?"

"Cloche?" Richard asked.

"Hat," Deanna and Arnaud said in unison.

Jeannie looked very well appointed in a pantsuit the color of an eggplant with matching hat. A smashing look. Though, as Richard scoured her face, he noticed her mood seemed not to match her smart appearance. Everyone sensed a certain energy around Jeannie though none could say exactly what it was. Vivian would've called her aura "troubled."

Oriane stood and extended her hand. "Nice of you to come." After she introduced everyone around the table, she invited Jeannie to sit beside her.

Deanna reached across the table—the new warm and fuzzy Deanna—to squeeze Jeannie's hand, but stopped when she noticed Jeannie clutching a copy of the poster she and Oriane had been handing out. "Delighted you could join us. Oriane tells me you saw Leandro Vasquez's New York premiere. Was he incredible?"

At the mention of Leandro Vasquez's name, a pallor crept across Jeannie's face. "Sorry. What was your question?" she asked softly.

"Was he incredible?" Deanna repeated her question. "As incredible as *The New York Minute* made him out to be?"

"I can't remember. The world is dark—to me," Jeannie said.

"Maybe you should take off your sunglasses," Oriane said, trying to be helpful.

Jeannie grinned at Oriane's suggestion though the expression appeared more pained than grateful. She removed her sunglasses and exchanged them for a pair of fashionable bifocals, tucking the former in her purse.

How could Richard bring up a subject like Vasquez's philandering with Jeannie Jacobs present? He'd either have to speak with each woman separately or bide his time for another moment. He didn't want Jeannie to think that guild business revolved around gossip. As luck would have it, Richard wouldn't have to wait to bring up a seedy conversation about Vasquez.

"I—thought he loved me," Jeannie said, now wringing her hands. "But his heart follows every fancy."

"Honey, as long as she's wearin' a skirt," Arnaud offered as if dishing about his best friend, "Leandro knows what to do."

"You thought who loved you?" Oriane asked Jeannie, in the same vein.

Jeannie's face became a perfect simper. She uncrumpled the poster in her hand and let it billow onto the table.

Another waitress, this one a lot younger than Arlene, sauntered over to the table with a pitcher of water. "Refill anyone? Hey, Dr. Rohrer, how can I get tickets to that show opening Thursday?"

Deanna leaned across the table. "She must have seen the poster, Richard! That poster's a winner."

"Or Arlene told her all about the big tip you're giving her," he said to Deanna. He turned to the thirty-something server. "I'm glad you asked, honey." He reached into his pocket. "Here are two tickets, third-row orchestra seating, for opening night. And don't forget to get gussied up. Opening night at the opera is a grand affair."

"For real?" She held the tickets up. "I got free tickets!"

A small horde of white-uniformed women, like a flock of seagulls, came hurtling toward the table where the guild was enjoying breakfast, saying things like, "Do you have any more?" and "How about me?" and "I want tickets" and "I love opera."

One woman began singing, "The Wedding March," then said, "They played it at my wedding."

Hmm. You're not getting free tickets for that rendition, Richard thought. "The Wedding March" is played at everyone's wedding.

Richard stood. "No more tickets today, ladies."

"Aww!" they all groaned in various keys and registers from coloratura to contralto.

"Just listen to WHNK this week," he said. "They're giving away free tickets all week."

"Are we advertising on WHNK?" Deanna asked.

"We are now," Richard said.

While everyone else seemed to be in buoyant spirits, Richard noticed Jeannie sat quietly, hands folded in front of her. It was never easy being the newcomer. He needed to try to bring her into the fold. Richard cleared his throat. "Time to get down to business. I know I speak for Deanna when I say that we're worried about our Lion Man. That all his newfound success playing Giovanni has gone to his head. That he's going to start—" Richard stopped himself before he said *whoring*.

"Is this discussion really necessary?" Oriane asked. "Don't we have other things to discuss besides—?"

Deanna cut her off. "Maybe we should talk about it." She turned her attention to Jeannie, softening her voice. "Is that?—pardon me for being indelicate," Deanna began, picking up and smoothing out the paper Jeannie had left on the table. "Did that happen to you?"

"I suppose—I brought it on myself," Jeannie said with an inflection sounding bereft.

At that moment, Arlene trotted over to their table, beaming, with plates of waffles in each hand and the others lining her arms. "Here we are, folks. Everybody good and hungry?"

"He's just a flirt," Arnaud said, a little too quickly. "He just can't help himself when it comes to women. Arnaud has proof. Arnaud found his black book and took some notes!" He took a piece of paper from his pocket, unfolded it and breathed deeply.

Richard noticed that none of the women paid a sliver of attention to the food on their plates. Arlene was taking an unnaturally long time passing out everyone's food. "Whose black book?" Arlene asked. "The hottie's?"

"Shhh," Oriane said. "Arnaud's trying to talk."

Arlene let out a wolf whistle that sliced through Richard's ear drum. "Gather 'round girls," she called, circling her arms to gather in her co-workers. "This is gonna be good."

At first Richard wanted to yank the book out of Arnaud's bony fingers. Then it occurred to him that all the scuttlebutt would be good for ticket sales. He decided to keep his sour old trap shut.

Here goes," Arnaud said, inhaling sharply and deeply, as if a recitation was bound to follow, as other waitresses clustered around their table. "Leandro's had five hundred and twenty women in France. Two hundred from the Rhineland. One thousand and three from his homeland, Argentina—in case you didn't know—and all the other Spanish-speaking countries where he's performed. Countesses, hotel maids, country beauties, ministers' wives. Young and lovely women. Old and plain broads."

The women who worked at the diner—six waitresses, including Arlene—punctuated each of Arnaud's statistics with groans of pleasure or dismay—Richard couldn't tell which. By the time Arnaud reported on his desire for slender girls in the summer and big-legged broads to keep him warm in the winter, all the women assembled held their breath. Even women in nearby booths were hanging on Arnaud's words.

"Wait a minute. Wait a minute," Oriane called out. "It's not what you think."

"You're right, Oriane." Arnaud shrugged. "He's only had ninety-one women in Turkey," Arnaud offered meekly.

Deanna cradled her head in her hands. "That's a relief. Only ninety-one in Turkey."

"Ninety-one in Turkey?" Arlene said, clapping Richard on the back. "Holy Moses! I didn't even know they had women in Turkey."

Jeannie's head dropped onto the tabletop, and she began sobbing into her elbows. Then she mumbled something. Richard couldn't quite make it out but it sounded like, "God knows how many in New York."

"He has all of this written in a black book?" Deanna asked. "In English?"

"A black book," Arnaud said, apologetically. "It's all written down."

"Why would he take notes in English?" Deanna asked. "He can barely speak it."

"He seduced all those women without speaking their language?" Arlene asked and the rest of the wait staff erupted in laughter. "Now that's a man's man."

Oriane leaned over to Richard. "Surely, you know he was reciting from the script, don't you, Richard? Even Jeannie knows. Look at her face. She's almost smiling."

Richard clapped his hands. "Oriane has something to say."

"Arnaud, you aren't the only medium in the crowd," Oriane said smugly, putting her hand to her forehead as if receiving a vision. "Did this black book have any words on the front, like *G. Schirmer* for instance?"

Arnaud nodded.

"Oh, that was lots of fun," Oriane said. "Everybody—Arnaud was reading from the libretto. Not Vasquez's actual black book. That crazy list is in the script. Vasquez hasn't had that many women in real life."

"He's young," Deanna quipped. "Give him time."

"Relax," Oriane said. "He's only a libertine on paper."

A chorus of oh's and ah's erupted before the ad hoc group disbanded.

Arlene surveyed the table. "Can I get you anything else?" she asked, but Richard had already dove into his waffle and just shook his head.

Suddenly, Jeannie's eyes flashed with anger. "On paper only? Indeed, Oriane! I know of his rakish appetites. He's a deceitful man."

Richard sat up straight, pressing his back into the chair. Vasquez had taken Jeannie as a lover? She must be forty years older than him. It was all right for a man to be that much older in a relationship but not for a woman. Was Jacobs another wealthy loony-toon? Even though Jeannie looked damned good for her age, Vasquez would never go for a woman Richard's age, would he? Unless he was a total reprobate. If Vasquez *was* a total reprobate, that meant Vivian couldn't have been party to his guest-room shenanigans.

"Deceitful," Jeannie kept repeating, wringing her hands. "He mistook me for a call girl."

Was Jeannie going to have a psychotic break right there in the diner? Richard asked himself. She couldn't. Not before he could get a commitment for a major gift to the opera house.

"Jeannie," Richard began, "If Vasquez thought you were a high-class hooker, he must have been drunk as a skunk. You're obviously a woman of quality. He's just a talented kid from Argentina whose star is rising fast, a young man without any obligations to temper his lust for life, who's getting his first real taste of the world opening up to him like an eager oyster."

"On this point, you are wrong, Richard," Arnaud said. "Our rising star has a wife and six children back in Argentina."

26
The Trietto

Vivian is in the great room, having morning coffee, wondering why Richard hasn't yet made an appearance.

Vivian hadn't slept well after last night's incident in the guest room and awoke with a slight headache. She wasn't certain whether it had been caused by the port or the lack of sleep.

She was taking her coffee in the great room instead of the living room. On a sunny spring morning like this one, her peach-faced lovebirds would be too chatty and chirpy and would ratchet up her headache several degrees.

"Ma'am," one of the house servants said, approaching with a piece of folded paper in her hand. "This was left in the kitchen for you."

"Thanks, Cissy," Vivian said, taking the note from her. She unfolded it, expecting it to be an apology from Richard for accusing her of inviting Vasquez into her bed. Vasquez was an incredibly attractive man. But she would no more go to bed with him than she would with Knobby. She wasn't particularly interested in having a sexual rendezvous with anyone. Her ex-husband Guido's sex drive was big enough for a lifetime, one reason she still referred to him as "Guido the Libido."

Things had been so comfortable earlier in the evening, what with Richard's inviting her to the gala as his date. She shouldn't have expected the conviviality between them to last. *Conviviality?* Was that a word?

She unfolded the note.

Dearest, darling Vivian. Leandro cannot sleep at night,
for Leandro dreams of your balmy cheeks of roses,
where sly Cupid reposes.

And of that pretty mouth of coral, that breathes of flowers.

Oh, brother! She laughed so loudly, she was making her own headache worse. It was remarkable, how much Vasquez's command of the English language had improved since yesterday. More flowery nonsense then:

Meet me tonight at nine-thirty.

In Leandro's dressing room. Come alone and ready for love.

Was this Richard's idea of a practical joke? He'd have some fun at her expense, would he? She'd had enough of this nonsense. She took another sip of her coffee, then she tore the note into tiny pieces, strode into the living room and deposited it into the bottom of the lovebirds' cage. Take that, Dr. Richard Rohrer.

Cissy met her on the way back to the great room.

"Ma'am, there's a Dr. Richard Rohrer on the phone for you."

"I'll take it in the kitchen," Vivian said. By the time she reached the kitchen, she knew exactly what to say and how to say it. "Hello?"

"Vivian, we just had breakfast at the Steel City Diner—everyone on the guild."

"How nice for you all!"

"I'm sorry you couldn't join us," he said, sounding apologetic. "Did you get my note?"

Now there was the good old Rohrer zinger she'd expected. "I most certainly did," she said and hung up on him.

* * *

Oriane loped up the steps to her second floor apartment, clutching the note from Leandro in her hand. She felt dizzy. Was it from the note or from the fact that she had eaten too many empty carbohydrates at breakfast? She let herself in and headed for the kitchen. She poured a glass of water from the tap, preferring it as close to room temperature as she could get it, took a sip, and set it on the counter. She threw open the refrigerator door. Nothing but a half-eaten can of tuna fish and a too-ripe avocado. She wasn't hungry anyway, not really. She closed the door and headed to her bedroom where she fell backwards onto her bed. She removed Leandro's note from her hand and had to read it again.

Dearest, darling Oriane. Leandro cannot sleep at night,
for Leandro dreams of your balmy cheeks of roses,
where sly Cupid reposes.
And of that pretty mouth of coral, that breathes of flowers.

She sighed. She just knew he cared for her more than the other
ladies on the guild. All during the afternoon's rehearsal, they
exchanged secret glances. She invented messages in her head and
thought hard about them so they'd be planted in his brain. She had
to read the rest immediately or she'd burst with anticipation.

You have undone Leandro.
Oh, grant Leandro the pray'r of your love.
Show Leandro mercy!
Than roses are you fairer and than honey sweeter.
Oh, come, fairest one. Be Leandro's love, Leandro begs you.
Meet Leandro tonight at nine o' clock.
In Leandro's dressing room. Come alone and ready for love.

Should she meet him? She wanted to, but part of her was afraid
to, terrified that her feelings for Leandro were already too strong,
and her expectations for the affair so great that she'd turn into
Jeannie if he rejected her.

Then she remembered. She could level the playing field by using
the spell Arnaud had told her about. She ran back into the kitchen
and tore open the box her voodoo doll came in. It had two sides—
male and female. So, she flipped it to the male side, and using the
fabric markers that came with the doll, began coloring it in, so it
looked more like Leandro—but no pants, of course. She didn't want
to wait for the kettle to boil, so she put a mug of plain water in the
microwave until it was scorching hot, then she removed the mug
and dunked the doll's feet in the water. That would take care of any
cold feet. What was next? That's right. Now he had to go in the
freezer. She threw him face down on the top rack—so his personal
parts would freeze first, and set the timer for two minutes.
Meanwhile, she removed the half-eaten tuna—as good as cat food—
from the refrigerator and stirred it up, so it was ready to slather on
the doll's body when the Leandro came out of his deep freeze. Was

there another step between the freezing and the application of cat food? She couldn't remember.

A few minutes later, as she smeared tuna fish on the doll, she realized she just had to tell someone about the note, someone she could trust. But who? How about Vivian? The more she got to know Vivian, the more she liked her. She'd read the letter one more time while holding the doll, and then give Vivian a call.

* * *

Deanna thought about the note while she lay on the couch with a warm washcloth over her eyes. Not yet. She needed five minutes of renewal before she had the energy to handle another problem. Maybe it wasn't a problem. Arnaud had insinuated that it was an expression of affection. Why was Arnaud getting in the middle of this anyway?

She removed the washcloth and reached for her purse on the coffee table and retrieved the little square of paper.

Dearest, darling Deanna. Leandro cannot sleep at night,
for Leandro dreams of your balmy cheeks of roses...

"Balmy cheeks of roses?" Who was he kidding? Was this guy off his proverbial Brazil nut? She skimmed the rest, noting how many times Leandro used his own name in a love note that was supposed to be about her. The note ended with a request to meet her in the dressing room at ten o'clock tonight. Deanna knew she was good looking and lots of men still found her desirable, which had more to do with her polish than raw good looks. Perhaps Vasquez had come onto Jeannie in just the same fashion. No, she said he thought she was a hooker. There was no such implication in this letter but that hardly meant she trusted its contents.

She was ready to stuff the note back in her purse when her cell phone rang. Caller I.D. said it was Vivian.

"I think we have a Leandro problem, Deanna."

"Oh, heavens. Now what?"

"This will give you a laugh. Wait. I'm going to conference in Oriane though she's not laughing. Oriane, are you there?"

"I'm here," Oriane said, her voice cracking.

Vivian continued, "Vasquez has set up little trysts with each of us. In half-hour increments. Tonight, in the opera house dressing room."

"Guess who's the ten o'clock girl?" Deanna said dryly.

"That creep!" Oriane said. "I recognized the text of his love letter. It's right out of the libretto. An unoriginal creep, too."

"It appears our creep had a little helper," Deanna said. "Like his own little pimp. Now who in all of our acquaintanceship would stoop to pimp for Vasquez? Can you think of anyone, Vivian?"

Vivian gasped in mock horror. "You don't mean that you think—*someone*—wrote that letter for Vasquez?"

"What was your first clue?" Deanna quipped. "The sixth or the seventh mention of *Leandro*, his own first name, in one little love letter?"

"Wait until I get my hands on that little balloon man!" Oriane said, her voice breaking. "I'll pull out his bleached-blonde hair strand by strand."

"He's more of a skunk than I thought," Deanna said.

"You're sure that it's not Richard who's helping Vasquez spread his seed, so-to-speak?" Vivian asked.

"We're sure it's Arnaud," Deanna said.

"Arnaud gave us each a note at breakfast this morning," Oriane said.

"I hadn't realized that," Vivian said. "Richard didn't have anything to do with it?"

"Not as far as we know. I think I'll give him a call before rehearsal tonight to make sure."

"Are you very disappointed, Oriane?" Vivian said.

"No-oo," she said, verging on tears. "When did Leandro, I mean, Vasquez, get to be so selfish?"

"Sometimes success changes people, Oriane," Deanna said. "Sudden success like he's been having can bring out the worst in people."

Oriane sniffled. "What do we do now?"

"Let's meet over dinner," Deanna said, "to plan our revenge. Who else has seen *Falstaff*?

"Me," Oriane piped up.

"Not me," Vivian said.

"Are we going to stuff Leandro into a wicker basket," Oriane said, "and throw him into the Schuylkill?"

"Not exactly what I had in mind," Deanna said. "Just our luck, someone would pull him out and suckle him like he was Baby Moses from the bulrushes. No, I think we need to hit him where it hurts."

"I know just the spot where you can really hurt a man," Oriane chimed in. "I saw it on a skit on television."

"Where is that spot, Oriane?" Deanna said. "Vivian and I haven't a clue."

"Well, um, I shouldn't actually—" Oriane began.

Vivian giggled. "Why, Deanna? What evil scheme are you concocting?"

"It's the *cojones*," Oriane said. "That's where he's going to feel the—pinch."

"Correct-a-mundo, Oriane!" Deanna said, "Oh, and whatever we decide to do to Vasquez, no one, and I mean no one, can trace it back to us."

Oriane cleared her throat. "You don't have to worry about me."

"We do worry about you," Vivian said. "You knew Vasquez before all of us—when he actually was a nice guy."

"I'm wise to him now, though," Oriane protested. "I'm not going to fall for any of his tricks."

"Dinner at the diner—around five-thirty?" Deanna said. "Have you eaten already, Oriane?"

"Five-thirty's fine," she said. "Rehearsal picks up at seven."

"I'll invite Richard. We could use a man's perspective, too." Deanna turned to Oriane. "No matter what happens during rehearsal, be strong."

"Don't worry about me," Oriane said. "I'm just a chorister. Now, if I were in an actual scene with Vasquez, you might have to worry."

27
The Terminazione

That evening, Knobby reviews the staging of Giovanni's musical numbers including "Là ci darem la mano," with Vasquez as Giovanni and Catherine Carnahan as Zerlina.

Catherine Carnahan had come highly recommended, Knobby recalled. Even though she was marking her vocals, as she rehearsed her duet with Vasquez, Knobby could tell her voice was first rate. But why was she marking the physical through-line of Zerlina? She acted like a block of wood in Vasquez's arms—bumping up against him rather than melting into his body. Jerking her head around like an ostrich.

"Hold it. Take five, Vasquez," Knobby said. "Catherine?" He walked toward the apron and gestured her to come closer. "This number only works if Zerlina is as turned on as Giovanni. I'm not sensing anything close to being turned on in your actions, your body language." He gestured her to come even closer and whispered, "Have you looked at your co-star lately? Taken a good look? It shouldn't take much to get you in the proper mood to do this scene."

"I'm a singer, Knobby," Catherine droned, crossing her arms. "Opera is the province of singers."

Knobby softened his voice to sound more like a teacher and less like the autocratic Maestro who barked at all the performers. "That's an old-fashioned model. The best operas are seamless expressions of acting and singing. Oriane? Oriane!"

* * *

Deanna thought she'd drop by rehearsal to see how the show was gelling. Since Oriane wasn't in the scene being rehearsed, she was probably in the green room, waiting for her next cue. Oriane's was the first scheduled rendezvous after rehearsal tonight, and Deanna wanted to make sure Oriane carried out her part in Operation *Cojones*—Oriane was the nine o'clock girl, after all. And to tell her that Knobby wanted her on stage—pronto. On the way to the green room, Deanna nearly collided with Vasquez.

"Ah—Deanna," Vasquez said, with electricity in his voice. "Fairer than—the rose. Sweeter than—the honey."

So, he relied on scripts for his sweet nothings. Then again, English wasn't his first language. And from the sound of it, it wasn't his second either. However, he looked delicious—better than a hot roast beef sandwich au jus. Those smoldering good looks. What other man could wear a puffy shirt and skin-tight pants and not look like a buffoon? Since she'd sworn off men, preferring smooches from Knobby's pooches, she thought she didn't have to worry about weakening to Vasquez's advances until she saw him. An exceptional specimen, in every way.

"Hello, Leandro," she mewed and held out her hand.

Immediately, he drew it to his soft lips, kissed it, and then began nuzzling on the underside of her wrist, all the way up her arm. "Ten o'clock—tonight, eh—*mi dulce*?"

"Ten o'clock. Can't wait," she said leaning in to feel his velvety smooth lips on hers. She had to play along, to let him believe things were SITUATION NORMAL, rather than what they really were going to be—the AFU part of SNAFU.

"Did somebody call me?" Oriane asked, sticking her head outside the green room door, just as Deanna's and Vasquez's lips locked in a suffocating embrace.

* * *

"I have an idea. It's *singspiel*. I'll just speak my lines," Carnahan said, taking a seductive posture, and clearing her throat dramatically. "*Andiam, andiam, mio bene*," she bellowed to the back of the house, with a force and precision only Sarah Bernhardt could match.

Knobby knew she was being facetious, but he had a show opening Thursday, and needed to get a decent performance out of her. "That's the intensity I want. But not speaking. Singing."

Carnahan fumed. "What you want is impossible. I'm singing Mozart."

Thanks for filling me in, Knobby thought, otherwise I wouldn't have known. He opened his mouth to level her—she was egging him on. But he resorted to the patient teacher again. "It certainly can be done." He clambered onto the stage. "It can and it will."

Oriane popped her head around the backstage curtain. "Did someone call me?" she asked. Oriane looked plenty piqued. Too bad. Knobby thought. Whatever you were doing, it can't be as important as what I need you for—not two days from opening.

He nodded. "Sing Zerlina's duet with Giovanni, beginning with *'Andiam, andiam, mio bene.'* Just like you did at the masque."

Oriane plodded onstage. "Should I go get Vasquez? He's hanging around the green room with Deanna. Yeah, I'd say those two are pretty darn cozy!"

"Forget Vasquez. I'll be Giovanni." Knobby extended his hand to Oriane and pulled her into his side. "Maestro?" he said, nodding his head for a cue.

Maestro nodded and signaled a violin player to play a note. In local opera, it was a wise practice, to keep singers from pulling their pitches out of the air.

Knobby turned Oriane's creamy lips to his. They sang the first line of the last refrain in unison. Her body quivered as his fingertips tickled the side of her face and caressed her neck. They sang the last two lines of the song with their lips inches apart.

Over the orchestra playing softly, about half as loud as during a performance, Knobby heard Carnahan bleating, laughing uproariously as if she were watching the funniest show she had ever seen. After the final note, he leaned Oriane backwards and kissed her full on the lips in a dramatic clench. Then he gently lifted her to her feet. "Thanks, Oriane. That'll be all. See what I mean?" he said to Carnahan, as Oriane backed away nervously, staring at Carnahan the whole time like she was watching a sideshow attraction.

Carnahan clapped four times slowly, very slowly, for emphasis, as if she had just watched something very poorly executed, and said, "Now, that's rich. You're using my understudy to teach me how to act?"

"No," Knobby said calmly. "Oriane isn't your understudy any longer. She has the role now, Catherine. Because you're fired."

"But—you can't—" Carnahan stammered.

Oriane stood with her jaw hanging open, riveted to Knobby, who was now laughing robustly—the only person laughing now. "I hired your ass. I can certainly fire it."

Maestro set down his baton and began to protest.

Knobby raised his hand to Maestro to silence him while finishing with Carnahan. "Consider your fat ass fired." He pointed his finger at her accusingly and then to the wings. "Get off my stage."

Carnahan stalked off the stage, mumbling, "Loser!" she called over her shoulder, directly to Knobby, running right into Vasquez as she exited. "Fucking losers. You're a jerk, too," she said to Vasquez.

Vasquez lifted both hands in the air as if to say, *What did I do?* "What is buzz—Know-bee?" Vasquez asked flustered.

"I just fired Carnahan," Knobby said, his brusque manner returning now that he was addressing Vasquez. "Oriane is going to sing the role."

Vasquez nodded offstage. "Why you fire?"

"She refused to act the role. Whoever's playing Zerlina has to act as much as the other female leads," Knobby explained. "You know Oriane, right?"

Vasquez smiled and held out his hand gallantly. "Mi gorrión. You a look—*magnifico*."

Oriane crept toward Vasquez—cautiously. He took her hand and twirled her around in one pirouette, then another and then one more. "First I have—*gordo* Zerlina. Now," Vasquez said, "I have—perfect—Zerlina."

Oriane rolled her eyes.

"You are cold to me, Señorita," Vasquez said.

"I'm . . . uh . . . saving myself for later," Oriane said, painting on a smile.

Knobby exhaled heavily. Had Vasquez planned to prey on every woman in the cast, acting like an oversexed conquistador during every minute of every rehearsal? "Let's go, you crazy kids. I want to see this number *con gusto.* And Vasquez, I don't want you pawing her during the whole song. Save the molestation for the last stanza, okay? Maestro?"

* * *

Deanna checked her watch. She was due back at the opera house in two hours. She had just enough time to swing by her house, take a quick bath, and shave her legs. During her appointment with Vasquez, she needed to whip him into a sexual frenzy while actually keeping him at arm's length this evening. But just in case things zoomed out of control—let's face it; her legs had always been her best feature—irresistible where men were concerned. At least, they wouldn't be all stubbly in case she had to climb between the sheets with Vasquez. Anything to uphold her end of the top-secret, risky business the three leading ladies of the Hankey Opera Guild had planned for Vasquez.

28
The Counterpoint

The evening's rehearsal has just concluded. Oriane slips into the dressing room to freshen up for her rendezvous with Vasquez. Now that she's singing Zerlina for the show, she's doubtful she can resist the Lion Man's advances.

Oriane dug into a few of the make-up pots scattered on the dressing room table. She wasn't what people would consider a natural beauty, but her face was definitely mutable. Whenever she wore stage makeup, her looks were enhanced and no longer nondescript. First she evened out her blotchy complexion with a light shade of pancake. Then using rouge and white highlighter, she gave herself cheekbones and used a pencil to augment the arch in her eyebrows. All of which led her to believe she was only beautiful on stage, which propelled her to do show after show after show, the rationale being, that she would rather sacrifice the regular social life many other women her age enjoyed to be ardently admired for her looks four nights, twice monthly, three hours at a time.

She unbuttoned the top two buttons on her cotton blouse because she had to play the vamp. Under no circumstances, however, could she succumb to her innermost desires—to be bedded by the Lion Man. "Give me strength to resist him," she prayed and switched off the lights above the vanity. Just as she was leaving the dressing room, Knobby walked in.

"Oriane," he said. "Glad I caught you. I have some notes on your performance."

Oriane smiled thinly. She glanced at her watch. "That's great, but I'm supposed to—"

Knobby eased himself into her personal space and placed his hand on her shoulder. "I don't have many notes. You're—really doing a fabulous job."

"If there aren't many, maybe it can wait until tomorrow." She shrugged. "I'll come in fifteen minutes early."

He grasped her arm. "Just a moment. I have to tell you something. Then I can get back to my work, and you can get going."

She blinked. "Okay." His eyes were dewy with sincerity. She noticed little green flecks that she'd never realized were there before, and that his pupils were growing as big as dimes.

Knobby swallowed. "In the party scene, I need you to be a little more conflicted just before Giovanni drags you away. He's a gentleman. A real gentleman wants to spend time with Zerlina, a country girl. You have no reason not to trust him. In fact, stand here beside me." He gently led her to his side. "I'm going to tell Vasquez to pull you aside and nuzzle your lips before he takes you offstage."

Oriane's eyes lit up. "You want us to kiss before he takes advantage of me?"

"Zerlina's expecting him to act like a gentleman. If you go with him willingly, it makes his coarse advances that much more impactful later in the scene."

Oriane studied his face. Earnest and handsome. Not as handsome as Vasquez. But neither was she as beautiful as some of the women Vasquez had been linked with, according to another "Page Six" exposé that ran in the *New York Daily News* the day after they snapped his picture with Jeannie. "Just a playful kiss?"

"More than playful. He needs to show he's in charge—like this," he said, and he pulled her face toward his. "May I?"

Oriane shrugged.

First, Knobby caressed her lips with his fingertips and plumbed them with his own lips.

She felt herself surrendering in his embrace. Then she remembered that she had an assignment. She needed to meet, no, she wanted to meet Vasquez to launch the first salvo in Operation *Cojones*. She wanted to exact her revenge. She wanted him to feel some of the pain that he'd caused her. Granted, *Cojones* was a strange name for a Special Op, but when they met over dinner, Richard wanted them to use the correct medical term, Operation Vasocongestion. He urged them not to resort to the seedy street language Deanna wanted to use—Operation Blue Balls—which Richard said was medically inaccurate and misleading. That's when Oriane suggested Operation *Cojones* as a compromise. "Knob— Carter. May I call you Carter?"

Knobby nodded.

If she didn't play her part, perhaps the rest of the maneuvers would fail. Or worse, she would be accused of not doing her bidding. "I have to go."

"I have a confession to make," he said. "I didn't have any notes for you. I just wanted to be with you. I made up this little charade, just to kiss you." He stroked the side of her face with her fingertips. "Do you know how lovely you looked in that yellow dress? Like a buttercup. Back in Ohio, I used to pick buttercups for pretty girls, just like you. Oriane, you're not like a lot of women I've met in this job. You're special. Now that you have the part you wanted and deserved, I hope you can forgive me for overlooking you to begin with."

He'd said he was sorry. And he'd noticed her dress—the dress she'd worn for Vasquez, hoping he'd remember seeing her wearing it in London, which he hadn't. Carter had just told Oriane that she was something special. It occurred to her throughout her life, that's all she ever wanted to hear—that she was someone special to someone. "You don't want me to kiss Vasquez before he takes me offstage?"

"I most certainly do," he said, "but I want you to be thinking of me. Because, most assuredly, I'll be thinking of you." He leaned in and began to kiss her again.

She pulled herself away. Knobby was being very sweet. She knew she shouldn't waste another second thinking about being with Vasquez, but she wasn't ready to give up on him—not completely anyway. She refused to believe he had a wife and six children in Argentina. He didn't even wear a wedding ring. That was just a publicity stunt conceived by his agent to make him more marketable.

SEXY GIOVANNI IS SECRETLY A HAPPILY MARRIED MAN would be the entertainment tabloid headline. An ingenious stunt which of course, makes all his female admirers want him more—because he's unavailable. She intended to ask him tonight during her part of the special op, to see if he denied it. "Carter. Thank you, but I have to—"

"Oriane," Knobby said softly and tenderly. "I was hoping to get to know you a little better—tonight. We've had precious little time with each other."

How much better? she wondered. A lot better. The kind of a lot better she'd been waiting for all of her adult life. "I'll stay for a minute more."

Knobby ran his hands through her hair. "Oh, Oriane," he groaned.

"Oh, Carter," she said, letting him smother her with kisses. He unbuttoned her blouse.

"Carter, I can't—" she said removing his hands from her body and straightening up her blouse. "I have something important to do. Really."

Knobby stopped. "Oriane, you've become more beautiful and more special to me every day since I've arrived. At one point, I thought you even liked me back."

"Oh, I did like you—I mean—I do like you back," she said, remembering that she had her own little fantasies of being Mrs. Carter Knoblauch at one time. "Are you married?"

"No—not married," Knobby said.

"Ever been married?" Oriane asked.

"Not even close. I saw a few women but they never understood my job. The hours involved in a job like this. It's not just a job."

Oriane wrapped her arms around his waist. "I understand, Carter. Absolutely understand—the demands of this profession." And she closed her eyes, and this time when he kissed her, she kissed him back.

* * *

Vasquez heard the click of the door handle. Was Oriane only coming to see him now? Couldn't American women tell time? He had told the girl nine o'clock. Arnaud said he delivered the note himself. These American women would be the death of him.

What a surprise to see Vivian coming through the door. Lovely Vivian with the aquamarine eyes and breasts as bountiful as her bank account. Someone once said conductors only needed two things to be successful—a good tuxedo and a rich wife. Rich wives were good for performers, too. Money gave singers the luxury of choosing the roles they wanted—only caviar, no fish scales. To clarify, he didn't want to marry Vivian. He was already married. But to have her be his generous American lover would be *bueno* by him.

"Ah, Bibian," he said. "*Mi dulce.*"

Vivian's face lit up in a gentle smile. "Oh, Leandro. I couldn't wait to see you."

Vasquez sighed, feeling more relaxed already. What a vision she was! Her red hair looked whippy, like the whitecaps on Lake Hermoso, where his cows used to wade. Her low-cut blouse excited him; her breasts strained against it, longing to be free and bouncing in his cupped hands.

"Mind if I get comfortable?" Vivian said, lowering herself onto a settee and hiking up her skirt, to reveal a set of garters attached to hose with seams running up the back.

¡Ay de mí! he thought. If American women were the cause of his demise, what a way to go. His head spun. He slunk over to the settee and settled himself on the corner, wrapping his arm around her waist. "Bibian," he said, nuzzling her neck. "I come—inside house— a last night—a see you—you no there."

"I'm sorry," she said, and he could tell by her inflection she was remorseful. With the tips of his fingers, he drew circles on her upper thighs where the hose had stopped, leaving her skin exposed. He felt himself hardening with each sphere he carved into her creamy skin.

Vivian fanned herself. "It's hot in here."

Vasquez chuckled. And getting hotter. I may not have had Oriane, but having waited, when Vivian and I get to it, it will be *fantástico.*

"Let me take off my jacket, *mi dulce*," she said, removing it from her shoulders. As she did, she raised her arm right in front of Vasquez's nose.

"Ay!" he said, shuddering. Her armpit was unshaven. And it smelled like moldy hay from a barn. "A gorilla!"

Vivian gasped. "Is that a turn-off? I went native a couple years ago. I thought you Latin types liked natural women. I'll put my jacket back on."

Vasquez reached for it in a flash and helped her into it. He exhaled heavily. "Way we were, eh?"

"*The Way We Were*," Vivian said. "I loved that movie. So romantic." She reached over and with one hand pressed her palm into the slight bulge in the front of his pants, rubbing until his manhood bounded back. With the other, she fingered her hair, lifting it in little wisps off her face. Then she shook her head lightly and began painstakingly rearranging her hairdo. "Do I look all right?" she said as she continued to rub him with the other hand.

"Beautiful," he said, his voice a raspy murmur.

"Are you sure?" she asked. "Does it really look all right? All of it? I want the feathering to look exactly like it should. I'd hate for it look less than perfect for our little rendezvous."

"*Sí, sí, bueno!*" he cried.

Just as he approached the point of no return, she yanked her hand away. He groaned and sucked in air, like someone had just thwacked him in the chest.

"Just got a text. One second." She reached into the side of her bag, pulled out a cell phone and flipped it open. "Oh," she said, giggling. "It's Richard. I never should've given him my cell number. Now, he texts me day and night, just like a little kid. Look at what he said." She shoved the phone in front of his face.

"Don' wanna see," he said, scowling.

"Can't see it, you say? 'Vivvy…' he calls me Vivvy. 'Vivvy, can I see you tonight after you're finished with Vasquez? Say, ten-fifteen?'"

"'Finished with Vasquez?'" Vasquez huffed. "What you do— with a goat?"

"I guess he is a goat, if goats like to go, go, go," Vivian said. "Richard can go, go, go for hours."

"Stop!" Vasquez leapt off the settee. "No talk—about Richard—in my—being."

"*In my being?*" Vivian began laughing uncontrollably. "You're funny, Leandro. Dumb as one of those hairy cows you used to herd in the Chaco. Your English is horrendous. Don't say *in my being*. Say *in my presence.*"

What a disappointment, this woman! This evening! First one did not show. Now this one! He thought he knew the kind of woman she was, and she turned out to be a sow with hairy armpits who gets him aroused then fusses too much with her hair for no reason. Then she stops what we are sharing, when I am so close, and talks to that old goat. While I am right here—me! Leandro Vasquez. Lion Man. What woman settles for a goat when she could have a lion. He felt a sharp pain in his groin. His head ached. He knew why, too. Well, he had one more chance with Deanna. "Somebody—should make—old a-goat—goulash."

"You're going to make Richard into goulash? That's too funny. Wait until I tell him."

"Time a go, Bibian. Go to goat."

"Well, if you insist." She rose with a protracted sigh. "I was just kinda getting warmed up."

He'd like to feed that old goat to a wolf. Let a ravenous *lobo* gnaw on his grizzled meat. Or hand him to a gypsy, who'll cook the old goat's flesh until it fell into strings. He knew a gypsy back in Argentina who would take care of Richard. First, she'd make wild, animal love to him. Then she'd roast him in her cook pot.

As quickly as Vivian had stolen into the room, she scooted herself out the door.

* * *

Deanna was waiting, silently. "Is it working?" she asked.

"He seems pretty frustrated," Vivian explained. "I don't think Oriane ever showed."

"That wasn't the plan, but if that's the case, all the better," Deanna said.

"He's not stupid. Surely he's caught on to what we're doing," Vivian said.

"His ego's pretty big. I think he believes what he wants to believe," Deanna said. "Imagine, arranging to see three women in one night, back to back, with a half hour slotted for each? At forty-two, it takes a half hour just for my engine to warm up. Hey, did your underarm hair stay in place?"

"If I held my arms straight up in the middle of a Category IV hurricane, that spirit gum would hold. Just hope I can remove the hair without ripping off my skin."

"Rubbing alcohol followed by warm soapy water. Oriane swears by it."

"You're getting help with your skit, right?" Vivian asked. "Do you think you-know-who will show?"

"I'm counting on her," Deanna said. "He's a very attractive man. Heaven knows, I'm a hard-up woman. She needs to make an appearance—to save me from myself." She gave Vivian a finger wave. "Wish me luck."

Three months ago, Deanna never would have thought she and Vivian would be working cooperatively to accomplish anything—not even a successful show. Oh, the power of a common enemy. She knocked on the door. "Leandro?" she called sweetly. "It's Deanna."

"Come in," Leandro called.

Deanna pushed the door open and gasped. There stood Leandro in a leopard-print thong. The rest of his clothes lay in a hasty heap flung atop the dressing room table. She should have remembered that she was slated as the third act of a three-act production—and the third act always contained the climax. Heavens, that woman better show or Deanna was an overcooked empanada. She hadn't been with a man in more months than she had toes and fingers, and right now, he looked like medium rare beef tips, ready to be sucked off a skewer. What could she do but go with the feeling and enjoy it while it lasted. She pressed the door closed behind her, feeling the doorknob to make sure it was unlocked.

"Pu-r-r-r-r," Deanna said, thinking she sounded like the Catwoman. "You are the Lion Man. Come here you big, beautiful hunk of cat."

Vasquez sidled toward her like the king of the jungle eyeing its prey. He wrapped his muscled arms around her and began their lovemaking with a deep lingering kiss. When he finally released her, she came up panting. So, she breathed in and out slowly then pulled his mouth toward hers until their lips were again locked.

He began unbuttoning her blouse. Deanna groaned as each pearled fastener came undone. Then in a move she thought only happened on the silver screen, he lifted her off her feet and carried her to the chaise longue across the room, where he laid her down on the plush red velvet.

To hell with their mission. She would make her body an offering to this demigod of opera. And heaven help anyone who tried to stop her.

Vasquez had unzipped her stretch jeans when Jeannie Jacobs burst into the dressing room. "Hold on, you wicked one," Jeannie cried out.

Vasquez, still lying atop Deanna, looked up, shaking with indignation. "Qué? Jeannie?"

While many men would stumble for words under these circumstances, this man had an international reputation for playing Giovanni. He knew exactly what to say. A froth of Italian flowed from his heart, into the air via his full, moist lips. "*Idol mio, non vedete ch' io voglio divertirmi.*"

Jeannie splayed her body across the dressing room door. "*Divertirti?* Ach!"

Deanna caught her breath and interrupted the drama ensuing between the Lion Man and his spurned accuser with the stuck crazy button. "Enough with the Italian!"

"He said," Jeannie began, "'did I not see that he was amusing himself.' To which I said, 'Yes, you cruel man. I know too well how you amuse yourself.'"

Deanna rebuttoned her jeans and pulled her shirt closed. She crawled out from under Vasquez and managed to get to her feet. At that moment, she felt as though they could not have selected a more apt name for a Special Op to bring down the Lion Man. Operation *Cojones*, indeed. She burned with longing for Vasquez. But just as Richard had said, if you're going to play with fire, you'd better expect to get scorched.

"Deanna." Vasquez turned to face her and reached for her hand. "This—damsel—gorrión—adore a me. I pity—no love."

"You wretched man," Jeannie said, with such vehemence it forced Vasquez to turn and face her.

It was clear that this was a painful part for Jeannie to play in this scenario. Deanna regretted asking her to be involved. But the scene had to be finished. And just as Jeannie had predicted, Vasquez lapsed into lines from the libretto. She continued hers as well, a variation on them anyway. "Into what horrible crimes has this wretch been plunged." She pointed to the heavens, or more accurately, the ceiling of the dressing room. "Already, I see a fatal bolt of lightning crashing onto his big head."

"What you mean—big head!" Vasquez said.

"Shhh," Deanna said, quieting Vasquez. "Now's not the time, Leandro. She's inconsolable." Deanna motioned to Vasquez to sit down. "I'll take care of her. We'll continue this later." She took Jeannie by the arm.

But Jeannie resisted and continuing spewing invective at Vasquez. "I see the abyss opening beneath you—you vile monster."

"Aaahh!" Vasquez shrieked. "She a scare—me. A witch, no?"

"No," Deanna said to Vasquez. "That's enough, Jeannie." Deanna pushed her out of the dressing room. She slammed the door closed and planted herself in front of it. "Good heavens, that's one case of crazy you're heaping on this man."

"You asked me to help you," Jeannie said, sounding broken, tears welling in her eyes. "I helped you."

"I'm sorry I did," Deanna said. "But now that it's done, we all have lessons to learn, don't you think? All of us."

"Despite what he is, I still pray for him," Jeannie said, adjusting the silk drape around her arms. "I pray for us—for Leandro and me—that one day we'll enjoy the love I know we can share."

Deanna shuddered in complete amazement at this woman, who might be in the midst of a nervous breakdown. "Pray for yourself, Jeannie. And pray for the guild." Deanna sighed with all the weight of the opera company's fate hanging in the balance. "We have a show to mount. And Giovanni has to be the single greatest theatrical sensation this town has ever known."

"I will pray for all concerned," Jeannie said and gently bowed her head. "Goodnight, Deanna."

Without speaking, she followed Jeannie out of the opera house and into the parking garage and watched her step into the back seat of a limousine and speed away. Then she strolled over to Vivian's driver and rapped on the window. "Your charge is ready. He's in the dressing room. He needs to go home and get some sleep."

"I think I'll let Walt take him home," Vivian said. "Let him stew in his vaso-whatever. Can you give me a lift?"

"Sure," she said. Ah, the merry, merry month of May, Deanna said to herself, heading to her own vehicle. Nothing like it. She dug out her cell phone and punched in Richard's number.

"How'd it go?" he asked.

"We might have overdone it. We may have broken him," she said, thinking she herself never felt lousier.

"I have a feeling he'll perk up when he sees tomorrow's paper. *The Hankey Herald* is running a feature on Vasquez tomorrow morning," Richard explained. "Tomorrow afternoon, a reporter from *The New York Times* is arriving for an interview. The story they want to run answers the question, "Are bold and beautiful opera stars the key to reviving a dying art form, from small houses up, rather than from the Met down?"

"Great!" Deanna said, climbing into her car. "The old double-edged Beauty and the Beast feature where once again Hankey plays the beast. At least Vasquez comes out smelling like a princess."

"That's what we need right now—to boost ticket sales."

"By the way, Oriane never showed," Deanna said.

Richard said nothing for a long moment.

"Richard?"

"I had a feeling that might happen. She might not have been able to summon the indifference needed for this special op."

"Did you know Knobby fired Carnahan?"

Richard was quiet again, but Deanna would bet money that he was pursing his lips. "Had to be done, from what I hear."

Vivian knocked on the window. Deanna depressed the door lock and waved her inside.

"That won't help Oriane overcome her crush," Deanna said to Richard. She held up her finger to Vivian as if to say, just a minute. "Speaking of killer crushes, Jeannie is scheduled to have everyone for dinner after dress rehearsal in her Hankey home."

"You mean her McMansion," Richard added.

"Right." This house lust coming from two people who have a higher standard of living than most of rest of the world. "Maybe we should rent a neutral space. She really doesn't need to be around Vasquez now."

"If he's as broken as you think, it shouldn't be a problem. Besides, it'll be a real treat for the regular choristers. I'll bet most of them have never seen anything like Jacobs Place. By the way, I gave the *Times* your contact number since you're the new guild chair."

"I'll be ready to spin if they call. I'll see you after dress rehearsal, then."

29
The Banquet Hall

The cast, crew, and guild members are enjoying a reception and meal at Jacobs Place after Wednesday's dress rehearsal.

Jeannie surveyed the crowd assembled for the party. They oohed and aahed from the moment they entered her home. She was delighted to have a reason to show off her beautiful homestead to the cast and crew. Perhaps she'd give up her New York residence altogether. People in Hankey were more charming and welcoming than she remembered and could scarcely be called nonplussed about anything.

Many guests already gushed their appreciation. Jeannie gave the caterer new marching orders: he must butler more hors d'oeuvres—no holding back. She wanted them to feel as though they were appreciated for the sacrifices they made. She knew that only selected members of the cast were paid, and that the rest received meager rewards compared to the time invested.

Earlier in the day, while getting a detoxifying facial at Font-o-Beauty, she overheard people who were thankful—even grateful for the opera company whose production garnered Hankey some attention from *The New York Times*. *The New York Times!* they squealed. Luckily, it was feature coverage and not an exposé.

If the writer endeavored to be objective from the get-go, you couldn't tell from the story that wound up in the nation's most sought-after Arts Section. But Leandro was magical like that. He just drew people to him. His life story—growing up in privation in a South American country, learning to project by singing across the open range, then finding a generous patron whose belief in him was unflinching, and winning the Operatoonity Contest as a nobody competing against a sea of privileged somebody's—was intoxicating. It was his unbridled talent and sheer magnetism that paved Vasquez's way into international stardom. Now that classic opera was going High Def at Cineplex showings around the country, the *Times* concluded that Leandro was the perfect complement to the new generation of beautiful opera stars.

"Oh, Mrs. Jacobs," gushed one of the girls in the chorus. "Your home is beautiful. Thank you for having us."

Jeannie called over a server holding a tray of martinis—an extraordinary looking young woman whose perfunctory ponytail only highlighted the exquisite bone structure of her face. "Drink, darling?" Jeannie said to the girl.

"Everywhere I've been this week—the mini-mart, the beauty parlor—especially at the beauty parlor—people, well women mostly," the chorister continued, "are talking about Leandro Vasquez. Leandro this and Leandro that. We're lucky to have him."

Jeannie grabbed a martini from the tray and handed it to the chatty young woman. "Have a drink. Have a good time," she said, straining to smile.

Jeannie had wanted her new volunteer affiliation to provide the sense of fulfillment in giving back to the community that she had sought and lost over the years with other arts organizations. Why had she become obsessed with Vasquez, with winning his favor? His affection, his love? People told her she was a charming woman. Perhaps what they really meant was that her money was the most intoxicating thing about her, and she was only appealing by virtue of her wealth. Where Vasquez was concerned, she simply couldn't resist him. Having lived in New York for the last thirty years—the Sutton Place area of Manhattan—she'd met plenty of self-important types. Some charismatic. Some charming. No one ever turned her head while Sol was alive. Then she lost Sol, and her view of the world shifted—dramatically. She saw everything afresh through the wide eyes of a teenager. When she met Vasquez, her world turned on its head. She knew she could never have him. But that hardly stopped her from wanting him—a perfect specimen of a man gifted with the music of the ages.

Around nine-thirty, all the guild members had showed. Deanna and Richard entered together.

"Why, Richard," Jeannie said. "You are a bon vivant in your nailhead blazer. Armani?"

"No, Boscov's," Richard said, referring to a local department store.

"Still, very smart on you," Jeannie said, while Deanna squeezed his arm.

Shortly before ten, Vasquez arrived at the party, followed by Knobby and Maestro. As he stepped into the foyer, the crowd assembled, chorus members, and supernumeraries applauded wildly. Their much maligned town had just received front page attention in *The New York Times* Arts Section, and Vasquez was the reason why.

Vasquez bowed deeply as if taking a Metropolitan Opera curtain call. The room fell silent, waiting for Vasquez to say something.

"Speech, speech," someone in the crowd called out.

"Gracias—lovely people—of Hankey," Vasquez said, using his best stage projection. "I am pleased—serve a you."

Deanna slipped her arm into Jeannie's and said softly, "I hated to do what we did the other night. But he seems like a changed man."

"We'll see," Jeannie said, with little emotion in her voice, but thinking that as long as there was a fresh supply of willing women, men like Leandro didn't change.

"How are you doing—anyway?" Deanna asked.

It was an elementary question, but Jeannie knew Deanna's implication. "Better," she said, hoping her watery eyes didn't give her away. "Ready to move on. I suppose I have to greet the divo. That way, he can go meet all his admirers." She stepped forward and ceremoniously welcomed in the trio on whom most of the success of the production now depended.

Most of the company's eyes were still on Jeannie and Vasquez. He lifted her hand from her side and kissed it. She blanched at the feel of his lips on her skin.

Arnaud rushed forward. "Leandro! Arnaud will take your coat."

"Gracias Señor Marceau." Vazquez twirled his cape from his shoulders dramatically to reveal another white puffy shirt, this time paired with tight maroon pants. He was a god on earth. How many men could pull off wearing a cape like that without looking like a toreador who'd misplaced his bull ring?

"Be right back," Arnaud said.

Deanna stepped forward. "Hungry?"

Vasquez gestured as if to say *starving*.

"Wait 'til you see the buffet Jeannie's set out for us," Deanna said, grabbing his arm and leading him out of the foyer.

From a distance, she followed Deanna and Vasquez to the buffet. Vasquez greeted Richard with a hearty, two-arm handshake. *The New York Times* article was a coup for the guild and everyone was giddy with the attention. Vasquez was charming to a fault, thanking everyone who wished him well on his opening while filling his plate.

Though she'd been many things in her life—a debutante (she was once as fresh-faced and lovely as the server toting the tray of martinis), a beautiful young mother, a dilettante, a philanthropist, and a society matron, most recently—Jeannie reminded herself that at her age, she simply wasn't good enough for this Adonis in the prime of life. Why hadn't she seen that before? It was a paroxysm, certainly, that rich old men retained the power and influence amassed throughout life while age alone stripped women of theirs. But a reality nonetheless.

* * *

Arnaud scurried past the hall closet, holding Vasquez's cape. He tried the doors to several downstairs rooms until he stumbled onto a spare bedroom with a full mirror on the closet door. He turned on the light on the nightstand. Then standing in front of the mirror, he pressed the cape to his face. What was that fabric? It was light and soft. Maybe it was llama hair. Did they have llamas in Argentina? And it smelled like Vasquez—like his cologne. Arnaud inhaled deeply, and it made his knees soften. He stood in front of the mirror, whipped the cape around his shoulders, fastening it at the neck. "I am—the Lion Man," Arnaud said in a deep voice.

"Mr. Vasquez?" a woman's voice called from the entrance to the bedroom.

Sheepishly, Arnaud turned to face one of the servers from the catering crew.

"Sorry—I thought you were—someone else," she said, hurrying away, her pert ponytail bobbing behind her.

Arnaud took the cape off and laid it on the bed. When Vasquez wanted to leave, only Arnaud could help him retrieve his cape. He turned off the light and scuttled himself back to the dining room.

"There you are!" Arnaud said, staring at Vasquez's plate, piled high with food, including three mounds of caviar. "Do you need a drink?" Arnaud snapped his fingers at a waiter passing by and lifted a martini off the tray. Then he led Vasquez to the high-top table reserved for him. "Delicious, no?"

"No!" Vasquez said. "Every day—I make squeeze—Oriane, she stinking like—dead fish."

"No!" Arnaud said, concealing his delight.

"Yes! She need a—how you say—"

"Fragrant bubble bath?" Arnaud offered.

"Sí. Bubbly bath! I must tell—that Know-bee," Vasquez said. "Where Know-bee?"

Arnaud shrugged, trying to stave off a smile.

The server with the ponytail trotted by with a tray of hors d'oeuvres.

"*Delicioso*," Vasquez said, drawing out every syllable in the word. From the back, the tight fit of her short-sleeved shift suggested a very shapely rear-end lurking beneath. Vasquez put his arm out and gently detoured her over to the high-top. "Not so fast. What you got—a me?"

Arnaud wasn't listening as the girl rattled off the appetizers on her tray. He was staring at the handsome Vasquez, observing the heat behind his eyes.

"What is name?" Vasquez said to the young woman, his eyes riveted to her.

Oh, if only Arnaud could be the object of such longing.

"Mindy." She smiled, revealing a row of sparkling white teeth, straight as fence posts. "Here you go," she said, placing a few goodies on a napkin beside Vasquez's plate. "Gotta circulate," she said. And as she walked away, Vasquez slid his hand across her perky derriere. Arnaud could almost see the smile creasing her face from the back of her head.

"Delightful—Mindy," Vasquez said, his pupils wide as saucers.

It was happening again. If Vasquez felt remorse over his philandering, it had vanished like the caviar he had piled on his plate. Vasquez was on the chase once more.

"Find Mindy, Arnaud." Vasquez popped a truffle in his mouth and licked his fingers. "Tell her—I want her." He drew his finger to his lips and brooded.

If only Arnaud were a glove upon that finger, that Arnaud might touch those lips. "Here?" Arnaud asked, his voice cracking.

Vasquez glanced at his watch. "Fifteen minute."

Arnaud faced him slack-jawed. "Her? She's a little trollop pushing appetizers."

"You owe—a me. You make a joke of me with Richard. I want Bibian but no get. I need women—bad need. Ever since Nuevo York, when I want 'the head,' but I get old cheese!" Vasquez poked him in the chest on *old cheese*. "Trollop—look a-tasty—to me. No old cheese."

Could Arnaud live through setting up a rendezvous with another would-be lover? What choice did he have? "There's a bedroom down the hall, three doors down on your left," he said, holding up and wiggling three fingers. "It's dark. You'll know it's the right one because your cape's lying on the bed."

"You find—trollop. I find—Know-bee," Vasquez said.

* * *

Vasquez swaggered into the living room, enjoying the reaction of each woman as he passed by. It was like watching candles melting. He saw his quarry in the corner, talking with Oriane. He dared not go any closer. Every time he got close to Oriane, his feet turned ice cold. Then in the next instant, he felt like he was burning up. And neither of those was the worst part. She was the most tasty morsel in rehearsal this weekend. He'd wanted to gobble her up. Now, she just about made him sick. Was this what happened with all American women? Once you decide to make love to them, they stink like old fish you forgot to clean for days.

"Know-bee!" Vasquez called. He cocked his finger, to make Know-bee come to him. He wrapped his arm around his shoulder until they were safely in the other room. "I no can—do love scene with Oriane."

Knobby cracked a smile. He sighed, shaking his head. "You're funny, Vasquez."

"No joke. She smell—like a fish. Like dead fish."

Know-bee's brow furrowed. He inhaled deeply. "Take it back, Vasquez."

"She reek—a fish!" he said.

"I'm a black belt in the black arts, Vasquez! You make one more nasty comment about Oriane," Knobby said, striking a martial arts fighting position, "and you might never sing—or love—again."

Vasquez shrugged. America is full of crazy people. "Fine. Go back—to a trout." He backed away, remembering he had a date with a ponytail. Why hadn't someone told him American women were so smelly? Would Ponytail smell like trout, too?

* * *

Jeannie didn't think it was wise for her to get up-close-and-personal with Vasquez this evening. But she certainly enjoyed looking at him. She'd position herself nearby to better admire him. He looked scrumptious from any angle. She scanned the crowd in the dining room but didn't see him. He might be relaxing in the foyer or the sitting room with others from the show. She strolled through the front rooms of the house. No Vasquez. He had dug into the food with such appetite, it was possible he was in the kitchen entertaining the catering staff, sneaking their canapés. She pushed open the swinging door that led from the dining room to the kitchen.

"Has anyone seen Mindy?" the captain of the catering staff was calling as Jeannie entered.

"Are you missing a server?" Jeannie asked.

* * *

Arnaud grabbed another martini off the tray. His fourth, but who was counting. It looked like Deanna approaching, but since she was a little fuzzy around the edges, he couldn't quite tell. "Deanna?" he said, trying not to slur the double n's in her name, which made it sound worse.

"Arnaud? You're plastered," Deanna said. "I don't think I've ever seen you in your cups before."

Arnaud turned his empty martini glass upside down. "Arnaud is out of his cups."

Deanna laughed easily. But then everyone in the guild had the front page Arts Section glow this evening. "Have you seen Jeannie?"

Arnaud shrugged. "Not lately."

"I wanted to run something by her about the gala. Maybe she's in the kitchen. Come with me," she said, leading him away. "Did you try those chicken livers? They were exquisite. With any luck, they'll be an extra one in here I can sneak."

They entered the kitchen, which was mostly deserted. Jeannie must have hired a half-dozen servers, all circulating. No Jeannie. A man stood over the work island, arranging salmon balls on a tray. He wore a black polo shirt with "Donny's" embroidered over the pocket.

"Excuse us," Deanna began. "We were looking for Jeannie?"

The man with the catering company looked in his early thirties. He had lots of sandy brown hair he flicked off his face several times while finishing the tray. His arms were as muscular as Arnaud's and evenly tanned. "Sorry, haven't seen her—for a while. When you find her, tell her Donny needs to talk to her briefly."

"Are you Donny of 'Donny's'?" Deanna asked.

"None other," the man said.

"Your rumaki were out of this world," Deanna said.

You're out of this world, Arnaud thought. Where has Donny been all my life?

"Melted in my mouth," Deanna continued. "Mine never came out like that. I'd love to know your secret ingredient."

Donny smiled. "I'll tell you. But then I'll have to kill you."

Arnaud looked at Deanna, whose cheeks had flushed pink. Donny was flirting with her. Another perfect man bites the sawdust. "No Jeannie? Come along, darling," Arnaud said, pulling her out of the kitchen.

"We'll pass along the message," Deanna said as they were leaving. She turned to Arnaud. "Boy, was he cute."

"Could you have been more obvious?" Arnaud said flatly. "Anyway, no Jeannie."

"How about Vasquez? He didn't skip out already, did he?" A wave of recognition splashed across Deanna's face. "You don't suppose that Jeannie and Vasquez—"

* * *

Jeannie unlocked the drawer in the nightstand. There it was, just as she'd left it earlier in the week, when she was thinking of using it on herself. She picked up the shiny 9 mm handgun, inserted the magazine, and pulled back on the slide, loading one bullet into the firing chamber. She exited the master bedroom and glided down the steps and headed down the hall toward the guest bedrooms. She rattled the doorknob on the first bedroom she came to. Locked. No light coming from under the door. She leaned her head against the door. No noise inside. She quickly ruled out the next bedroom. Which meant they could only be in the last one, the only one she'd left unlocked in case the caterer needed extra storage.

She crept to the door, which was open a crack, and peered inside. There, gleaming in the moonlight, was the bare rump of Leandro Vasquez. Underneath him, writhing in pleasure was presumably the server who'd gone missing—Mindy? Was that her name? Such a beautiful ass, she thought. Such a pity to have to ruin it. Jeannie took a deep breath, raised the gun, aiming down sight at the target like her instructor had taught her, and placed her index finger on the trigger.

* * *

"How many times does Arnaud have to say he is sorry?" Arnaud was telling Deanna. "Arnaud only tried to make our star happy. He got carried away. Think of the good Arnaud has done the guild over the years. Forgive this one indiscretion. Please."

"Up until Vasquez, you have been a good friend to the guild," Deanna said. "But no more pimping."

"On Arnaud's life, he swears, *after tonight*, no more pimping."

"After tonight?" Deanna's eyes widened with the certain knowledge that Arnaud was up to something. "What did you do for Vasquez—tonight?"

"No chance of Vasquez being with Jeannie, I'm afraid," Arnaud said.

"What did you do for him?" Deanna said, searching his eyes. "Tell me!"

"What?" he asked.

"Don't *what* me, you stinker. You—"

Without warning, the crack of a gun rang through the house followed by a blood-chilling scream.

"Oh—God!" Arnaud cried and the glass slipped out of his hand. He bolted for the front door and ran out of the house, certain that whoever had a gun was going to shoot him next.

* * *

Richard tore off toward the sound of the gunshot. Deanna and other guests followed close behind. When Richard reached the bedroom, he found Jeannie holding a smoking gun, and Mindy cowering behind a naked Vasquez. Neither was bleeding though both appeared terror struck. Her first shot must have missed. He watched as Jeannie raised the gun, aiming it at Vasquez's belly button. Her arm shook violently. If she fired again, although it appeared that she wasn't an experienced shot, she might shoot off that grandioso package of his.

"Who was shot?" Deanna called into the room. "I'll call an ambulance."

"No need. No one was hurt," Richard said, in a soothing tone. "If Jeannie puts the gun down, things will go back as they were—no harm done."

"I hate him," Jeannie said. "I want to put a bullet through his heart."

Vasquez cried. "You *loco*—"

"Keep quiet, Vasquez," Richard scolded him. "Jeannie, put the gun down."

"I love him," she said, tears staining her cheeks.

"We don't shoot people we love, Jeannie," Richard said, as if talking to a kindergartener. He gently placed his hand on top of hers. "He's not worth it," he said. "You're better than what he has to offer. He's just a stupid kid who's full of himself right now, but even he doesn't deserve to be shot." Miraculously, Richard eased the gun out of Jeannie's hand—as if someone else was helping to pry open her fingers. He felt a pressure on the right side of his body, as though someone unseen was standing beside him. "Thank you, Mary," he whispered. Mary's pulsing energy reorganized itself into a little blast of wind and blew out the open window, fluttering the curtains on her exit.

"Richard—what you—" Vasquez began.

"I told you to keep your mouth shut!" Richard commanded, now holding the gun. "Or I'll shoot you myself."

"Richard," Deanna cried. "Don't you dare."

Richard wrapped his arm around Jeannie and eased her into Deanna's arms. "But if I have to shoot him," he told her, lowering her voice. "I'll aim for the *cojones*, not the vocal cords."

He turned around to face the naked couple, slipping the safety back on the gun. Vasquez's face was filled with terror. "Get your pants on, Leandro." Then he stuffed the gun in the back of his pants.

Vasquez reached for a pile of clothing in front of him. "You can—a leave now," Vasquez told Richard. He handed Mindy her underwear and her shift.

Without saying a word, Mindy, now dressed, picked up her shoes from off the floor and hurried out of the bedroom.

"I'm sticking with you until that butt of yours is parked in that limousine and headed home. Yes, the Lion Man sleeps tonight. By himself," Richard said as Leandro buttoned his shirt. "You're opening a show tomorrow."

* * *

After Richard escorted Leandro to the front door of the carriage house, he walked to the back door of the Frantz estate. Vivian was seated at the kitchen table in a house robe, having a hot cup of something. Deanna said Vivian begged off the dinner party because of a migraine. Richard figured she was still avoiding him. He was just about to knock on Vivian's kitchen door when his phone rang. He pulled it out of his pocket and glanced at the display.

"Marlena?"

"Hi, Dad. I got your message. Did I catch you at a good time?"

"No problem," Richard said, lowering his voice. "So, how's everybody?"

"We're all fine. Did you call me about something special?"

"We've got a world-class singer coming in for *Don Giovanni*. Thought you might want to fly out."

"Sorry can't. Sonny has little league. How about next time?"

Should he go into the fact that there might not be a next time, that this might be their last show? "Sure, I'll call you in a month or two. Take care, honey."

Vivian must have heard him talking. The porch light came on and the kitchen door opened a crack. "Richard? Come in," Vivian said. "Would you like some tea?"

Richard slipped inside the door. The kitchen smelled like bergamot. Vivian had made herself some Earl Grey. "No, I just wanted to apologize. I insinuated that you—well, you know—that you invited him into your bed. It was wrong of me. I see now that he's incorrigible. That you were blameless."

"Come in," she said and pointed to a kitchen chair.

"No, thanks," he said and remained standing. "I can't stay."

Vivian sat down and wrapped her hands around her tea cup. "It was bothering me, and I accept your apology. Deanna called.

She said you were a real hero tonight. That you saved Jeannie from a jail term. And you saved Vasquez. That you saved the show."

Richard shrugged, but he felt pride coursing through him when Vivian mentioned his intervention, just the same. "I did what I had to do. Anyway, about that gala tomorrow night. I want you to be my guest—my date—like we talked about before. Would you like to join me, Ms. Pirelli?"

"Why, yes," Vivian said. "I would like to be your date, Dr. Rohrer."

30
The Prima Recita

It is Thursday evening in downtown Hankey. The magic of an early evening in May has blanketed the town like a cascade of falling stars. A newly scrubbed statue of the city founder glistens atop the marquee, standing sentinel over a parade of lit bulbs, giving the opera house the glow of a Broadway venue. It is one hour before curtain.

Deanna and Richard huddled in the back of the opera house box office.

"So many without tickets or reservations," Deanna said, eyeing the line of people extending out the door and out of sight. "It's only seven o clock."

"Dozens of first timers. That's a great sign," Richard said. "We'll have to open another window. I'll man it. You have other things to do." He reached under inside the desk and pulled out a cash box. "Perhaps our Don's not such a devil after all."

"Last night, standing at that bedroom door. That was the scariest night of my life," Deanna said. "You were amazing. It was an extraordinary hostage negotiation. I am in awe, Richard."

"And I you, Deanna," he said.

"Can I count that for you?" she asked, pointing to the box.

"Already counted," Richard said, setting the box inside the till and lifting the shade to signal a new window was open. He called into the crowd, "If you need tickets, the line starts here."

"I'll make sure they're standing in the proper line," Deanna said, heading into the crowd. She grabbed the stanchion and set it in the middle of the entrance. Someone reached out and grabbed her arm. Startled, she whirled around to see a younger man smiling in her direction.

"Need help?" Donny of Donny's Catering asked. He was wearing blue jeans and a tweed sport coat.

Jeans? She should've told him about what was considered customary attire for opening night at the opera. Deanna gasped. "You're here?"

"After last night's little drama," Donny said. "I wouldn't have missed this. I gave away my Alan Jackson tickets for this."

"Now I'm impressed," she said, thinking that he looked good in jeans. Like he'd been born to wear them.

"What are you doing?" he asked.

As Deanna directed him to grab the other stanchion and string the red velvet ropes between the two poles, she thought of her third-row orchestra seats—a pair, a hundred bucks a pop. She was going to invite her new trainer to opening night and then things got too hectic, and she forgot to ask him. She was relieved to fill that empty seat tonight with such a fine pair of blue jeans. And did it really matter that he had worn jeans? Jeans on Donny looked better than tux pants on most men.

* * *

Knobby approached Vivian, who offered to open the house. "Everything backstage is perfect. The performers feel comfortable," he said. "Thank you for everything you've done. Oh, and did Oriane get the flowers?"

"I delivered them myself," Vivian said. "They were so fresh, they had dew on them. She was floored."

"Very good," Knobby said. "I'd say, ten minutes. Then you can herd the masses in."

Vivian fiddled with her earring. "You were just backstage? How was Vasquez?"

"Sounded great in warm-ups. Let's not forget, he's a professional," Knobby said, "bound for greater houses than this little music box," though he himself had grown to love Hankey and admire the guild. Standing in that house on opening night, he felt like he was home.

"I thought we'd 'cured' him, with our charades Monday night," Vivian said. "That's some kind of cad who can pretend nothing's wrong after what happened last evening."

"I think one more dose of 'castor oil' will do the trick," Knobby said.

"You have something else up your sleeve?" Vivian said, worry creasing her face. "It won't compromise the show, will it?"

"Now, you know me better than that."

"Know-bee!" Arnaud called from the front of the house. "Know-bee!"

"I'll go round up my ushers," Vivian said.

Knobby was poised to take the biggest professional risk of his career. The women's shenanigans hadn't humbled Vasquez for longer than a day. When Vasquez hooked up with a server last night, he almost got his ass shot off trying to get a piece of hers. What Knobby planned for Vasquez would either cure him forever or ruin them both. "What do you think, Arnaud?"

"They will do as Arnaud asked," Arnaud said, clasping his hands in the middle of his chest. "Arnaud will stake his reputation on it. I will give you the cue—I promise. You follow that, and everything will work out." Then he removed a hankie from the breast pocket of his jacket and waved it until he got Maestro's attention and blew him a kiss.

* * *

Deanna felt an energy in the house like the first time she'd been to La Scala. Just like La Scala, every seat was filled. The murmur of expectation for the show to begin, issuing from twelve hundred people, reminded her of an enchanted forest humming on an early summer evening.

The houselights dimmed. Deanna's whole body trembled. Her hands clutched the armrests as the spotlight emerged for Maestro's entrance. Richard had stopped by to say the house was sold out—they had to sell standing-room-only tickets—and not to look for him, that he had exchanged his seats with two subscribers who normally sat in the back row. Vivian claimed to be too nervous to sit for the time being, Richard explained, and asked if they could stand for a while along with Hankey's first-ever SRO crowd behind the orchestra seating.

An older woman with opera glasses and her husband, presumably, slipped into the seats beside Deanna just as Maestro lifted his baton.

Deanna leaned in close to the woman and pointed to her glasses, "I'm not sure you'll need those glasses in the third row."

"I most certainly do!" the woman snapped. "I want to see every inch of the Lion Man when he peels off his shirt."

Good to know they selected the right photo for the poster. Deanna fell silent, and let the overture wash over her like anesthesia. It was one of her favorite parts—six minutes of calm before what augured to be a tempest of a show. When she returned her hand to the armrest, Donny's hand was already covering it. She slipped hers inside his and held it tightly.

* * *

What a magnificent sound! Maestro's orchestra sounded better than Richard ever remembered, even richer and fuller than last evening. The excitement was building and building toward his favorite section of the overture—the allegro. Richard had to keep from laughing as the Maestro's comb-over flopped back and forth with the downbeat. During the tremolos, Maestro kneaded the air with his fingertips at the same speed the violinists' bows flew over the strings.

What a genius Mozart was! His overtures hinted at the conflicts in store for operagoers—subtly clever and musically resonant. One hardly needed to be a musician to appreciate the tension between Giovanni's arrogance and the higher power that eventually destroys him foreshadowed in the overture. Mozart was one composer who always rewarded careful listeners.

Richard massaged his lower back with his left hand—he wasn't keen on standing for the entire show. In fact, he'd not "stand" for it, and Vivian would know as much after the first act. Perhaps he could coax her into taking a seat. He heard the new, plodding tempo, which meant Leporello's appearance was imminent—the overture had concluded. He closed his eyes and prayed silently. "Wish us luck, Mary. Wish us luck." As the curtain peeled open, he felt a cool breeze wafting over the back of his neck.

* * *

Don Giovanni was never Mary's favorite work by Mozart. She preferred *The Marriage of Figaro,* which was clever and light and not so complex. Unlike most fans of *Don Giovanni,* her favorite character was Don Ottavio. Typically, opera lovers regarded him as a wimp. But Don Ottavio was simple, and his trials were essentially simple. Everything he did, every note out of his mouth, underscored his abiding love for Donna Anna.

These days, the darkest parts of *Don Giovanni* had to be played as black as the libertine's heart—the postmodern era demanded such cynicism; otherwise, the piece lost any relevance whatsoever, becoming almost laughable. To her mind, Giovanni wasn't sexy at all—just an overconfident man of privilege who had nowhere to go but down, destined to self-destruct. She would do her part—and then some—to ensure that when Giovanni faced his darkest hour this evening, it would be horrific in an extra dimension.

* * *

At Vasquez's first appearance in a mask and cape, the audience swooned. He was a presence. The woman beside Deanna panted like a startled cat and whipped on her opera glasses. The moment Vasquez opened his mouth, it was as if the entire audience held its breath, to catch every vibration of his every note.

During the set change from scene three to scene four, Donny whispered to Deanna, "That Giovanni's something! Real eye candy for the ladies."

Was that just an innocent statement or did Donny truly regard Vasquez as eye candy? Did Donny like men more than women? Did he like both? He had a metrosexual kind of appeal. She hoped he wasn't bi. She'd barely survived Stu's cheating on her with another woman. She'd die if she had to worry about her lover stepping out on her with another man.

"I didn't realize the actors talked in opera," Donny said.

"In Mozart they do," Deanna said, sneaking a glance at his legs. She could see hints of well developed thigh muscles straining against his jeans. The fact that he worked out was no help in determining his sexual preference. Gay man often had hot bodies. "Well, not just Mozart."

"What was that?" Donny asked.

"Shush!" the lady next to her said. "They're starting."

Deanna laughed to herself. In ten years, she never remembered subscribers being that attentive during scene changes. She wasn't sure if Donny was liking the show, but she felt pretty sure he'd appreciate the humor in scene five.

* * *

Richard had read about the production of *Don Giovanni* James Levine conducted at Tanglewood in 2006, and had thought of a bit of humorous business for the Maestro. Richard was the only one who could suggest such a thing. The shtick complemented Maestro's healthy ego, per Richard. Lo and behold, Maestro agreed to try it opening night—surprising even the orchestra.

Just after Leporello tells Elvira that she is hardly the first woman Giovanni has abandoned, that women in every country, every city, every village have known his exploits, and moments before he sings, *"Madamina, Il Catalogo,"* Maestro walked out of the pit and onto the stage and handed Leporello the score of the entire opera. Elvira snatched it from him, greedily searching for her name in *Il Catalogo*. The audience roared.

"A great gag," Richard said. "They loved it. Want to take our seats now?"

"I hear the clinking of the coins, Richard," she said. "Gold is coming."

* * *

At intermission, Deanna was thrilled that people couldn't shut up about Vasquez. She waited in the ladies room line just to eavesdrop.

"I've died and gone to heaven," one of the subscribers said.

"After this production," another subscriber said, "maybe you'd prefer to go to hell—with you know who!" And they both laughed uproariously.

"Imagine, that little girl from Hankey being seduced by—him!" another said, and every woman within earshot sighed.

By him! Deanna thought. Already, Vasquez had been elevated to godlike status and need only be referred to as *him*, the great *him*. If they only knew *him*.

The houselights flashed three times. The next act—the second act—would be their triumph or their undoing. It was a tricky one— very sophisticated technically, symbolically, musically. Deanna wasn't a praying woman, but she shot up a quick communiqué anyway. They'd come too far and endured too much to fail now.

* * *

Mary loved what Knobby was doing with the second act. Giovanni became more menacing, more crazed with each scene, which made perfect sense to her. The audience must be made to feel that Giovanni deserves the end he gets. Not to mention that it made the task expected of Mary that much easier. Oh, wasn't Giovanni the hell-bent lothario? Seducing Elvira's servant right under her nose. Taunting and mocking the ghost of a man, a military hero, slain by his own hand. Rivaled only by Vasquez himself. Chasing all the women on the guild. Loving and then abandoning Jeannie Jacobs because she wouldn't "give him the head." Seducing the serving girl at Jeannie's party right under her nose. Calling Richard an old goat and fantasizing about his being devoured by a ravenous wolf or stewed by a gypsy. Tonight was Mary's chance to let Vasquez know that her old goat was off limits to all, including wolves with fangs and gypsies with goulash.

Finally, the stage lights came up on the final scene in Act II, The Banquet Hall. How was Vasquez dressed for the last supper?

Shirtless. Hundreds of opera glasses flew to hungry eyes. Women gasped. Some moaned at such a magnificent sight. And Mary's job was to devil this don? This was going to be fun.

The crowd was rapt as Giovanni, the beautiful anti-hero, one destined for his own self-destruction, taunted his manservant with his words and terrified him with his actions while his hands ranged over the maidservant's shapely form. How would the audience react to the risky business coming up? Giovanni sat the maidservant on the end of the table, facing him, slid his head under her skirt and said the line, "*Ah che piatto saporito!*" When the supertitle, "Here's a dish to be commended," flashed overhead, some in the audience spit out their false teeth. Mary noticed that Deanna's date threw his head back and belly laughed at that line. Classic opera for the twenty-first century. Knobby knew how to keep operagoers on the edge of their seats.

The lights onstage dimmed suddenly, the scene was progressing—or retrogressing, more accurately. The ghost of the Commendatore loomed upstage in silhouette. As more lightning flashed, the Commendatore's twisted, decaying face was illuminated. Though the audience found him terrifying, to Mary's way of thinking, the Commendatore looked a lot like the statue of Henry Hankey atop the marquee, right down to the tri-corner hat. Here we go, she thought, stilling her essence to give her the ability to summon her friends.

When Giovanni drops his sword and falls to his knees—that was to be her cue, Arnaud had said. She waited and waited. More lightning, then artificial fog—dry ice—eked into the banquet hall. The audience shivered at the gothic special effects Knobby was unleashing in this scene. Vasquez turned to face his ghostly accuser and drew his sword.

Suddenly, as the pillars flanking the Commendatore turned to fire, Mary spotted the ectoplasm of another ghost flying into the scene. Paylor! What was she doing here? No one had invited her. Paylor swooped in on Giovanni, her shrieking nearly drowning out his line about having no fear. Several in the audience screamed.

Giovanni hadn't yet dropped his sword, but Mary had no choice but to appear now.

"Let's go," she cried and Mary and her ghostly band descended onto the opera house stage.

"Good—a god!" Vasquez cried to the back wall of the theatre, flinging his sword away two lines early out of sheer terror.

Another ghost rushed in to possess the body of the actor singing the Commendatore. With inhuman strength, this one grabbed Vasquez by the arm and dragged him backstage to the fires of hell with such brut force it was as if Vasquez was a forty-pound waif, not a strapping baritone weighing almost two hundred pounds. Who was this new ghost? Mary needed to know.

"Gahhh!" Vasquez cried at the Commendatore's iron grip on his arm.

Donato Bianco? What was he doing here? Didn't he have better things to do? It certainly wasn't Hankey's fault that he'd been run over by an ice cream truck. He'd brought that on himself. Vasquez was Mary's to devil, doggone it. No one should have the pleasure of that task but her—and her friends.

"Aaaahhh," shrieked the actor playing the Commendatore as Mary rushed to his aid, trying to extract Bianco's ghost from him. Just as she got Bianco to leave the poor Commendatore, Paylor threw herself into Vasquez's body.

"Zahhhh!" Vasquez cried as if shot through with a bolt of electricity. Mary saw black smoke streaming from the top of his head.

She and her friends had agreed to *frighten* Vasquez—not *kill* him. The guild needed him to survive. He had to deliver six stellar performances of Giovanni for the opera house to stay afloat. She and her friends didn't have the power and couldn't inflict the terror that poltergeists could.

She had to stop Paylor and Bianco, who would stop at nothing to ruin the show. Like freakish bands of green slime, Mary and her friends streaked over to Paylor and began pummeling her to get her to release Vasquez, whose head swung violently backwards. Then it jerked right. In the next second, he took an uppercut to the left.

While Paylor rendered Vasquez immobile, Bianco threw him a couple of blows in the stomach. It was as if Vasquez were in a boxing match with three or more invisible and deadly opponents.

Another ghostly presence swooped in and clawed at Bianco. Who was this new ghost?

"Don Giovanni," the ghost bellowed. Vasquez, recognizing the voice of his rescuer, wailed, "*Señor Garcia! ¡Socorro!*"

Who in the name of all things sacred was Garcia? Whoever he was, they needed him. "Señor Garcia! Help us!" Mary cried.

"*Dond' escono quei vortici. Di foco pieu d'orror,*" Vasquez wailed. "What mean these dreadful gulfs that open to devour me?" flashed overhead as supertitles. Certainly, no two lines had ever been sung with more verisimilitude in the last three hundred years than in this particular production of *Don Giovanni*.

With Giovanni's fateful and final words, the Commendatore is supposed to push Giovanni off the platform at the back of the stage into hell. Vasquez didn't wait for a shove. He dove off the back of the platform.

"Fires of hell—now!" Knobby shouted in the headset.

Chorus members onstage and a cluster offstage gawked at the spectacle, trumpeting their final lines, "*Tutto a tue colpe e poco. Viene c' è un mal peggior.*" The English translation, never more prophetic, "Horror more dire awaits thee. And dread is thy dark doom" appeared overhead simultaneously. That's because Vasquez came rocketing out of hell, back into audience view, suspended in the air by the energy of the ghosts tussling over him.

"He's mine," Paylor shrieked, tugging on one arm.

"Not on your wretched slimy soul," Mary cried, yanking on the other.

Bianco and Garcia continued to battle overhead, with each new blow, careening into Mary and friends, causing them to lose their grip.

Back and forth they pulled on Vasquez's arms, his legs, then his arms and legs at the same time.

By now, Vasquez howled like a wounded hyena.

Knobby saw Arnaud on the other side of the auditorium waving furiously at him, drawing a line across his neck, mouthing, "Cut! Cut! Cut!"

No more light, no more ghosts, that's what Arnaud had said. "Blackout! Blackout! Now!" Knobby yelled through the headset.

Instantly the stage fell dark. Deprived of energy-giving light, the connection to the spirit world was broken, and the ghosts released their grip. Vasquez fell to the mattresses piled below him in a heap.

Before Knobby's crew had the lights back on, before Vasquez could stumble to his feet for curtain call, the audience had stormed out of their seats, applauding thunderously.

31
The Encore

The post-opening night party is in full swing at Luigi's, Hankey's most popular Italian restaurant. Gala attendance is the highest ever and includes most of the guild members.

There weren't a lot of places in Hankey that could accommodate a crowd in excess of three hundred. Luigi's was always the restaurant tapped for events with huge numbers to feed. For tonight's gala, Luigi pulled in every friend, every relative, and every friend of a friend and relative of a relative. He promised Deanna no one's glass would be empty that night and that everyone would eat their fill, or he wasn't Luigi Leggione!

Deanna was standing in the corner with Donny, waiting for the cast to arrive when Luigi approached. "How you like so far?" Luigi asked Deanna.

"Fantastic, Luigi!"

He patted her on the face lightly.

"Luigi, this is Donny. He's also a—" Deanna stopped. She'd charmed an extraordinary deal out of Luigi. If she mentioned that her date was a caterer, that tidbit alone might jeopardize future opening night parties at Luigi's. And make no mistake, after tonight's success, there would be plenty more galas for the Hankey Opera Guild. "He's also an opera lover."

Donny shrugged. "I loved *Don Giovanni*, that's for sure. Nice to meet you, Luigi."

Luigi shook his hand briskly and smiled. "Where is Don Giovanni, eh?"

Good question, she thought. "He has to get out of costume and make-up. He'll be along shortly, I'm sure."

"You say he come soon, eh?" Luigi said, taking Deanna's face in his hands and kissing her on the lips. "I trust you, eh? Back a work."

She looked across the room and caught Richard's attention, mouthing the words, "Where is he?" and looked at her watch. Knobby'd agreed to bring Vasquez. Knobby told Deanna that Vasquez was his charge and that he'd keep him on a short leash—his leash—for the rest of the performances.

Richard held his hands up as if to say, "How should I know?" and wrapped his arm around Vivian's waist.

She looked radiant, Deanna thought. A little earth-girlish in her batik skirt and lace-up boots, but happy and perky alongside Richard.

"Deanna," Donny said. "The show was fabulous. I never knew I liked opera."

Donny just said the word *fabulous*. All evening long, she'd been looking for clues that might reveal Donny's sexual preference. She felt sparks whenever she looked in his eyes. But she no longer trusted her judgment with men and relied on the thinnest of clues to help guide her behavior. *Fabulous* was one of the words that gave her pause to consider if whether his overtures were romantic or merely friendly. The other question that plagued her, that she tried to avoid thinking about since the banquet at Jeannie's house was his name. Donny. Not a superstitious person by nature, more than ever Deanna was certain all the Dons of the world existed to vex her and her beloved opera guild. First, it was Don Blank. Then it was Donato Bianco. Then it was Donna from Bronsky and Greenburg. And of course, *Don Giovanni* itself. A show that brought on more horrors and challenges than she'd ever signed on for. Only a moron or a woman in complete denial could overlook the significance of all the Dons in her life.

Donny leaned over and kissed Deanna on the lips. "I never knew opera attracted such beautiful fans either. Smart, beautiful, sexy fans," he said, planting more kisses on her lips with each word.

"It's easy to see how you arrived at sexy and beautiful," Deanna said, kidding. "How did you know I was smart?"

"As I recall, you said, 'This is the best rumaki I ever tasted.'" He ran his fingers through her hair. "It takes a smart woman to know when she's been beaten by a man."

Now that was a decidedly chauvinistic remark. It did her heart a world of good to hear some good old-fashioned sexism tumbling from the lips of an achingly handsome man.

Another man approached. It was Benny Lebowski, the arts editor for the *Hankey Herald*, and a fickle friend of the Opera House. Sometimes Benny would slam a production just because he could.

"Benny, glad you could come," she said. "Benny? Donny," she added, making the necessary introductions.

Benny's eyes lit up. "Donny? Is that your name? We've never met. I'm sure of it," he said with a distinctive purr in his voice. "I would've remembered you."

Benny was flirting with her date. Would Donny flirt back? She wouldn't give him the opportunity. "What did you think of the show, Benny?"

"It was extraordinary. I've never seen anything like it. Vasquez is a first-rate singer. How on earth did you find him?" Benny said, stroking the stem of his martini glass.

Jesus, could he be more obvious? Donny seemed unfazed by what Benny was doing with his hands.

"And the direction, Deanna? It was lively, provocative. I like what Carter Knoblauch is doing with his talent," Benny continued. "I saw people in the audience I'd only ever seen at the bank or the grocery store. How in God's name did you accomplish all this?"

"How about the local girl in the show?" Donny asked. "Wasn't she great? Who knew we had that kind of talent in Hankey?"

"For a local girl, she wasn't half bad," Benny said.

"No, she was great, Benny. Absolutely great," Donny said. "I've read your columns. It's a real shame that you feel fine performers can only be imported. Won't you excuse us? Deanna and I have other people to see." Donny grabbed Deanna's hand, dragging her in

Richard's direction. "That man was an ass. Did you see what he was doing with his glass, the whole time he's talking to us?"

So, he'd noticed. Was that good or bad—that he noticed? "You shouldn't have insulted Benny. He's the god of his section at the *Herald*. We need him and his reviews. Even the stingy ones," Deanna said.

Secretly she was glad he'd put Benny in his place. She'd been wanting to for years.

She and Donny were halfway across the room when the double doors at the front of the restaurant peeled open. Oriane entered first, and the crowd applauded generously. Then Vasquez entered, and the crowd gave him an ovation beyond even Deanna's expectations—cheering, clapping, blowing noisemakers, and clinking glasses. Bravos and more bravos. For some reason, his nose was turned up—just like Deanna's did when she smelled day-old fish.

Deanna rushed ahead to the front of the restaurant to congratulate Oriane.

While Donny was busy greeting Oriane, Deanna extended her hand to Vasquez, who grabbed onto it like he was drowning and she'd just thrown him the last lifesaver. "Qué? Qué?" he said, his hand shaking violently in hers. Then she noticed Knobby and Arnaud holding him up from behind.

"What's the matter with Vasquez?" Deanna whispered.

"He's a little shook up," Knobby said. "He'll get over it. In time. With a little food and a couple drinks. Maybe more electric shock therapy."

"All he can say is, 'Qué? Qué?'" Arnaud said, snorting. "He still looks fabulous, no? As long as you look good, what else matters?"

Deanna burst out laughing. "Qué? Qué?" she said. "Oh, no!"

"It's not a big deal. People will be chalking his behavior up to the language barrier," Knobby said. "No need to worry. I'll be glued to Vasquez all night."

"You don't have a gun stuck in his back, do you?" she asked.

"Now, why didn't I think of that?" Knobby said.

"Carter, I hope you won't be glued to Vasquez every minute," Oriane said. "See that love seat? Over there? From the moment I met you, I've wanted to sit there with you on opening night."

"I think we can fit in some time for that," Knobby said, taking her hand and giving it a squeeze while Luigi hurried forward and crushed Vasquez in a bear hug.

"Bravo—Giovanni!" Luigi said.

"Gahhh!" Vasquez cried, an agonizing sound like a bull being castrated.

"Gahhh to you, *pisan!*" Luigi cried, hugging him harder.

"Qué? Qué?" Vasquez said, weeping openly.

"Qué? Qué?" Luigi aped, crying on Vasquez's shoulder.

* * *

For the next several hours, until two in the morning, cries of *Qué? Qué?* and "Gahhh!" rocked Luigi's—the crowd's mimicking but signs of affection for the handsome and talented, albeit humorous opera singer whose English proved to be especially problematic that evening.

Richard felt obliged to entertain the crowd from the hospital who came out to Luigi's. He and Deanna hardly talked all night. When Deanna snuck off to the ladies room, Vivian cornered her there. "I don't like that the crowd is mocking Vasquez. All this '*Qué? Qué?*' business is getting out of hand," she said. "What can we do?"

"That's what happens when people are partying. I'm not doing a damn thing about it," Deanna said. "Vasquez is young. He's still standing. He'll rebound, mark my words. And no one in Hankey will forget this night as long as they live."

Deanna and Donny seated themselves on a red leather banquette, his arm wrapped around her waist. Knobby was as good as his word, remaining glued to Vasquez all night, except for one stint of canoodling on the love seat with Oriane. Should Deanna offer to take Vasquez back to the carriage house? That might give him some time alone with Oriane. Then again, Oriane was enjoying the limelight—dancing, laughing. This was her coming out—hardly a time to be cemented to Knobby's side all evening.

"What do you say we blow this crazy joint," Donny whispered in her ear, "and go to my place for a little late-night rumaki?"

Deanna was exhausted. She couldn't remember whether she drove to Luigi's or where she'd left her car or whether she needed to sign for anything before they left. Hell, Luigi knew where to find her. He had people, the kind who would hunt her down if she needed to be found. Her stomach hurt from laughing. Her hands were sore from clapping. Even her eyebrows ached. She'd never seen a more draining scene in a operatic production than the banquet scene Vasquez survived tonight.

Suddenly, she was flooded with emotions. What a shame that Jeannie had committed herself to Serenity Acres that morning! She was sorry that Vivian had had such a crummy childhood. It made her sad that Oriane's gifts would always be discounted in Hankey because she was a local girl. She regretted toying with Vasquez's affection and plotting to teach him how to be a better human being. Ironic, considering, she wasn't the world's greatest human being herself. Mostly, she felt like she had a big, gaping hole where her heart should be. Should she open herself up? Let Donny rush in and fill it for her, with her?

She looked into Donny's brown eyes. "Ready when you are," she said, wondering what he'd meant by "late-night rumaki." If it meant what she hoped it meant, she'd definitely have to find someone else to chair the guild. She needed to get busy having the love affair of her life.

32
The Cognoscenti

On the morning of the final Sunday matinee, Knobby is conducting an interview on "Weekend Edition" with host Liane Hansen via telephone in his opera house office, his first ever appearance on NPR, and Liane's last as host of the popular show.

"This afternoon marks the last performance of *Don Giovanni* presented by the Hankey Opera Company of Hankey, Pennsylvania, a small Rust Belt town trying to keep opera alive for future generations," Liane began. "Joining us is Carter Knoblauch, general director. Against all odds, your production was a smashing success."

"We did encounter some problems, yes," Knobby said. "We lost our original Giovanni in an unfortunate accident. Then we scheduled a preview to boost attendance, and the replacement Giovanni hired as his replacement developed strep throat. Two days before we opened, we had to let one of the professionals go, the woman hired to sing Zerlina.

"Apparently, at least according to the critics, you slotted in a local woman who delivered a breakout performance," Liane said. "Aren't you forgetting a very important complication just as production began?"

Knobby cleared his throat. "I actually suffered a heart attack during my interview for the job and underwent a heart catheterization. They said I died on the operating table. But seconds before all brain function ceased, they revived me."

"Then, you had one guild member who had to be hospitalized?"

"She suffered from emotional exhaustion. It's very stressful producing opera today. It requires the stamina of a pro-athlete and nerves like a NASCAR driver."

"I understand she was going to head up a new fund-raising event—the Hanukkah Music Fest?"

"It can just as easily be a holiday sing along—that would sell tickets, too."

Liane clucked her tongue. "No one construed all these bad breaks as omens that you shouldn't do the show?"

"We didn't have a choice, Liane. We had to mount a successful show or close our doors."

"And succeed you did, my friend. One critic said, and I quote, 'Hankey's mounted the most heart-pounding Giovanni ever produced in the continental United States. Whoever believed opera was boring never saw a production in Hankey, Pennsylvania. The banquet scene alone,' he said, 'could scare the head off the Headless Horseman.' Quite an endorsement. How did you create such terror during a live production of an opera?"

"At its core, *Don Giovanni* is a ghost story. We tried to make the most of that thread."

"Hired a couple equity ghosts, did you?" Liane asked, chuckling.

"Something like that," Knobby said. "You can do a lot with special effects these days."

"A reviewer from *The New York Times* came to the show and commended you for your willingness to reach out and grow an appreciation for classic opera in the broader community by hosting opera raps and a free matinee for all-comers. I understand you'll be broadcasting future productions on the side of the opera house."

"That's the plan. A bit of Lincoln Center on the Schuylkill."

"Very exciting, Carter. And speaking of heart-pounding, what a Giovanni you stumbled onto."

"Leandro Vasquez is a truly electrifying talent," Knobby said. "Very humble. Easy to work with. He'll go far in this business."

"Now that you're in business for a while, what's next for Hankey?"

"This summer we're producing a concert version of our first modern opera—an original show based on my near-death experience this spring, entitled, *Heavens! Hold That Elevator!* Oh, and good luck to you, too, Liane. This being your last show and all."

"Why, thank you, Carter! That was General Director of the Hankey Opera Company, Carter Knoblauch," Liane said, "commenting on the success of their recent production of *Don Giovanni.*"

The Epilogue

Now that the opera company's survival is ensured for another year, it's time to turn the reins over to a new chair. I've inherited three puppies, who need lots of attention, as well as hooked up with a local caterer, which means some sweet catering deals for the guild.

— Deanna Lundquist

I can't tell you how much I enjoy those opera raps. Knobby's offered to let me conduct the fall rap on Rigoletto. *Marlena's even coming and bringing my grandson — in support of the old basso buffo. But the best thing I accomplished for the guild this year was securing a new major underwriter — the Frantz Foundation — who's established a $500,000 matching gift challenge.*

— Dr. Richard Rohrer

Though I loved all the critical acclaim from my portrayal of Zerlina, I don't intend to pursue fame and fortune in New York or even in Chicago. Just like cable television has created more opportunities for work so that professional actors don't all have to work in porn, regional opera offers real opportunities for singers like me.

— Oriane Longenecker Knoblauch

One of the most exciting developments stemming from my work with the guild is a new upscale line of fine condiments — Salsa Verdi, Berlioz Béarnaise, and Wasabi Wagner.

— Vivian Frantz

It's a good thing I handed over the dachshund puppies to Deanna. Oriane and I are expecting twins in February. I've heard dachshunds aren't good dogs for children.

—*Carter Knoblauch*

Imagine! Arnaud Marceau, whose family barely had two sou to rub together, the new Chair of the Hankey Opera Guild. But success spawns many friends, which means more guild members, people! Especially if Leandro Vasquez returns next season.

—*Arnaud Marceau*

I love—my wife—my children. I will—return a Hell—before I—return a Hankey.

—*Leandro Vasquez*

I look forward to new, inspired leadership on the guild. Especially since the new guild chair is my new roommate—and life partner!

—*Maestro Schantzenbach*

(Mary Rohrer has crossed over and is unavailable for comment.)

The Glossary

Arpeggio A broken chord in which notes are heard in succession, not at the same time.

Aside A dramatic device in which a character speaks to the audience. By convention the audience is to realize that the character's speech is unheard by the other characters on stage.

Basso Buffo A bass voice taking a comic part.

Burletta Musical term generally denoting a brief comic Italian (or, later, English) opera

Claque A paid group of singers (mostly standees who are hired by individual singers or the management to applaud loudly at the correct moment (after an aria or an act when curtain calls are taken).

Cognoscenti The critics or those in the know, a term that dates back to early classic composers

Comprimario A junior lead or second principal part.

Counterpoint The simultaneous combination of two or more melodies.

Deus Ex Machina Plot device in which a person, group, or thing appears at the exactly appropriate moment to conveniently help a character overcome a difficulty previously believed insolvable.

Dissonance Intervals and chords that jar the ear because they lack resolution.

Divina A quintessential diva, e.g. Maria Callas

Dramma Giocoso An opera in which elevated characters appear alongside the peasants and servants of *opera buffa*.

Elektra Complex A psychoanalytic term used to describe a girl's anger towards her mother. Also a one-act opera by Richard Strauss, in which Elektra plots to kill her mother.

Fioritura Ornamental figures making a plainer melodic message more fancy.

Fugue A composition for a given number of parts or voices; built on one or more themes. Voices enter in imitation of each other.

Impresario Manager of an opera company

Pastichio Musical piece openly imitating the previous works of other artists, often with satirical intent.

Pedal Point A note sustained below changing harmonies above.

Proscenium The space between the curtain and the orchestra on stage.

Singspiele German for "sung plays."

Soubrette Light soprano comedienne

Stagione A system of staging opera that concentrates on one over a period of weeks instead of a different opera every night (repertory).

Terminazione A termination or firing.

Time Beater Disparaging term for an orchestra conductor

Tragic Flaw A flaw in the character of the protagonist of a tragedy that brings the protagonist to ruin or sorrow.

Traumatic Hook An extremely distressing, frightening, or shocking event used to engage the reader or audience.

More Great Reads from Booktrope Editions

Riversong by Tess Hardwick (Contemporary Romance) Sometimes we must face our deepest fears to find hope again. A redemptive story of forgiveness and friendship.

Throwaway by Heather Huffman (Romantic Suspense) A prostitute and a police detective fall in love, proving it's never too late to change your destiny and seek happiness. That is, if she can take care of herself when the mob has a different idea.

Jailbird by Heather Huffman (Romantic Suspense) A woman running from the law makes a new life. Sometimes love, friendship and family bloom against all odds...especially if you make a tasty dandelion jam. (coming fall 2011)

Ring of Fire by Heather Huffman (Romantic Suspense) Wealth, beauty and power are somehow not enough. Maybe if you add in smuggling and rare diamonds? (coming fall 2011)

The Printer's Devil, by Chico Kidd (Historical Fantasy) a demon summoned long ago by a heartbroken lover in Cromwellian England, now reawakened by a curious scholarly researcher. Who will pay the price?

Thank You For Flying Air Zoe by Erik Atwell (Contemporary Women's Fiction) Old enough to know better, young enough to do it anyway...

Moonlight and Oranges by Elise Stephens (Young Adult) Love, fate, a secret dream journal, a psychic's riddle, a downright scary mother of the beau. A timeless tale of youthful romance. (coming fall 2011)

The Dirt by Lori Culwell (Young Adult) The beauty, the nerd, the tomboy and the missing sister. The wealthiest family has the darkest of secrets, but then, nobody's perfect! (coming fall 2011)

Sample our books at www.booktrope.com

Learn more about our new approach to publishing at
www.booktropepublishing.com